ADAPT OR DIE . . .

From the great height of  looked down on the spreading for a quar swollen with the first an entire day in the a venture out in the day~~~~ ~~~~ ~~~~ sleep and a meal from her soggy backpack had refreshed her. At nightfall she had slipped out and left the vicinity of the highway, heading not east toward the main thoroughfares but west, through a series of empty housing developments which crowded the brink of the highland on this side of the river. She had to move slowly in the darkness, and she'd lost time rummaging through houses along the way to refurbish her supplies. . . .

Now another day was dawning, and Twila needed to move inside out of sight. It was her second day of freedom, but she was too hungry and too worried to enjoy it. This was a foreign and hostile world. Besides having Security hunting her, there were the local hazards of poisonous snakes, poisonous spiders, and wild animals. She had no real plan for the future except to stay alive. . . .

MOTHER GRIMM

Catherine Wells

A ROC BOOK

ROC
Published by the Penguin Group
Penguin Putnam Inc., 375 Hudson Street,
New York, New York 10014, U.S.A.
Penguin Books Ltd, 27 Wrights Lane,
London W8 5TZ, England
Penguin Books Australia Ltd,
Ringwood, Victoria, Australia
Penguin Books Canada Ltd, 10 Alcorn Avenue,
Toronto, Ontario, Canada M4V 3B2
Penguin Books (N.Z.) Ltd, 182–190 Wairau Road,
Auckland 10, New Zealand

Penguin Books Ltd, Registered Offices:
Harmondsworth, Middlesex, England

First published by Roc, an imprint of Dutton Signet,
a member of Penguin Putnam Inc.

First Printing, November, 1997
10 9 8 7 6 5 4 3 2 1

Chapter 1

Twila Grimm was eight years old when they put her grandfather Outside.

"It's not fair!" Twila's mother shrieked, characteristically hysterical, her arms stretched dramatically across the plate-glass window that divided her from her father. Twila, clinging to her Aunt Patricia, gave her mother a guarded look. Mother wasn't going over the Edge, was she? Unconsciously Twila twined herself into the folds of her aunt's habit: a pale, flowing garment.

But there was Grandfather, calm and strong and reassuring as always—even if he was sealed away in a bare little room. "Calm down, Roxanne," he admonished firmly from inside the isolation chamber. "You're frightening Twila."

At the mention of her name, Twila looked up, large dark eyes peering out from under the hood of her habit. It hid a tumbled mass of dark curls, for Trish had hurried her out of bed and into the bulky robes, without bothering to strip off the little girl's pajamas, much less comb her hair. Together they had fled across the spongy grass of Quad Seven and grabbed the transit for Medical, already ten minutes behind Roxanne. They had raced through corridors, waving their clearance badges at people, down an elevator, through more antiseptic halls, to this place: the Isolation Unit of the Numex biodome's Medical Center.

Now Twila looked up at her grandfather, the only man she had ever seen up close. He looked so tall and so strong—how could he be sick?

"You're a doctor," her mother was sobbing, beating her fist against the glass. "Can't they make an exception? You got it doing their stupid research, can't they—can't they—"

"Keep me in isolation forever?" Grandfather finished. "No, Roxanne. I can't claim any special treatment just because I work for the Medical Authority. What kind of message would that send to people? And besides, I'd go over the Edge if I had to stay in this cramped little room the rest of my life. No, Roxanne. I have the CM virus; I am a danger to everyone in the biodome. The only thing to do is for me to go Outside. Now, get control of yourself or I will have Krell sedate you."

At that Roxanne drew away from the window, the hood of her habit sliding carelessly off her shining blond hair. Twila wanted to tug at her sleeve and tell her mother to pull the hood back up, but just then Aunt Trish scooped her up and carried her closer to the glass.

Twila looked through the window at her grandfather, and there was a hurt in his eyes that made a lump form in her own throat. Up at this height, she could see the tears spilling down Trish's cheeks, but it made her proud that her aunt didn't wail the way her mother did. Twila firmed up her own trembling chin and faced her grandfather squarely. "You don't look sick," she said bluntly.

A little smile touched his lips. "I don't feel sick, either," he told her. "That's the way it is with this disease, Twila. You can be sick for ten or even twenty years without ever feeling sick."

"Then, why can't you stay with us until you feel sick?" Twila wanted to know.

"Because even though I don't feel sick," he explained, "the disease is inside me, and I might give it to someone else. To your mother. To Aunt Trish."

"Is it CM-B, then?" Trish asked him. Twila did not know then the difference between the A and B forms of the virus her grandfather had contracted. She only guessed that B stood for bad.

Carlton Grimm looked at his younger daughter. "Yes, it's B," he said; and Twila knew as surely as she knew anything that it was a lie. She had never heard her grandfather lie before.

"Will you die Outside?" Twila asked, and she felt a warm tear stealing down her own cheek.

"No, no, precious!" Grandfather exclaimed. "Not me. I'm strong and I'm smart, and I'll be all right for quite a

while. I'll go to one of the old cities, to Sante Fe or Albuquerque, and I'll find things there that I need to survive.
You see?" He pointed to a pack that sat in a corner of the
room. "They're not putting me out with my bare hands.
That pack has food in it and tools, and a good map to get
me where there's shelter and maybe even stored food.
And there are seeds. Do you know what I can do with
seeds, Twila?"

"Plant a garden?" she asked.

"Exactly. I'll plant a garden and grow my own food,
just like we do Inside, and I'll find a house to live in—one
with a fireplace."

"A real fireplace?" Twila's face lit up. "Like the one in
the book you read to me, where the children hung their
stockings, and the man slid down and got all covered with
soot?"

"Just like that," he promised.

Just then the door opened, and a cloaked figure entered,
sending Roxanne skittering across the room to the far side
of her sister and child. "It's all right" came a deep, reassuring voice. "I've just come from Blood Check, I'm
clean." As proof he flashed a clean tag; then he moved a
step toward the window, watching the man on the other
side. "Grimm," he said softly.

"Krell."

There was a moment of silence, a moment heavy with
the expectation of dreaded things. Then, "I'm sorry," said
Dr. Krell.

Something flashed in Grandfather's eyes so that Twila
turned and stared at the man in the room with her. "We're
all sorry," Grandfather said, and Twila knew from his
voice that he was saying more to Dr. Krell than just those
words. But when a sob broke from Krell's throat, Twila
was so startled that she forgot about the unspoken message. Why was this man crying? Did everyone feel this
badly that her grandfather had to go away?

"I'll look after them for you," Dr. Krell told Grandfather in a choked voice. "Especially Twila. I'll take care
of them all. Rest easy on that count."

"Rest easy?" Grandfather echoed in a hollow voice.
"No, my friend." He looked very tired, and Twila wondered if having a disease made one tired like that. "I have

not rested easy since Sharee died; I doubt I will rest easy ever again."

Then Grandfather turned from the window and picked up his pack. Shouldering it easily, he faced the window one last time, his voice steady, his eyes dry. "Good-bye, Roxanne. Good-bye, Twila. Trish—you have to be the strong one now. And, Krell . . ."

There it was again, that look. It was harsh and cold and silent—hadn't Grandfather called Dr. Krell his friend? This wasn't the kind of look you gave a friend.

"We'll lick this thing," Dr. Krell promised. "Someday we'll lick this thing."

Again there was the heavy silence as Grandfather looked the hooded Dr. Krell square in the eye. Twila knew he wanted to say something; but when he spoke, it wasn't really what he wanted to say. "At least one person will" was all Grandfather said.

Then he turned to the door in the back wall of the room, put his hand to the seal, and opened the passageway that would lead him out of the biodome, where he had spent forty-nine of his fifty-six years, into the unknown world of Outside.

Twila clipped the last of the sucker growth from the peach tree and stood up, straightening the crick in her back. Then she reached out for one of the twigs near her head, and eyed it critically. Yes, there was definitely a blossom forming there. She examined another branch, and another. Dozens of blossoms were starting to form. Soon her little crossbreed would bear its first fruit, and Twila smiled. *Me, too,* she thought. *I'm twenty-four, and I'm almost through with my degree, and I've had my application in for four years. They have to approve me for insemination this year, they just have to.*

From a speaker pole some twenty feet away, a gentle voice sounded. "Ms. Grimm, are you through with the pruning shears?"

Twila sighed. "Yes, Ralph, I'm through."

"Please return the shears to the utility box at the corner of the orchard by the wall," the gentle voice told her.

With a grimace of disgust, Twila turned and trudged along the line of fruit trees toward the translucent wall of the biodome. *I'll bet he had a camera trained on me the whole time I used those shears,* she thought sourly. *Pruning shears! What does he imagine I could do with them? Cut off a few fingers? Go for the jugular?*

It was, of course, exactly what the security monitor was concerned about. There were too many people in Numex walking the Edge. It was a hazard of biodome living that their great-grandparents had not imagined when they retreated into these sanctuaries to escape the disease which ravaged their world. Twila herself had never seen an incidence of the violence that could occur when someone went over the Edge, but it had touched her life before she was born. Her grandmother Sharee had been murdered in Quad Twelve while on her way home from Stores. The murder weapon—the cut lid of an aluminum can.

So Twila hiked obediently to the concrete box at the edge of the orchard, and dropped her shears into the return chute. Tomorrow after classes when she returned to tend to her project and put in her Required Labor in the orchard, she would go through a quick psycheval with the monitor. Then from his control room, Ralph would release the lock on the utility box so she could get her cultivators and probes and other tools, and work her solo shift among the fragrant trees.

As the shears clattered into the box, Twila stood up and glanced at the thick, translucent wall beside her. Through the latticework of inverted pyramids that supported it, she saw in the glass a dim reflection of herself; of a wide brow and a pointed chin, of rounded features and even teeth, of curling dark hair pulled back and tied with a scarf. She was dressed in shorts and a sleeveless top, for here near the wall the air was warm, heated by the greenhouse effect to a temperature the inner part of the complex did not enjoy. Her light brown skin glistened with a faint sheen of perspiration.

Then her gaze passed through her own reflection to the world beyond the wall. Outside, it was spring, but it was a colder spring than in this protected place. The native plants were still brown and bare, giving the mesas beyond the dome a desolate cast. Unexpectedly, Twila thought of her grandfather and shivered. Sixteen years it had been since he had been put Outside. Sixteen years was as long

as anyone infected with *cerebral mortis* could expect to
live. But if he were still alive, out there, somewhere . . .

"What was it between you and Dr. Krell, Grandfather?"
she whispered to the bleak horizon. "Won't you ever
come back and tell me?"

From a speaker above the utility box came the gentle
voice. "Are you ending your shift, Ms. Grimm?"

Twila sighed. "Yes, Ralph, I'll be leaving now." Slowly
she turned and made her way back through the orchard to
the city side.

Her habit waited on a speaker pole. Warm as she was, it
did not occur to her to venture into the populated areas of
the biodome without properly cloaking herself in the
flowing garment. Not that that would help if someone
went over the Edge. But her mother had taught her not to
call attention to herself, and if it was a feeble defense
against irrational violence, at least it was something. So
like the rest of the population of Numex, Twila wrapped
herself in wheaten anonymity to steal silently through the
common areas of the dome.

"Blood!" she swore in disgust now, using the filthiest
epithet she knew, as the habit slipped out of her fingers
and landed in the soft soil of the orchard. Now there
would be smudges on the pale garment. She brushed it off
as best she could, but her dirt-grimed hands were poor
tools for that task. Finally she gave up and threw the habit
on over her head, hoping the many folds would conceal
any traces of dirt. Adjusting the hood to shadow her face,
she headed for the chalk line that divided the orchard
from adjacent gardens. "I'm leaving my red zone now,
Ralph," she called toward the speaker pole. "You can
green it as soon as I hit the walk." The she hurried toward
the cement path that led out of the horticulture unit and
back toward the transit stop.

The security monitor was not the only one who watched
Twila go, her graceful, feminine body muffled in the non-
descript habit. From the edge of a berry patch two zones
down, a pair of steel-gray eyes watched her breeze along
the walk toward home. It was as close as he could get to
her; while she worked in the orchard it was a red zone,
and anyone crossing the chalk line into it would have trig-
gered an alarm that brought an MA security team on the

double. Even venturing into an adjoining zone would have put Security on alert, and he would have been warned to leave the area while Twila was working. Isolation was safety, the Medical Authority's solution to the twin problems of infection and insanity.

So he only watched, this time, watched and wondered how he could get closer. Somehow, he must get closer.

The transit hummed along a gravel path that wound from the orchards through rice paddies filled with tilapia, along legume fields, where the bent sprouts of beans were just pushing their way through the rich loam, across the savanna and back toward the habitation zones. Overhead the ceiling of the biodome was clouded with condensed moisture, for it had "rained" from the misters here during the morning hours. The proper humidity for each of the biomes of Numex was carefully monitored and maintained. The cultivated areas through which Twila rode were quite moist compared to her living zone near the northwestern wall.

Several miles away to the southeast, Twila could see the dark green canopy of the rain forest biome. She rarely ventured there; seventy odd years of growth had turned it into a crowded place, one of the few wherein harvesters and botanists hacked their way regardless of damage to the foliage. Radical pruning was necessary to keep the lush vegetation from overbalancing its nutritional base. As a botanist, Twila understood the need for that; but anywhere that people worked with large razor-sharp blades was a place she avoided.

The savanna was more to her liking. Ambling across it now in the ungainly electric transit, Twila looked out across the rolling sweep of arid land. This was the most unrestricted view in the entire biodome, golds and greens and browns blending in a tapestry of persistent life flung out like a worn comforter across the land. There were no buildings, and the tallest plants were shrubby mesquite trees. Even though the ceiling was not fifty feet overhead, it had a feeling of openness and space that always lifted Twila's spirit. It was, Grandfather had told her once, at least five miles across.

Overhead a fine layer of dust muted the glass, collecting

more heavily along the seams of the square panels. Twice since the complex had been constructed, repair crews had had to go Outside in environment suits, to blow and wash away the accumulated dirt so that it did not impede the sunlight. Everything in the biodome depended on two things: the hydroelectric plant, which supplied their power, and the sun. Without enough sunlight, the food crops would not grow, and the rain forest would not manufacture enough oxygen. Just before the last cleaning, the situation had been serious enough that the energy ration for other industries had been decreased so that grow lights could be electrically powered to counteract the solar deficiency.

As the transit drew within sight of the habitation zone, the gravel track it rode upon became smoother, raked more often by younger students doing their Required Labor. Less dust was kicked up by the small tires, and the vehicle seemed to bounce less. Twila relaxed a little in her molded plastic seat as the ride became more comfortable.

The transit had eight stalls on each side and two in the back. Once, Twila knew, people had ridden *together* inside vehicles, not in compartments that opened to the outside, but kept each passenger isolated from all the others. But that was Outside, before CM-A made people afraid to jostle up against each other, made them afraid that casual contact would transmit the anaerobic virus from one to the next.

The aerobic form, CM-B, had sprung up within a generation of the discovery of A, and had not the sealed habitats already existed, humankind might not have survived. Borne on a cough, a sneeze, on the very wind itself, it spread across the globe in a matter of months. Twila's grandfather and great-grandmother had been among the last admitted to the Numex biodome before all traffic with the Outside was stopped. It was just too risky, the Medical Authority decided. They could not allow anyone, or anything, else Inside.

For several years after that, people had come to beat on the doors of the habitat, begging for admittance, screaming that they were clean. Those had been terrible years for the inhabitants, working their gardens and tending their livestock behind the impenetrable glass while wretched humanity wailed on their doorstop. But the Medical Authority was adamant, and the numbers of plaintiffs dwindled as symptoms of the disease began to manifest in the population. Finally the Outsiders stopped coming. For several more years there was still electronic contact with the Outside; the Medical Authority diligently transmitted all its research results to exiled doctors, who continued to work toward a cure for CM. But by the twentieth year of isolation, no more messages came into the biodomes. The catatonia that characterized the advanced stage of the disease had overtaken the last despairing researcher; the MA turned its efforts away from cure and back toward prevention.

Oddly enough, the aerobic form CM-B, which decimated the world Outside, had been virtually eradicated Inside, except for laboratory specimens; any breach in the integrity of the biodome's structure caused air to rush *out*, not in. So it was the anaerobic A form that, after all this time, still plagued the domizens. The tests for it were less accurate, and it had been known to lie masked in the bloodstream for weeks before it was discovered in a routine book check, and its carrier ejected.

And then there was the fear of another mutation . . .

As the transit wound its way through the habitation zone, Twila shifted her tired muscles and looked with longing for her stop and the end of her journey. The Quads of the habitation were green with grass and shrubbery, the buildings straight and solid with their walls of earth-tone block. Here and there a cloaked figure scurried along a walkway, bound for home or Stores, or perhaps a late shift of Required Labor. Rarely did two walk together. Even those like her mother and aunt, who shared living quarters and worked in the same animal husbandry zone, usually traveled separately.

The transit swung around a sharp corner, pressing Twila up against the side of the compartment. Its top speed was twenty miles an hour, the only safety restraint a simple cord that clipped across the opening. Twila wondered sometimes if her grandfather had been exaggerating when he told of vehicles that once zoomed across roadways on the Outside at speeds in excess of sixty miles an hour. How could people take their lives in their hands that way? What if two of those vehicles should collide? Even if the long-projected tunnel connecting Numex with the Dafow biodome was ever completed, and vehicles sped along it at the hundred miles an hour engineers thought feasible, they would be strictly scheduled. How could it be that hundreds of thousands of such vehicles had once gone where they pleased, when they pleased, with such minimal regulation? It just wasn't reasonable.

Now the transit slowed, and Twila unhooked the cord in preparation of jumping out. She surveyed Quad Seven carefully as they approached. Nothing looked out of the ordinary, no one loitered or dawdled or watched furtively as the transit pulled to a stop. When she stepped lightly out onto the spongy green grass, two other habited figures also disembarked, but each headed directly toward a building. As Twila hurried toward her own building, one final person stepped out of the transit and headed in the same direction, but she/he waited respectfully while Twila gained some fifty yards before following. If it was an Edgewalker, it was a polite one.

Still, Twila felt a wash of relief as she closed the apartment door behind her. Mother and Trish's habits hung by the door, ready to be deposited in the laundry cart when it came around later that evening. "Mom, I'm home!" Twila called as she threw back the hood of her habit and checked again for the dirt smudges she had acquired. After tagging them with laundry pins, she bent over at the waist and flipped up the back of the garment, letting it slide to the floor over her head.

When she stood up again, Trish was coming into the room. At forty-five, Trish was beginning to exhibit care lines around her eyes and mouth, though the eyes still sparkled a lovely blue and the mouth smiled as she greeted Twila. "Hi, sweetie, how was your day?" she asked, coming to give her niece a hug.

"The most astounding thing happened," Twila replied, returning the hug quickly. She knew better than to let her mother catch them. Mother wouldn't hug anyone, and could hardly stand to watch other people do it. But there's nothing dirty about it, Twila thought defensively. Grandfather used to hug me all the time.

"Astounding? What's that?" Trish asked, curiosity in her eyes.

"Well, I was standing in the orchard pruning fruit trees when this purple bug crawled off one of the leaves into my hand," she began, "so I brushed it off onto the ground, and suddenly it started to grow. In just fifteen seconds it was the size of a goat, and then a horse, and then an elephant—"

Trish cocked a blond eyebrow, realizing she'd been had. "An elephant?"

"Just a small elephant," Twila qualified. "But it was still purple, and it had this ugly bug face, and it made this funny humming noise that got the glass to vibrating . . ."

"Enough!" Trish gave her niece a gentle cuff on the arm. "Better watch out, or Security will haul you away as an Edgewalker."

"Me?" Twila squeaked. "I'm so sane, it's painful. So are you. In fact, the only one here in danger of going over the Edge is—"

"Twila? Twila, is that you?" Roxanne's shrill voice penetrated the living room before she made her entrance. She wore comfortable lounge pants and a loose-fitting sweater, the softness of which only served to accentuate her graceful carriage. Her hair tumbled free, and her pale skin glistened from a fresh scrubbing. Despite gray strands in her blond locks and hands that were rough with many years' labor, Roxanne Grimm was still lovely, looking somehow younger than her younger sister.

It's because you hide, Twila thought. Because you hide in the nursery with the baby animals, and in your music and your pills when you get home, and you let Trish deal with everything. Everything.

"It's not her fault," Trish had told Twila once when Twila blurted out that accusation. "Before your grandmother died, she was just your regular mean, bossy, big sister. But that broke something inside her, and she was just never the same."

"It didn't break you," Twila had persisted.

Then Trish had smiled, although Twila could see the tears in her eyes quite clearly. "Then, I'm the lucky one, aren't I?" she'd said.

Yes, Twila thought now as she glanced at her aunt, you

are the lucky one. You got to share hugs with Grandfather long after Mother stopped, because "it wasn't decent." And you join committees that study problems in the biodome and make recommendations, which the Medical Authority ignores anyway. And you got to tell me all about reproduction and menstrual periods because Mother didn't know "why they don't just remove all that surgically, since no one uses it anymore"; and you got to call up the MA school administrator to argue when they wouldn't let me into the advanced-studies program in medicine, and you logged an official protest over the matter, which will probably mean you'll never be approved for more advanced studies yourself. You *are* the lucky one—because all of that, and putting up with Mother, and having a few lines around your mouth and eyes, is worth it for just one of Grandfather's hugs . . .

"You're awfully late," Roxanne worried.

"Got to my shift late," Twila apologized. "I was pruning fruit trees, and I didn't want to have to ask for the shears again tomorrow, so . . ." She smiled and shrugged in what she hoped was a disarming way. Then she turned and hung her habit beside the other two.

"It's not safe, you know," Roxanne lectured Twila's back. "It was dusk when your grandmother was killed. It's a very unsafe time of day to be out and about."

"Oh, stuff it, Roxy," Trish growled at her sister. "If someone's going to go over the Edge, they aren't going to wait for dusk to do it."

Now Roxanne turned on her sister. "No, but if they're going to stalk a victim, they just might. You look at the statistics, Patricia. You look and see if there aren't more murders and—and—*rapes*"—she could hardly get the word out—"at dusk than at any other time."

"Rapes? Really?" Trish arched an eyebrow. "Then, I think I'll start hanging out around Medical at dusk. Have you seen some of the young doctors and techs they show on those panel discussions? Mmm, mmm. And they're all clean, guaranteed. Not to mention the judgment a girl might get if the doctor had any assets when they put him Outside."

Roxanne's jaw dropped, and her eyes bulged. "Pa-*tri*-cia!" she shrieked. "How *dare* you say such a thing in this

house! In front of Twila! Why—why—that's—that's—
obscene, it's—it's—"

"A joke," Twila finished, turning back to her mother.
"Mom, it's a joke. Don't you know by now when Trish is
teasing you?"

Roxanne flushed a deep red. "Well, it's not funny!" she
snapped. "Obscenity is never funny!" Then she turned on
her heel and stalked into her bedroom, slamming the door
behind her.

Trish sighed. "I'm sorry," she apologized. "I just can't
seem to resist. She's so rigid! I just wish . . ." She sighed
again. "I don't know what I wish. Well, it looks like she
won't be joining us for dinner tonight. The meal cart
came by just before you did—it's goat stew and salad.
You want to set the table while I warm the entrée?"

"Sure," Twila agreed, feeling a little guilty for being
glad her mother would stay in her room until they were
through eating. She and Aunt Trish had the best conversations over dinner when Roxanne wasn't around. There
was nothing Twila could say that would scandalize her
aunt, no question she could ask but what she would get a
calm, reasonable answer. She could even show Aunt Trish
her new dancing costume . . .

Twila looked down at her sweat-stained shirt and grimy
knees. "On second thought, Trish," she said, "let me bathe
first. I'll be quick; just give me about five minutes before
you nuke the food."

Bathtubs were legends in the biodome, where economy
of space was a way of life. Even the shower stalls were
small, with barely enough room to turn around in. In addition, with a restricted water supply, the push of a button
would activate the sprayer for only one minute; bathers
were expected to rinse, then lather without the water running, and press the button again for another rinse. Even
so, Twila knew how her mother would howl if she heard
Twila running the shower for a second time in one day.
So instead she grabbed her robe, slipped into the tiny
toilet room, and proceeded to strip out of her sweaty
clothes. Filling the sink with warm water, she dipped in
her washcloth and began to scrub.

Poor Aunt Trish, she thought as she started with her
face and neck, first rinsing away the surface dirt and then

lathering with soap for deeper cleaning. She doesn't say those things to aggravate Mom nearly as much as she says them to liven up her own life. She should have been an instructor—not just because she was so talented with computer graphics, but because then she could interact with students on the net for most of the day—instead of following her sister into animal husbandry. Sure, it's great to be outdoors so much, and have all the animals to cuddle and care for, but it's not like having someone to talk to. I mean, I enjoy my time with the trees, but I enjoy my advanced studies in botany as much for the communication with instructors and students as for the knowledge I gain. And if I couldn't go dancing every night . . .

Just the thought of it made her heart pound and her breathing grow rapid. Interaction for education was all done flatscreen, either by live or taped image. Business communication was also flatscreen, unless you were involved in some major committee work for the Medical Authority. But social interaction—social interaction was holographic. Afraid of physical contact, the domizens had devised a safe way for people to come together for conversation and communal activities via special rooms equipped with three-dimensional, integrated, computerized imagery. They sang in choirs, performed in plays, and had athletic competitions, all without leaving their apartments. Twila and her friends met every evening at a dance hall called Papa Joe's, a place that existed only in the binary bits of a network server.

And wait till they see me tonight, she thought as she finished her bath and slipped into her robe. I'll turn heads when they see me tonight. With my new outfit, and my hair *au naturel* . . .

She tugged the bandanna out of her hair, and let the black locks tumble down around her shoulders. Pity there was no time to wash it, but it took hours to dry. No one would notice, anyway, for the raven curls still glistened and swirled when she shook her head. Whoever her father had been, she was eternally grateful to him for his genetic gift of raven hair. As beautiful as her mother was, as dearly as she loved Aunt Trish, she had no desire to emulate their pale golden tresses. From her first dance solo at age twelve, when she had taken center stage and heard the audience gasp, Twila had known that her hair made her a standout.

In a world of anonymity, it was the one thing Twila wanted most to be.

The message came back quickly on the screen: "YOU ARE NOT AUTHORIZED TO ACCESS PERSONAL INFORMATION ON TWILA GRIMM."

His steel-gray eyes glared at the obstruction, then narrowed at the thought of how he could circumvent it. Punching function keys viciously, he exited the Public Information program, exited the shell, all the way back to the operating system. For a moment he stared at the blinking cursor; then he typed very carefully, "BIOMED."

Again the response was quick. "AUTHORIZATION CODE?"

Still he hesitated. He had not used the code in twelve years, and then it had almost gotten him thrown out of school. If they tracked his usage now, the repercussions could be even greater; these days he had more to lose.

And more to protect himself with. Thrusting doubt behind him, he keyed in the code.

This time the response was slower, for it was an old and cumbersome program, too much information hidden behind too many layers of security. But finally the request screen appeared, and he typed in: "PERSINFO%GRIMM_TWILA@MEDAUTH.NUMEX.MED."

And there it was: her parentage, her education, her psycheval, her history. Most of it he already knew. Scanning quickly he skipped from screen to screen, until finally it leaped out at him: dance. Twelve years of dance instruction, three years as an assistant instructor, a request from Fitness that she be diverted from Botany into their program. MA had declined the diversion, and Twila was never told about the request, but it didn't seem likely that someone with such talent and persistence would drop the activity altogether. There were holo dance halls, he knew, where the dancing was both wild and wicked. Would Twila spend her off hours in such a place?

He exited the program quickly, knowing the less time he spent in it, the less likely his usage would come to someone's attention. Yes, that would be like Twila, he thought. Safe in her apartment, she would transmit her image to the holo dance hall, to flirt with men who could never touch her, never invade her life. Conventional little Twila. Safe little Twila.

He laughed bitterly.

You don't know how safe you really are.

Chapter 2

Twila stretched gracefully, feeling the muscles pull and then relax all through her leg and back and upswept arm as she held the posture six, seven, eight, nine, ten. Then she reversed the stretch and woke up the muscles on the other side: hold, hold, feel the release of tension, feel the circulation increase, seven, eight, nine, ten. With a practiced flourish of her arms, she bent at the waist and reached down to clasp her ankles, mentally counting the disks of her spine, making herself aware of each one from lower pelvis to medulla oblongata. Then she raised herself slowly, vertebrae by vertebrae—

"Twila!"

Her heart thudded as her mother's stern voice came over the speaker in the room. She groaned and went reluctantly to the controls. "Yes, Mom."

"Did you ask Aunt Trish before you booked this room for *three solid hours* again tonight?" Roxanne demanded.

"Yes, Mom," she replied with more patience than she felt. "Aunt Trish is working on her morph art tonight. She's never afraid to tell me when she wants the room. Besides,"—Twila glanced at her watch—"it's after nine; she'll be going to bed soon. She has early shift tomorrow."

"And you have a medical appointment," Roxanne reminded her.

Twila wanted to stamp her foot and shout, "Mother, please, I'm twenty-four years old! I can keep track of my own medical appointments." But she knew how far that would get her, so she refrained. Instead she said, "Ten-thirty, I know." Then, with just a trace of mischief, which Roxanne would never pick up, she asked. "Did *you* want the room tonight?"

"I don't need that room!" Roxanne snapped, and the connection went dead. Smiling to herself, Twila keyed in the program for Papa Joe's dance hall.

She had already set two stools and a chair on their marks in the room, so when the images materialized around her, there was no adjusting of furniture to do. The ballet rail, which they'd installed when she was eight, became part of the bar. A small attachment on the ballet bar held three glasses of water at countertop height, her refreshments for the evening. The exercise equipment that her mother and aunt used were masked by the instruments of a jazz quintet set up in the corner. The walls seemed to expand as tables and chairs appeared in their place, and the floor was suddenly a scuffled parquet, dingy in the low light. Twila thought about going into a nonparticipa-tive mode, just to see who else was here tonight, but she decided against it. It didn't really matter; she was going to dance tonight anyway. She looked around just once to satisfy herself that everything was as it should be; then she positioned herself in the "doorway" and called out to the computer, now responding to audio input as part of the program.

"Papa Joe: live participation."

Suddenly the dance hall was filled with people: men and women in outrageous clothing, an aging bartender who polished glasses with a white towel, musicians wailing on their instruments. Music filled the air—rhythmic, sensual music that seemed to slip under Twila's skin and draw her toward the dance floor. She stood only a moment in the doorway, watching as one or two people looked up and noticed her entrance; then she moved slowly into the center of the room.

There was a change in the tenor of the general commo-tion as she took her place. Here and there she heard her name as friends recognized her and called out to others that Twila was here. Slowly she began to sway with the music, letting it flow through her, giving herself up to the thrumming of brushes on snare, the insinuation of the saxophone. The two or three other people occupying the dance floor slowly moved off to one side, there to sway and watch as Twila made her debut dance.

Twila reveled in their attention, knowing she could

rivet friend and stranger alike with her performance. Her dress was new: charcoal black, it seemed to shimmer in the low light as she twisted and snaked her body in time with the music. Its style was drawn from a dance costume she had seen in an old flatscreen movie. The skirt swirled out as she turned, its panels strips of cloth three inches wide and cut to varying lengths. They fluttered and clung to legs that showed golden brown through transparent stockings. The bodice was sleeveless and backless, a mere halter that hooked behind her neck and plunged to a deep, open V just inches above her navel. Had she worn it in the hallway of her own building, she could have been arrested; here in the holo dance hall it was elegant for its simplicity, sensuous for its modesty.

She finished her dance with one foot propped on a stool, and her body draped over her extended leg, luxurious black curls falling over her face. There was a moment of silence; then the applause burst forth. She could hear her friend Marc leading the others. "Papa Joe!" he called out. "Play a samba for Twila! A samba so Twila and I can dance!"

Others echoed the request: "A samba! Yes, a samba!" When the computer had registered enough responses, the wizened bartender looked over at the band and nodded. The musicians conferred a moment, then struck up the requested motif. Twila responded gleefully as Marc approached and beckoned her back onto the dance floor. He was a small man, only a meter and two-thirds in height, but he was still several centimeters taller than Twila. He had dark hair and a thick mustache, which, together with a rectangular face, prevented him from looking like a cherub. The two of them fell easily into the steps of the dance, for they were old partners. Others joined in as they strutted across the floor, never touching, only moving in synchronization. Touching only spoiled the illusion in holo dancing.

Joy flooded through Twila, the joy of the dance, the joy of companionship, the joy of being a standout at Papa Joe's with all eyes on her. She smiled widely, white teeth sparkling in her brown face, hair flying wildly as she tossed her head to one side, then the other, then back.

Keeping Marc ever in the corner of her eye, she glanced out into the crowd to see who else was here tonight.

There were Shannon, Elise, and Sybil, all at the same table, of course. They never went anywhere without each other, though they were as diverse as people could be. Shannon was blond and well built, a fitness instructor who lived somewhere off Quad Twenty-three, near the ocean, and never left her apartment. Elise was tall and angular with mousy-brown hair, a mechanic whose Required Labor had taken her inside more buildings than the rest of the people at Papa Joe's would ever see. Sybil was a chunky brunette who worked as a cook; from her kitchen came the food for three buildings off Quad Twelve, not far from the botany lab. Twila thought she had spotted the buildings once, but she never mentioned that to Sybil. It would be gauche to tell someone you knew where they lived or worked.

Larry the Lurch was there—Twila and her friends had adopted the big lug, who had no grace and no beauty, but adored watching the others dance. Charlene and Max sat at a table together making sensuous eyes at each other and playing almost touching games with their images. No doubt before the evening was over, they would establish a private link, dropping out of Papa Joe's to indulge in whatever self-gratification they could encourage each other to.

Karen and Piers seemed to be flirting with a relationship as well, although Karen was so changeable, she might well drop Piers and take up with Mickey or Don before the evening was over, or even both of them. Karen only turned up at Papa Joe's one or two nights a month. Rumor had it her standing gig was role-playing a stripper in a program that was very popular with members of the Cowboy Conference.

But as on any given Friday night, there were at least a dozen strangers participating at Papa Joe's. Whether they were regulars elsewhere, or simply skipped from program to program throughout the holo world, Twila never knew or asked. It was enough that she had never seen them before, or they her. These were the people she danced to impress; these were the ones she baited and teased and tried to tempt. Oh, she had lured most of the men in her circle into private links at one time or another, but there was always that embarrassment of seeing them again at Papa Joe's, and either wanting or not wanting to establish a private link with them again. She wasn't sure which was worse. She knew Marc still hungered to go private with her, but she was not at all inspired by him; and it was a miserable seven weeks she had spent after her one episode with Patrick, trying desperately to lure him off again, when it was obvious he preferred the charms of a girl named Ramona from his Renaissance art class.

But rugged Patrick with his cleft chin and wavy hair was not here tonight, Twila saw as the dance ended and she went to drag her real chair over to Marc's table. No one had seen him or heard from him in some time. Piers, who played holo baseball with him on Tuesdays, had indicated that Patrick was on his way to forming a monogamous relationship with Ramona. Twila wondered if it was a virtual marriage or a real one that Patrick was thinking about. She could accept the concept of a virtual marriage—in fact, she hoped one day to form one of her own, with a terribly exciting dancer who could converse intelligently on the flatscreen and didn't spend all his time wrapped up in the conferences. But although she knew her grandparents had shared a real marriage, it was something beyond the scope of Twila's experience, and she wasn't sure the idea was at all attractive. For one thing, Roxanne would never allow a stranger into the apartment, so Twila would have to move out. It would mean learning a new building, perhaps a new part of the biodome. And what about Trish? Would Trish defy convention in order to visit Twila in person, or would she be cut off forever from the physical presence of the aunt she loved so dearly? Then, of course, there was the primary consideration: to let a man actually *touch* her . . .

It was too much to think about, and so Twila pushed it out of her mind. Perhaps it was just as well she had never gotten Patrick into a second private encounter. He had never appeared the radical sort, but Trish had warned her that men were funny that way. So many of them had old-fashioned ideas about relationships with women.

"Outstanding!" Marc was raving now, buttering her up as usual. "Larry, didn't you think Twila was outstanding?"

Larry the Lurch nodded enthusiastically. "You were *both* outstanding."

Shannon leaned over from the next table, blond tendrils drifting across her exquisitely made-up face. "Nice outfit, Twila," she commented. Her own dress was a see-through affair of white organdy with blue piping and tassels. Twila thought it revealed too much too soon—where was the mystery in something like that? But two strangers at the bar gawked openly as Shannon minced over to ask the bartender for sake. The drink appeared magically on the bar; Twila wondered just how many of those Shannon had made up ahead with the stipulation that they not appear in the participative mode until she called for them.

But as Shannon turned and glided back toward her seat, drink in hand, Twila was startled to see that one stranger at the bar was not watching Shannon at all. Instead he seemed to be staring directly at Twila; and as their eyes met, he flinched slightly and dropped his gaze. It was, of course, what Twila expected—to have men watch her. But this man looked almost angry at being caught. She studied him a moment: a young-looking man, past thirty but not by much. His hair was a common shade of dark brown, his beard a slightly lighter shade and trimmed fashionably short. His body was trim; but then, with a few genetic exceptions like Larry the Lurch, everyone in the biodome was trim. There simply wasn't enough food issued for anyone to get seriously overweight.

Yet there was something in the way this man had looked at her that was not common. Even before she caught him staring, he had looked almost angry. But with whom? With her? With himself?

The music began again, a rollicking jazz tune that had the dancers on their feet and headed for the dance floor. Twila joined them, losing herself in the complex rhythms. But even as she strutted and stomped and twirled in her magnificent new costume, she could feel his eyes on her. She glanced his way now and then—never long enough to make him uncomfortable, but often enough to pick up a few more details. He was fair-skinned, but with a healthy tone to his complexion. He wore a plain khaki pullover and khaki pants, suitable for the casual atmosphere of Papa Joe's. His shoes were hard-soled, which indicated that he had occasion to go outside his apartment and his building to work. On his left wrist he wore a broad leather band, and on his right a narrow one—no slouch at fashion, then. His bared forearms were coated with dark hair, and a few curls twisted through the open neck of his shirt. He had the look of someone whose Required Labor was physical; yet his hands bore no trace of calluses or chafing. A tech of some sort, perhaps, or a security guard for the Medical Authority—although he was not really muscular enough to be the latter.

By the time the dance ended, Twila had decided to satisfy her curiosity. Leaving her friends, she walked straight to the bar where the man sat. He appeared to be on one of the stools she had preset; for a moment she was tempted to slide it out from under him, just to see how he would react to her playing with the illusion. That, however, would be construed as an insult, and she didn't think she wanted to insult this man. Not just yet. Instead she reached over to the other stool she had set, and slid it into the image of the one next to his.

Surprise flickered in his eyes as he saw the illusion broached temporarily; but he recovered himself and turned his attention studiously to his drink. Twila perched herself on the stool beside him, and stared frankly at his profile.

His eyes hardened as he realized she was watching him unabashedly. A scowl darkened his countenance, and he gave her a furtive sideways glance.

"Do you dance?" she asked him.

He turned his eyes cautiously in her direction. They fixed on her mouth first, then slid up to her dark eyes before darting quickly away again. "No," he replied.

"Just like to watch?"

Again he lifted his eyes grudgingly to hers. They were gray eyes, and their expression was not so hard now as it had been, but it was still very guarded. Apparently he was not accustomed to participating in holo bars.

"My father taught me to appreciate art," he replied after a moment, and there was a heavy current of irony in his voice. Then his eyes slid back to his drink.

"Your father." Twila did not even know who her donor father had been, and many of her friends were in a similar situation. Here was someone whose father had been involved in his life, although she was unsure from the man's tone of voice how he viewed that involvement. "Do you live with him?" she asked.

"Work with him." The man stirred his drink carefully with its swizzle stick.

That reminded Twila she was thirsty from the previous dance. She turned to the bartender. "Papa Joe, may I have a glass of water?"

The bartender smiled softly, and indicated the row of glasses Twila had preset. She walked up the bar to where they stood, retrieved one, and walked back to her reluctant companion.

His eyes, she noted with satisfaction, had followed her the whole way up, though he had pretended not to be looking as she rejoined him. "I've never seen you here before," she said brightly. "Your first time?"

"Yes." He sipped at his drink, then studied his glass at eye level.

"Well, I really enjoy it," she went on conversationally, leaning toward him slightly with her shoulders back, chest thrust out. "My friends from dance class recommended it, and I think they have the best music here." She sipped at her water, gazing steadily at the man. "Who recommended it to you?"

He turned slowly, his eyes caught at first by her boldly displayed bosom, then he brought his gaze up to meet hers. The anger was there again—not hot anger, but a smoldering resentment. *Of me?* Twila wondered. *Why? I've never met you before. Or is it what I make you feel, that you resent?*

"Actually, it was a computer program," he said frankly. "I was looking for a holo dance hall where a beautiful woman might come to dance, and it recommended this one."

Twila recognized the compliment, however generic, and a smile spread slowly across her face. She held his eyes, daring him to keep looking at her; he did, his own eyes bright with challenge. *That's more like it,* she thought. The haunting music fed her mood.

"Dance with me," she invited.

A smile quirked one corner of his mouth, but he shook

his head slightly. "I didn't come to dance," he told her. "I'm sure you can find another partner."

She rose slowly from her stool, still smiling, knowing she had scored points in this first encounter. And it was only a first encounter. She would bother the man at the bar again.

"What's your name?" she asked abruptly.

He hesitated only a moment. "Jon."

"Jon." She rolled the name around her tongue, still watching the tight-lipped stranger. It was as though he had raised a shield around himself, one which conversation might threaten. "Is that a shadow name?" she asked.

He looked puzzled. "Shadow name?"

Could it be he didn't know? "Just for holographic encounters," she explained.

Now he flushed. "No," he admitted. "I wasn't smart enough to think of that."

He really didn't know, then. "Jon what?" she prodded.

"Jon Shadow."

Twila gave a throaty laugh at the quick response. "Touché. Come dance with me, Jon Shadow. I'll teach you, if you don't know how."

Still he shook his head.

She set her glass on the bar as the band took up a bluesy tune. "You haven't asked me *my* name," she chided.

"I already know your name."

Cold fingers tickled the back of Twila's neck, and her smile faded. "Really?" she asked in a voice made breathy by the touch of fear.

With a wave of his hand, he indicated her friends at the nearby tables. "They shouted it when you came in, remember?"

Relief washed over her. Of course, they had all called greetings to her across the room. For a moment she'd been afraid . . . But that was silly. Why should this man know her? He didn't even seem to want to talk to her—although he certainly wanted to look at her. She bent her face close to his so that he drew back slightly.

"Dance with me," she whispered one more time.

"No," he whispered back. "Thank you."

But she could feel the current of electricity passing

between them. As she walked back onto the dance floor, the evening suddenly held a new feeling of excitement.

Jon watched her go, drawn by the suppleness of her movements and the dark, rich beauty of her. He'd met other people with that golden-brown complexion and the smooth, rounded features that spoke of Hispanic origins, but in all his life he had never seen such luxurious curls. Light glinted off them now as she tossed her head and beckoned to the man who had danced with her earlier. He joined her eagerly on the dance floor, and they began to sway in time with the music, their images the barest fraction of an inch apart, moving in perfect synchronization.

Painfully Jon tore his eyes away from her. This was not at all as he had imagined. He had only wanted to see her up close, to hear her voice, and know her face—He gave a bitter laugh. He had seen her up close, all right. His blood still raced from the closeness of that encounter. Strange sensation, this holographic interplay. The images were exquisitely real, and the voice duplication almost flawless, but there was no scent of human musk in the air, no radiant heat from the image of a body—never mind. He had generated enough heat for both of them. The illusion was frustratingly good.

His gaze slid back to where she danced, pulsing with the sleazy tones of the saxophone. Her movements were slow and suggestive, marked by sensuous bends and pelvic thrusts. Her partner shadowed her every move, arcing his body over hers, running his hand along the length of her outstretched arm just an inch away from it, undulating in perfect rhythm. It was an outrageously bawdy display, the kind that seventy-five or a hundred years ago would have been considered indecent in a public place. But, in truth, this place was no more public than the flatscreen of an old-time movie house; it was less so, because Twila and her partner weren't even in the same room. She need never fear what carnal desires she stirred in him, or in the men who watched them.

Innocent Twila, so well protected. Or so she thought. If only she knew what was perpetrated against her, without her knowledge—

She was watching him again. Jon turned away. It hadn't

occurred to him before he entered this holographic program that Twila might single him out for a flirtation. He had wanted to be just one of the crowd. But the minute their eyes had met, a shock had gone through him, and apparently she had felt something, too. He hadn't imagined that could happen holographically. Yet his heart still pounded at the memory, and he found himself turning to look at her once more . . .

Of every dance partner Twila had ever had, Marc was the best. In this most lascivious dance his hands wandered over her undulating body exquisitely close to her skin without once spoiling the illusion by actually brushing her image. Yet while Marc's perfect dancing sent a thrill through Twila, his virtual presence did not. Her mind kept wandering to the man at the bar, the man with the compelling gray eyes who was watching her every move . . . Jon . . .

The dance ended, and Marc encircled Twila's waist with his arms, preventing her from moving without breaking the illusion. "Who's your friend?" he asked.

"Calls himself Jon," Twila replied, finding it difficult to sound casual. Then, because the notion was so foreign, she added, "You know, I don't believe he's ever been in a holographic encounter before."

"Really?" Marc's eyebrows shot up. They were as black as his hair, and nearly as thick as his generous mustache. "A virgin, eh? I didn't think any still existed."

"Well, there's always my mother," Twila commented dryly, gesturing for Marc to release her. They walked slowly back to the table.

"He can't really be a virgin," Marc continued. "I mean, you can't really take a sports class without using the holo programs. And he doesn't look like the sort of guy who hibernates. Maybe he's just not used to dance halls."

Twila grinned wickedly. "Maybe he goes in person."

"Oh, stop!" Marc scoffed. "He's putting you on, that's all. He wants you to *think* he's a virgin. Some women find that exciting."

Twila considered that. Was that part of Jon's appeal, this apparent inexperience with holographic encounters? No. No, she had felt the magnetism long before she had

wondered about his virginity. It had something to do with
the way he looked at her ... Suddenly she was conscious that Marc was watching her. "Why would anyone
find that exciting?" she asked, to cover her drifting attention. "Virgins are clumsy."

"Don't ask me," Marc defended. "I don't pretend to
understand it." The quirk in his mouth was both teasing
and petulant as he eyed her and said, "But you're going to
go talk to him again, aren't you?"

"I don't know," she lied, not happy at being so easily
read. In fact, it was simply a matter of how long she
should wait before she approached Jon again. His gaze
was like a tangible touch on her skin—but, of course,
people accustomed to holographic encounters learned to
be sensitive in that way: feeling the hand that made no
contact, the breath that was only imagined. He was naive
in the ways of holographs; he did not know how obvious
he was being.

Or did he?

Maybe Marc was right. Maybe it was all an act, to
arouse her interest. If so, it was working very well. But
Twila, accustomed to manipulating men, did not like the
idea that one might be manipulating her. *I'll ignore him,*
she thought. *I'll make him make the next move.*

But Jon stayed on his bar stool and looked away each
time she turned in his direction.

Half a song slipped by. *I'll wait two songs,* she thought,
and see if he doesn't make his move. She pretended to
watch the dancers on the floor; most of them were very
good. *I'll wait till the end of this song, at least,* she
promised herself. There was plenty of time, the evening
had only begun.

Abruptly she rose from her chair. "I forgot my water at
the bar," she announced, and went to retrieve it.

Jon gave her a sidelong look as she approached. She
said nothing but simply reached for the glass, standing
close to his image, between the two stools. Then she
drank deeply before pausing for breath, letting her chest
heave just slightly for effect.

"Flatscreener," she announced simply as she put her
glass back down on the bar.

He did not look up; but he did answer. "I assume that was directed at me."

His voice was not as deep as Marc's, but not as high as Patrick's. A pleasing register, she decided. "My mother's a flatscreener," she continued, keeping her own voice midrange and noncommittal. "Everything she wants is in letters and pictures."

He was leaning on the bar with one forearm, his other hand stirring his drink slowly with a swizzle stick. He seemed intent upon the motion of the liquid in the glass. "And that's bad?" he asked her.

"No," Twila admitted. She perched on the adjacent stool again, but did not look over at Jon, focusing instead on the glass in her own hand. "I guess it means she has a really vivid imagination."

"Or she's very repressed."

The remark caught Twila by surprise. That was, of course, her own opinion of her mother, and of flatscreeners in general. But why should he think that? She studied his face carefully, trying to see past the brooding look to the man beneath. What kind of man was he? Why did he show so little knowledge about holographing, yet disparage flatscreeners? Was it himself he was disparaging? There was no clue on the closed face. "Which is your case?" she asked finally.

He looked at her then, and something like amusement shone in his eyes. Or was it incredulity? Maybe flatscreeners didn't ask such bold questions.

For a moment he let his gaze slide over every inch of her face with that same half-smiling expression, but without letting his protective shield crack in the least. It was almost condescending, the way he looked at her, as though her face were a book that he could read without her being able to read his. Finally he asked, "What if I told you neither?"

The skin along Twila's arms prickled. There was something in his tone that annoyed her. It was as though he addressed his words to a child, or to a mental inferior. He seemed to be teasing her because he didn't think she would understand what he really meant. It was like his remark about learning to appreciate art from his father: it meant something to him that those words did not convey to anyone else. But Twila was accustomed to the respect of her peers, both in dance and in studies; she did not appreciate his assumption that she would not or could not fathom his remark. Her dark eyes grew hard as she adopted a defensive posture. "You're not repressed *or* imaginative?" she asked, feeling around the words carefully, looking for the trap he apparently expected her to step into.

"I'm not a flatscreener," he replied. "At least, not the way you mean."

Not a flatscreener, my privilege card! "You don't know your way around a holo," she challenged.

"Not an intimate one," he agreed.

Intimate. The word sparked Twila's sense of mischief. She could play games as well as he. Once again she leaned close to his image, but this time he did not shy away. Instead he held his ground as she brought her lips within an inch of his, hoping the holo projector on his end was precise. "Intimate?" she whispered. "Is that how you see this?"

"Oh, yes," he whispered back, and she was pleased to note that there was just a slight shake in his voice. "I understand now what you find here."

A slow smile spread across Twila's lips, although her eyes still glittered. She drew back from Jon, then turned with a brisk movement that sent her long dark locks whipping around behind her. Stalking out onto the dance floor, she gestured for Marc to join her. "Papa Joe!" she called out. "Play 'The Horn Possessed.' "

For the next hour she danced virtually nonstop. She changed partners, she danced solo, but she always danced. One moment she whirled like a demon, the next she swayed slowly, seductively. Sweat glistened on her skin; it trickled from her temples, it dripped from her chin, it slid between her breasts. Around her, couples and triples were beginning to vanish. She herself declined three offers to "go private."

Marc lingered, hoping she would change her mind, but a slender brunette was making advances toward him, and Twila knew that soon he would go, too. As the music turned soft and sensuous, she beckoned him for one last dance. The brunette looked petulant; Marc shrugged and declined Twila's offer.

There was a movement from the bar, and Twila saw a man approaching—not Jon, but another stranger. He was taller than Jon, a bit more heavily built, and not unattractive. Still, Twila was in no mood for a substitute. What was there to a private encounter, if not the fascination, the chemistry? She did not know this man, did not feel any attraction when she looked at him. Slowly she drew herself up to face him, bowed with a graceful flourish, but turned away.

"Oh, come on," the man cajoled, circling an arm in front of her so that she could not go forward without breaking the illusion. "I can't hurt you. One dance."

She had seen him on the floor and had not been impressed. "Another time," she said graciously, smiling back at him and then sliding sideways.

But he slipped around in front of her. "No time like the present," he persisted hopefully.

Any other night Twila would have danced with him, even toyed with him; but tonight that did not suit her, and so she declined again. "My time has run out," she told him, the holo jargon meaning that someone else in her living unit had the room booked, and she must give it up.

He looked a bit miffed at that. "You had time for a dance with your friend," he replied, waving a hand at Marc, who was now headed across the room with the brunette, undoubtedly bound for his controls to key in a private link.

"Please," she said patiently, not wanting to insult the man, for he had done nothing as yet to merit that. "I just don't feel—"

"What the lady means," a smooth voice interjected, "is that she was saving this dance for me."

Twila looked up to lock eyes with Jon, and a jolt went through her as powerful as an electric shock. Even the stranger must have felt it, the moving of worlds as a magnetism as old as humanity connected and bound them. He faded away; Twila hardly noticed that he'd gone. All she could see was the fair-skinned, close-bearded face of Jon standing in front of her.

"You promised to teach me," he said softly.

A long, bluesy sax note slid toward them, seeming to curl itself around them, heightening the delicious tension. "It's very simple," Twila said, hearing the huskiness of her own voice. "You move with the music . . ." Deep notes from the string bass thrummed through her; she felt them reverberate in her chest and groin. "Gently . . . Just gently . . ." She began to sway her hips, letting the movement ripple up through her torso. "And you try to stay as close to me as you can without touching my image."

The soft shuffle of brushes on drums seemed to caress her. Jon moved in close to her, finding the pulse of the music, echoing her sinuous movements. Twila bent to one side, stretching her arm out and back; Jon let his hand slide slowly along its image to the very tips of her fingers, bringing his chest close to hers. She took a careful step back as she drew up out of the posture; he brought his foot next to hers, the image of his thigh only inches from the fluttering panels of her skirt.

Twila raised her arms slowly over her head, back slightly arched. Jon raised his hands so that they cupped the outside of hers; then he ran them slowly down the image of her arms to her slender waist. Curling one arm around behind her back, he pressed his image close to her pulsing bosom, his eyes still locked at hers. Heart pounding, Twila let her head drop back, exposing her sweat-sheened neck. She saw him lower his head, saw his lips purse, and could almost feel the coolness of the breath he blew against her image.

Bracing her feet a little wider apart, Twila gradually began to lower her head toward the floor, arms curving up and behind her to help control her descent. Jon's arms stayed behind the small of her back, seeming to support her. He moved his knee into position between her thighs, still moving it in time to the music. As she dropped back toward the floor, fingertips brushing the parquet, she could no longer see him standing over her, yet she felt his virtual presence acutely. It was almost, she thought, as though she could smell the scent of him, or feel the heat of his flushed skin.

The heady complaint of the saxophone seemed to glide over her vulnerable body, tickling her bare skin, brushing against the soft cloth of her dance costume. Slowly Twila lifted herself back up. Excitement pulsed through her to see Jon bending to meet her, his lips air-tracing the curve of her neck up to her chin, then along her jaw to her ear. She slid the fingers of one hand deep into her hair, holding it back away from her perspiring face.

"Do you know what a private link is?" she asked him.

"I have some clue."

"If we left now, we could have an hour alone. More, if we want. There's no competition for my room."

"Oh, yes." The irony was back in his voice. "Your mother is a flatscreener."

She brought her hands up, palm forward, and he echoed the movement. Carefully she circled both hands out and around, bringing them back to her waist; he stayed with her without letting his eyes leave her face.

"You're very good at this," she told him. "Are you sure you haven't done it before?"

"Holo dancing?" He shook his head. "Never before tonight."

A strange chill ran through Twila. Holo dancing? What else could he have thought she meant? From the back of her mind came a thought she had dismissed long ago, a snatch of an argument between her mother and Trish. In one of her baiting moods, Trish had claimed that people in the Medical Authority indulged in physical relationships.

"They do not!" Roxanne had spat at her sister. "That's a sick and vicious rumor! They of all people know how important it is to be pristine. You just watch your mouth, Patricia Grimm. Our father was a doctor!"

"And how do you think *we* got here?" Trish had challenged.

The reminder of her carnal conception was too much for Roxanne. She had stormed out of the room.

Now Twila looked into Jon's gray eyes and wondered. He claimed to be no flatscreener, nor to have any experience with "intimate" holographic programs; yet it was obvious that he was no stranger to desire. There was always the possibility that Jon was in, or had been in, a real marriage. At the moment, the thought did not seem as repulsive to Twila as it had earlier that evening.

Or could it be the old rumor was true?

"Are you a doctor?" she asked bluntly.

That brought a smile to his lips. "If you want me to be," he evaded.

His fingers brushed by the image of her neck, and Twila shivered. "I want you to go private with me," she said frankly, "and I don't usually ask a man twice. I don't usually ask a man at all. But you seem to be a virgin in this, so here it is. The two of us, in any sort of room you care to imagine. Doing whatever you want us to do."

"Discussing philosophy?" he suggested.

"Or the place of art in the biodomes. Anything." She was not going to be put off this time.

He curled an arm around her waist again, looking down into her dark eyes as their bodies continued to sway with the music. "A tempting offer, but I must decline."

The absence of regret in his voice annoyed her. "Perhaps you have a better offer," she suggested in a voice edged with that annoyance.

His eyes left her face then to watch as his finger traced a path along the edge of her plunging neckline, the merest fraction of an inch from her image. He had the steadiest hands she had ever seen. "No, I doubt there's an offer that could match yours," he whispered, and now the regret showed through. "But it would be very, very foolish of me to accept it. I have not gotten where I am by being foolish."

"And where are you?" she asked.

The music stopped, and Jon stood still. "On a treacherous mountain slope," he said softly. "One imprudent move could be my undoing."

"And mine?"

At that his lips twisted into a bitter smile. "Oh, no, Ms. Grimm," he told her. "You have nothing to fear from me, or anyone else. There's not a soul or a sensation in this biodome that could undo you."

She knew there was a buried meaning here, but what it was eluded her. "Is that a compliment?" she demanded.

"It's a fact," he said simply. Then he called out, "Papa Joe: end participation."

Immediately his image vanished, but Twila stood stock-still, knowing he could still see her because he had only ended his participation, not the program. For a moment she was so wrapped in the heavy emotions of the evening that she could hardly think, let alone move. Nothing in the biodome that could undo her—why would he say that? What made him think she was so unassailable? Or did he mean something else entirely?

Suddenly she flinched, and her eyes grew wide. "Blood on you!" she hissed, heart pounding wildly. "How did you know my last name was Grimm?"

Chapter 3

In all the years Twila had been coming to Medical for her regular medchecks, she had always been put in the same examination cubicle. The pictures had changed: today there was a geometric print that she didn't think had been here last month, and a photograph of Clara Tomhurst, the woman who financed the original construction of the Numex biodome. The technicians had changed: the masked woman in greens who had brought her from the filtration room to this cubicle was shorter and had more lines on her face than the woman who had done the same job for three years before. The multimedia show on the entertainment monitor had changed, too, according to Twila's age: lately the audiographic litany had smacked of cubism and Wagner, a combination that was reportedly the rage with people taking advanced studies. But it was the same examination cubicle she had been put in as a child, when they used to bring her toys in sterile wrappings to keep her amused until the doctor came in.

If they knew anything about me at all, Twila thought impatiently, they wouldn't waste their time putting that garbage on the entertainment monitor. They'd know I don't watch videos; I dance. And I don't care if Wagner is "in," I prefer jazz. And I wouldn't mind in the least if they'd bring me a package of toys to play with while I wait.

Just then there was a knock, and the door slid back into the wall to reveal yet another masked tech in greens. "Hello, Twila," greeted a rich motherly voice as the woman held up her wrist to display her clean tag. "May I come in?"

"Sure," Twila replied listlessly. This face was familiar. It was Sophie, the same anesthesiologist she'd had for the past fourteen years, an unflappable woman who paid no attention to Twila's occasional complaints about having to come in every month, when most of her friends came only twice a year.

"You're very special to Dr. Krell," Sophie would always reply. "Your grandfather asked him to look after you, you know, and he takes that very seriously."

Twila wondered if Sophie knew anything about the day Dr. Krell had made that promise, and what it was between him and her grandfather that neither had voiced. Probably not. It was some dark secret between the two of them that had made the promise bittersweet to Carlton Grimm, or so Twila believed. Was it the reason she seemed never to be through with these medical appointments?

"Dr. Krell promised to look after my mother, too," Twila had pointed out to Sophie once, "but *she* doesn't have to come in every month."

"Your mother has a different medical history," Sophie had told her smoothly. "She doesn't have the tendency to anemia that you do, and she doesn't play in the dirt like you botany students. We give each patient the attention she needs."

Then, why, Twila wondered privately, do you keep telling me I'm special to Dr. Krell?

"Ready for a nap?" Sophie asked now, handing her a modesty sheet before reaching up to the controls on the IV that ran into Twila's arm.

"I don't know why I have to be asleep for this," Twila grumbled, flicking the sheet over herself as she stretched out on the examination table. "They stick that needle into my arm every time; the other things they do they can't hurt much more than that."

Sophie laughed. "Just a precaution," she said—as she had said the last time Twila complained. "People aren't accustomed to being poked and prodded by other human beings; sometimes they react adversely. Anesthesia is so safe and simple these days; there's no need for you to be uncomfortable, and there's no need for us to worry about what you'll do. Now, say good night, Twila."

"Good night, Twila," Twila sighed heavily.

Then she was awakening slowly, feeling slightly disoriented, as usual. She also felt sore in places she'd rather not be sore, but that was as usual, too. "What do you do to me when I'm asleep?" she murmured as things began to come into focus around her.

"Blood samples, tissue samples, pap smear, the usual," the anesthesiologist responded in her calm, implacable voice. "Now, just rest there a bit, and let me know if you feel sick at all."

"Just sick and tired," Twila sighed. "How many years do I have to go through this?"

"That's up to Dr. Krell," the woman replied. "I'd guess another five or ten, depending on how your bone marrow responds to this new medication. Now, you know the routine—no dancing or other strenuous activity for forty-eight hours."

"Can't you take this thing out of my arm now?" Twila asked, indicating the IV. "You know I never have an adverse reaction to the anesthesia."

"The nature of an allergic reaction," Sophie told her, "is that it occurs, not the first time you are exposed, but after repeated exposure. Just relax."

"How can I relax with this thing in my arm?" Twila shifted awkwardly onto her side, holding her arm out of the way. "When they have this anemia thing under control, do you suppose I can have a baby?"

The tech lifted her eyebrows. "That's for Dr. Krell to say," she answered, "I'm sure I don't know. But I'd wait a while, if I were you. You're young, you like to dance— why trouble yourself with a pregnancy?"

Twila shrugged as best she was able to, lying on her side. "The nesting instinct, I guess. Or—or because I've always thought I could do a better job than my mother did."

"I think your mother did a fine job," the woman placated. "You didn't turn out so badly."

"Do you have a child?" Twila asked.

She could not see Sophie's mouth behind her mask, but she saw the eyes crinkle up in a smile. "A little boy. Actually, a big boy now. He went off to live with his uncle when he was eleven, so I still remember him as little, but that was eight years ago."

"How could you let him go?" Twila wondered. "I mean, I'm not exactly the joy of my mom's life, but if I'd been a boy and had to go to another living unit when I reached puberty, I think she'd have screamed bloody murder."

"It was best for him," Sophie responded, but Twila thought she heard a catch in the woman's voice. "I live with my cousin who has a girl, whereas my uncle had two boys he was raising already. It's easier for teenagers to be in unisex living units."

Twila wondered about that, although she said nothing. When her mother and aunt were children, no one had thought twice about Carlton Grimm raising his two daughters, and Trish, at least, had turned out quite normal. But before Twila was born, the complexion of biodome society had changed. The radical teachings of Elizabeth Modecko, an early resident of the biodome, steadily won followers until people like the Grimms with their actual marriage and nuclear family were the exception rather than the rule.

A forceful speaker and prolific writer, Modecko had inundated the domizens with her message of sexual segregation. The only safe sex, she said, was no sex; and the only way to insure no sex was to eradicate all contact between male and female from the time of puberty. To prove her point, she had sent her own son out of her home to live with his father, her estranged husband; as far as anyone knew, she had never seen the boy again.

At first her ideas were rejected as being excessive, the reaction of a wounded spouse in a bitter separation. But as the years progressed and the anaerobic form of the CM virus kept cropping up, Modecko's solution was given more and more credence. Finally, just after Twila's grandfather had gone Outside, the Medical Authority gave its tacit endorsement to the philosophy of sexual segregation. As though this vindication were her release, Elizabeth Modecko had passed away a year later from a wholesome, but deadly, heart attack.

Roxanne had been a believer in Modecko's way, even before her father became infected and was banished from the biodome. Twila wondered sometimes what her mother would have done if Carlton Grimm had not become infected. Would she eventually have demanded that her father leave the living unit, or would she have left herself? Or—most likely, in Twila's mind—would she have continued to live out the principles of sexual segregation, while conveniently ignoring this rather large gap in their observance?

Now there was a rap on the door, and it slid open. The figure standing there was in a habit, not greens. Twila had been expecting him.

"Hello, Dr. Krell."

He flashed his clean tag just as the tech had done before stepping into the room. It was standard courtesy in any face-to-face encounter. But he did not let the hood slide away from his face. "Hello, Twila," he greeted her warmly. "Thank you, Sophie, you can go. I'll monitor Twila's recovery."

The anesthesiologist left, and Krell took up a stool near Twila. "How have you been feeling, Twila?"

"Fit as a fiddle," she replied quickly. "Dr. Krell, how much longer do I have to come in every month like this?"

"Oh, a little while," he told her. "But I have good news. Your red count has been stable for six months now—it looks like we've finally found a medication that is doing the trick. You keep taking it, and in—oh, say twelve months—we'll start cutting back the dosage. The object is for your bone marrow to start manufacturing enough red cells without artificial help."

"But the bad news is I still have to come every month," Twila guessed.

Krell sighed. "I'm afraid so. Especially when we start cutting back the dosage, it's important for us to keep close tabs on you. I'm sorry. I know it interferes with your lifestyle."

"I really did want to go to Papa Joe's again tonight," Twila admitted. "But I can't stand going and not dancing. Can I at least get my next appointment on a Monday instead of a Saturday? The most interesting people show up on weekends."

"We'll see what we can do," he promised, reaching over to tap on a keyboard attached to a console that faced away from Twila. "I know how you love Papa Joe's."

Twila sighed and lay back on the table, adjusting the modesty sheet around her. "Not that he'll ever show up there again."

"He?" Curiosity vied with amusement in Krell's voice. "Ah, has the lovebug bitten you again, Twila?"

Her face wrinkled in a frown. "I'm not sure. It was all very exciting, but—annoying, too. I'm not sure I could take too much of this man."

Krell cast an evaluative glance her way, then continued tapping on the keyboard. "Sounds like the lovebug to me."

"But this man was very different," Twila protested, raising herself up on one elbow. "He was so—dark. Not in looks, but in personality, if you know what I mean. And mysterious. Like some character out of a Victorian novel."

"I see." The amusement lingered in Krell's voice as he tugged on a pair of rubber gloves. "I think we can take that needle out of your arm now; you seem to be doing just fine. And is he a dancer, too, this dark and mysterious Victorian protagonist?"

"No," Twila said, pushing back the sheet as she struggled into a sitting position with her feet dangling over the edge of the table. "I mean, he danced a little, but he's not a dancer. And that's not like me to be attracted to someone who isn't a standout dancer." She extended her arm as Krell reached for the jar of sterile wipes. "But there was something about Jon—"

Crash! The jar of wipes smashed on the floor and splintered into fragments. Krell jumped back, and Twila flinched away onto the table. "Damnation!" Krell exclaimed, his voice shaking. "I'm sorry, Twila, it just slipped out of my hands. Are you all right? You aren't cut, are you?"

Twila inspected herself quickly. "No, I'm fine," she reported. "It just frightened me. And you?"

Krell shook out the folds of his habit, and there was the tinkling of glass as a few shards dropped to the floor. "Just fine, the habit protected me. Just sit there a minute, Twila, while I get someone in here to clean this up."

Then Krell left hastily, and the door slid shut behind him.

Twila found herself shaking now, a natural reaction to the simple shock, she knew. Or was it? There was no one in the room monitoring her recovery from the anesthesia. How unlike Dr. Krell to leave without calling someone else in first! Perhaps the equipment was being monitored somewhere outside the room. But if so, why did they always have a tech sitting in with her? Dr. Krell was just startled, that was all, and he forgot. Startled by the breaking glass—or had he been startled by something else, which had caused him to lose his grip on the jar in the first place?

Don't be silly, Twila, she chided herself. Dr. Krell is as unshakable as Sophie. Besides, we were only talking about the nightclub, about Papa Joe's . . .

Still Twila found herself shivering uncontrollably. She caught up the modesty sheet and wrapped it around her shoulders. Is this normal? she continued to wonder as the minutes ticked by. Why is it taking Krell so long? Should I call someone? The console Krell was using—if the standard shell is on the monitor, there should be an intercom icon. Mindful of the broken glass on the floor, Twila reached out with her foot and tapped the monitor so that it swiveled toward her. It was filled with lines of type, something Krell had been looking at before he stopped to take the IV out of her arm. By squinting, she could make out the words:

CHECK PARTICIPANTS IN PAPA JOE'S DANCE HALL 03-07-2082

Why, he was checking up on her! Checking to see who had come to the holo dance hall last night!

PARTICIPANTS IN PAPA JOE'S DANCE HALL 03-07-2082
WERE

0783315	BENNISON, MARGARET
0786882	CORSA, MARCUS
0859271	DIAL, SHANNON
1395710	FINGLE, PAUL
1624719	GRIMM, TWILA
#######	PROTECTED IDENTITY

The list went on, but Twila stopped reading. How could Dr. Krell get a list like that, anyway? Names of participants were not available through PubInfo. But of course, this was not the Public Information system; it was a special Medical Authority system, and the MA had access to all kinds of information the general public did not.

Then, what was this "Protected Identity" business? Who could protected their identity, even from the Medical Authority? Someone with an awful lot of power. Was that Jon? He had hinted at some elevated stature within the biodome: "I haven't gotten where I am by being foolish," he had said. Certainly she did not see his name anywhere else on the list, and he had let it slip that Jon was his real name. Protected Identity. The only people who might possibly be able to protect themselves from a Medical Authority search were, of course, members of the Medical Authority—and not mere technicians. It would have to be a doctor or a researcher, probably someone fairly well up in the hierarchy. Perhaps a member of the governing board—but no, he was too young for that, wasn't he?

Just then the door slid open, and a tech with a broom flashed her clean tag. "Had a little accident, I see," the woman joked. "What was it, just a jar of alcohol wipes? Oh, that's nothing." She plied the broom deftly, rounding up all the broken glass. "As agitated as Dr. Krell was, I thought it was blood serum or something."

The thought sent a new wave of goose bumps down Twila's spine. The sheet around her upper body provided some warmth, but her feet were bare and cold. "Can you reach my shoes and socks for me?" she asked the tech, pointing toward the chair in the corner where she had left her clothing.

"Oh, sure. You want me to glove first?" the tech asked.

"No, your clean tag's good enough for me," Twila responded. "Just hand me the things, my feet are freezing."

The tech obliged, then finished her cleanup job as Twila struggled into the ankle socks and hard-soled shoes. "Is Dr. Krell coming back?" Twila asked as the woman started out the door.

"I don't know; he was headed somewhere in a hurry," she replied. "You want me to get someone for you?"

"No, that's all right," Twila said hastily. "I'm sure Dr. Krell hasn't forgotten me."

As soon as the tech was gone and the door shut, Twila eased herself off the table. She was still connected to the IV, but she pulled it with her until she could slide into the chair by the computer console. As long as this Medical Authority system was up, there was some information she'd like to retrieve from it. Like more about her medical history than Krell was telling her. Like a list of all the doctors presently serving the Medical Authority.

She studied the phrasing on Krell's request that still showed on the screen. Then she typed in one of her own. LIST DOCTORS NOW SERVING MEDICAL AUTHORITY.

It took only a second of two for the response to appear. IMPROPER SYNTAX; PLEASE REPHRASE YOUR COMMAND.

Improper syntax? Twila studied the screen. LIST was the command, DOCTORS the object, and the modifiers were NOW, MEDICAL AUTHORITY, and SERVING . . . Of course. She was looking at it from a layman's perspective. To someone in the MA, the doctors were serving the patients, not the MA. How many times had her grandfather told his family that? Twila tried again. LIST DOCTORS IN SERVICE 03-08-2082.

This time a list began to scroll rapidly across the monitor. Twila tried to catch it with a scroll lock, but she had already missed too much by the time she found the right key. So she let it pass, then typed again. LIMIT PREVIOUS LIST TO DOCTORS WITH FIRST NAME JOHN. As an afterthought she added, OR JON*.

This time she sat with her finger poised on the scroll lock, but it was unnecessary. The list was short.

> BLANCHARD, JOHN
> MARKOWICZ, JOHN
> STEINER, JOHN
> SMITH-HORTON, JOHN
> TIGRANO, JOHN
> VOLK, JOHN
> GREER, JONATHAN
> KRELL, JONATHAN

Krell! Twila sat back in surprise. In all the years she had known him, she had never thought to ask Dr. Krell his first name.

Footsteps sounded in the hall outside, and Twila quickly cleared the screen, hurrying back to perch on the edge of the examination table. But the footsteps went on by. After a moment she ventured back to the keyboard.

Now what did she want to ask? How could she figure

out which of these men might be her mysterious companion of the previous evening?

LIMIT PREVIOUS LIST TO DOCTORS AGE 30–40, she typed. There, that ought to help.

The list came back quickly:

JOHN MARKOWICZ
JONATHAN KRELL

Krell! But Dr. Krell was her grandfather's friend, nearer to sixty than forty. Something prickled at the back of her neck, and Twila typed: GIVE CURRENT POSITION OF DR. JONATHAN KRELL.

For a moment she thought the program would balk and refuse her request. Then it popped up on the monitor. DR. JONATHAN KRELL, CHIEF OF RESEARCH—IMMUNOLOGY.

Chief of Research, what did that mean? Was that what they would call the Dr. Krell she knew? In truth, Twila did not know what his title was. He had always been her family physician, her grandfather's friend. She had assumed he was fairly important, only because he had worked so closely with her grandfather, and both Trish and Roxanne had insisted their father was on the governing board of the Medical Authority.

Curious now, Twila typed again. LIST ALL DOCTORS IN SERVICE WITH LAST NAME KRELL. It did not surprise her when two names appeared: Jonathan Krell and Samuel Krell. So she typed, GIVE CURRENT POSITION OF DR. SAMUEL KRELL.

Again there was a slight delay before the answer appeared. DR. SAMUEL KRELL, CHIEF OF STAFF—MEDICAL AUTHORITY; CHIEF OF RESEARCH; CHAIR—GOVERNING BOARD.

Something went cold in the pit of Twila's stomach. Abruptly she cleared the screen, marched back to the examination table, and curled up on it with the sheet wrapped around her.

Her Dr. Krell was chief of staff? Chair of the governing board? Why, that made him head of the whole Medical Authority! Why did he bother himself with the personal administration of her case? True, he had promised her grandfather, but it would have served just as well to turn

her over to some other competent doctor who could report
to him.

Guilt, said a little voice inside her. *You heard it in his
voice the day they put your grandfather Outside. There
was guilt in his voice as he promised to look after
you. "Especially Twila," he said. And what was that in
Grandfather's eye as he stared at his friend? A threat? An
accusation?*

Silly, she chided herself. Silly fantasies of an eight-
year-old girl. Silly, to make so much of this. So my grandfather's friend is now head of the MA, and he still takes
time to look after me personally. That's not so odd. They
were friends, after all.

And chief of research, what did that mean? Jona-
than Krell was chief of research—Immunology, but
Samuel Krell was simply chief of research. All research?
Did that mean Jonathan Krell reported to Samuel Krell?

Then it clicked in Twila's mind. "I called him by
name," she whispered aloud, remembering their conversation just before Krell had dropped the jar. "I said there
was something about Jon . . ." The computer had told
Krell that an unidentified doctor had been carousing at
Papa Joe's, and Twila had called him Jon—

I've given him away, she realized suddenly. To his
supervisor, and his—what? Father? Uncle? Cousin?—to
the head of the whole Medical Authority, for certain! I've
given him away—

But why should anyone care? So a young doctor, on
his off hours, did a little holo hopping and wound up
at Papa Joe's—it was perfectly acceptable recreation,
even encouraged by the MA. People who released their
sexual tensions were healthier than those who repressed
them; that's why programs like Papa Joe's had been
written. That's why there was a holo room in every apartment. Why should anyone care if Jon—or any other
doctor—had a drink or two and watched the dancers at
Papa Joe's?

Because he didn't just happen to be there, Twila knew.
Because he came there looking for me. That's why he
knew my last name, because I'm the one he was looking
for. But why?

Why?!

Anger flushed Twila's brown face. There were too many mysteries here, and she didn't like it. There were things they weren't telling her about herself, secrets being kept from her about her own life, and she *did not like it*! Angrily she pushed off the sheet and jumped to the floor. The IV tugged at her arm; annoyed, she snatched up a jar of gauze pads, fished out one of the little packets, and tore it open. Clamping the gauze over the needle with her free hand, she seized the rubber tubing in her teeth and yanked. Her arm stung as the needle was torn ungracefully from it, but Twila was too angry to care. She pressed down on the wound for a moment, then grabbed up her clothing from the chair and began to dress.

Blood on Dr. Krell! He had no right to keep things from her, no right at all! It was her body, it was her health, and if there was something—something that another doctor would want to come and *gawk* at—

She stopped short in the act of pulling on her shirt. Perhaps it was nothing medical at all. Perhaps the elder Krell had merely mentioned to the younger what a lovely girl . . . what a stunning beauty the daughter of his old friend . . . Was that all?

If it is, she vowed silently, then they'd better tell me that. They'd better tell me something. Because I've had just about enough of mystery and secrets and evasion.

Cloaked in her habit, Twila peered out into the hallway. There was no one in sight. So she stepped out boldly, casually, as though she were simply through with her appointment and going home now. But she did not turn to the right toward reception; instead she turned left and started deeper into the maze of corridors and cubicles that was Medical.

One last inquiry of the MA computer program had told Twila the location of Dr. Samuel Krell's office and Dr. Jonathan Krell's lab. It had even drawn her a convenient map. Not wanting to look out of place, she had refrained from printing a hard copy but had instead committed the route to memory. Down here and to the left, then right to the elevator. Dr. Krell's office was actually on the ground floor, but it could not be reached directly. One had to go down to the basement level, past the immunology lab,

where Jon worked, and then up a broad flight of stairs to a
suite of offices tucked up against the biodome wall.

There were techs in the hallway, but they were all
bound somewhere specific, coming and going from the
examination rooms, carrying medicines, pushing equipment. Twila walked purposefully as though she, too,
walked these halls every day. It pleased her that no one
took any notice; but, then, why should they? The advantage of a habit was that no one could tell who she was or
that she didn't have any business prowling the corridors
of Medical.

. As she approached the elevator, a ping announced that
its car was just arriving. Twila slowed her steps to give
anyone debarking a chance to clear the area before she
approached. But the tech who stepped out of the elevator
seemed unconcerned by her presence in the hallway.
Mask down, he actually smiled when he saw her and
nodded in greeting. "Good morning, Doctor," he called as
he passed by only inches from her shoulder.

"Good morning," Twila murmured back, trying to conceal her start. It was true, then, the jokes they made about
people who worked for Medical—daily monitoring of
their clean status made them lax about interaction with
each other. Twila took a deep breath and stepped into the
elevator.

When the elevator came to a stop and the doors slid
open, Twila hesitated, suddenly aware of how different
life in the bowels of Medical might be. How long would it
take them to notice that she didn't fit? Would some auto-
matic reaction of hers be spotted as that of a stranger?
And what would they do to her if she were caught? Would
they just escort her off the premises, or were there penal-
ties beyond that which she must endure?

Silly flamingo, she chided herself. What can they do?
You're clean, you've just been checked, so you're not
endangering anyone. Besides, Dr. Krell won't let them do
anything much to you—he was Grandfather's friend, and
he promised to take care of you.

So Twila stepped boldly out of the elevator—

—and into another world. Oh, it still had the white,
sterile look of Medical, with the smell of disinfectants
heavy in the air. The techs she saw in the hallway were

still dressed in greens, but few wore masks. Twila had never seen techs without masks. Furthermore, they walked and clustered *together,* in twos or even threes. They talked to each other, and the sound of laughter filtered to her ears.

Twila stood staring dumbly for several moments before she realized that standing there gawking would certainly give her away. So she turned briskly to the left and marched down the wide corridor toward her destination. On the way she passed a large open room equipped with comfortable chairs and low tables—*lounge* was the word that came to her mind. Twila had never seen a lounge, let alone used one. Most of the lounges originally designed in the biodome buildings had been turned into something else. This one, it seemed, still functioned in its original capacity as a gathering place, for the chairs were worn and the tables stained.

How strange it felt to pass people in the halls and make eye contact! To do so anywhere else in the biodome would have been unthinkable. What if one of them were an Edgewalker, and that innocent contact caused him to single you out as the target of his madness? Twila suppressed a shudder, then wondered if a shudder might give her away in this place of casual socialization. Should she put down the hood on her habit, she wondered, to blend in better? Probably—but somehow she couldn't bring herself to do that.

A right turn took her down a longer corridor that was not quite as wide as the trunk she had come in on. From the map she had studied on the computer upstairs, it should run almost the length of the building, stopping only fifty feet short of the biodome wall. Large rooms opened off this corridor—laboratories, she guessed from discreet glances through windowed doors as she passed. Most of the doors were shut, and beside them were standard badge readers. In her schooling, Twila had been issued a badge to access the common teaching labs. There, of course, times were rigidly scheduled so that no two students would encounter each other in the lab. Here, she watched people badge their way in to where three or four other techs and researchers worked together.

Other doors along this corridor stood open. One looked

like a laundry room, and another appeared to be a meeting
room of some sort. For holo conferences? She wondered.
Somehow she had always imagined that those conference
rooms she saw on the flatscreen were just simulations,
with participants safely ensconced in their own holo
rooms. It seemed now that this was not always the case—
at least not in Medical.

Angry voices from a room up ahead stopped her short.
Cold fear ran through Twila; there was genuine hostility
in these voices. When her mother grew angry with her or
Aunt Trish, the anger was dramatic but only blustery, an
anger of defense rather than aggression. This was something else. "What have you got, shit for brains?" the one
voice demanded. It was a man's voice, hot with outrage.

The other voice was cold. "Don't push me, Murphy."
Its coldness sent a chill through Twila. She had witnessed
true anger before, but only on the flatscreen. Once there
had been a "brawl" in Papa Joe's, but it was a ridiculous
thing: two women smashing at each other's images
because of jealousy over some man, each trying to
degrade the other by shattering their illusion. In the end
someone had called Security to tune them out, and the
disturbance had been promptly removed. Here, the two
voices came from the same room—two people face-to-
face, where they could actually strike each other, and
there was no way to remove them from each other, or
from her route.

"You're the most ignorant, incompetent bonehead I
ever saw, you know that?"

Twila trembled, afraid to go closer, afraid to go back.
Could they be dangerous? Violent? Panic seized Twila.
What if one of them went over the Edge? What if she just
happened to be walking by, and one of them—

Ridiculous, she told herself, trying desperately to calm
her pounding heart. This is Medical, these people
probably have psychevals more often than anyone else.
There can't be an Edgewalker here. Just because your
grandmother encountered one . . .

Slowly, carefully, Twila forced herself to move forward, closer to the angry voices. She forced herself to
walk normally, to hold her head up and not cringe when
she approached the door. That was what her mother had

always taught her: don't do anything unusual, and maybe they won't notice you. Maybe you won't attract the Edge-walker's attention, and you'll be safe. You'll be safe.

She was even with the door now, her heart thumping wildly, but she kept going. What did my grandmother do, she wondered, that caught an Edgewalker's attention? Nothing, Aunt Trish says. Nothing. She just walked out of Stores, carrying her packages, and there he was. No warning, just this madman in her face, and before the security monitor could sound the alarm, he'd slashed her throat—

The voices were behind her now, growing muffled as her trembling knees carried her farther away. Gradually her pulse slowed and her mind began to clear. These were the halls of Medical, not the open streets and plazas of Numex. There was less fear here, that was obvious, and Grandfather always said it was fear that caused people to go over the Edge—fear and frustration. But it was not until she was nearly at the end of the corridor that Twila could ignore the feeling of a great menace at her back.

Ahead the corridor came to a T, and she would need to go left. A double doorway stood on the wall where the corridor ended, and above it hung a sign: ISOLATION.

Twila shuddered. That was where her grandfather had been held before he was put Outside. She had been here before, then, though all she remembered of it was an elevator ride and a maze of corridors with white walls. Beyond that sign somewhere was the glassed-in room with its tunnel to Outside . . . There were no windows in the doors, and the simple badge reader beside them seemed somehow inadequate to control them. *This is where people were taken,* Twila thought, *when they were infected. This is where they were dragged, screaming sometimes, and forced Outside. This is where Grand-father went, of his own volition, and it was only my mother who screamed . . .*

An ache welled up in Twila, squeezing her heart. Sixteen years. Oh, Grandfather, I still miss you. I can't help thinking how different my life would be if you hadn't had to leave us. And I can't help wondering what it was like for you . . . at the end . . .

Resolutely Twila turned the corner and went on toward

her destination, quietly putting distance between herself
and the frightening word: ISOLATION.

Ten yards down this corridor, she turned right again
and her pulse quickened. The immunology lab was just up
here on the left. If Jon and Dr. Krell were not there, she
would have to continue to the elder Krell's office. She
hoped they were here; this trip through the corridors of
Medical was more unnerving than she had ever thought it
might be, and she didn't want to continue it. But what if
the lab door had no windows, and she could not see in?
Undoubtedly it was locked, and she had no badge to let
herself in. What would she do? Pound on the door and
demand to be let in? How childish. And what would she
say to the person who opened the door, if the Doctors
Krell were not in the room?

Voices carried down the hallway to her. These were not
angry voices, like those she had heard earlier, but they
were forceful. Slowing her steps, she saw that the door to
the immunology lab stood wide open, held that way by a
broad, habited form that looked familiar. The voice was
familiar as well. Twila approached silently, listening
intently.

It was the elder Dr. Krell's voice, smooth as butter,
eminently rational, with just a hint of amusement in it.
"For the love of God, Jon, you can be so stone-headed
sometimes. What was the point?"

"Scientific curiosity." That was Jon's voice, laden with
irony. It sent a strange tingling through Twila. There was
no doubt about it now; this was the man she had tried so
hard to tantalize last night.

Now Dr. Krell laughed. "There are better ways to satisfy your curiosity, boy, and better women to satisfy it
with."

The comment puzzled Twila. So did the following
pause, pregnant with a heavy tension she could feel, even
out here in the hallway. She stood silently just outside the
door, her slender form shielded from Jon's view by
Krell's broad back. "That would be your response," Jon
said, voice frigid with contempt.

But Krell did not flare at his tone, choosing to ignore
the hostility in it. "Come, now," he cajoled. "I know I'm

not the perfect father, but I haven't done so badly by you, have I?"

"Considering what a shock I was to you."

"Not so." Krell's voice was low and aggrieved. "Jon—you've been out there too much, you're starting to think like one of them."

One of them? Twila wondered. What "them"? And out where? Outside the MA?

"I was raised out there, remember?" Such bitterness! It was both balm and bane to Twila to hear it—balm that it was not she alone who came in for it, bane that anyone should live with such pain inside him.

"And are you sorry I changed your life?" Krell countered, still without rancor. How patient he was! "Sorry I took responsibility for you, gave you the opportunity to be where you are?" He stepped out of the doorway now and into the lab, and the door began to swing shut behind him.

Twila caught it, her quick movement lost behind Krell's broad habit. She stood motionless even as Jon's retort stopped Krell short.

"Carlton Grimm gave me the chance to be where I am."

Krell seemed to sway a little, as though a transport had passed within inches of his face. Then, with a steady, deliberate movement, he stepped to the left and leaned against the bank of cupboards that was just inside the door. Twila could see Jon now on the other side of the room, his body turned profile to his father as he worked at some equipment there. His face was hard and full of anger that filled his voice. Krell tried again, his voice still calm. "Carlton gave us all the chance—"

Suddenly Jon straightened up, and Twila knew he had seen her at last. Krell broke off his speech, following Jon's stare, and turning, saw her as well. "Who the devil—!" he exclaimed. "This is a secured area—"

"What has my grandfather to do with this?" Twila demanded, stepping into the room and allowing the door to swing shut behind her.

"Twila!" Krell exclaimed.

The two men looked at her in shock. Krell's hood was thrown back, and Twila's first thought was, I've never seen him unhooded before. Her second thought was, His eyes are gray, too.

Jon was not habited, but wore a white lab coat over dun-colored pants and a light kapok shirt. He looked older than he had last night—perhaps it was just the paleness of his skin in the harsh light of the lab. But it was his face that fascinated Twila. In those brief moments when he first saw her, a dozen emotions warred across his face: surprise, anger, joy, guilt, hope, fear. Twila watched them struggle, wondered at the complexity of them, and then saw them solidify into a mask of coldness in which his gray eyes blazed like molten stone.

"Twila, what are you doing here?" Dr. Krell asked with apparent solicitude, but he had the look of a man trying to cover a bad fright. "How did you find your way?" He reached out to draw her farther into the room, but Twila shied away. There was an office to her right, just inside the lab door; it made a small corridor with the cupboards on the left, and she stood her ground like a mouse to the entrance of its tunnel, secure as long as escape was close at hand.

"No questions, Dr. Krell," she told him flatly. "It's time for some answers."

Krell moved back a little, gesturing for her to come out of the aisle. "Patients can't just wander about, it's not safe," he was saying. "Did someone tell you—"

"I'm a very bright girl," she flared, staying where she was. "And I'm not going to tell you how I found you until you tell me one or two things."

That brought the cruel twist of a smile to Jon's face.

"All right, then," Krell said with measured candor. "What do you want to know?"

You're going to lie to me, Twila thought. Even before the words are out of your mouth, I know you're going to lie to me. You don't want me to know what's going on. But I have to know. I have to get it out of you somehow.

"Am I dying?" she asked bluntly.

Jon gave a sharp, incredulous laugh, and Krell looked flabbergasted—but not for long. "No, no, Twila," he assured her with that infuriating touch of amusement in his voice. "You are not dying."

That, at least, had the ring of truth. She forged ahead. "Am I some kind of freak?"

Instantly the amusement was gone. "No, Twila," Krell said quietly. "You are not a freak."

But the truth was written on Jon's face, if not his father's.

"Liar," Twila whispered.

"Twila—!" Krell threw up his hands in exasperation. "You are not a freak! You are a normal, healthy young woman with a long and normal life ahead of you."

"Provided I come here every month for you to put me to sleep and run tests I never see the results of, and poke me and bleed me and—" Turning sharply away from him, she marched across the room to Jon and stood directly in front of him, glaring up into his face. It seemed to her he drew away from the forcefulness of her approach. "Why did you come looking for me last night?" she demanded.

The answer lay just behind his eyes, but she could not read it; it lay just on the tip of his tongue, but he would not open his mouth to speak. He only gazed down at her and wanted her to know. Once again she felt a shock, as though their two souls had come into alignment, as though they had locked into place and no force on earth could pull them apart. Tell me, tell me, tell me! her eyes pleaded.

I can't, I can't, I can't, his eyes replied.

"You misunderstand," Krell interjected gently.

With an effort Twila tore her gaze from Jon's to look back at the elder doctor. Unhooded, his face bore the marks of his sixty-odd years: it was worn and a bit fleshy, though only as suited his broad shoulders. His hair was dark like Jon's but graying at the temples, and a gray streak ran from his forehead back over the crown of his head. He looked weary, his frame sagging a little as she turned on him. "Twila," he said calmly—too calmly, she thought. He was prepared to lie to her again. "When you were a little girl," Krell began, "your grandfather—"

"Made you feel guilty as sin about something," she finished, angry that he continued to treat her like the child of whom he spoke. "What was that between you, the day he went Outside? You fell all over yourself offering to take care of us—'especially Twila,' you said. And for a minute, for just a minute, he looked like he wanted to kill you. Why was that, Dr. Krell?"

Krell's mouth dropped open. His eyes flicked ever so briefly to his son, then back to Twila. His jaw worked once, then twice, then his mouth snapped shut and his eyes dropped to the floor.

"Because it was my fault," Krell whispered hoarsely.

Now Twila's mouth gaped. From the corner of her eye she saw Jon jump, saw the look of shock on his face, saw him take an involuntary step toward his father.

Krell groped for a nearby stool and sagged onto it. "It was my fault he was infected," the older man rasped. "I was working here in the lab, and I had an experiment running—I should have posted the warning first, I always posted the warning first, but that day I thought—" He broke off. "It doesn't matter what I thought. I failed to post the warning on the door before I took the culture out of storage. And when I heard someone badge the door, I turned to wave him off—and my elbow hit—" Again he stopped, fighting for control of his voice. "It was Carlton, and he was unmasked. Of course, we both had to go through Filtration and Sterilization, and I kept hoping—" Krell turned miserable eyes on Twila. "He was unmasked. When the test results came back . . ." Krell could not finish. He dropped his head into one hand.

Twila looked at him, slumped on the stool, the picture of wretchedness, and she couldn't help wondering, *Truth or fiction? Truth or fiction? Is this really a burden you've carried for sixteen years, or is this a story designed to tug on my heartstrings and shut me up?*

Over the years Twila had tried very hard not to wonder too much about just how her grandfather had become infected with the deadly virus. If it was truly CM-B, as he'd told Aunt Trish, then somehow, in his work at Medical, he had breathed it in. Then, Krell's story could well be true.

But in her unguarded moments, when her thoughts wandered where she did not want them to, Twila remembered how sure she had been that Grandfather had lied to Aunt Trish. And if that were the case, how could he have gotten CM-A? It was anaerobic, needing to pass from host to host directly, without coming into contact with the air. Had he touched an infected patient? Had he drunk from a contaminated container? Whatever the case, it ruled out Dr. Krell's story.

Was it all my childish imagination? Twila wondered. My grandfather never told lies; what made me think he was lying then?

What makes me think Krell might be lying now?

Twila turned to look at Jon. He seemed disarmed by his father's confession, uncertain why Krell had chosen to share it. But he did not seem to question it. If Jon, who hated him so, took this story at face value—

"But what does that have to do with me?" Twila asked unexpectedly, turning back to the elder Krell. "What does that have to do with me? With Jon coming to find me? With your chastising him for doing that? Tell me, Dr. Krell, what's wrong with *me*."

From outside the door came the sound of shouting, but Twila hardly heard it. She fixed her gaze on Krell, still slumped on the stool, and waited for an answer.

Slowly Krell lifted his head and stared at her. How soft his gray eyes were, how painted with misery! How strange that those same eyes, in Jon's face, were always so hard, so defensive . . . "You don't understand," Krell said softly. "You don't understand. You were so precious to Carlton. When he—when I—I promised to look after you, Twila. It was all I could do. But I couldn't take over his role, I couldn't bear to see you every day and be reminded . . . so I look after your health. I'm a doctor. That I can do."

The noise from outside intruded again. A crash, a scream perhaps, but muted, distant.

"And if my health doesn't need looking after, do you make something up?" Twila demanded, unimpressed by his outpouring. "Drag me in once a month and put me through a battery of tests, just to ease your conscience? Because if that's the case, Dr. Krell, I have no intention of coming in for any more medical appointments."

Now Krell looked up sharply. "You have to!" he exclaimed involuntarily.

"Why?" She took one step toward him. "Why, Dr. Krell? *What's wrong with me?*"

A heartbeat. The lie formed. "Your medication—"

"Liar!" She swung around, back to Jon, and her habit swirled out, jostling a beaker on a nearby table—

Jon lunged for it, catching it in gloved hands before it tipped. Twila froze, suddenly conscious of the threat that might exist in this laboratory. "What's in that?" she asked in a small voice.

Jon glanced at her and saw the terror on her face. "Just an enzyme solution," he assured her, his voice gentle with understanding. "Don't worry, we don't leave live cultures lying about. They're all secured in the coolers, there." He nodded toward the wall across from the door.

Twila could not suppress a shudder. Maybe Krell's story about her grandfather was true after all. It was certainly plausible.

Suddenly she was conscious of Jon's gaze on her, and she glanced up into his eyes. There was no hardness in them now. Yet even the gentleness in them was different than the gentleness his father had shown. It flowed out, whereas the softness of Dr. Krell's eyes had tried to draw her in . . .

Behind them Krell rose from the lab stool. Jon turned away, but not before Twila saw the coldness come back into his eyes. He carried the beaker off to a counter at the far side of the room.

"Twila, I know you think it's a lot of fuss over nothing," the elder Krell began again, "but the truth is—"

He was cut off by a shrill voice from the lab's intercom. "Dr. Krell, emergency!" Both Dr. Krells jerked toward the sound. Twila's heart lurched inside her.

"Yes, what is it?" Jon demanded as he strode toward a wall console.

"Emergency alert, there's been a security breach. An unauthorized person is in your area. Please double-secure your lab."

Was that all! Twila found it ironic to be relieved that she had been discovered. All three relaxed, and a small smile tugged at Jon's lips. "Yes, I know," he answered dryly. "She's standing right here—"

"No, no, this is a male," the voice interrupted, still urgent. "A tech with a research badge, but he's unauthorized and considered dangerous. He appears to have gone over the Edge—"

Without preamble Jon turned to the bank of storage units lining the wall. "Code the door!" he shouted at his father, punching in the locks on the individual cabinets.

"Code it how?" Krell roared back. "I haven't got the sequence!"

"It's in my desk—" Jon made one move toward the office, then stopped. "Damn, never mind!" He turned back to the cabinets. "Just—throw something in front of it. Twila!" he barked. "Help me lock these things. Just push in every button you can see."

For a moment Twila stood numbly. Over the Edge . . .

"Twila!"

Jon's sharp voice jolted her. Locks. Blood, the locks! Yes, she must help Jon, because they couldn't let anyone get at the cultures in those coolers—Heart pounding, Twila scurried around a lab table toward the row of storage units. Which ones had the virus? She should lock those first, of course. But live virus—Jon was advancing toward her along the wall, slammed his palm against the protruding locks as he came. Jon was wearing gloves.

I'll let him get those, Twila thought, steering to her left and beginning to smash the locks into place as she had seen Jon do. I'll let him get those, he has the gloves.

Behind her she could hear Krell grunting as he dragged a chair from the office and propelled it toward the door. "How the hell did Security let this happen?" he was fuming. "Jon, this is ridiculous, this chair won't—"

Suddenly he broke off, and Twila could feel the draft as the door was thrown open. *Keep working,* she told herself. *Keep locking the cabinets*—But she could not resist. Slowly she turned to see what madness looked like . . .

He wore greens, his mask dangling around his neck. In his hand was a small silver tool stained red; in his eye was a coldness that froze Twila's blood, and her hands. With one sweep he seemed to take in the room: Krell shoving the chair at him, Jon slamming home the locks, Twila motionless as a mouse before a cobra. There his gaze stopped.

It's happening, Twila thought in panic as the eyes bored into her and the silver tool glinted in his hand. It's happening to me, just like it did to my grandmother Sharee. He's seen me, he's fixed on me, and I don't know why.

She never knew why, but she died in the street, and I'm going to die here—

With one foot the demented tech flung the chair back at Krell. Then he bounded over it, knocking Krell aside, heading straight for Twila. "No-o-o-!" she could hear Krell's stricken cry as the green menace bore down on her. "No-o-o! God, no-o-o!"

There was a flash of white, and the green blur shifted suddenly to her left. Reality snapped back into focus for Twila, and she saw Jon on the floor, on top of the man in greens. But the Edgewalker was a big man, bigger than Jon. It took only one arm to fling the young doctor aside. "Twila, run!" Jon shouted.

Twila ran for the door.

But she could not leave. Turning, she saw Jon scrambling to lock the last of the cabinets, the ones that she had bypassed out of fear. She saw the twisted smile on the tech's face as he discerned Jon's objective. She saw him grab Jon by his lab coat and haul him back, sending him sprawling. She saw him look at the coolers, saw him reach out, saw him yank one open. An alarm shrieked.

"Masks!" Jon yelled, pulling his own into place.

Masks? Twila fumbled at her hood. Masks? Terror seized her. *Masks?*

Flinging her arm up over her nose and mouth, Twila staggered toward the door, but the chair was in her way. Behind her she heard the tinkling of glass as numerous vials and dishes hit the floor and shattered. Small, desperate noises escaped her as she stumbled around the chair and tried to reach the door . . . the door . . .

Faces stared back at her through the glassed upper part of the door, two faces of MA security guards. Why didn't they come in? Why didn't they rescue her? Isn't that what Security was supposed to do? But even as her hand grasped the handle of the door, she knew it was locked against her. She knew why the security guards did not come in, and why they could not let her out.

From somewhere came a sharp cry of pain. Hopeless, helpless, Twila spun around and saw the elder Dr. Krell grappling with the tech. There was blood on Krell's habit, but a mask was in place over his nose and mouth. Then as she watched, the tech slowly sagged, his struggles decreasing, until he slipped from Krell's grasp onto the glass-strewn floor. From his throat poured blood in a scarlet stream.

Now Jon staggered to his feet, favoring his right knee. As quickly as he was able, he crossed to where Twila stood engulfed in horror. His arms reached out, hesitated, then slid gently around her.

Twila was hardly aware that he was touching her. She looked up at him, her habit sleeve still pressed uselessly across her mouth and nose. "I don't have a mask," she whimpered.

He lifted his right hand to brush a strand of hair out of her eyes, winced at the motion, and changed hands. "It's all right," he soothed, his voice made strange by the filtration mask.

But she knew better. "I've been exposed, haven't I?" Her voice came in little sobs. "I've been exposed just like my grandfather was, and now I'm infected and I'm going to die."

"No, no, no," he whispered, hugging her close to him. "No, you're not going to die. You're not infected, you don't ever have to worry about being infected, you're the safest person in this room. Twila." Through the hood of her habit his voice was muffled, but his words were clear. "You're immune."

Chapter 4

Jon shoved a filtration mask toward Twila. "Put this on."
She took it slowly, turning it over in her hands, examining the inside. It was lined with mechanical and chemical screening devices that were one-quarter to one-half inch thick, and that made it heavier than its size and crisp white texture made it appear. A spongy rim insured a tight fit against varying shapes and sizes of human faces.

"But I don't need this," she objected numbly, still dazed from the stream of events over the past two hours.

"You know that, and I know that," Jon said curtly. "But every tech working this evac doesn't need to know that."

Still numb, Twila lifted the mask and slipped it into place as bidden. She wished Jon had put it on her; she imagined his hand brushing her cheek, lingering in her hair. It was safe, after all—all those things she had only pantomimed in holos, the physical contacts she had both dreaded and craved; they were safe for her now, with Jon. He couldn't hurt her, and she couldn't hurt him.

But Jon limped away to unlock a sterilizer built into the wall, and started loading it with equipment from one of the lab tables.

"How did I get to be immune?" she asked abruptly.

Jon continued to work, using his left hand. His right wrist was bound, either sprained or cracked in the scuffle with the mad tech. He glanced up at Twila, his eyes scowling above the bleached-white circle of his filtration mask. "Ask the other Dr. Krell," he said.

You're not angry with me, she thought. *You're just afraid—afraid someone will have noticed how tender you were with me, how you cradled me like a child in your arms. You're afraid someone might think there's a soft spot in you somewhere. And there is. A very large one.*

But his soft spot would not allow him to answer her question. Reluctantly Twila turned to look at the elder Krell. He was on the visicom in Jon's office, talking to techs in the hallway as they moved an evac unit into place over the lab door. Krell was garbed in dark pants and a light shirt; he had removed his bloodstained habit and draped it over the body of the tech. It had been the tech's blood, not Krell's, that had stained the habit during the fight. *A powerful man,* Twila thought, *to stand up to that tech in his madness. Physically powerful, and emotionally powerful, to disarm him like that and then cut him with his own weapon . . .*

"Sealed?" she could hear Krell ask. "All right, I'm going to open the door and take out the blood check kit; then we'll load this fellow in. Dump him in the crematorium and blow the ashes Outside; there's no point in trying to decontaminate him."

It was an unusual fate for a domizen—even an Edgewalker. Bodies of humans and animals alike were normally treated with chemicals to make them decompose faster, then buried where their nutrients would enrich the soil that fed the community. To be so spurned, so despised, that even in death there was no place made for you . . . Twila's stomach grew queasy, and she turned back to Jon. "I'll ask him later," she whispered, her eyes on the floor. She didn't think she could talk to Krell right now.

Jon paused in his work, eyes softening as they rested on her ashen face. Then he turned and called to his father, who was coming out of the office, "Can't we send Twila out first?"

Krell looked up, his hand on the lab door, and saw Twila perched on a lab stool, looking small and forlorn in her muslin habit. "I'm sorry, dear," he apologized. "It will only take thirty minutes or so to dispose of this rubbish; then we'll get you out of here and into a decontamination chamber. I can give you something to sleep then, if you want."

Neither his offer nor his sympathy charmed her. "No, thank you," she replied quickly, not meeting his eyes. "I think I've done enough sleeping for today."

There was a slight pause as Krell took that in. Then he

opened the door and removed a tray from the evac unit outside. "Jon," he called, "can you give me a hand with this fellow?"

"If one is all you need," Jon said dryly as he limped over to the corpse.

"You ought to take up martial arts, son," Krell jested. "You'd be able to handle an Edgewalker like this."

Jon made no reply, and Twila was sure the remark hurt him, despite the lightness of Krell's tone. It was not just that Jon's father was bigger physically than he—for now, without his habit, Twila could see that he had a good forty pounds and several inches on his son. But by position and reputation, Krell cast an awfully big shadow. Worse, it seemed to Twila that he kept reminding Jon of it.

With some difficulty the two men loaded the body into the evac unit. Jon was hampered by his injured wrist and knee, and Twila knew she ought to offer to help, but somehow she could not make herself do it. She had never seen a dead person before, never seen a body torn by violence and soaked with blood. A great wave of cold washed over her just thinking about it. She couldn't even use Krell's discarded habit to mop up the blood congealing on the floor. Immune or not, the thought of touching anything bloody repulsed her. She let the doctors take care of that, too.

When they had accomplished their task, Krell closed the lab door again and waved to the techs outside to take the evac unit away. Then he picked up the tray that he had set aside before and turned to Twila. "I'm afraid we need one more blood sample from you, my dear."

Resentment prickled Twila. With the gruesome body gone, she felt less queasy, but her anger began to bubble. "Why, if I'm immune?" she demanded.

Krell shrugged, unaffected by her testiness. "Jon and I will have to provide samples, too, even though we were masked. Call it insurance. In your case, call it a chance to observe what your blood does when exposed to the virus under uncontrolled circumstances."

Reluctantly Twila pushed up the sleeve of her habit and extended her arm. "Is there any chance I'm not immune under 'uncontrolled circumstances'?"

"None," Krell replied flatly, wrapping a piece of rubber

tubing around her arm to find the vein. "Rest assured of that."

But Twila wasn't sure what to believe of Dr. Krell anymore. "How did I come to be this way?" she asked again.

Deftly Krell inserted a needle in the bulging blue vein, loosened the tube, and reached for a sterile vial from the tray. "It's something in your blood," he told her as he extracted the sample. "We're not sure what to call it, really; it's not actually a bacterium, not an antibody—antivirus is the most descriptive term. Your body manufactures it—we think in your bone marrow, but we're not even sure of that. Whatever it is, it destroys the CM virus before it ever gets to the nervous system. We've watched it in cultures: it engulfs the virus and more or less digests it, excreting waste materials that bear no resemblance to the original virus. Even the DNA is altered! But we don't know how."

"And that's really why I have all these medical appointments, isn't it?" Twila asked as he covered the needle with an alcohol wipe and drew it out.

Krell pressed a gauze pad against the tiny puncture. "Hold that," he instructed. "Twila, we've been trying for twenty-odd years to replicate this agent in your blood, or to concoct some kind of blood serum, or in some way to transfer your immunity to other people. But it doesn't work. As soon as the agent is injected into a host, it loses potency and becomes ineffective. There's something unique to your body chemistry—perhaps to your DNA—that allows the antivirus to live in you, but not in any host environment. At least, not for long."

"But why didn't you just tell me this?" Twila demanded, the strain of the day putting her on the verge of tears. "Why all the secrecy, all the pretense? I'd have been happy to trot down here and give you a pint or two of blood whenever you needed it, or sit through whatever tests you wanted to perform. Why keep it secret from me?"

Krell sighed. "At first you were too young to understand. And then we were afraid what the knowledge might do to you. Adolescence is a tough time, Twila—being immune would have made you feel even more of an oddity than a teenager normally feels. And if you should

slip and let the secret out—can you imagine how other
children would have reacted? You'd have been the target
for more resentment and hostility than I care to think
about. Besides, we didn't want the whole community to
know; they would have expected too much too soon, and
we were having such poor luck with our research. It just
seemed simpler to keep it all quiet."

"And now that I'm grown up?" Twila persisted. "Do
you still not trust me? Do you think I might go running
out into the street shouting, 'Nana, nana, I'm immune and
you're not'?"

"Of course not," Krell scoffed. "I know what kind of
fine, responsible person you have become, and I know
that you will treat your condition with the confidence it
requires. And undoubtedly I could have told you—maybe
should have told you—years ago. But we'd established a
story, a routine—it was just easier not to change it."

"Easier?" Twila snorted. "Easier to drug me and
deceive me and—" She broke off suddenly and turned
back to Jon. "Is it true?" she asked bluntly. "Is that what
all this has been about, running tests on me, on my blood,
to find out about the immunity?"

"Twila—!" the elder Krell exclaimed, pain in his voice.

She swung back to him. "You've lied to me all my life,
Dr. Krell. You'll forgive me if I want a second opinion in
this." She returned her gaze to Jon. "Is it true?"

Jon had gone back to loading the sterilizer, but now he
stopped and glared at them both. "Yes, it's true," he said
after a moment. "That's my research here; I've made a
career out of studying your blood, trying to find a way to
transfer your immunity to other people."

"Well, he's had a little help," Krell commented dryly.
"Your grandfather and I started the research; then I went
on to another area and Jon took it over. And he has a
number of assistants who, thankfully"—here he nodded to
the empty lab—"don't work on Saturday." Then he
looked across at his son, and there was the softness of
muted pride in his eyes. "Jon's had some intriguing
experiments going lately, though; we're very hopeful."

"This batch will have to be run again," Jon said with a
gesture toward the tables in the lab. "They've all been

corrupted by our friend's little—interruption." He went back to loading the sterilizer.

Twila watched him and wondered if the activity wasn't more to keep himself distracted than to get the task accomplished. "How will they sterilize the whole room?" she wanted to know.

"They'll come in wearing SCEs," Jon told her. "Same kind of suits they wear to go Outside. What can't be loaded in portable sterilizers will be trashed. Then they'll divide the lab into sections"—he pointed at tracks in the ceiling—"and change the air, one section at a time. And finally, we'll stay out of it for two weeks. The virus needs a host to survive. As long as there are no plants or animals in here to nourish it, it'll die out in about ten days."

"And us?" Twila turned to the elder Krell. "How long will it take to decontaminate us?"

"Twelve hours," he replied. "Unfortunately, we have only one Decontamination Chamber, and it will only accommodate two people at a time. You'll go first, Twila; Jon and I can continue the cleanup process in here until it's our turn."

Twelve hours. Twila shrugged. "I guess I'd better call Mom and tell her I won't be home for supper."

"I'll do that," Krell said hastily, crossing toward Jon's office. "I'll arrange for you to spend the night here at Medical, when you're through in the Decontamination Chamber. You don't want to be going home at that hour; too many Edgewalkers about in the dark." He disappeared into the office, and Twila could hear him tapping out the code to call her mother.

She turned back to Jon, who was now tearing down equipment at one of the lab tables. "Well, I couldn't go dancing tonight anyway," she sighed.

The trace of a smile quirked Jon's eyes, his mouth invisible behind his mask. It was a refreshing break in his surly mood, and Twila decided to pursue it. Sliding off the lab stool, she came to stand beside him.

"Why did you come looking for me?" she asked softly.

The smile faded, and for a moment she was afraid he would grow cold and angry again. But then he shrugged. "I'd never met you," he said. "I know the elements of your blood like the keys on my terminal, and I'm on intimate terms with your DNA, but I'd never met the woman." He stacked several petri dishes, and pushed them toward the back of the table. "That didn't seem right."

It touched her. It showed the sentimentality she knew was there, locked behind the coldness of his gray eyes. She liked knowing he had this sense of rightness, a set of principles that he marked his life by. It intrigued her even more than the dark mystery he had projected in Papa Joe's. Standing so close to him—*physically* close— she felt a resurgence of the strong magnetic attraction between them. "Why did you wait so long?"

His face clouded, and instead of answering, he said in a low voice, "If you are wise, you'll not show too much interest in me in front of the old man."

Twila's eyebrows flew up in surprise. Then slowly, casually, she turned to look at Krell, where he sat at Jon's desk. He was indeed watching them through the open doorway.

So she walked boldly across the room and into the office.

"How did my mom take it?" she asked.

"Oh, I told her we were just keeping you overnight for some more tests. I didn't see any point in alarming her with words like 'exposure' and 'decontamination.' "

Another lie! But a justifiable one. If her mother knew she'd been exposed to the CM virus, Roxanne would go absolutely over the Edge—

Suddenly Twila's mouth went slack as she realized the implication. "She doesn't know, does she?" Twila asked. "She doesn't know I'm immune."

"She thinks you have a rare blood condition that we're studying," Krell admitted.

"And Aunt Trish?"

"We've told her the same story, but she's more astute than your mother, and I don't think she believes it." He grunted. "I'm not sure what she does believe."

Twila wasn't sure, either. All these years, and Aunt Trish had never so much as hinted that—

Then something else occurred to her.

"Why isn't my mother immune?" Twila dropped into a chair beside the desk and looked at Krell with dark, questioning eyes. "If I'm immune, didn't I have to inherit that from someone? Either my mom or my donor father? Or one of my grandparents? Someone?"

From the corner of her eyes, she saw Jon step up to the countertop nearest the doorway and begin to empty containers into the trash. But she knew he was listening.

Krell sighed. "What you have could be a mutation, Twila," he said. "A genetic fluke. We don't know why mutations occur, but they are the reason that humankind has been able to survive——"

"Tell her," Jon interrupted, coming into the doorway.

Krell glanced up uncertainly at his son.

Jon's face was hard again, his tone determined. "Tell her—she has a right to know."

For a moment longer Krell hesitated; then he shrugged and frowned a little. "I suppose it can't hurt anything," he conceded. "Somewhere along the line, Twila, this immunity was a mutation; but in your case it is inherited."

"From whom?" Twila demanded, her heart pounding.

"From the woman who brought you here," Krell replied. "From the woman who pounded on the wall of the dome where your grandfather's office window looked out. From your birth mother."

All the strength drained from Twila's limbs, and she sat limply, staring at Dr. Krell.

"She looked like a wild woman," Krell went on. "Hair matted, clothing torn, covered with dirt. Carlton had seen them before, these wretches who would come and pound on the walls and beg to come inside, screaming they were clean—but not for years. We knew there were still people Outside; Security made occasional forays Outside in SCEs, retrieving hardware and chemicals and other things it was difficult to manufacture Inside, and they reported seeing people. But they didn't seem to have any interest in bothering us.

"Then this woman showed up." Krell massaged his temple, as though the memory was one he wanted to erase. "She had found Carlton's window somehow, and she knew his name—maybe someone who was put Outside told her about him. Anyway, she pounded on the wall and called out, 'Dr. Grimm! Dr. Grimm!' Normally he would have lowered his blinds and left the office—he told me once he could never bear to listen to their pleading. But when she called him by name, he stopped. Then she said, 'I have something you want,' and she went back to a clump of yucca and pulled you out. You couldn't have been more than three months old."

Krell leaned forward, resting his arms on the desk. "Carlton called me in from the next office, and pointed to the pair of you standing just outside the wall. 'Krell,' he said, 'I want to bring them inside.' I was dumbfounded. 'You can't!' I said. 'They have to be infected. It's been nearly forty years since the virus went aerobic.' But he said to me, 'The virus manifests its symptoms in ten to fifteen years—twenty at the very most. Look at her, Krell. Look at the age lines in her forehead, the wrinkles around her eyes.'

" 'A life of hardship will do that,' " I argued.

" 'To a teenager?' he said. 'No, Krell, look at the proportions of her body, the contours of her face. She is no teenager. She's too physically mature.' Then he crossed to the window and asked the woman, 'How old are you?' And she answered, 'I lose count, but I know it's past thirty.' " Krell blew out a breath. "Past thirty. She should have been dead for ten years. Either the virus had mutated again, or"—he leaned back in the chair—"she was immune. Either way, we had to know. So we brought the two of you Inside."

"What happened to her?" Twila whispered. "Where is she?"

Krell shook his head sadly. "She couldn't handle life Inside. She—"

"She couldn't handle being strapped to an examination table," Jon interrupted, "and jabbed with needles and drugged and—"

"Were you there?" Krell asked quietly.

"Carlton told me," Jon defended. "Carlton was there."

"Yes," Krell said pointedly. "He was." Krell let the implication of Carlton's knowledge and participation in the woman's treatment hang for a moment. Then he went on. "We had to put you both through Decontamination before we could examine you," he told Twila. "Then we tried to explain the tests, tried to explain why we needed to draw blood, to—" He gestured helplessly. "It was so

totally outside her experience, she couldn't understand.
Couldn't deal with it. You were undernourished, with a
parasitic infection, so we had you isolated from her,
hooked up to an IV—Anyway, she left. Tricked an
orderly into releasing her restraints, then clubbed her and
ran. She was still in Isolation, and the tunnel was right
there, and she was gone. We tried sending Security after
her in SCEs, but she knew the country out there, and they
didn't. She just vanished. Just vanished." He looked up at
Jon. "Is that what Carlton told you?"

   "Yes," Jon agreed. "That's the way Carlton told it,
too." Then he turned and went back out into the lab.

   Krell watched him go. "Twenty-two years," he said
softly. "Twenty-two years since his mother sent him to
me; twenty-two years, and the hate is still there . . ." Krell
tapped idly at the keyboard. "He adored your grandfather.
It was Carlton who got him interested in medicine, not
me. He wanted to take his advanced studies with Carlton,
but—a lot of things got cut short when your grandfather
went Outside."

   Twila heard the pain in him and knew she ought to be
affected by it, but she was too numb to respond. Still
reeling from the shock of her immunity, now she
struggled with the knowledge that Roxanne was not her
mother at all; that some Outsider had given birth to her in
the contaminated ruins of civilization and brought her
here to be deposited on Carlton Grimm's proverbial door-
step. *Who was she?* Twila wondered. *Was it from her that
I got my dark hair and golden-brown skin? All these years
I thought it was from my donor father . . . Then, was I
conceived in the natural way? Of course, there can be no
artificial insemination Outside. People never live to be
more than fifteen or twenty, they have only the artifacts
left by a former civilization and what primitive things they
can develop themselves by that age. But if my mother was
nearly thirty . . . Are there more, then? Are there more
people Outside who are immune to CM? If so, shouldn't
we let them in?*

   Do they want *to come in?*

   "I'm afraid all this has been very stressful for you," Dr.
Krell said gently. "And the decontamination process is
not going to be very pleasant. Why don't you let me give

you something, something very mild, just to help you relax. Not sleep, but—"

"No!" Twila screamed, jumping up from the chair, suddenly trembling with rage. "You can't make it go away by drugging me, don't you understand? You can't make anything change; you can't take back all the lies that have been told me; you can't make it any easier to bear—You can't erase the pain, Dr. Krell. I have to feel it, I have to deal with it, I have to get past it. If you drug me, you only put it off, and that doesn't help—it only makes it worse. Just let me hurt! Leave me alone and let me hurt."

With that Twila stumbled out of the office and into the lab, flinging herself into the farthest corner from Krell and sinking to the floor in a sobbing heap. She heard Krell start to come after her; Jon stopped him. "Let her be," Jon hissed. "Can't you honor even one simple request?"

Huddled in her misery, Twila knew that although she did not want the elder Krell anywhere near her, she wanted desperately for the younger one to come and comfort her. She wanted to be held and rocked, and she wanted Jon to do it; but Jon did not come. Was he just honoring her request? Or did it have more to do with what he'd said earlier about not showing too much interest in front of "the old man"?

Grandfather, I need you! her mind cried out. *If you were here, you would hold me. If you were here, you would explain to me why—why? Why did you never tell me I was not Roxanne's biological child? And although I understand why you couldn't tell her where I came from, why couldn't you tell Aunt Trish? Or did you? Does Trish know any of this? And why did you give me to Roxanne to raise, and not her?*

Twila looked down at her hands, at the slender brown fingers roughened by work in the orchards. *Are they my mother's hands?* she wondered. *Did she have the same slender ankles, the same wide brow and pointed chin, the same curling dark hair? Did she want to leave me behind, is that why she brought me here? To be rid of me? To give me a better life? Did she think they were hurting me, hooking me up to an IV, sticking me with needles and drawing blood? Did she try to take me back? Did she only try to save herself?*

And if she was truly immune, is she still alive? Outside?

Slowly Twila began to control her sobbing. She'd come to this lab in search of answers and found only more questions. Questions with no answers. Questions with answers she dreaded. She needed to talk to Trish. *I'll tell her everything,* Twila thought. *I'll tell her everything I know, and then maybe she'll tell me everything she knows. Maybe by putting those pieces together, we'll make some sense of this chaos . . . But did she ever know my real mother? Ever see her? Probably not. I don't think she could have kept it a secret from me, if she knew my mother was from Outside. But who would have seen her besides Dr. Krell? Some of the techs? How could I ever find out who they were? And would they remember how a wild woman looked twenty-four years ago?*

Suddenly she drew herself up and looked back at Krell. He was helping Jon tear down the equipment on the lab tables, but he looked up when she moved. Hope showed on his face.

"Do you have footage of her?" Twila asked in a voice made rough by her tears. "Do you have footage of my real mother?"

Krell hesitated. "There might be some in the history files," he said. "I'll look."

Twila waited patiently while he tapped out commands on a terminal in the lab, flashing through screens of information, coming at last to a segment of video. "Here," he called to Twila. "This was taken while you were still in Isolation with her."

Slowly Twila approached the monitor, looking over Dr. Krell's shoulder. The video had been recorded through the glass of the isolation chamber—the same one, she thought, where she had last seen her grandfather. There were glares from the glass, but she could see the grubby figure inside. Long dark hair blocked any view of the woman's face, hair tangled and windblown and littered with pieces of dry grass, as though she had slept on the ground. Her arms and legs were bare, but a dirty white blouse covered her back as she huddled in a corner of the room. Bulky cloth-and-rubber shoes encased otherwise tiny feet, and a spreading skirt of a gaudy floral fabric was stained and torn.

Then as Twila watched, she lifted her head. Dark hair lifted from her breast, and now Twila could see the child cradled there, a tiny bundle of dirty bunting with a head thickly coated in fine, dark curls. Something knotted in Twila's stomach. It could be, she thought. It could be that tiny, tousled waif is me. But my mother—I wish I could see her face—

As though she had heard the request, the woman in the video lifted one brown hand to brush the hair from her face, and Twila gasped. The eyes were sunken and surrounded by dark circles; a long scar ran along her left jaw, and a smaller one above one eyebrow; but there was no mistaking the familiarity of that face. The mouth, the nose, the narrow chin and wide brow, were like those Twila saw in the mirror every day. It was an older face, and had its own unique character, but there was no doubt in Twila's mind that the woman holding the baby was her own mother.

"She—She looks—" Twila did not know how to finish the sentence.

"Used?" Krell asked. "Life is harsh Outside, Twila. The climate is harsh. The unfiltered sun is harsh. The labor required to produce food is harsh. On top of that, there were signs—that people are harsh. To each other. No wonder she wanted something better for you."

For me, Twila thought. But not for herself?

Krell switched off the video.

"Why did you stop?" Twila demanded.

"I'll make you a copy," he said gently. "So you can take it with you. Please—be sensitive with it. Don't show it to your mother."

No, it wouldn't be wise to show it to Mother—

"You mean Roxanne," she said aloud.

"I mean your mother," Krell repeated. "She has been your mother for twenty-four years, Twila. The fact that she did not give birth to you doesn't change that."

No, it didn't change that. But the fact that Trish had raised her as much as Roxanne gave a new irony to the situation. Why did you want me, Mother-Roxanne? And did you regret your decision afterward? Or were you just unequal to the task, and willing to let Trish take over the hard parts . . .

"They'll be coming back with the evac unit soon," Krell told her. "I know how upsetting all this is, and your natural reaction will be to talk about it—Please, give some thought before you blurt this out to the first person who'll listen. Think how other people will react if they know you were brought in from Outside. Think what would happen if they knew you were immune. You need to give yourself time to adjust to all this, Twila, before you decide to share any of it."

Twila found her hands were shaking, and she found she could not control them. "I can't keep it bottled up," she whispered. "I can't keep this all inside myself!"

His large, strong hands reached out to clasp her trembling ones between them. "You can talk to me," he urged. "You can say anything you want. You can yell and scream, you can hit me if it makes you feel any better. Call day or night, I don't mind. Say whatever comes into your head, whatever accusations, whatever frightening things occur to you. I'll be here for you, Twila. I promised your grandfather, and I promise you now: I will always be here for you."

Twila lifted dazed eyes to his. Talk to Krell? The propagator of this deception? What good would that do? She was filled and flooding over, drowning in emotions and hurts that could not be contained—She needed someone to soak up the overflow, someone who could sponge it up and drain it away—not Krell. Krell was too slick; his polished surface would never absorb a thing that Twila poured out. It would only puddle there and stagnate. She tried to pull her hands away.

He would not let her go, searching her face earnestly. "Tell me you'll think about it, Twila," he pressed her. "Promise you will consider who you are speaking to before you speak, and the impact your words will have."

Twila's eyes flashed. "No, I'm going to stand in the middle of the Quad and shout it out. What do you think?"

"Don't talk to techs," he continued. "Don't talk to your schoolmates. Don't talk to—"

"Can I talk to Jon?" she interrupted, afraid he would name Aunt Trish next.

There was a hesitation. Krell released her hands. "Of

course, you can talk to Jon," he said, but there was no
sincerity in his voice. Why didn't he want her to talk
to Jon?

"As though I'll ever see him again," Twila muttered, by
way of diversion. "I'm not eight years old anymore, Dr.
Krell. I will be careful."

A small smile curved his lips. "That's all I ask, Twila.
That's all I ask."

As though on cue, the evac unit arrived back at the lab
door. Krell brought up the visicom on the terminal where
he sat. "Time for you to go now. The decontamination
process is not very pleasant; you'll be stripped and
scrubbed and bathed in various chemicals and radiation,
not to mention having to breathe into a machine for hours.
I'm afraid you'll have a long time to dwell on what's been
said here. Try not to—Try to understand why we didn't
explain all this earlier. Try to see it from our point of
view, Twila, your grandfather's and mine. You are a very
special young lady to me, as you were to your grandfather, and not because of your immunity. But those of us
in authority have an entire community of eight thousand
people to think of. Sometimes we make decisions we
don't like personally."

He spoke now to an evac tech outside the door. "All set
out there?"

"All sealed, Dr. Krell," the woman replied.

"We're sending Twila Grimm out first," Krell told her.
"Jon and I will clean up in here until you're ready for us."

"We'll take good care of her, Doctor."

Does she know? Twila wondered. Does she know the
name Twila Grimm, and who I am, and what is in my
blood?

Krell ushered her toward the door. "You are your
grandfather's granddaughter," he told her as he tugged the
heavy lab door open. "I trust the depth of your wisdom,
and the breadth of your perspective."

You might as well, Twila thought uncharitably. You
don't have much choice.

But as she stepped out of the room and into the tiny
evac unit, she thought about Grandfather going Outside
with his bulging pack of supplies. Even if they had not

required him to go, he would have gone, for the good of the biodome. It was the kind of person Carlton Grimm was.

It was the kind of person she would always try to be.

Jon would not watch as Twila stepped out of the lab into the claustrophobic evac unit. She looked too small to bear such a burden. He wanted to push past his father, cram himself into the unit with her, and stay with her for the whole decontamination process. He wanted to be with her when they stuffed her garments into waste bags for incineration, to soothe her through the humiliation of being touched by strangers in dehumanizing plastic suits. He wanted to hold her hand as they hosed her with anti-septic solutions and cradle her head when the nausea from the radiation set in. He wanted to speak one last word of comfort before they sealed her into a capsule to lie for eight hours breathing, just breathing. He wanted to be there when they finally unsealed her sterile coffin and helped her out, and he wanted to hold her—

God, how he wanted to hold her!

The knowledge made him flush under his beard. He had always known she was lovely. He'd seen pictures of her, even before he began to look for her out in the biodome, so he'd known she was an attractive woman. But when she'd sashayed up to him in the holo program and looked him squarely in the eyes with bold invitation, he'd been totally unprepared for his own reaction. Desire had surged through him like water through a sluice gate. Had she been an MA tech or another doctor, he'd have had her back in his office in minutes, his arms wrapped around her, his face buried in that raven hair.

But she wasn't a part of the MA, wasn't someone he could approach to satisfy his sudden, instinctive lust. She wasn't someone he should even know socially. She was *Twila Grimm*. She was his research. What was it his mother had said when he'd told her he was going into research? "Don't get too attached to the mice."

But like a fool, he'd wanted to know who she was. Carlton had known, after all, and it hadn't affected his research that the child whose blood he studied day and night was his adopted granddaughter. So Jon had read her public file, peeked at her academic record, watched her at work in the orchards. Each glimpse only frustrated him more. He'd only intended to watch her in the holo program—why had he even used the participative mode? Although he couldn't have heard her conversation, he could have seen the pride in her bearing, the confidence in her step, the high energy in her dance. All those things would have helped to paint a picture of who she was.

And left me aching for more, he realized. *I wanted to see her face-to-face, to talk to her, to know what she thought and how she felt. I got what I wanted.*

I just didn't expect to give anything in return.

He heard the lab door close and seal, heard the whine of the evac unit's motor sealing the booth-like apparatus shut, and knew his opportunity was gone. Twelve hours of close confinement with Twila—how sweet the thought! But it was not worth the price. The price for his trip to Papa Joe's holographic dance hall would be heavy enough.

Jon felt rather than saw Krell approach, and his stomach knotted with anger. "Poor thing," Krell said sympathetically. "I wish there were some way to make all this easier for her."

"Time," Jon said curtly. "That's the only thing that will help."

He could feel his father's searching eyes on him. "It hasn't helped you much," Krell observed softly.

Jon's eyes flashed. "Different situation," he snapped, limping toward another lab table to disassemble the last equipment there.

Of course, it did no good; his father simply followed, pitching empty cultures and chemicals into sewage bags, all to be carted to a disposal tube and blown Outside. For a moment they worked in tense silence. Then, "Just what do you think I should have done differently?" Krell asked in an easy voice. "Denied paternity when your mother finally told me? Sent you to someone else, instead of taking you in? Denied you advanced studies in medicine?"

"It's not what you did then—"

"Maybe I shouldn't have given you your own lab when

you were twenty-three. Maybe I shouldn't have made you chief of research last year, with a chair on the governing board. Maybe—"

"—it's what you're doing now!" Jon forced his voice over his father's. "This—this double standard for Medical, this secret lifestyle we have here—"

"Do you want to give it up?" Krell asked pointedly. "Do you want to go to work every day in a place where people hide their faces from each other, where they're afraid to be in the same room together, let alone speak to each other?" His voice lowered. "Do you want to give up your little affair with Dr. Mintz? Or the freedom to have another with someone else?"

Jon burned, as he burned every time his father named names, names Jon tried desperately to keep private. "*No* one should have to give it up," he hissed. "That's the point. Why should they have to live differently outside of Medical?"

"They don't!" Krell cried, throwing his hands up in the air. "Jon, I don't make them do it. I didn't set up the social structure out there. But we're talking a paranoia that's taken the form of a religion. You don't go around toppling people's gods, Jon, they don't like it. They don't want it. The people in this biodome have chosen that way of life because it's what they want. It's what they need to make them feel safe. Everyone wants to feel safe, Jon."

"But they don't!" Jon erupted. "If they felt safe, they wouldn't hide from each other!"

Krell gestured helplessly. "I'll never make you understand. This whole society is built on the belief that isolation is necessary to survival. You can't tear that down overnight! What we need to do is not concentrate on its destruction, but its deliverance. We need the vaccine, Jon. We need something we can give them to make them believe they're safe, as safe as those of us in Medical. Either your research, or my research, has to come up with something we can offer to every domizen in Numex—it's the only way out of this mess."

Jon wanted to smash the petri dishes on the floor. Instead he slammed one on the lab table. "Your research is a dead-end," he hissed.

"My research keeps you and me from Carlton's fate," Krell hissed back.

"I will find the answer," Jon insisted doggedly. "I will find it, because I won't have my daughter growing up in the kind of world Twila has."

Chapter 5

"**G**ood morning, Ms. Grimm."
    The voice came from the speaker above the bed. Twila pulled her head out of the closet she had been searching and looked back at it, but it was an audio intercom only; no face looked down at her. "Good morning," she grumbled back, thinking it wasn't really very good at all. She wondered how they knew she was up—unless, of course, they had video on their end. She gave her hospital gown a self-conscious tug, hoping her posterior was better covered than it felt. "I was just checking to see if anyone left clothes for me," she told the intercom. "They took the ones I was wearing, and told me they'd find others for me." Did they burn them? she wondered. Or just irradiate them until they looked as bleached and brittle as she felt?

"Did your doctor say you were to go home today?" the faceless voice asked. It was a woman's voice—a condescending woman's voice, Twila thought.

"Of course, I'm going home today, I'm not sick," Twila answered impatiently, although she felt weak and a little shaky. That came of not eating for twenty-four hours, and then losing what little was in her stomach during the final stages of the decontamination process. "Dr. Krell just arranged for me to sleep here last night because he didn't want me out in the common areas at midnight."

There was a slight pause. Twila wondered if the faceless voice were trying to assess the implications of that, or if she were checking something on her terminal. The voice said, "Why don't you have some breakfast? The cart should be coming around in about five minutes."

Breakfast! There was nothing Twila wanted more—except to go home. And she got the distinct impression she was being stalled, or placated, or both. "If the clothes are a problem," she persisted, "I'll just have my Aunt Trish bring some from home."

"Why don't you wait until after your doctor has seen you?" the voice suggested.

"Because," Twila snapped, "he's going to be a little busy until noon, and I have studies to do!" She had seen Dr. Krell only briefly before they wheeled her away to her room on a gurney. He and Jon had been crammed into the tiny evac chamber together. Jon had looked sullen, until he saw her. Then something in his face softened. Twila managed a weak smile and waggled her fingers at him. The senior Krell smiled and waved back at her; but in that instant before he saw her gesture, when it was only he and his bitter son in that tiny, tiny space, he had looked . . . tired. Just tired.

"There's a terminal right in your room," the voice replied. "You can access your studies from here."

"Did Dr. Krell say you were supposed to keep me here?" Twila demanded. She wanted to go home. She wanted to get out of this antiseptic environment, to go roll in the rich soil of the orchard, to get dirt under her nails and feel sweat prickling on her scalp. She wanted to see Aunt Trish; she wanted to hide in her room; she wanted *out of here.*

Again there was the slight pause. Was her use of Krell's name getting through? Twila hoped so. She hoped something was penetrating the rigidity she heard in the faceless voice.

"Patients are never discharged before rounds—"

Spit and blood! "I'm not a patient!" Twila exploded. "Dr. Krell arranged for me to have a place to sleep last night because I didn't get out of the Decontamination Chamber until—"

"Good morning, Twila!" This voice came from the monitor beside the bed, and there was a face to go with it. Twila moved to where she could see it better. It was the face of a woman in her thirties, a handsome woman with some Oriental blood. "I'm Dr. Mintz. Dr. Krell asked me to look in on you this morning."

"May I please go home now?" Twila asked testily.

"Certainly." Dr. Mintz could be seen tapping some keys

on her terminal. "I've authorized your discharge. Is there anything else I can do for you?"

Now it was Twila's turn to hesitate. After so much resistance, it seemed too simple a release. "Why was I being held, anyway?"

Dr. Mintz snorted. "Bureaucracy. To get you a bed, we had to admit you, so to get you out, a doctor has to sign a discharge. I didn't imagine you'd be up this early, or I'd have taken care of it before."

It made sense, but Twila was still irritated from her encounter with the faceless voice. She plopped herself on the bed, staring sullenly at the monitor. "I don't have any clothes to wear home," she complained.

"I'll have housekeeping bring you a habit."

"Thank you."

"Anything else?"

Twila studied Dr. Mintz, who seemed to be studying her. There was a certain curiosity in the older woman's eyes; did she know about Twila's immunity? "Have you worked with Dr. Krell a long time?" Twila asked.

A small smile glimmered, was quickly suppressed. "I hardly ever work with Dr. Krell."

"Then, why did he ask you to look in on me?"

This time the smile would not be forced away. "It was Jonathan Krell who asked me to look in on you, not Samuel Krell."

Jon? "Will you get in trouble with Dr. Krell—Dr. Samuel Krell—for releasing me?"

Now the smile spread, and it made Dr. Mintz's face lovely. "Heavens, no! I'm the one who admitted you; as I said, it was the only way to get you a bed. Jon's not a physician," she added. "He couldn't make the arrangements himself."

"I thought his father was going to."

Dr. Mintz shrugged. "That Dr. Krell hardly ever does his own detail work. He delegates; it's good management."

Just then the door to Twila's room swooshed open, and a robot cart buzzed in laden with food trays. "Housekeeping already?" Dr. Mintz asked, able to hear the cart but not able to see what was on it.

"Breakfast," Twila replied.

"Take advantage, if you like," Dr. Mintz invited. "Housekeeping may be a few minutes."

Twila considered refusing on principle, but not for long. Her stomach was a gnawing, empty pit; she lifted a tray from the cart, and pushed the go button to send the vehicle on its way. Then she peeked under the lid and wrinkled her nose.

"It's the same fare you'd get at home," Dr. Mintz told her.

"I know, but it always tastes worse in Medical. I just hate being here, that's all. Too many unpleasant memories." For six weeks when she was twelve, Twila had been housed on the hospital floors of Medical while they ran numerous tests for her supposed anemia. She wondered now what they had really been doing all that time. Injecting her with the CM virus, just to make sure she was immune?

Dr. Mintz started to say something, then hesitated. Twila looked up inquiringly. The doctor glanced away, moistened her lips, then said, "Would you rather come to my office to eat that? I can have housekeeping bring the habit here for you."

It took Twila aback. People did not invite other people into their homes, or offices, and they did not invite them to eat with them. The virus could be transmitted carelessly during eating. But this was Medical—and Twila was immune. "I'd love to," she replied fervently. "Where are you?"

"I'm two floors up," Dr. Mintz replied. "The elevator is at the opposite end of the corridor from the nurse's station. When you get off, go straight ahead; I'll be the third office on your right."

It felt strange, padding down the corridor of a hospital floor of Medical in her bare feet, her gown flapping loosely around her. Twila kept expecting someone to object to her being out of her room; but no nurse was at the station, and no security monitor registered a protest. Still, she was glad to slip into the elevator and punch a floor button, and gladder still when the doors opened onto an empty corridor. Dr. Mintz's door was open.

"Come in," the doctor invited, rising to greet her. Standing behind her desk, she appeared much smaller than Twila had imagined. "You're welcome to one of my lab coats, if that would make you more comfortable."

Twila looked at the white coat hanging on a hook beside the door. Wear someone else's clothing? But she was immune—it didn't matter. She took the coat. "Thank you."

Dr. Mintz was not rude enough to approach her, gesturing instead to a chair set at a comfortable distance from the desk. Twila slid into it and opened her breakfast tray. "So are you a friend of Jon's?" she asked around a mouthful of rice, hoping to find some tactful way of inquiring whether the doctor knew of her immunity.

"You could say that."

It seemed an unnecessarily noncommittal answer, and Twila realized suddenly that doctors who were friends saw each other face-to-face—not through holographic encounters as Twila and her friends did. Had it been rude to suggest that Dr. Mintz and Jon met in person? "You work together, I suppose," she tried to amend.

"No, Jon's work is research; I'm a physician."

From bad to worse, Twila chided herself. "I'm sorry, I don't mean to be personal," she apologized, spooning curds of cheese into the remainder of her rice and mixing it together. "I was just wondering—how much you knew about me."

"I know about Jon's research, if that's what you mean," Dr. Mintz replied gently.

Twila could feel the doctor's eyes on her, studying her. It's only natural, she told herself. If I met someone who was immune, I'd be curious, too.

"Jon said you only just found out yourself," Dr. Mintz went on.

Twila felt a burning in her cheeks. Why should I be embarrassed? she demanded of herself. All these years I didn't know—didn't even suspect—am I that stupid? No. I suspected something. I just thought—

"I thought there was something wrong with me," Twila explained. "Sometimes I thought I had some rare disease, that I was dying or something—I don't know. Something so terrible they wouldn't tell me about it. Other times I thought they were making a mountain out of a molehill, just poking me and running tests because they had nothing better to do, because I was such a gullible subject. Gullible." She snorted. "I had no idea how gullible."

"It's a touchy subject," Dr. Mintz observed. "There are just a few of us in Medical who know about it. We can't offer it to everyone, so . . ."

Twila looked up. "Offer what to everyone?"

For just a beat Dr. Mintz froze; then, "Your immunity," she continued smoothly. "We can't offer it to others, so until we can . . . I don't think it was right to keep you in the dark, but I understand the need to keep this quiet."

Twila nodded agreement, but she watched Dr. Mintz's face closely. It betrayed nothing, except a desire to keep the conversation moving. What had she meant, if she hadn't really meant Twila's immunity?

"I was a teaching assistant when Jon took his advanced studies," Dr. Mintz went on, the change in subject only a slight one, but Twila was sure it was just that—a change in subject. "He was a bright boy, and we—we hit it off well. Then I started my residency, and I didn't see much of anyone except hospital staff for a long time. About a year ago I ran into Jon . . . at a meeting." That didn't ring true, either. "We sort of renewed our friendship. I like his company."

"I only met him for the first time Friday night," Twila said. Only that, the night before last? It seemed much longer. "I—" She was going to say she liked his company, too, but a prickling sensation crept along her back and neck as she realized that here in Medical, where people were not afraid to touch each other, it might have a different connotation than it did in the rest of the biodome. "I think I'd like to know him better." That, at least, was honest. Whatever its implications.

Dr. Mintz's brow furrowed slightly. "It might be better for Jon if you didn't."

Twila stopped with a last forkful of papaya halfway to her mouth. "Why is that?" She remembered what Jon had said about not showing too much interest in him while his father was watching.

"I'm no psychologist," Dr. Mintz said, "but you have to be blind not to see the tension between Jon and his father. The old man is—well—possessive, I guess. And manipulative. He loves Jon, I truly believe that, but—

he wants to know who Jon sees, and when, and why. He wants to know everything there is to know about Jon—I think, in order to control him. Or to try. Jon's not very controllable."

"I'd have guessed that," Twila murmured.

"So the old man takes hostages, so to speak. 'You want your own apartment, Jon? Take your medical boards. You prefer research? I can give you your own lab, just remember where you got it. You like that girl? I have her career in my hands.' " Dr. Mintz frowned. "From Jon's point of view, he doesn't dare care about anyone. But Jon is"—she searched for an appropriate word—"very passionate. About what he believes. About what he does. So when he wants to care, but is afraid to . . ."

At first Twila saw it only as it applied to herself: Jon wanted her, wanted to be close to her as much as she to him, but he wouldn't let himself be set up by his father. Then she realized that Dr. Mintz spoke from personal experience. It was written softly just beneath the features of her face: she cared for Jon, and Jon would not allow himself to care back. "I'm sorry," Twila whispered.

Dr. Mintz's eyes showed start, then she forced that emotion from her face. "It's harder on Jon." She shrugged. "It wouldn't have worked for us, anyway. The last thing under the dome that I want is to have a family and all those attachments; Jon has one daughter already and wants more."

The fork slipped from Twila's fingers, and flew clattering to the floor. Cheeks burning, she bent over to retrieve it. A daughter! It had never occurred to her. How did a man come to be raising a daughter? Of course, her grandfather had raised two—"A daughter." She cleared her throat as she sat back up, trying to look nonchalant, knowing that she was failing miserably. "To spite his father?" she asked.

Dr. Mintz gave a lopsided smile. "Probably. He tried to keep her a secret from the old man, of course—paid a host mother, can you imagine? I suppose he thought the old man was keeping too close an eye on his girlfriends—I'm sorry, I must be shocking you with talk like this," Dr. Mintz apologized.

"Oh—just a little," Twila admitted in a small voice.

That was why Jon didn't know much about holo programs. He didn't need them to release his sexual urges. She shivered, but she couldn't help thinking . . . what it would be like . . . "My grandfather had an actual marriage," she told Dr. Mintz, "and raised two daughters when my grandmother was killed by an Edgewalker. I think Jon idolized him, and—well, maybe that has something to do with it."

Dr. Mintz nodded. "It could be. Jon spoke of Dr. Grimm often when I knew him as a student; although it's been years, I'm sure your grandfather made a lasting impression on him."

Just then a robot cart hummed in with a clean habit and slippers in its basket. Trading her empty tray for the garment, Twila shook it open and tossed it deftly over her head. "Thanks for the use of your lab coat," she said, slipping out of that and the gown before putting her arms through the habit sleeves. "I'm not very modest in holo programs, but . . ."

"Don't apologize," Dr. Mintz laughed, rising. "I'm the one who should apologize, all those things I was saying— I just wanted you to understand Jon, but I'm afraid I've painted a rather decadent picture—"

"You have a different lifestyle here in Medical," Twila interrupted. "I'm sure if you saw me in holo programs, you'd think *I* was decadent." The habit settled in place, Twila looked once more at Dr. Mintz—an attractive woman, she acknowledged, and a sincere one. Jon had good taste, at least. "Thank you for inviting me to your office, Doctor. I have—appreciated—this conversation. And its honesty. That seems to be in short supply around here."

She saw the flash of guilt in Dr. Mintz's face. There was something else, then, that this woman had avoided telling her. What? "I didn't want you to think ill of Jon when he doesn't contact you anymore," Dr. Mintz said. "It's not because he doesn't want to."

"Oh, he'll contact me," Twila said with assurance. "Because if he doesn't, I'll walk into his lab to see him. And you can tell him that from me."

With that Twila turned on her heel and left the room.

* * *

Aunt Trish was waiting when Twila entered the apartment. "What are you doing here?" Twila asked in surprise.

"Playing hookey," Trish quipped. "The chicks and ducks will have to put up with your mother alone today." But there was worry poorly hidden behind the roguish smile.

"How much did Dr. Krell tell you?" Twila asked bluntly.

Trish sighed. "He said you'd found out Roxanne isn't your birth mother. He said maybe you shouldn't be alone for a little while."

Suddenly Twila felt very weak in her knees. Trish reached out for her, and she virtually fell into her aunt's arms, clutching her tightly as though she were the only solid thing in her shaky life. In some ways, it was true. "Aunt Trish," she said through clenched teeth, "I want to tell you everything that happened. Everything I learned. And then I need for you to tell me everything. Everything that has to do with me, what you know and what you suspect. All of it. I need the truth, Trish. I've stumbled into a morass of lies and deceit, and I desperately need for someone to tell me only truth."

"You've got it," Trish vowed.

They sat in the living room, and Twila let the entire story flood out of her, from meeting Jon to using Dr. Krell's computer access, to the Edgewalker, to the revelation of her immunity and birth outside the biodome. Trish sat silently, and by the end of it she was pale and thin lipped, but she stayed calm. "Well," she said when Twila had finished. "Well. That answers some questions I've had."

"And raises as many more," Twila said. "Did you never suspect any of it?"

"Immunity? No. No, that never—" Trish gave a nervous laugh. "That never crossed my mind. But I never believed that goat manure about a rare blood condition— although I guess, in a way, that was the truth. And I used to pester your mother to—to find out more, but she wasn't curious; and they wouldn't tell me anything because you weren't my daughter."

"I wasn't hers, either."

Trish let that pass. "I suppose that's why they didn't

want you to take advanced studies in medicine, either," she speculated. "They didn't want you to know."

"But why not?" Twila demanded. "If I became part of the MA, why would it matter if I knew I was immune?"

Trish shrugged. "Maybe . . . they were afraid it would give you too much power. You'd have something you could use for political clout: to give or withhold your blood for study."

But Twila shook her head slowly. "There's got to be more to it, Aunt Trish. There are still pieces missing from the puzzle."

"And probably always will be." Trish rose stiffly, and Twila saw that her hands were trembling somewhat. "I'm thirsty, how about you?"

"Parched."

Trish crossed to the kitchen area and opened the fridge door. "Something with some nutrients, I think. Juice? Lemonade?"

"You don't have any ale stashed in there, do you?"

"Where your mother can find it?" Trish snorted. "No, but I've got something in my room that will give this fruit juice some kick."

"I'll take it."

Trish disappeared for a moment, then returned with a pint jar of amber liquid. "Your mother thinks it's plant fertilizer," she explained, pouring carefully into two glasses. At first she poured one shorter than the other; but with a glance back at Twila, she evened them up. "Don't drink it too fast if you're not used to it," she advised as she added the fruit juice. "It has quite a kick, but you won't feel it until you stand up. I wouldn't want your mother to come home and find you half-crocked."

"Why aren't you my mother?" Twila asked bluntly.

Trish took a moment to steady herself on the counter, then picked up the glasses and brought them back to where her niece waited. "I wasn't consulted," she said frankly. "For that matter, neither was Roxanne. Dad—your grandfather—brought you home and said you needed a mother, and Roxanne would be it." She seated herself across from Twila once more. "I was as angry as I had ever been with him. I had the same questions: why her and not me? And he said what he always said. 'She needs it more, Trish. You're stronger than Roxanne; you'll be fine on your own, but Roxanne needs something, someone to pull her outside herself. She'll never find a man, never look for one, so a baby is the next best thing.' "

Twila sipped at the fruit juice. It had a mellow flavor, both less sweet and less tart than plain juice. "Didn't work, did it?" was her comment.

Trish gave a wan smile. "Oh, to an extent. When you were little, when you demanded so much—but Roxanne never learned how to surrender. She accommodated your needs, but she never learned how to really surrender to them." She reached out a hand to Twila. "Don't be too hard on her. It's just that she wants—stability, consistency, in her life. She wants everything to be framed out with no surprises. Children are full of surprises."

Twila was tired of people explaining other people's behavior. Trish explained Roxanne; Dr. Mintz explained Jon; Krell explained himself. Wasn't that odd? Usually people tried to explain away the shortcomings of people they loved, but Krell only tried to explain his own . . .

"Did Grandfather ever talk about Jon?" Twila asked quietly. Jon had been, she calculated, in his late teens when her grandfather left. If, as Dr. Krell had indicated, Jon had idolized Carlton, had Carlton been aware of it? Had he been fond of Jon, too? Had he worried that Jon's devotion to him wounded Dr. Krell?

Trish thought a moment, looking back to a time she seldom thought of anymore. It seemed forever since her father had been here with them, sharing the breakfast table, holding Twila on his knee over Roxanne's protests. How different that time had been! Something to look forward to each night—Dad coming home, late. Face-to-face conversations on sociology and ethics. Watching tapes of Twila's dance lessons together and exchanging smirking comments. Laughing. Glowing. So long ago.

There had been less of that toward the end. Carlton had seemed preoccupied, distracted. Never inclined to talk about his work or the politics there, he now ceased to speak of that aspect of his life at all. Had he mentioned Jon? "Not that I recall," Trish replied. "If he did, it never registered with me that it was Krell's son he was talking about. I never suspected Krell had a son. Never wondered about it."

Twila nodded. "Me, too. It was such a shock. I guess I never think about people having children. Not grown children, at least." She was just beginning to feel the soothing effect of the alcohol, so she took another large swallow of juice to hurry it along. "There are just too many things I don't understand," she sighed. "Too many pieces of the puzzle still missing, and Dr. Krell isn't going to tell me any more than he has to."

"Make him have to," Trish suggested.

"How?"

"Refuse to cooperate with these monthly appointments unless they tell you what's going on."

Defy Dr. Krell? Something about that raised the hairs on the back of Twila's neck. He had always been gentle and patient and reasonable with Twila, but he had always gotten his way. Even, it seemed, if he had to deceive and manipulate her to get it. "I don't think it's a good idea to threaten Dr. Krell," Twila said uneasily. "I don't think that's a good idea at all."

Twila felt hotter and grungier than usual by the time the transit pulled into view at the junction of the legume fields and the orchards. For two weeks she had thrown herself into her Required Labor with a vengeance, cultivating, cleaning irrigation ditches, composting. Now it was Friday, and a rain day in the orchards so that the humidity was up, and she felt that she wanted nothing more than to stand under a hot shower for hours and hours and hours. To hell with Papa Joe's—she was too tired to dance, anyway.

But I must go to Papa Joe's, she thought. I have to give Jon one more chance. He might look for me there; and oh, how I want him to look for me there! Then, if he doesn't come, if he doesn't come and doesn't call—Monday I'll go to his lab, because the two weeks of decontamination should be up then. I'll go to Medical and say I have a sore throat or something, and when they put me in an examination room, I'll slip out and go to the lab. But I'd much rather he came to Papa Joe's.

What should I wear tonight? she wondered as the transit

slowed in its approach, the gears grinding as it down-shifted. My fishnet leotard with a dance skirt? The red string dress? I want to be absolutely devastating if he shows up—but I don't want to deal with other men if he doesn't. Maybe the strapless skin suit with a tunic; I can always lose the tunic if he shows . . .

The transit crunched to an almost stop on the gravel path, and Twila stepped toward it. There was another passenger visible in the front nearside compartment—unusual, she thought, this far out. Someone working the legume fields, most likely, although they usually boarded the other side. Twila stepped back again, planning to grab the last nearside compartment.

Then the habited passenger tugged back his hood, and she saw it was Jon.

He motioned her to get on. She did, jumping to catch the still-moving vehicle and swing into the compartment next to his. The transit picked up speed, growling under the load as it toiled through the cultivated land toward the savanna.

For a moment Twila just sat there, heart pounding, aware of the nearness of Jon through the molded plastic compartment wall. Jon! How many times during these two weeks had she wondered if she'd imagined it all, imagined the dark attractiveness of him, imagined the magnetic connection between them. But one look at his face had banished all doubt. She felt herself trembling, waiting for the next step.

But nothing happened. The transit rumbled on, and Jon said nothing. Should I speak? Twila wondered. Is he waiting for me to start? But no—he started by coming here; he must have something planned. Or is he testing me to see if I'll really pursue this? Does he want me to ask him questions? Is he just sitting there waiting for me to ask him something before he'll speak? What should I ask? How should I start?

Just as she opened her mouth, Jon began to whistle. She could hardly hear him through the divider, over the steady hum of the transit motor. But he was definitely whistling. She recognized the tune. It dated to the early days of biodome life: "Safe in my Solitude."

Was that supposed to mean something? Was it a signal

of some kind, a code? Was he telling her subtly to leave him alone? Or did he mean that here in the transit, separated from each other, it was safe to talk?

They passed a potato/tomato field with its two separate species occupying the same growing space and came upon a grainfield. Jon switched songs. This one was a bawdy tune, sung mostly by adolescents who had just begun to experiment with holographic sexual encounters. The lyrics went, "Under the rubber plant, deep in the rain forest, I'll come with my machete if you'll come with your grass skirt." It went on with several suggestive lines about encounters in the rice paddies, and by the ocean, and in the stargazing room atop Medical. Twila wondered at Jon's choice. But then, perhaps he was only whistling, to pass the time, and to keep her from speaking.

At the end of the grainfield the land sloped upward to the savanna, and the transit slowed to about five miles an hour as it labored up the incline. Jon stepped out.

Startled, it took Twila a moment to react. Then she unclipped the safety cord and jumped out after him. They stood on the road some ten yards apart as the transit growled on through the dust, leaving them behind.

Jon had left his hood down. He looked strange in the habit, his dark hair and short beard making his head seem small atop the voluminous kapok garment. *I should take my hood down, too,* Twila thought. But she remembered how dirty and sweaty she was, her hair tied back and her brow undoubtedly smudged and streaked. She left it up.

For a moment Jon only stood there looking at her, gray eyes neither angry nor glad. Finally he said, "Carolyn told me you threatened to walk into my lab if I didn't contact you."

Twila was unprepared for the fluttering of her heart when she heard his voice. It took her a moment to respond. "I would have, too," she said bluntly.

"I have no doubt of it. That's why I'm here."

Still she could not read any emotion in his voice. Was he upset with her? Taken with her audacity? Neither?

"Are you sorry to be here?" she asked frankly.

His eyes lowered. "No," he admitted. "I'm not sorry for a chance to . . . talk with you. Or even just to see you."

Twila lifted a hand self-consciously to her sweaty face. "You haven't exactly caught me at my best."

A smile quirked his lips. "I've seen you worse." Then, because she looked alarmed, he explained, "I came to the orchard a couple of times. Before Papa Joe's. Watched you from a couple zones away. I thought that would be enough."

His look told her it wasn't. Twila flushed and felt herself uncharacteristically tongue-tied.

He started walking then, up the road after the transit. Twila fell in step beside him. He no longer limped, she noticed, although his right wrist was still in a brace. "Up ahead is the junction with the rain forest road," he told her. "There'll be another transit coming down it shortly. It won't slow down much, but someone as agile as you shouldn't have any trouble jumping on. If you go to Stores, then home, no one will know you switched transits in the middle of nowhere."

"Why should anyone care?" she asked.

"My father will care." He walked at a temperate speed, as though he were accustomed to wilderness travel and knew how to pace himself. "My father will be watching you very closely from now on."

"But why should he care if I talk to you?" she persisted. "He said I could. I asked him, and he said I could."

"He didn't mean it."

"I know that," she admitted, "but what I don't understand is why."

Why? Jon avoided looking into that naive face with its sensuous full lips and dark, exotic eyes. *Why? Because he is a man of passions himself, and he knows very well what I feel when I look at you. Because he's afraid of what you might learn if we get too close. Because he knows I don't agree with what he's doing . . . and neither would you . . .*

Jon took enough time to formulate a more careful answer. "He has a lot invested in you," Jon said slowly. "He has plans for you. And they don't include me."

"I don't care what his plans are," Twila snapped. "I make my own life."

So sure of herself! "No, you don't," Jon replied. "You think you do, but you don't." He tried to remember a time when he had felt so arrogant. Long ago, before Carlton

Grimm had gone . . . Time for a little disillusionment for
Twila. "You applied for advanced studies in Medical,
didn't you? Who do you think put the kill on that?"

He saw her face burning at the implication, but he knew
it was only a pinprick. There was plenty more. "And
remember Professor Llewska, who started to get friendly
with you when you were an undergrad?" he went on.
"Remember how he suddenly got professional?"

Now her fists clenched unconsciously as the level of
her anger—or perhaps her embarrassment—increased.
Did it occur to her to wonder how he, Jon, knew about
Llewska? Had it dawned on her yet that her private life
was common discussion between the researchers whose
subject she was? Not yet, he thought. "And a holographic
program you tried once," he pursued. "Rhapsody in
Rain?"

"Oh, that was so stunning!" Twila exclaimed. "You felt
like you were actually Outside before CM, with clouds
overhead and the shimmer of rainfall all around—it was
so real, I could practically feel the drizzle—"

"It scared the spit out of him," Jon told her. "He was
afraid you would develop a taste for Outside and want to
try it yourself—and being immune, you could. He shut
the whole program down."

Twila stopped dead in the road. "He has no right!" she
protested.

"Who's going to stop him?"

A coldness swept over Twila, and she could not look at
her companion. Who, indeed? she wondered. Dr. Krell
was head of the entire Medical Authority. If he decided a
holo program was inappropriate and ought to be shut
down, it would most certainly be shut down. If he decided
a certain young lady ought not to be admitted to advanced
studies in medicine, then she would not be. If he didn't
want a liaison between a student and a professor . . . did
that mean he could have gotten to Patrick, too? Did he
know about Patrick?

Did he know about *everything*?

Her cheeks burned hotter as she thought about the intimate moments transmitted via the biodome's central computer system. Could Krell see those? Surely not, they
were protected! A student-professor exchange was one

thing, but a private social—that is, a private link—no one should be able to—

"Is that why you wouldn't go private with me after Papa Joe's?" she asked in a low voice, wondering if she would ever be comfortable in a private link again. "Were you afraid he was watching?"

Jon gave an embarrassed cough. "He was busy that night; I saw to it. It was the only way I dared come."

"Busy?" Her head spun with the implications.

"Busy." Jon turned his steady gray eyes on her as he made it plain. "A new applicant for advanced studies in medicine. Redhead. Twenty-one. Very eager. Do you take my meaning?"

"Yes," she answered, her voice cracking just a little. She cleared her throat and forged on. "He doesn't need holo programs. Neither do you, that's why you knew so little about them."

She could feel his eyes on her, boring into her, but she could not meet them. "That's right," he said bluntly.

"Because you have Dr. Mintz." Why did that fascinate her?

"Had," he corrected. "We've decided to take a break from each other for a while."

Now she looked at him, looked at the dark and brooding face with the grim set to its jaw. "You've both decided, or just you?" she asked, remembering what Dr. Mintz had told her.

"I won't let the old man play with her career, trying to get at me. I have too much respect for her to do that to her."

"And maybe just a little affection," Twila chided.

He stopped short and glared at her, and Twila congratulated herself at having scored points again. "Listen, little girl," he snarled, "I can't afford the luxury of caring too much." But Twila knew it for the ruse it was, a ruse that only fooled Jon.

"The problem is," she told him softly, "you don't know how not to."

For just a moment the mask fell away, and she saw that other Jon, the one who had held her in the lab and crooned in her ear that it was all right, that she would not die, that she was safe. That Jon looked oddly bare, and young, and confused. An image flashed to her of a seventeen-year-old boy who'd just been told that Dr. Grimm had gone Outside that morning, without a word of forewarning, without saying good-bye—

But the bitterness clamped itself back on his features, and he started down the road again muttering, "Jesus Christ, Twila, you don't know the first thing about it! You live in that apartment with two other women; what could you possibly know about what men feel?"

"I've had a few relationships," she insisted. "Holographic, yes, but you've seen how real that can be. What did you call it? 'Intense'?" She smiled as he growled. "And my grandfather lived with us, and he was very wise and very loving. I'd call that a rather good example."

He snorted. "You were eight years old."

"The formative years, isn't that what psychologists say?" she persisted. Then, because she wanted to keep pushing at him, "I understand he had an influence on you, too. That's what your father said."

"Yes, and we saw what happened to him, didn't we!" Jon snapped.

Twila stopped dead in the road. "What do you mean?"

Jon was several paces beyond her before he stopped and turned back. He looked defeated. "Nothing. Nothing, forget it. It was something to say, that's all."

Slowly she came toward him, brain numbed with the idea. "Do you think your father intentionally infected him? Because he was jealous?"

"No, I don't believe that at all," Jon said quickly. "The old man loved Carlton. Carlton was everything he thought a man should be, everything his own father wasn't. Besides"—Jon turned and started walking again—"he's obsessed with beating CM in his lifetime; it set the research back years when Carlton left. My father may be a manipulative bastard who believes he knows what's best for everyone in the biodome, but I don't think he'd compromise his work to punish me. It's not in his profile."

Twila tried to evaluate that assessment, but all she could think of was the look her grandfather had given Krell on the day he went Outside. Did Grandfather believe Krell had infected him? It sent a chill through her.

She hurried to catch up with him again, and for a

moment they walked in silence. Then, "What would happen," she asked slowly, "if I refused to come in for my next medical appointment?" Moving along briskly in their habits made them both warm, even though the kapok fabric was lighter than cotton. Perspiration glistened on their brows. "What would your father do, do you think?"

Jon shrugged. "He'd take the rational approach first," he told her, "try to talk you out of your 'stubbornness,' as he'd call it. For the good of the biodome, and all that. He'd get your mother to put pressure on you, and everyone else you respected. And if that didn't work"— Jon shrugged again—"he'd have you declared an Edge-walker and detain you in Medical indefinitely. You can't fight him, Twila. There's no point."

She didn't buy it. "You fight him."

Again he turned those cool gray eyes on her, as though measuring her. But the disdain was gone, that look of condescension that had crept into his features when they met in Papa Joe's, and earlier today when he'd tried to shock her with his father's wickedness, and his own. Progress, Twila thought.

"Yes, I fight him," Jon agreed. "Every chance I get, on every front I get. I always lose, but I always fight. I can get away with it." He blotted his forehead with his habit sleeve. "It took me awhile to understand that, but once I did, it gave me great freedom. You see, my father has a plan for everyone, and part of his plan for me is that I take over the MA when he steps down. Not that he ever will, you know; he'll die in office. But he intends to leave the work, and the leadership, to me. I'm his legacy, his immortality. I'm his chance to rule even after death."

Twila wondered if that were really true, or if the judgment were too harsh. Or too lenient. Was there a point beyond which Jon ought not to push his father? "If you do become chair of the governing board," she said, "or whatever it takes to be kingpin in Medical, you won't rule the way he does, will you?"

"No, I won't," Jon said adamantly. "I don't believe in this double standard he's established for the MA; I don't believe it's healthy for people to be afraid of each other, afraid of physical contact. I believe the risk of contracting

CM is less than the risk of going over the Edge, and immensely preferable."

Twila suppressed a shudder. It was a radical point of view; she didn't know what to think of it. "Does your father know you feel that way?" she asked.

"I've made it abundantly clear."

"Then, why does he still want you to follow him? Why doesn't he pick someone who will carry on his own philosophy?"

Jon's smile was sardonic. "He still thinks he can change me. He thinks he's persuasive enough that eventually I'll come around. And I'm his son. Blood of his blood." The smile faded, and he studied the ground where he walked. "You wouldn't think that would matter, but somehow it does. It really does."

Twila watched him carefully. "Is that why you had a child?"

He raised startled eyes to hers. Anger flashed through them, but it faded quickly into the sullen, brooding look he had worn at Papa Joe's. "No," he said. "I had other reasons. But that's one of the things I learned from it. That's not to say I couldn't love a child who was a combination of someone else's genes, but in this goofy, warped, repressed society we have, it's become important to me that she is mine. Truly mine."

"Even if she was conceived in a petri dish?"

Now his eyes flashed angry again. "Who told you all this?"

"Dr. Mintz."

"Remind me to thank her," he growled.

"It just slipped out," Twila told him, although not too repentantly. "Girl talk, you know."

They were approaching the intersection of the two transit tracks. Jon stopped in the shade of a mesquite tree and looked down at her. "My father doesn't want you inside the MA," he told her flatly. "Understand that. And while I can fight him, I don't think you should. Be a quiet, obedient little girl; don't give him any reason to think you're going to spoil his plans. He can hurt you—I don't mean physically, he's not that kind. But emotionally. He can make your life miserable, so I'm telling you, don't aggravate him."

An impish smile tugged at her lips. "Can I aggravate you?" she asked provocatively.

"You're not going to see me again."

"The hell I'm not!"

His scowl only made him seem more handsome, more magnetic. "Twila, you're not hearing me," he admonished. "If he thinks there is anything between us, he will try to use that—to manipulate you, to manipulate me. We can't meet again. We can't talk."

"Are you saying we just surrender?" she demanded.

"Not surrender, just stall," he qualified. "It's not forever. I'm making progress, Twila—in my research." His voice grew more animated; it seemed his passionate nature knew more than one channel. "I'm learning things about this agent in your blood that we never knew before. Somewhere in your DNA there's a key, and when I find it and turn it, it's going to open the door on a whole new way of life for the people in the biodome. When we can inoculate against CM, we can blow the seals on this microcosm and get out from under his thumb. Once the fear is gone, he has no power. People can take charge of their own destiny again. I just need time, Twila," he urged. "Five years, ten years—I can break his grip. In the meantime, I'm planting the seeds of sedition in Medical. Others may be afraid to disagree with him in public, but if I'm careful—if I say it right—I can, and others can't help but hear my message. Give me time, Twila. I can turn it all around."

"All by yourself?"

"No, not by myself," he said impatiently, waving off her objection. "But it has to be done from within the MA. We have to do it from inside, and as I said—he'll never let you in."

"Because he fears me?" she challenged, eyes bright. There was still something going on that she did not understand.

Jon hesitated, arrested as much by the eyes as by her suggestion. "Yes, I believe he does," he told Twila. "In your immunity, you have something he needs, and he's afraid of losing control of it. He's afraid of the power it could give you."

There's more to this, insisted a voice in her brain.

There's more to this than just the agent in your blood. If all he needed was your blood, he would let you have a child—lots of children, and then there would be more donors. Isn't it logical that if he wanted a blood serum to inoculate eight thousand people, he'd want more donors? What else is it that Dr. Krell needs from me? "So you want me to trust you," she said to Jon. "Trust you, but not your father. Even though I know bloody well you're not telling me everything, either."

Jon looked caught. Twila knew she was right. "Believe in me," he whispered, pleading. "Believe in what I'm doing. Believe my way is better than his."

Intensity was written in every feature, every fiber. Dr. Mintz had been right; behind the sullenness and the reluctance churned a passionate soul. But then, Twila had never doubted that. She had sensed it in their first meeting at Papa Joe's. Jon was a raging torrent dammed up tight, with one or two spillways giving only a hint of the powerful emotions held in check. She could feel it now like a tangible force, pulsing from him . . . pulsing through her . . .

"I believe in you," she said quietly. "But I will have answers to my questions. And I will see you again."

Jon struggled inwardly. Why couldn't he make her understand—? But then, did he really want to? No. He really wanted to see her again. Somehow, somewhere, without his father's knowledge. But that would not be easy, now that the older Krell knew Jon had been curious enough to seek her out. "Not here," he told her finally. "We have to keep changing the place, or he'll spot the pattern."

"Where?" Her eyes were earnest, and there was need in them. It kindled his own need, and he knew he was lost.

"I'll let you know," he promised.

"How?"

That part could be done. "I have access to an old computer system," he explained, "one the old man can't get to. He can tell it's been used, but he can't break into my files. I can send you a message in real time. It will only flash on your screen and erase itself."

"Can I contact you?" she wanted to know.

Fear struck him. "No." Then he considered, thought of

a possible solution. "Maybe. I can set up a mud—that's a multi-user domain—and we could both be on the same system—but he'd see where you logged in, even if he couldn't see what we said." Jon frowned. "Better yet, I'll see if you can use my password to get in and leave a file. That way I don't think he can track the source."

"When?" she demanded.

He bristled. Why was he doing this for her? He'd never done this for anyone else, no matter how strong the attraction—but this was not anyone else. This was Twila Grimm. "Whenever," he said obliquely.

"Next week?"

"I don't know!" he flared. "When it works out, that's all. When it works out." He drew his hood up, needing to shut her out now, needing to let his head clear so he could think. "I have to start walking. There will be people on the transit when it comes, and we can't afford to have them see the two of us together. After it makes its turn at this intersection, run and jump into one of the rear compartments—they always fill last. I'll wait up the road where there's a thick clump of desert broom. With any luck, no one will see us; and if they do, there's less chance they'll think anything is unusual if we board separately. They won't be tempted to call Security." He started to turn away.

"Jon!" She reached out instinctively to catch at his sleeve, then let go when she realized how rude that was.

But you're immune, said a voice inside her. *And he is accustomed to being touched.*

So she reached out more deliberately and clutched, not his sleeve, but his arm. It was firm beneath the light habit—an arm of real flesh, not a hologram she could only pantomine holding.

"I will wait for you to contact me," she said evenly, "but you must do something for me first."

He stood looking down at her, a head and then some taller than she. "And that is?"

"Kiss me," she whispered. "Like in the old flatscreen vids. I've always wondered what it would be like." *More so since you held me in your arms and told me I was immune.*

He stood stock-still, and Twila was afraid he would

refuse. But then he reached out and cupped her face in both his hands—strong hands, the palms slightly damp with perspiration. She caught the scent of him and felt the longing in her grow. Then he bent down and placed his lips on hers.

It was not the sensation she had expected. In fact, it felt awkward. Twila didn't know what to do with her hands. She raised them to touch him but found his elbows in the way, so she started to lower them again. That didn't feel right, either, so she tried moving her hands around behind him and letting them rest lightly on his lower back. His lips on hers were warm, but it didn't seem that she was participating in this expression, and she thought she ought to be. Then it was over, and Twila felt a surge of disappointment that this first kiss had been none of the things she had expected.

But Jon did not release her. Instead he kissed her again—patiently, it seemed to her—and again, more insistently. Twila forgot about her hands as her mouth began to respond to his touch. Finally on the fourth kiss, Twila felt a wrenching that started in her groin and traveled up through her chest to where the kiss had suddenly become electric. Jon's hands left her face and circled around her, drawing her tightly up against his body, demanding closeness of her. A wave of blackness swept Twila's mind, and for a long moment there was nothing but this incredible new sensation that banished all coherent thought and left only feeling.

And then the kiss ended, and Jon stood holding her, his breathing rapid, his cheek resting on her head. "I'll contact you," he promised. "One way or another. Soon."

Chapter 6

"**Y**ou don't look well," Roxanne observed. "I think those tests Dr. Krell gave you a few weeks ago were hard on you."

Twila looked up from her supper with a look of weary incredulity. Did her mother have any clue what had happened at Medical? Of course not. Krell would have spun her some tale, and she'd have believed it implicitly. And Twila did not feel up to disillusioning her. In fact, Twila was not sure she could. Roxanne had always believed whatever Krell or any other doctor told her. They were her saints.

"It's just my period, Mom," she lied, going back to picking at the food on her plate. "I get kind of dragged out."

"Are you going dancing tonight?" Roxanne asked.

"I don't think so." Jon wouldn't be there, she knew that now; and somehow the idea of facing all her friends, of listening to their idle chatter, dragged at her mood even more. Sometimes she wondered if she would ever feel like going to Papa Joe's again.

"You should exercise," her mother advised. "It'll make you feel better. You don't have to go to that—place. Just put some music on and dance."

"Maybe I will," Twila agreed reluctantly. The week had come and gone since she'd walked with Jon along the roadway, and he had not contacted her. Perhaps dancing would lift her spirits.

"Papa Joe's would be good for you," Trish put in. "You didn't go last weekend, or any night this week—your friends will wonder what happened to you."

"She can contact her friends flatscreen," Roxanne snipped, rising to collect the dinner dishes. "I think it shows maturity on Twila's part that she doesn't need that—other kind of—socialization."

If you only knew, Twila thought wickedly, just how far that other "socialization" could go. She doubted Roxanne had any inkling of what went on in a private link. But a private link no longer interested Twila, not with anyone she knew, or could imagine. It wasn't just the gnawing suspicion that it wasn't really private. The real reason was that she only wanted Jon, and not in any holographic program. She wanted to touch him, to feel his arms around her, to be kissed again—

"Don't forget to take your medicine," Roxanne reminded as she carried the dishes to the kitchen. She always prewashed the dishes, regardless of the fact that once the meal cart took them back to be reused, they were thoroughly washed and sterilized.

Twila sighed and went back to her bedroom to get her pills. As she shook one out of the bottle into her hand, she stopped and studied it. It was a small tablet, pink with tiny red flecks in it. What was it really? she wondered. Something to build up her blood, so they could keep drawing off more for research? Or was it part of that other thing, the thing that no one would tell her? She would get it out of Jon yet. Somehow.

Jon. Twila looked at her silent monitor a moment, then reached for the keyboard and rapidly logged on. Maybe tonight. Maybe tonight there would be a message . . .

Nothing. Her mailbox was empty. But it wouldn't come as a mail message, she reminded herself. He said it would flash across her screen. What if she wasn't logged on when it came? Would it wait till she was on the system? Not likely, not if it would leave no trace. Did Jon have a way of knowing when she was logged on? The idea made her shiver. People in the MA knew too much about other people's business. Especially Dr. Krell.

Trish appeared in the doorway. "Your mom almost encouraged you to go to Papa Joe's," she joked. "You'd better do it just for the novelty of having her approval."

Twila smiled wryly but shook her head. "I just don't feel like it."

Trish glanced at the monitor, glowing with the cheering

colors of the PubInfo shell. Quietly she slid the door closed behind her. "You're waiting for him to call, aren't you?"

Twila shrugged, then admitted, "It's some secret, secret system, and I have to be logged to get his message."

"Twila—" Trish came in, sat on the edge of the bed, and clasped her hands together. Twila recognized the gesture; it was confidence time. "I know all this has been upsetting," Trish began.

"There's more, Trish," Twila insisted. "There's more than they're telling me. And Jon knows what it is." And Jon is dark and compelling. "If I could just talk to him . . ."

"Maybe there is more," Trish agreed. "But maybe there isn't. Look, I know you're awfully taken with this guy Jon, but—" Twila blushed. "But this business, this animosity, between him and his father—it worries me. Something must have happened between Jon and his father, and I'm afraid whatever that is, is coloring his judgment."

"How Jon feels about his father has nothing to do with me," Twila defended.

"Doesn't it?" Trish had propped her elbows on her knees and was twisting her fingers together, not in an anxious gesture, but in a thoughtful one. "Just about everything negative you've told me about Krell, you learned from Jon."

Twila's cheeks burned. "He lied to me, Trish," she insisted. "Dr. Krell lied to me. He lied to us all."

"So did your grandfather."

It stung. Twila felt a knot tighten in her breast. "But Grandfather would have told us. When I was older. He would have told me, anyway, and you, if not Mom. He wouldn't have kept that kind of secret from us."

"Probably not," Trish agreed. "But, Twila, your grandfather had some good reasons for doing what he did when he did it. Maybe Dr. Krell had good reasons, too."

"Oh, yes, he told me his reasons," Twila snapped. "Only I didn't think they were very good."

"Maybe he hasn't told you all of them," Trish pointed out. "Maybe that's what it is they're not telling you, a good reason for all of this. Maybe it's something you won't want to know."

Twila's jaw tightened. "It can't be any worse," she pronounced, "than not knowing."

For a long moment Trish just gazed at her. Then, "I hope you're right," she sighed, rising to her feet. "I've lived with a bitter woman all my life, Twila. So have you, for that matter. You know how slanted her point of view can be. If Jon does call you—try to take a step back, that's all. Try to take a step back from his bitterness and see things through your own eyes, not his." Trish left the room, closing the door behind her.

Alone again, Twila sat staring at the glowing screen. There was more than a little truth in what Trish had said. Jon's hatred of his father did seem excessive as she thought about it. Roxanne was no picnic to live with, but Twila didn't hate her mother. What was it Krell had said when they were alone in Jon's office? "He hates me. After all these years . . ." What had happened to form the breach between father and son? And was Jon's claim that his father spied on him, and on Twila, based on fact or paranoia?

But Dr. Mintz had confirmed Krell's manipulative behavior where Jon was concerned, his desire to control not only Jon but anyone whom Jon might care about.

Then again, Dr. Mintz had been Jon's—what? Girlfriend? The term seemed inadequate to the kind of relationship Twila suspected they'd had. "Lover" was a better term. She had been his lover; and wouldn't she have been as influenced by Jon's perception of his father as Twila found herself being?

But Dr. Krell lied to me! her mind screamed. *He lied, he lied, he lied!*

Grandfather lied.

And Jon lies with his silence. To withhold truth is no better than to lie.

Twila reached out to snap off the monitor.

She froze with her hand on the switch.

A single line of letters sprawled across the screen. "SAT 15:30 MEDICAL NORTH DOOR."

Tomorrow! Twila's heart began to pound, and all thoughts of truth and paranoia and righteous indignation fled temporarily from her consciousness.

* * *

Twila forced herself to walk slowly, carefully placing herself at least ten paces behind another person on the walkway that skirted Medical. She'd gotten on a transit as though bound for the botany lab, which she had scheduled for three hours; but just past Quad Three she had slipped off the moving vehicle and crossed three blocks to the avenue that housed the major public buildings of Numex: Stores, Planning, and Medical.

She had never been in Planning. In the early days of life in the Numex biodome, it had been a beehive of activity, peopled by administrators, schedulers, governing committees. But as outbreaks of CM continued, even after the habitat was sealed for the last time, fewer and fewer people were willing to meet there in person. Administrators began to work exclusively out of their homes. Committees met only holographically, or they conducted business on computer conferences. No one knew exactly what went on in the Planning building now; one rumor said the MA had taken it over, just as they had taken over most of Planning's functions. Another rumor said it had been converted to housing, although no one knew anyone who lived in it. Still another rumor said it was inhabited by old-time planners who lived communally and didn't realize they no longer ran things.

The concrete bulk of Planning disappeared from her peripheral vision as Twila continued carefully toward the north end of Medical. There were more people in this vicinity than she normally encountered in her daily routine, with habited figures swirling this way and that across the Quad, along the walkways, avoiding each other tactfully, moving purposefully toward their destinations. Twila longed to move as briskly as the rest of them, but she had decided to disguise her walk as that of an older person. Besides, she was early.

This is crazy, she thought as she rounded the corner and moved toward the single door set halfway back along the northern wall. There's no one watching me. How could there be anyone watching me? *Why* would there be anyone watching me? Security has better things to do than to see if I got off the transit where I was supposed to. Dr. Krell has better things to do, too. Trish was right, Jon is paranoid. All this secrecy stuff is utter nonsense—

The door swung suddenly open, and Twila froze in her tracks; but the figure in the doorway was Jon, his white lab coat open, his countenance dark and handsome. "Come on," he snapped. Twila hurried the last few steps to join him, her heart thumping.

"It's thirty minutes till shift change," he told her as the door swung shut behind them. "We need to clear the elevator before people start heading out." Taking her arm, he guided her swiftly around two corners to a bank of four elevators. One sat open; Jon stepped quickly inside, drawing her with him, and jabbed a button.

Then he moved away from her, leaning up against the elevator wall and gazing at her.

Twila gazed back, feeling suddenly shy. What was she going to say to him? What questions should she ask? And why should he give her any answers at all?

Jon fished something out of the pocket of his coat and reached over to clip it on her habit. It was an MA badge. "To make sure you don't look out of place," he told her. "Not that people are very observant, as you may have guessed from the fact that you were able to walk through an entire floor of medical personnel to my lab without being stopped."

Twila fingered the badge. There were some numbers on it and two red stripes. "What does this tell people I am?" she asked.

"A student. Student badges are fairly easy to appropriate."

"Does it work?" she wanted to know. "To open doors, I mean."

He shrugged. "I can hardly call Security and ask them if a particular stolen badge is activated or not."

"And your password?" she pressed. "You said you'd see if I could use your password to leave you messages on that secret computer system of yours."

For a moment she thought he would refuse. Then he fished in another pocket and withdrew a slip of paper. "Get out of the public shell," he told her, "and type this on the command line." Twila reached for the paper, but he held it back. "Memorize it. Don't say it out loud; just memorize it and give it back to me." Then he relinquished the paper to her.

Twila looked at the sequence, gave it a logic she could remember, and handed the paper back.

"He'll know you're using it," Jon told her, "so save it for emergencies." Then he tore the paper into thumbnail-size pieces, which he stuffed back in his pocket.

"Aren't you going to eat them?" she asked dryly.

"Not without a good burgundy," he replied.

The elevator slowed, and Twila glanced up at the floor markings. Seven. They were on the top floor. "What's up here?" she asked as a ping announced their arrival.

"Offices. Lounge. Solarium."

The door rumbled open. "Solarium?" She was puzzled.

"A sunroom. This building butts right up against the outside wall, you know." He took her arm again and steered her out of the car and down a short corridor to the right, then sharply left. "It used to be considered therapeutic for patients to sit in a room lit by natural sunlight."

"And now?"

His mouth twisted in a wry smile. "It's considered therapeutic for doctors to sit in a room lit by natural sunlight."

"Is that where we're going?"

Jon shook his head. "No. Someplace better. Someplace only the elite have access to, those who are in my father's very best graces." On the right a door was marked STAIRS. Jon slid his badge into the reader beside it, opened it, and gestured for her to precede him.

"I thought Medical was only seven floors tall," she wondered aloud as she began to mount the steps.

"It is," he replied. "And one subterranean. Haven't you ever heard of the Stargazing Room?"

Twila stopped so short that Jon stumbled into her. He grabbed her to keep them both from falling; for a long moment they stood thus, Jon clutching her, their bodies locked close together.

"The Stargazing Room?" she repeated weakly. Twila had heard of the place, of course, but she'd never imagined she would get to see it—except, of course, holographically. She had used it once as the setting for a private link with Patrick. The night had not been what she expected, and since then she hadn't found anyone that she wanted to use it with. Now she was going to be there in the flesh—with Jon.

Slowly he released her, took a step back, and motioned her to proceed. She did so reluctantly, afraid and unsure why.

The chamber at the head of the stairs was circular, about twenty feet in diameter. Eighteen inches above floor level it mushroomed out, crowned by a glass dome constructed of squares of glass like the outside wall, but smaller to accommodate the greater curve. Also like the outside wall, supporting the glass globe was a framework of black triangles. A window seat encircled the room, covered with red plush cushions. All that was exactly as it had been in the holo.

But the center of the room was not bare, as it had been when Twila had visited it holographically. A circular divan rested there, covered by a mound of pillows that spilled over onto the floor. A low table near it sported a decanter and glasses of cut crystal. Another squat object appeared to be part furniture, part appliance, for it was encased in cabinetry but hummed as though electrified. Twila's jaw slipped open as she wondered why Jon had chosen this place.

Following her gaze, he seemed to read her question. He cleared his throat, embarrassed. "Only a dozen people have access to this room," he explained. "And most of them are in meetings right now. They usually only come here at night, anyway. I, uh, thought it might be the safest place we could meet. To talk."

Twila lifted nervous eyes to his; he flushed and walked toward the window.

"Come here," he called, kneeling on the window seat and gazing down on the land below them. "Here's a sight I'll bet you've never seen."

Twila joined him, kneeling as well, and all apprehension fled as she was caught up in the wonder of the vista beneath them. Outside the biodome to the east, a line of great mountains thrust skyward, their western slopes dotted with desert chaparral. Twila had caught glimpses of them through the southern biodome wall, but she had never been to the rain forest from which the best ground-level view was had. At any rate, she doubted it could compare with this aerial view from eight stories up. Somewhere in the valley at the feet of those mountains lay the old city of Albuquerque, but none of it was visible from here. There was only the thick stand of trees, which marked the course of the Rio Grande, slicing through an otherwise desolate land.

When she had recovered her breath, Twila ran to the western windows and looked down at the broken terrain below. Steep-sided mesas stretched all around, but from unseen mountains beyond the horizon a silver ribbon of water snaked ever closer to the biodome until it spread out into the bubble of a lake. The biodome itself sat atop a mesa on the lake's northern shore.

Next Twila ran to the south side of the room and peered down, trying to see where the lake lapped at the foot of the mesa. There she saw the earthen dam that bottled the river's water to form the lake, allowing the flood to spill through only after it had spun the great turbines of the hydroelectric plant, which supplied Numex with its power. But too much of the biodome itself lay between her and that facility; she could not see any of the installation, only the far bank of the river, dotted with pale green succulents and scrubby little wildflowers. Overhead a pair of hawks glided on a thermal.

"I should have brought binoculars," Jon apologized, seating himself on the cushioned window seat beside her. "You could pick out a water tower and a couple other buildings in the suburbs north of Albuquerque."

Twila strained at the glass, trying to see. "And the wind harvesters?" she asked. "I hear there's a whole forest of them on the west bank of the Rio Grande. Do you need binoculars to see those?"

"If you can see them at all," he told her. "There are ten miles and a lot of high ground between us and them. Next time I'll bring the binocs, and we'll try."

Next time. Suddenly Twila sat down and gazed up at him. His pale skin flushed under her scrutiny, and she could see a jaw muscle twitching beneath his close-cropped beard.

"What kind of plans does your father have for me?" she asked bluntly. "Last time we met, you said he had plans for me. What are they?"

Jon shrugged and looked away. "To keep control of your life. He likes to control people, and he's very good at it."

"Good enough to control you?"

It was a saucy remark, and Twila expected an angry response; instead she got silence. Then, in a very low voice, Jon replied, "Maybe more than I like to think."

Twila was too stunned by the confession to continue. She had hoped to goad Jon with the question, to get him to tell her what he didn't want to tell her; she was not prepared for his capitulation.

"He's crafty," Jon continued after a moment. "Half the time you don't even realize he's pulling the strings. He sets you up so you think it's your own idea, when really . . . He even uses my anger toward him to push me in the direction he wants." Jon pulled one foot up onto the window seat and leaned back against the black tubular framework that held the glass in place. "When my mother first sent me to live with him, all he had to do was tell me not to do a thing, and that's what I'd do."

Twila was curious about Jon the boy. She was curious about everything that had to do with Jon. "How old were you?" she asked.

"Eleven." He grimaced. "That's the 'proper age,' you know, for children to go live with a same sex relative."

Just another boy, shunted off to live with his father when he reached puberty. "Did you know him before then?" she wondered.

Jon shook his head. "All I ever heard about my father was what a bastard he was, how he'd used my mother's affections, how he'd lied to her and misled her—I guess she thought she was the only woman in his life, and one day she walked in on him with another tech. Anyway, all I got for the first eleven years of my life was this diatribe about his sins; then suddenly I was sent to live with the monster."

"How could she do that?" Twila marveled. "If she hated him so much, how could she send you to him?"

"Social pressure." Jon sat forward, leaning his arms on his knees. "You really can't raise an opposite-sex child in your household these days—not outside Medical, anyway. And she didn't have anyone else. She really didn't have anyone else."

What if that happens to me? Twila wondered. *If I ever get approved for insemination, and my child is a boy, what would I do? I have no male relatives. Where could I send him for his teenage years? I'd be in the same straits Jon's mother was in. But would I ever know who his father was? Jon at least knows who his father is—unlike me.* "Hadn't your father made any attempt to contact you?" she persisted. If she knew she had a child living somewhere in the biodome, she knew she would want to see that child, to talk to him. "No visicom calls, no Christmas gifts—Maybe your mother just didn't tell you."

Jon barked a laugh. "The old man is who she didn't tell," he said. "The detestable Dr. Krell didn't know he was a father until my mom couldn't find me any other home. Like everyone around here, he was scrupulous with his use of condoms. She had to connive to get some live semen from him and have herself inseminated. Thought if it was a done deal, she could turn his thoughts toward marriage. But she made her devastating discovery before she ever told him she was pregnant—and then she refused to tell him. Quit Medical and found anther job. He never missed her."

"So you hated him from the beginning." Twila was remembering Trish's speculation abut Jon's prejudice.

Jon read her intent. "Oh, I've had plenty of evidence of his character to substantiate my mother's opinion," he assured her.

"But he took you in," Twila reminded him. "He didn't have to do that." *I'd take in a child of mine. Any child.*

"Sure he did," Jon snorted. "Can you imagine the bad press if it got around that the great Dr. Krell wouldn't take in his own son?"

Bad press! Twila shook her head. "You're such a cynic, Jon."

"I've know him longer than you have."

Twila tried to detach herself from Jon's bitterness, tried to assess the situation as an impartial outsider. It was difficult when she didn't really know Dr. Krell. There was only that impression of a problem between him and her grandfather—one he had explained. And those monthly visits with their idle chitchat about her studies and her dancing—never about him, she realized. She really didn't know any more about Dr. Krell than he had decided to show her. But other people, people who worked with him, knew him. "Dr. Mintz thinks he really loves you," she told Jon.

Jon shifted uncomfortably. "She's mentioned that."

"You don't believe it?"

Now he rose and began to pace. "I believe he loves the idea of me: a son of his loins, all that. But I don't think he really knows who I *am*." He stopped near the divan and cast a brooding look at the looming mountains. "I hope I never make the same mistake."

"With your daughter?"

There was caution in his eye as he regarded her. Then, "She has a very distinct personality," he told Twila. "Very—independent. A mind of her own, even though she's only four. I hope I never do anything to squelch that, the way my father tried to do to me."

Twila found this tender spot in Jon very intriguing. The little girl was very precious to him, that was clear. "And when she gets to be the 'appropriate age' . . ."

Now his eyes flashed. "She stays with me," he said harshly. "No one separates me from my little girl."

"Not social pressure—"

"There's no pressure of that kind inside the MA, and I don't have any relatives or friends outside it anymore. Even my mother is back working as a tech."

She couldn't help it. Twila found herself thinking what it would be like to have a child whose father was this committed. She wondered what it would be like to have Jon's child. She wondered if they could do as her grandparents had done, and live together in an actual marriage, sharing the child rearing . . . and other things . . .

"Hell," Jon was saying, "inside the MA they don't care what you do, as long as you turn up clean at every Blood Check."

Twila pushed herself to her feet, and found that her knees trembled a little. Flushing slightly, she forced herself to walk the few steps to where Jon stood and turn her face up into his. "And you do a great many things, don't you, that we don't do in the rest of the biodome. Things we've been told are wrong."

She felt his passion change its course, focusing now on her, on her upturned face and her slightly parted lips. Twila gave her head a slight shake to dislodge her hood, bringing her mass of dark hair into view. For a long moment she stood waiting.

Jon's hand with its wrist brace drifted out as though of its own volition and touched the mountain of curls. Slowly his fingers twined themselves in those raven tresses; Twila felt her pulse grow more rapid. Then reluctantly he withdrew his hand, stroked her cheek once, and let his arm fall to his side. "They don't care what I do," he whispered, "but they care very much what you do."

"Why?" Twila demanded petulantly. She wanted him to kiss her again, and it seemed unfair that he stopped himself. "Why should they care what I do? I'm immune, what difference can it make?"

Jon's face grew dark and closed again, and he turned away from her, crossing back to the southeastern windows and staring out toward the mountains. "They care," he muttered obliquely.

"And that matters to you," she challenged, following him. What were they not telling her? "Because they—no, your father. Because your father has some kind of plans for me that you won't tell me about, you won't go against his wishes." Beyond him the bulk of the mountains loomed with an almost active presence. "It doesn't make any sense, Jon."

"There are constructive ways to buck my father's authority, and destructive ways," he snapped. "I'm trying to stick to the constructive ones."

"And why is it constructive not to tell me what's going on?" She caught his arm—a solid, flesh-and-blood arm that was really Jon—and tugged him around to face her. "What's constructive about that?"

His mouth opened to make a heated reply, but froze for an instant. Then suddenly his lips were on hers, crushing hers, and his arms were crushing her to him. Caught by surprise, Twila resisted; then, as his hands began to grope her body through the kapok habit, she panicked and tried to fight him off, frightened more by the savageness of his

demeanor than the unfamiliar sensation. In that moment
of struggle she realized how far she was from any rescue,
how helpless in the grip of superior physical strength.

Finally she broke free—or was allowed to break free,
she had no delusions about that. Retreating a few steps to
the foot of the divan, she stood panting and eyeing Jon
severely.

"That's what you wanted, isn't it?" Jon asked in
mocking tones.

"You know it isn't," she hissed. "Not like that."

"There's lovemaking and there's rape," he told her
coldly. "There's use and there's abuse. There are exciting
secrets, and there are dangerous ones." He passed the
back of one hand across his mouth, as though to wipe
away a trace of something unpleasant. "Go home, Twila.
Go finish your botany degree. Go do your Required Labor
in the orchards. Go dancing at Papa Joe's and have your
private links with strange men. Forget about being
immune, because it really doesn't change anything for
you. Just like knowing who you are didn't change anything for me."

Twila straightened up, believing he lied. Her whole life
had changed. His had to have changed, too. This had
touched him—*she* had touched him—but he wouldn't
admit it. "I'll have my answers, Jon," she vowed.

He stood straight and tall in the bright spring sunlight, a
dark and commanding presence. "Not from me."

"Then, I'll have them from your father. But one way or
another, I will have the truth," she promised. "I will have
the truth."

Krell stared at his monitor absently, hardly seeing the
images anymore, wondering when enough was enough.
She'd seen Jon again, he knew that; she had signed up for
the botany lab earlier today, but not badged in. Where had
she gone? Where had they met? It got harder and harder
to keep tabs on Jon because he would walk into the
savanna or the rain forest and just disappear for hours
where there were no cameras. Security tried to tail him for
Krell, but they were busy and Jon had gotten quite clever.
And now he was teaching Twila.

What did Jon tell you? Krell wondered as he watched

the players at Papa Joe's on his monitor. Twila danced like a demon—not with her customary seductive artistry, but like a wild thing, exhausting herself in frantic motion that could not exorcise the dark spirit that possessed her tonight. *What did he tell you when you were alone together? Is that what's making you this way—or is it that he wouldn't tell you anything? I don't know how he could, not without compromising himself.*

It could be an advantage, Krell mused, that Jon had developed this attraction for Twila, and she for him. They could provide a useful check on one another. Twila would cooperate to assist Jon with his research, and Jon would be careful to say or do nothing that might hurt her—or would he? What had touched her off tonight? What had Jon done, or said, to make her so angry? If he only knew where they had been, there might be a Security tape . . .

Twila's friends were drifting off now, casting worried looks in Twila's direction as they left. Seeing her behave so strangely, they had tried to find out what was wrong, but her only response was a manic laugh and a demand that they dance with her. Soon only faithful Marc was left. Twila slithered up to him and invited him to share a private link with her, and Krell thought he would have let that go, but Marc shook his head. "You're not yourself," he told her sadly. "Twila, I'd risk Outside for a chance to be with you, but with *you*—not this thing that's inhabiting you tonight."

"Party pooper" was her dismissal. Then Krell watched in dismay as she turned to survey the stragglers at the bar, apparently searching for some other man to lure off. If she was this hungry, then Jon had not touched her—a good thing, at this point in her cycle. Perhaps she had invited him and he had turned her down, knowing what was at stake; hence her frustration and anger. Jon might protest, Krell thought, but his instincts were good. He knew how much was riding on this research.

But what of Twila? What was he to do with her tonight? He couldn't afford to have her talking with strangers, not when she was like this. In this mood she might decide to broadcast her immunity. Or it might just slip out. Either way, there would be grave consequences. He must stop this. Krell's hand moved toward his keyboard.

* * *

Twila had decided on the thinner on the two men at the bar, a young lanky fellow with an easy smile. He would do. All she needed was someone to help distract her and help relieve the tensions that dancing had failed to banish. She didn't need Jon, didn't need his physical touch for that. Holographic sex was cheap, and safe, and with a stranger there were no recriminations or broken relationships—

Suddenly the program crashed, and Papa Joe's disappeared from around her.

"Twila," said a sad, familiar voice.

She wanted to weep. It was not Jon's voice.

"Twila, I'm so sorry," whispered Dr. Krell. "I feel this is somehow my fault. Please. Please, come to my office after school Monday. I'll waive your Required Labor. Please come and talk to me. Please."

Hot tears streamed down Twila's face as the sense of invasion mounted. "And what will you tell me, Dr. Krell? More lies?"

"No. No more lies," he promised. "Please, I can't bear to see you like this. I promised your grandfather I'd look after you, and I feel that I've failed . . ."

"No more lies?" she demanded. She'd always felt safe at Papa Joe's—this was her world, where her mother couldn't intrude, where her studies didn't matter.

"Nothing but truth between us, Twila."

"Will you tell me how you can *crash my program*!" she shrieked. It was one thing for him to have checked on who the participants where; it was another for him to have watched her dance with her friends. "How you can walk into my connection *without my permission*?" Violation! Was there any part of her life that had not been violated?

There was a slight pause. "I'm going to send over something to help you sleep," Krell told her. "Please take it. You need to rest. Things will look better tomorrow. Monday we'll talk, and we'll get this all straightened out. I promise."

His absence when he broke the connection was tangible. The last vestige of Twila's strength vanished with it, and she collapsed on the floor of the holo room. When the robot cart arrived with her sleeping pills, its monitor saw that there was no longer any need for them. The pills were deposited on the table in the kitchen, and the cart withdrew.

Several hours later, when Roxanne rose to prepare for her Required Labor, she found the pills on the table and Twila on the floor of the holo room. She managed to coax her daughter up and into bed, and dutifully forced the pills on her. Twila, barely conscious, swallowed them down without caring what they were. Then, exhausted and drugged, she slept for the next twenty-four hours.

It took Twila some time to realize that Sunday had vanished from her life. She was late for class, and suffered a "Good of you to join us, Ms. Grimm," when she tuned in. But the sleep had been healing; by the time she caught the transit for the botany lab, she was feeling more like herself than she had in three weeks. She was looking forward to her time alone in the lab, and the following Required Labor, when she logged on to the computer in the lab and found two messages waiting for her.

The first was from Medical, reminding her of an appointment with Dr. Krell. Twila groaned, and wondered if she couldn't just call him and tell him she was feeling much better and wouldn't really need to talk to him today. Now that she had begun to feel normal, the last thing she wanted was to listen to him beat his breast for his sins and continue his harangue about only wanting what was best for her.

While she considered the feasibility of declining the appointment, she opened the other waiting message file. It was from her lab partner Natasha, bringing her up-to-date on the status of the experiment they were jointly running. Twila noted the procedures Natasha had used, and ran an eye over the results she had recorded. Interesting. The meiosis in the cells in Group A was exactly as they had postulated. Now, if Group B also ran according to their hypothesis . . .

The last line of Natasha's message read, "Call me. I have great news!"

Curious, Twila placed a call to the woman at home. "Hi, Tash, what's up?"

Natasha's dark, dimpled face fairly radiated joy from

the flatscreen. "Twila, you'll never guess! I've been approved for insemination."

Twila's eyes grew wide. "You're going to be a mommy?" she shrieked. "Tash, that's great! That's wonderful! When?"

A broad grin split Natasha's face. "I don't know for sure. They've just put me on a fertility drug. See?" She opened a case of pills, and held it up toward her monitor's input. "I'm supposed to take these to increase egg production—that increases the chances of success. Then, when I ovulate, they'll call me in for the insemination procedure. If it doesn't take the first time, I'll stay on the pills and they'll try again the next month. Oh, Twila, can you believe it?"

"No," Twila murmured, stunned. "No, I can hardly believe it." But she had ceased to listen to Natasha's bubbling. Instead, she stared at the pills cradled in their individual compartments within the case that her lab partner held. They were tiny pink pills, flecked with red.

Chapter 7

Twila upbraided herself all the way from the lab to Medical. How could she have been so stupid? Why hadn't she guessed it before? It was so obvious—where had her head been? Had she been so dazzled by Jon that she couldn't think straight?

How stupid, how naive, how totally, absolutely blind—

Monthly appointments, followed by vaginal soreness. An agent in her blood that could not be transferred artificially to another person. An agent they wanted in quantity for research.

The were harvesting her eggs!

How many children do I have? she wondered. I, who have been denied insemination for so many years! How many children have been stolen from me, planted in surrogate mothers, raised up by someone else so that I can continue to be the—the—the *prize pullet* for their research! Are they all hidden away in a nursery somewhere, being bled on a regular basis for Jon's research, waiting till they mature sexually so that they, too, can be robbed of their seed? Or are they scattered across Numex, being lied to by foster parents, led along in the same dance that I've choreographed for twenty-four years?

The receptionist in Medical looked up in alarm as Twila swept up to the window glowering. "I have an appointment with Dr. Krell," Twila snapped, flipping her id into the courier basket. "Twila Grimm."

The receptionist checked her computer terminal, then pulled the basket to her side of the window and checked the id. Her face relaxed a little. "Have a seat, Ms. Grimm. I'll have a tech escort you—"

"I know the way."

The woman hesitated, then called down to Dr. Krell's

office. A moment later she buzzed the lock on the door beside her station. "Dr. Krell says you can come down."

Habit swirling, Twila flung open the door and marched down the corridor. It seemed as though she had been through it a hundred thousand times. Eleven years of monthly appointments; fertility drugs to produce multiple eggs; she could have nearly four hundred children by now! It wasn't likely, of course; in vitro fertilization was never one hundred percent successful. But even with a twenty-five percent success rate, which didn't seem unreasonable to her, there could be a hundred. A hundred children she had never met. A hundred little boys and girls, from infancy through adolescence—

Anger boiled inside her as she reached the elevator and descended to the clandestine lower floor of Medical. A hundred little dark-haired babies, of whom she had not seen one! A hundred little girls and boys who were *hers,* and yet she had not witnessed one birth, not held one in her arms. Did they have pointed chins, too? Did they have dark eyes, and warmly tanned skin, and tangled curls? Did any of them like to dance?

No wonder you quailed to tell me, Jon, she thought viciously. No wonder you berated your father's silence with your eyes but would not break it with your voice. You were afraid to tell me that I have a hundred children already and will have a hundred more, but that I'll never, ever, be allowed to bear one in my own body. That was what you meant, wasn't it, by your father having "plans" for me.

People passed her in the halls now and nodded, but Twila ignored them in her single-minded march. She passed classrooms filled with real people and did not notice; she passed laboratories, where teams of four and five worked in the same room, but did not slow her step; she passed a couple openly caressing and did not give it a second thought. When she drew near Jon's lab, she fumbled through the slit in her habit to the pocket of her shorts, fished out the badge Jon had loaned her on Saturday, and thrust it into the reader beside his door.

Jon looked up in surprise when she entered. So did three other people working in the lab, but Twila did not see them. She did not know what she intended to say until she opened her mouth and the words spilled out.

"Where are my children?"

Jon did not flinch; instead his face grew hard and inscrutable. Putting down a beaker he had been holding, he stripped off his rubber gloves and came toward her. Without a word, he took her by the arm and piloted her back out the door.

"They've been stealing my eggs, haven't they?" Twila demanded as they continued down the corridor to the west. "That's what the monthly appointments have been about, isn't it? That's what you wouldn't tell me, what none of you would tell me. You've been stealing my eggs and creating children that I've never seen!"

Jon did not speak, but ushered her onward at a brisk pace.

"How many are there, Jon? A hundred? Two? What's the success rate with in vitro fertilization these days? Do you have trouble finding host mothers? Or are you foisting them off on women as their own children? Do you milk them for blood already, or are they still too young? Got them on vitamins? Are you fattening them up, like Hansel and Gretel?"

But nothing seemed to penetrate Jon's resolve or tempt him to respond.

"Do you think I hold you less responsible, because you don't participate in the robbery process? They do it to feed your experiments, don't they? You're just as much to blame for your silence, anyway. You're just as much to—"

They were going up a broad flight of stairs now, out of the institutional corridors of Medical and into an area that was more open, and richly carpeted. There was something familiar about it that penetrated Twila's tirade and made her stop to consider it.

Grandfather's office. She had been there only once as a child, but it had looked like this. They were back on the main level of Medical now, in the area of the administrative offices.

Jon rapped perfunctorily on a wooden door, and opened it without waiting for an answer. Dr. Krell looked up from behind a large oak desk.

"Twila has a question for you," he announced coldly,

"which I refuse to answer." Then, propelling Twila into the room, he closed the door on her.

For a moment Twila stood staring at Dr. Krell. He was an impressive figure, seated at the desk with sunlight streaming in through the windows behind him. His broad shoulders, his distinguished countenance, looked exactly as a chief of staff and chair of the governing board ought to look. And out a window like this, out there, was where her birth mother had first approached the biodome, first begged for admittance for herself and for Twila—

"Have a chair, Twila."

The gentle voice brought her back. Its message did not register. "Where are my children?" she demanded.

Krell gave a sigh and closed his eyes. "I was afraid you'd come to that conclusion."

"Are you trying to tell me," she raged, advancing toward his desk, "that you're not stealing my eggs on a monthly basis and fertilizing them to create children with my immunity?"

"Oh, for God's sake, Twila, stop being so melodramatic!" Krell exploded, leaping to his feet and sending his great swivel chair sliding backward. "Yes, we harvest your eggs. What would you have us do? This agent in your blood is the only thing that can stave off the extinction of the human race!"

"Now who's being melodramatic?" she accused. "Last I heard there was still a waiting list for approval to have children. If the demise of the human race is so imminent, why is population so strictly controlled?"

"God Almighty," Krell swore in frustration, "you're a bright girl, Twila, you can figure it out. We can't live in these domes forever! Slowly, surely, our support systems are deteriorating." He passed a hand over his face and began to pace in front of the window. "We don't have the population or the space for the industry it takes to support our own technology. We've been scavenging from the Outside for decades; but good quality forage is getting scarce because things are deteriorating out there, too, and there's no new source of manufacture. What happens, Twila, when the alarm system goes out and we can no longer tell when the dome has been breached? What happens when the hydroelectric plant goes down, and we don't have the right parts to get it running again? We lose our power, we lose our computers, we lose our communications, we lose our ability to manufacture—we lose everything!"

The words struck Twila like a blow to the chest. Raised in the insular community of the biodome, she had gone through life under the assumption that the dome would go on forever. The possibility of a power shortage due to drought was often discussed, but never what would happen if the power plant failed entirely. It seemed as remote a possibility at the sun falling out of the sky.

"The clock is running on humankind," Krell told her, coming to tower over her and wag a finger in her face. "That agent in your blood is the only thing that can help us in time. And even so, there's a question of whether or not we can exploit it fast enough. We need chemicals, all kinds of chemicals to carry on our research—where do you think they come from? Outside, most of them. But they have a limited shelf life. We don't have twenty years, Twila, to complete our work. We'll run out of critical supplies before then."

Twila groped behind her for the chair Krell had offered her earlier, and eased herself into it.

"Yes, we harvest your eggs," Krell went on, his voice mellowing now. "And yes, we use them to create children with your immunity. And it works, Twila. In every instance, the children have carried the antiviral agent in their blood. That's the *good* news. No matter what happens to the rest of the human race, your children will live."

"You could have told me," she whispered. "You could at least have told me."

Krell sighed again. "And I can see now that we were wrong not to. Twenty-twenty hindsight once again, Twila. But you were a child when we started all this, and it seemed too great a burden to place on you. I can see that was an error in judgment on our part—you're very strong, and you always have been. But we were frightened, and you were our only hope. We didn't want to jeopardize that hope." He knelt down in front of her and gently took her small hands in his large ones. "We were the weak ones. Can you forgive us, Twila?"

How tired he looks, Twila thought as she gazed into his eyes. And how old. It's a terrible responsibility he bears—I wouldn't want it. And yet I have it. It's mine now as well. If I don't continue to cooperate—

They'll force you, she could hear Jon say. Would they? Yes, they probably would, she realized. But wouldn't I, if I were in their place?

Outside the window a gust of wind sent dust swirling through the air, then died suddenly and allowed the dust to settle.

"How many children do I have?" she asked.

"Not that many, really," Krell told her. "Eight girls and four boys born, with two incubating."

Twila's jaw dropped. "Is that *all*?"

Krell hesitated. "We have several embryos frozen as well."

"Frozen!" she shrieked.

"It doesn't harm them," he soothed. "We can thaw them and plant them in a host mother sometime in the future; they have every bit as much chance of survival as embryos that haven't been frozen."

"But why freeze them?"

Again the hesitation. "There are advantages to having them be different ages."

Her hackles began to rise. There was something more here, her instincts told her, something more that he still was not telling her. "I want to see them." she said bluntly.

Krell sat back on his heels, "What?"

"I want to see these embryos you have frozen. I want to see my children."

"Twila—"

"You promised me the truth, Dr. Krell!" she flared. "You said nothing but truth between us anymore!"

Krell drew a deep breath and rose to his feet. "Very well," he said quietly. "Come with me."

They found Jon lingering outside the office door. "I was waiting to see if I should rush in with a fire extinguisher" was his droll comment.

"Twila wants to see her children," Krell advised him coolly. "That is, the frozen embryos. We're going to my lab, if you care to join us."

Jon said nothing but fell into step with them. Twila

looked up into his face. He was worried about something. A strange sense of foreboding filled her.

Dr. Krell's laboratory was off a different corridor than Jon's, farther north. Twila was surprised to see an actual security guard at its head, who nodded to Dr. Krell as they passed. Why wouldn't a badge lock be enough security for Dr. Krell's lab?

"What kind of research do you do?" Twila asked as they continued.

"It's different than Jon's," Krell replied obliquely. Then, after a moment, he added, "It's cellular, but not hematologic."

"You're not looking for a blood serum, then?"

"It began as neurological research," he explained. "As you know, CM attacks the brain cells; although the virus is transmitted through the blood, it is basically a neurological disease. But there are certain cells, called T-cells, which can at a particular point in time take the imprint of whatever cellular mass into which they are injected. That is, if you inject them into brain tissue, they become brain cells, and they function as brain cells. Healthy cells. That's where I first got the idea."

"I don't understand," Twila said, shaking her head. "Do you treat CM patients here? I thought they were all put Outside, like my grandfather."

"Well, I tried the procedure with one or two patients," Krell admitted, "but the remission it gave was only temporary. So I've branched off into other areas."

"Such as?" she pressed.

"We've had some success with injecting the T-cells into the bone marrow of healthy individuals," Krell said calmly. "The T-cells become marrow cells, but because the donor carries the immunity to CM, these marrow cells manufacture blood with the antiviral agent in it."

Twila stopped short. "Then, you have a cure," she said. "You have a cure for CM."

"Not a cure, a preventive," Krell hastened. "And not a permanent one. Unfortunately, the immunity only lasts about three months. Then, the marrow cells cease to manufacture enough of the antiviral agent to combat the CM virus, and the patient needs a new infusion of T-cells."

"Where do you get these T-cells?" Twila asked. "From my blood?"

There was a long, chilling silence. "You understand the critical nature of our research, Twila," Krell began. His eyes pled for understanding, although his voice was calm. "You understand what a desperate battle we are fighting."

"You don't get them from my blood," she guessed. "That's why it's not hematologic, this research of yours. Where do you get them?"

"We have to be able to go Outside, you know that. But it's dangerous, even with the SCEs. And those of us who work every day with the CM virus—there's a tremendous risk involved. Look what happened to your grandfather. An immunity, even a temporary immunity, cuts down the risk of contamination and increases the speed with which we can work. And if we can stretch that immunity to longer periods—if we can, at last, make it a permanent immunity—that's what we need, Twila. That's the saving of the human race."

A cold knot formed in Twila's stomach. "You get these from my children."

Krell swallowed. "We have to get the T-cells while they're still blank, before they've taken on the individual imprint that will cause tissue rejection. It's a small window; the fetus has to be between nine and twelve weeks old."

Now the coldness was all around Twila, creeping in on her from the edges of her vision, turning it black. "And what happens to the fetus after you've extracted these T-cells?" she asked, her voice trembling. "What happens to my children then?"

"They're not children," Krell replied. "They're not viable at that age, Twila. Don't think of them as children."

"They die, don't they," she said simply, and the blackness took over. "When you extract the T-cells, it kills them. You are *killing my babies*!!!"

Twila woke to a view of florescent lamps shining down in her face. She screwed her eyes shut again, and knew she was in Medical, but she thought it was just one of her appointments, and she was rousing from the anesthesia. Then she heard Jon's voice, softly, just beside her. "Twila . . ."

Memory rushed back, and she wrenched herself up from the couch on which she lay. Immediately Jon's weight bore her back down, pining her gently to the couch, and his lips were at her ear whispering, "Easy, easy. Stay calm, or he'll sedate you."

"Easy!" she shrieked, struggling against him. "No, I won't take it easy! Don't you think for a minute that I'm going to take it easy, because you're a damned lot of *butchers,* that's what you are. Butchers! Carving up my unborn babies for—"

"I said take it easy!" Jon hissed, still with his lips at her ear, still stretched across her and pinning her with his own body. "He's right there with a syringe. Is that what you want? A needle in your arm? Drugs in your veins? What good can you do your babies if you're drugged senseless?"

Finally his meaning penetrated her outrage, and Twila stopped struggling. She could, indeed, feel Dr. Krell's presence nearby, although she kept her eyes clenched shut. Slowly she forced the rage back—back down to where it was pinned as securely as Jon held her. No, she couldn't help her babies if she were drugged. But, then, most likely she couldn't help them at all. A wave of helplessness swept over her, and tears flooded her tightly closed eyes.

"You can't just kill my babies," she sobbed.

"I know," Jon soothed. "I know." And for the moment Twila was satisfied that he did. She allowed him then to lift her gently and enfold her in his arms, cradling her head against his shoulder as she wept hot, bitter tears.

"They're not white rats," she sobbed—quietly, so that only Jon could hear her. "They're not laboratory animals. They're my babies. You're killing my babies."

Jon brushed her tangled hair back from one ear, and pressed his mouth close to it again. "I know," he whispered. "I know it's wrong. I know it's wrong."

For several moments, Twila could not speak for the grief that overwhelmed her. She clung to Jon, letting him rock her and stroke her hair and whisper empty, soothing words in her ear.

Finally Dr. Krell tried to speak. "You mustn't think of them as—"

"Ssh!" Jon silenced him harshly. "Let her be. Let her grieve, for Christ's sake."

"But they're not—"

"How would you know?" Jon snapped. "You never wanted a child."

Krell recoiled as though struck. Then slowly he straightened himself, and with great dignity asked, "How do you know what I have and have not wanted in my life?"

Twila felt a tension snap through Jon.

"Did anyone ever ask me?" Krell continued. "Did your mother? The first I knew of your existence was when you were eleven years old. No one ever asked me how *I* felt about it. But think, Jon. If I didn't want you, would I have opened my life to you?"

Jon brushed at Twila's tangled curls, refusing to look at his father. "A man in your position couldn't afford to do otherwise."

"Now, that's about enough!" Krell flared. "For twenty-two years, Jon, I've listened to this asinine self-pity of yours, and if you're determined not to believe the truth, I can't help that. But for God's sake, grow up! In every argument, you fall back on that old complaint. I didn't want you. I didn't love your mother. Even if that were true—which it's not—don't you think it's time to put it behind you?"

Jon turned from Twila to face this attack. "That's not the subject," he snarled.

"You made it the subject!"

Fascinated, Twila propped herself on still trembling arms to watch the two combatants. Krell was a grand presence, large of frame and deep of voice, projecting an air of great authority. Jon was smaller, more intense, with the righteous zeal of a crusader.

"The subject is human life and human dignity!" Jon insisted. "The value of the individual—of Twila, as an individual. Of her children, each as individuals. Your problem is, you can't see them as individuals. To you, they're only tools, only specimens in your research."

Twila's heart lurched as he voiced her pain. Her babies. Dear God, her babies! Conceived as sacrifices, created only to die. It was a form of prostitution worse than slavery.

"Not true!" Krell's voice was anguished. "Not true at all. Twila is my patient, and I have always acted in what I believed was her best interest. And the fetuses are *not* children, but there are children—real children, conscious and aware—who are going to die if we don't find a cure for this disease! Your daughter, Jon. What happens to her if the dome is breached? What happens if the pumps that drive the sprinklers go out?"

Again Twila felt it: the wrenching of her world. Dizzied, she staggered to her feet, leaning against the wall for support. What *would* happen if the dome were breached? All the inhabitants of Numex—her mother, Aunt Trish—all infected . . .

"Don't you understand, Jon?" Krell persisted. "Every person in this biodome—every individual—is precious to me. They are *my* children. All of them."

"But some are more precious than others," Jon sneered. "They're the ones who get the immunization."

"Some are at higher risk than others—"

"*Stop it!*" Twila screeched. "Just *stop it,* both of you! I will not be a battleground for your enmity."

She stood leaning shakily against the wall, panting. Jon started toward her, but she held up a hand to ward him off, edging toward the door. "Do you get this—this immunization, too?"

He blanched and stopped short.

Twila felt her limbs begin to tremble.

"I won't anymore," he whispered.

The blackness crept in on Twila once again.

NO! she shouted at herself. *No. I will not faint again. I will not let myself be helpless before them.* She took one deep breath, then another. *I will not be the cowering victim, inviting an Edgewalker to practice his mania on me. I will be strong. My anger will make me strong.*

"Twila," Jon whispered, pleading. His face was a picture of abject remorse.

It put the strength back into Twila's legs. "*He* justifies it," she said bitterly with a nod of her head toward Krell. "But you—you know it's wrong—and you still do it."

"I used to justify it, too," he told her. "I can't anymore."

Damn you, she thought. Damn you, Jonathan Krell, that was the right answer. Why did you have to give me the right answer? I'd have been happier if I could hate you, too.

Finding nothing left to say, Twila turned and fled the room.

Jon stopped by his father's office at eleven o'clock. The light was still on, so he knocked and opened the door. "Did she get home yet?"

Krell shook his head. "Not home, not the orchard, not the lab."

"It's been dark for three hours," the younger man observed. From long practice he managed to keep his voice even, but his soul was ragged with guilt and worry.

"I know." They were silent, father and son, trying not to think about the possibilities for a young woman in such an unbalanced state, away from the protection of Security.

"I'm going home," Jon said finally. He was ineffably weary, wearier than he could ever recall being. "Let me know if she turns up."

Krell looked up at his son, an attractive man by any accounting. The moodiness that Krell found so frustrating seemed only to draw women to him. Women like Twila. "You may know before I do," Krell suggested.

"I doubt it." Jon was innocent of his own magnetism, but all too aware of Twila's wrath. Justified wrath, he thought.

"We are right," Krell told him, as though reading his thought.

But Jon shook his head. "No, we're not. You're not. I can't be part of it anymore."

"Jon, you can't be serious!" his father exclaimed. "You work with the live virus on a daily basis, you can't go without this protection!"

"Carlton did," Jon said simply. "I will, too."

"Jon—nine-week-old fetuses are not people," Krell insisted.

Jon straightened himself and looked his father squarely in the eye. "That's a philosophical question," he said. "One of personal choice and conviction, not scientific fact. They are people if you believe they are."

"And I don't."

"But Twila does." Jon's eyes as he faced his father were gentler than Krell had seen in a long time. "And they are hers—not ours."

Krell could not answer that, and so he turned away from his son.

Jon started out.

"Jon—"

The younger man turned back. Krell was still facing the window, gazing out into the star-flecked night. How many times had Jon carried on his conversations with that broad back? "Give my love to my granddaughter, will you?" Krell asked.

"No," Jon replied bluntly.

Krell repressed a sigh. "What do you hope to prove by keeping her away from me?"

"I don't intend to prove anything," Jon told him. "I intend for her not to know you, and you not to know her. You use people, and I will not have her used."

"I would love her," Krell said quietly.

"That's what I'm afraid of," Jon replied, and left.

Twila huddled under a date palm by the northwestern wall of the biodome and stared out at the eerie shapes of mesas etched against a glittering sky. Far to her left the moon balanced momentarily on the edge of a mesa, then seemed to roll down its sloping side toward the horizon. Its pale light made the palm cast a faint shadow of deeper darkness in the night. In that shadow Twila sat motionless, listening to the trilling of crickets and other insects, far from the human habitations of the biodome.

How long will it last? she wondered. How long before something breaks that can't be repaired? Was Krell exaggerating? How imminent is the danger?

It doesn't matter, she realized. When it happens, it happens. I can't let them keep killing my children.

But how can I stop them? Jon was right. Dr. Krell can declare me an Edgewalker and do pretty much what he likes with me. And if I tried to protest, tried to tell someone what was going on, who would believe me? And how long could they survive in this community if they opposed Krell? He has so much power, much too much power . . .

Outside, a solitary cloud drifted across the sky from the east, a dark, wispy, insubstantial thing. Stars peeked in and out of it like sequins through a threadbare habit. The moon was sliding rapidly from sight.

I can't let them keep doing it! Twila raged inwardly. I can't let them keep killing my babies. It's not as though these were fetuses that died in the natural course of things, their donated cells the spark of good in an otherwise tragic situation. These fetuses are created for their tissue, and then killed for it. That is an obscenity.

One I am helpless to stop.

So what will I do? Wait here until they find me, like a recalcitrant child hiding in her closet? Or go back on my own, like a lamb to the slaughter? What's the right choice? Grandfather, what would you do? If you were here, and not out there, what would you have me do?

But it had been too many years, and the memory of him was too clouded. His shade was too insubstantial to give advice, his character too obscured by time and childhood perceptions to set an example. Twila knew the answer had to come from herself, from her own convictions and her own intelligence and her own courage. Not even Aunt Trish could help her with this one—not that Trish would try. Roxanne was the only one who ever tried to make decisions for Twila; Trish had long since forced Twila to make her own. Now more than ever, Twila realized, she needed to make her own decision. If she did decide to fight Krell somehow, she dared not involve her family in any way.

So, then, logically, what courses were open to her? If she did not want Krell to keep robbing her womb of the fruit she wanted to bear, what were her options?

And as the last trace of moon slipped below the horizon, Twila knew what she must do.

*   *   *

Krell found Twila waiting in his office when he came to work the next morning. He did not ask how she had gotten there; he knew about the badge Jon had appropriated for her; and was, in fact, counting on her using it somewhere so he could track her whereabouts. He'd given Security instructions to locate her, but not apprehend her unless she seemed bent on injuring herself. Having monitored her passage through Medical, they had probably been trying to reach him as he walked from his apartment in the old Planning building to work. All of that made sense to him, and so he was not troubled. The important thing was that she had returned, and on her own.

Now she sat in his chair behind his desk, a tiny figure dwarfed by the large window behind her. Her habit was soiled from having slept out of doors, and her face beneath the hood was shadowed and weary.

"You didn't even look for me," she accused.

"Jon's idea," he admitted, saying nothing of the covert Security alert. "In retrospect, a good one. Not that I'm surprised. With the exception of his hatred for me"—he quirked his lips in a deprecating smile—"he really has excellent judgment."

The silence grew long between them, but Krell waited patiently. She had come here for a reason, and eventually she would get to it. The longer she stayed calm and reasonable, the greater the possibility that he could persuade her to be cooperative.

"I don't suppose there's anything I can do to get you to stop killing my babies," she said finally, the gravel of weariness in her voice.

"Twila." Krell crossed behind the desk and squatted down where he could look up into her dark eyes. They were red and puffy, but dry. "Imagine you had ten children, and they were all dying. Then you learned that you could save two, maybe three, but at the cost of the others. What would you do, Twila? Watch all ten of them die?"

Twila said nothing.

"If a child dies, Twila, it's a tragedy," Krell went on. "If a community dies, that's a catastrophe. But Twila—if the whole human race dies . . ." He let his words hang on the air.

Finally a leg muscle began to cramp on him, and Dr. Krell rose and extended his hands to Twila. "Go home," he told her gently. "Let me take you out of advanced studies this semester. You'll draw extra shifts of Required Labor, but maybe that will be good for you. Give yourself time to adjust to all this."

Slowly Twila put her hands in his and allowed herself to be drawn from the chair. "Shall I have a Security scooter take you home?" he asked.

"No, thanks, I'll walk." Her voice was flat.

"Stop and see Jon on your way out," Krell suggested. "He's been worried about you." Perhaps it would do good to encourage a relationship between them, now that the truth was out. It might provide her with some stability, something to focus on other than the fetal research. Who knew? It might be good for Jon, too.

Twila nodded dumbly and left the room. Her movements were sluggish, her mien weary. Defeated.

With a sigh of relief Krell relaxed into his own chair. Then he snapped on his workstation and keyed up the Security program.

Jon was alone in the lab when Twila let herself in. From the pallor of his face and the darkness of his eyes, she knew how little he had slept.

As little as I? she wondered bitterly

He stood looking across the room at her, his face a mask except for his eyes. Everything showed in his eyes: the shame, the regret, the anguish for what he'd done.

"So when the live virus was in this room," she began abruptly, "you really didn't need that mask."

Reflexively Jon touched the filtration mask, which hung from his neck. "Insurance," he said. "I was near the end of my immunity, and I'm never sure . . . And for show, I guess. Not many people in Medical know there's an immunization available. We try not to flaunt it."

"I can understand that," she said sardonically. "Just how many people can you keep immunized?"

Now the mask broke and anguish spread across Jon's face. "I don't know," he said miserably. "Twila, my father keeps that close to his chest, and I never wanted to know. I never wanted to know what was really going on with his work. I just wanted to succeed here so that he'd stop. It's the only thing I know to do."

"But you took the injections yourself."

"I didn't know what they were at first. That is, I didn't think about what they were. I just thought I could move ahead faster in my work if I didn't have to worry about— Then, when my daughter was born, I began to think. And the more I thought, the sicker it made me. I tried to tell myself if I didn't get the injections, he'd only give them to someone else . . ." Jon shook his head. "There's no excuse. I don't have an excuse. You were right: I'm worse than he is."

Twila let him carry that in silence for several moments. Then, "If I stay out of your life," she began "from here on out . . ."

"You'll be better off," he finished.

"And you?"

A wry smile flickered across his features. "Oh, I'll be better off, too," he assured her. Then he added softly, "But I think I'll hate it."

Now she crossed the room to stand directly in front of him. "You realize you've absolutely ruined holographic encounters for me."

He looked startled, then managed a weak laugh. "Well, you've done a fair job on my actual relationships." His voice dropped to a whisper. "I can't touch another woman without thinking about you."

"You'll get over it," she said flatly. It hurt him, and she was not sorry. But she stood on tiptoes and brushed her lips against his. "Good-bye, Jon."

With precision she turned and walked to the door, wishing she could see his face later in the morning when she sent him a message on the protected computer system he had told her about. THAT WAS FOR THE CAMERAS, it would say. MEET ME FRIDAY, STARGAZING ROOM, TEN P.M.

Chapter 8

It was like looking at a star chart, with the host of bright dots sectioned off into grids by the latticework structure that supported the glass dome of the Stargazing Room. With all the interior lights off, Twila sat on the circular divan in the center of the room and tried to imagine she was sitting Outside, looking up at that same night sky.

But she couldn't make it work. The struts were still there, holding back the velvet night, holding in the frightened settlement of Numex.

Jon stood by the southeastern windows, as he had since they'd come in, staring out toward the lump of blackness that was the Sandia Mountains thrown into relief by the spangled sky. Twila remained gazing upward, held by the hypnotic glitter of the stars.

"It's really a prison, you know," she said after a moment.

As she'd stepped off the elevator, her habit draped over her arm, and made her way back to the Stargazing Room, she'd half expected to find his father waiting for her instead of Jon. Only when she'd seen him leaning against the wall, waiting for her, had her apprehension vanished. Without a word he had unlocked the door and held it open, then followed her up the stairs to this place, now enchanted with night magic.

She had dropped her habit in a corner formed by the stairwell and the window seat, and kicked off her shoes. Immediately she'd stretched out luxuriously on the round divan, knowing he was watching her sinuous movements. She wore loose khaki trousers and a form-fitting knit top of forest green. Her neck and ears were hung with malachite set in mock gold, and golden bangle bracelets cluttered her wrists. Her feet were bare, with nails carefully polished.

"More like a goldfish bowl," Jon said finally, turning from the windows to look at her again. "We may not like our confinement, but it beats gasping your life away Outside."

Now she turned to look at him, really look at him. What made him so attractive? He was not bad-looking, but no stunner, either. Average height, a nice build but nothing extraordinary. His features were regular, his hair thick and well-groomed, but the same could be said for Marc. His eyes were his best feature, bright orbs in a face darkened, not in pigment, but in mood. That was it, Twila thought. It was that impression he gave of deep, internal conflict. She found herself always wanting to jostle his control, to strip away the mask and see what really dwelt underneath. Basic primal passions lurked there, at war with his careful judgment. They fascinated her.

He flushed under her scrutiny and turned to take in the spectacular array of stars once more. "It is breathtaking, isn't it?" he commented.

She glanced at the sky again. "I wonder if this is what it was like to travel in space?" she asked.

He came to her then, and sat not beside her on the upholstered divan, but on the floor at her feet. Why? she wondered. Why make that choice?

"I think," he said, "that space travel was never this grand. Those capsules were tiny; even the couple of space stations they managed were designed for efficiency, not stargazing. This room was designed for this—just this."

His head was near her knee, dark brown hair fashionably short, and he smelled of something spicy. This was so different from a holographic meeting; there were never any smells, and no sensation of radiant warmth from another body. Twila found herself intrigued by the texture of his hair—was it soft, or coarse? There was a way to know. Slowly she reached out with one hand and touched it.

"When the dome was first built," Jon went on as though he had not noticed, "this was a lounge area: sofas, chairs, pillows on the floor. People used to come here from all over the biodome to read in the natural light, or to sit on

the window seat and just gaze out. But after the first case
of CM-A inside the dome, when the ban was put on gathering in public—"

Twila trailed her fingers through the short, thick hair. It
was like her own for texture, but the length of it made it
behave differently. It wanted to go in one direction only,
and when it was drawn another way, it would spring back
and settle slowly into place.

"After that, no one wanted to wander through the halls
of Medical if they didn't have to, anyway. You might
catch something. So it was naturally only used by MA
people."

The shortest hair, that around his ears and toward the
back of his neck, gave her fingers a different sensation as
she passed them through it. An almost prickling sensation, as it brushed across her skin, each hair intent on
returning to its accustomed place.

"I don't know who started limiting access to it. Maybe
someone got tired of finding empty bottles and garbage
up here from the med student parties. Anyway, it got to be
an exclusive thing, to have access to this place. And since
it was only inhabited by a few people at a time—mostly
just two at a time—they changed the furnishings."

For lovers, then. Twila had guessed that, from the circular divan on which she sat. This tried to be a plush and
intimate place, with the mundane sights of Numex shut
out below and the intoxicating panorama of Outside all
around them. The small mechanical item on the floor
nearby had turned out to be, upon inspection, a refrigera-
tion unit—just the right size for a bottle of spirits and two
glasses. And nowhere was there a computer monitor or
anything that resembled a microphone or lens.

"Is it truly shielded from prying eyes?" she asked. "And
ears?"

Jon gave a brief snort. "My father brings his bimbos
here," he told her. "You can be sure there's no way
anyone can spy on him."

Why, she wondered, are they "bimbos" when he brings
them, but not when you do? For I know without asking
that you have brought ladies here, many times. You are
too self-righteous, Jon.

But she said nothing, only stroked his hair and reveled in the tactile sensation of that simple caress.

After a moment his hand reached up to capture hers and draw it down to his lips. He placed a kiss in her palm, then held her hand cupped against his bearded cheek. "Do you hate me for what I did?" he asked softly.

Twila felt oddly disturbed that she could no longer move her hand in the soothing motion of stroking his hair. She wondered about reaching for him with her other hand, but it seemed too awkward. "Grandfather always said," she told him, "we don't hate people. We might hate what they do, but we don't hate the person."

"I don't want for you to hate me," he whispered.

"You were wrong to go along with it," she said bluntly. "You can't criticize the slave trade and keep a slave in your house. It doesn't work."

"I know. I've stopped." He kissed her palm again. His mustache tickled, and his breath was warm and moist against her skin. "Can you forgive me?"

"Does it put you in much danger?" she asked. "Not to have the immunity?"

"Some," he admitted. "Not much. We worked without it for years; we can again. It just means more precautions, more time. And more tension." He gave a weak laugh. "I already have an ulcer, so what's the difference?" He curled her fingers around his own and kissed their tips. "Forgive me?" he persisted.

"Yes."

"Thank you." And with that he turned and buried his face against her thigh. Twila was startled, thrown temporarily off guard by the action. Her first impulse was to push him away, for the gesture was one she had never encountered before, and therefore it must be somehow wrong. But she restrained her hands. She had not asked him here to push him away. She took one deep breath, then another, and then hesitantly placed her hands on his hair. Once again she found that trailing her fingers through it was somehow soothing.

"Do you know where my children are?" she asked after a moment. "The ones they let live. The eight girls and four boys."

He tensed, then sat up and turned his face away again. "Depends on what you mean by 'where.' "

"I mean, are they all stuck in a nursery somewhere? Or do they have families? Mothers? Does someone love them?" Twila found her heart aching even to speak of it.

"They're like all the other children of Numex," Jon replied carefully. "They each have at least one parent, and the parents love them. They don't know, Twila. None of the parents know."

"Do they look like me?"

He gave a great sigh. "Some."

"Can I see pictures of them?"

Now he rose to his feet and crossed to the huge windows. "I don't think that's a good idea, Twila. You're only asking for more pain."

Springing up she followed him. "I'm asking for more reality," she said tightly. "It's not real to me, Jon, none of this is real, and I need it to be! I need to know that everything I've gone through, everything I have yet to go through, is to some purpose. Those children. *My* children. I want to see them. I want to know what they look like."

But Jon shook his head. "My father will spot it the minute you try to access their files, and close you down."

Twila remembered Papa Joe's crashing around her. Yes, if Krell thought it was bad for her to become attached to her children, he would shut down her first inquiry.

"You access them for me," she urged.

"I did once," Jon told her. "When I began to be curious; when he wasn't watching too closely. But he's wary now. We used to share research files, but he's blocked me out now; and if I try to use PubInfo, he'll spot that, too, and know it's for you. Leave it alone, Twila. It will only get you into trouble."

"I've been a good girl all week," she told him. "I've been the perfect little sheep, doing as I was told, not kicking up a fuss, taking my medicine. I need to see my children, Jon."

"I'm telling you it won't happen."

"Go in under that secret system of yours," she challenged.

Jon shook his head. "Too dangerous. It creates heat for

me every time I use it. It drives him crazy because he can see the activity, but he can't get to the files or tell what I'm doing. It was you grandfather's id, you see, and my father was junior to him; so Carlton set up this id with so many locks not even Security could break them. And as long as I don't use it too often, it'll stay that way. It's the only place I can hide information, Twila; I won't jeopardize it so that you can see pictures of children who belong to someone else."

Twila drew back. "That's how you see them? As belonging to someone else?"

"They have parents," he repeated. "They have lives, and you're not a part of those lives. You want reality, Twila? They don't need you. That's reality."

Tears brimmed in her eyes, and her lip quivered. Abruptly Twila turned on her heel and stalked back to the divan, where she threw herself full length on its plush surface.

After a moment Jon came and sat beside her. "It can't do any good," he told her in more soothing tones. "Concentrate on things that will do some good."

Twila rolled onto her back and gazed up at the bedizened night sky. "And do you have any bright ideas on what that might be?" she asked him.

Jon stretched out beside her and looked up at the latticework dome. "No. Not yet. I have plans to undo him, but I don't know how you can help in that, not yet."

"I don't care about undoing your father," she said. "I just want him to stop killing my babies."

"The only way to do that is to remove him from power," Jon repeated.

They were silent for a time, watching the stars glide imperceptibly across the dome. Twila reveled in the feel of him lying so close to her, their arms touching, the scent of him drifting to her nostrils. After a moment his hand sought hers, and he clasped it, twining his fingers through hers. Twila felt a special warmth spreading through her and wondered if he felt it, too.

In his apartment, Krell was entertaining when Security overrode his lockout. "Dr. Krell."

Reluctantly Krell loosed his hold on the attractive

brunette. "Duty calls," he whispered. "Don't go anywhere." She giggled as he left the room to sign on the
workstation in his den.

"This better be good," he told the Security officer
gruffly.

The officer was a young man in his late twenties, and
obviously nervous about having disturbed the most powerful man in Numex through a lockout. "It's the Grimm
woman, sir," he said in a deep voice that contrasted
sharply with his slight body. "She's badged her way into
Medical. We've tracked her to the Stargazing Room."

"So?" Krell was not impressed. "She's not likely to do
any damage up there."

"Your son has joined her."

Now Krell stopped and considered, stroking his jaw.
"Hm. Interesting." She had made it sound as though she
didn't want to see him again. What was she up to? Were
they plotting something together, or just in search of a
little privacy?

"Don't do anything," he instructed the officer. "See
where they go when they leave, that's all. Leave a message
for me. And don't call here again unless they head for my
lab." He signed off, but sat for a moment thinking. That
might be her plan, to rescue the frozen embryos, although
there wasn't anything she could do with them. Maybe she
had some hope that she could talk Jon into implanting one
of the embryos in her. He snorted. She'd have better luck
coaxing him to implant a baby the natural way. Jon had no
knowledge of surgical procedures. Unlike Krell, the boy
had gone straight into research. Either way, it didn't
matter. A pregnancy was easily taken care of.

Pushing the situation from his mind, Krell went back to
the brunette.

They still lay side by side, hands clasped, but Twila did
not know how to make the first move, and Jon did not
seem inclined to do so. Instead they gazed at the moon
drifting toward the western horizon. "Have you ever been
Outside?" Twila asked.

"Once," he admitted. "In an SCE. I didn't like it."

She propped herself up on one elbow and looked at him
curiously. "Why not?" She had always imagined that

would be an exciting, exhilarating experience—like this Stargazing Room, only better.

"I'm accustomed to walls," Jon told her, not meeting her eyes. "It made me dizzy, not having a roof over my head." He refrained from telling her that he had gotten wretchedly ill, vomiting inside the environmental suit, and that the Security people with him had laughed. "I was glad to come back Inside."

"Has your father been Outside?"

"Oh, yes." Jon hated to be reminded how his father took in stride so many things that Jon had no stomach for. "He goes out a couple of times a year, on foraging expeditions. He knows what to look for. It takes him less time than it does anyone else, and there's less danger to him because—" Jon broke off.

"Because he takes the injections," she finished.

Now Jon turned and wrapped his arms around her, pressing his whole body against hers. "Please, let's not talk about it anymore," he whispered in her ear, his breath warm and moist through the locks of her hair. "I've had enough anguish for today. I just want to be here with you, to hold you, to touch you . . ."

A mild panic enveloped Twila as she experienced the pressure of his weight bearing down on her. But she forced the panic away, coaxed her own body to relax and savor the contact. Then slowly she allowed herself to melt into his embrace.

It was a warm and comforting sensation, even without its sexual overtones. Twila felt safe, and loved, with the gentle pressure of his body surrounding her. "Why can't everyone live like this?" she murmured after a moment. "People holding onto each other in their hurt and their weariness . . ."

"The sad part is, they can," Jon told her. "With current controls, the chances of contracting CM here in the biodome are less than point zero two percent. It's just people's fear that keeps them apart." He nuzzled his face against her ear, which sent shivers through her body and distracted her momentarily.

Then, "Give them a placebo," she suggested.

Jon laughed, and when he drew his head back to look at her, she was surprised to see him smiling. It was an amused smile, as much in his eyes as in his mouth. It flattered his features even more than his customary brooding look. "A placebo? Twila," he chided. "You're the one who keeps demanding truth."

"Give them the truth," she countered. "Tell them that if they take this medicine, their chances of contracting CM are less than point zero two percent."

He laughed again and cuddled back up against her. "Oh, God, you're wonderful!" he sighed. "I wonder what the old man would say to that idea."

Krell dozed on the sofa, where they had concluded their lovemaking, feeling gratifyingly spent. The brunette was dressing, and he slitted his eyes for one last glimpse of that tantalizing body, but the heaviness of his lids soon won out. After a moment, he heard the front door open as she left. There was the satisfying click of the lock behind her, and he drifted off again.

It was near midnight when Twila slipped away from Jon. They were lying cupped together like spoons, for it had become obvious after his first one or two advances that she was not yet ready to finish what they had begun. Her conditioned reactions would take some time to break down. So he had contented himself with holding her close, his face buried in her hair. He was half asleep and stirred when she moved. "Where's the nearest toilet?" she asked him.

"Mm . . . downstairs and to the left," he murmured. "Second door."

"Thanks."

"Hurry back," he told her.

"I will," she lied. With careful nonchalance she picked up her habit, where it lay in a heap, firmly grasping the backpack hidden in its folds. Then she slipped into her shoes and moved quietly down the stairs. The corridor was deserted; she kept the habit over her arm and the bag as she headed for the elevator.

When she reached the basement level and found no one in the halls, Twila began to run. How long it would be before Jon became suspicious, she did not know. Neither did she know if Krell were somehow monitoring her, or if Security would spot her roaming the corridors off shift and stop her. She still had the badge, of course—necessary to her plan—but she couldn't risk an encounter with Security. So she ran with the strength of years of dancing, along the route she had first followed on her quest for truth: past empty classrooms, past locked doors, and down a long, wide aisle toward the double doors with their frightening sign, ISOLATION.

Her hands trembled as she fumbled the badge into the reader beside the heavy doors. There was no way to know if a student badge would work in this lock, except to try it. For a prolonged instant there was no reaction, and Twila's heart sank.

Then there was the telltale *chunk* of the lock releasing, and Twila flung the door open. She was in! Her heart pounded wildly. To the right, she knew, was Filtration and Sterilization, where she had spent twelve uncomfortable hours one month ago, but to the left—She darted in that direction and found what she sought, a series of glassed-in rooms. She had caught a glimpse of them as they wheeled her in, all with heavy-looking locks that did not open to a badge, all empty with their doors propped open. And in one of these rooms—at least one of them—

Yes! The last room in the row held what she wanted: the door to the tunnel that led out under the biodome wall. It was the door through which her grandfather had gone sixteen years ago; it was the door that would take her out from under Krell's thumb forever—

"Dr. Krell!"

Krell lurched awake, knowing it must be an emergency of some sort, but not remembering for a moment what the situation was.

Then it came back to him—Twila. Twila and Jon in Medical. He stumbled across the room to a console and logged on. "Yes?"

The Security officer was sweating now. "Sir, I know you said not to disturb you, but—"

"Spit it out, man!" Krell snarled impatiently.

"Ms. Grimm has gone into Isolation."

"Isolation?" He was still groggy. Isolation? What was in Isolation that would attract Twila? It was a grim and painful place when in use. At the moment it was empty. Why Isolation? Then it dawned on him.

"Good God, man, stop her!" he roared. "She's headed Outside!"

Was that a sound? A distant shout? A door opening? Twila did not wait to find out but bolted into the isolation chamber, pulling the inner door shut behind her. Even in her haste, she took pains not to risk having any infected outer air get into the biodome. She was relieved to hear the door lock, sealing this environment from the rest of Medical. The first hurdle was crossed; anyone coming after her would have to suit up against possible contamination before coming in.

Slinging the backpack onto her shoulder, she turned her attention to the other door. Like the one behind her, it was metal with elaborate seals and flashings. A light beside it was red—why? She tested the handle and found it would not budge. Panic gripped her. But it had to open, Grandfather had opened it so easily—Just then the red light went out and a green one beside it lit. With relief Twila realized that this door would undoubtedly be locked out until the other one was entirely sealed, to prevent any accidental contamination. Blood roaring in her ears, she put both hands on the handle and yanked. The door moved this time—reluctantly, unused for many years, but it did swing open on creaking hinges. A wave of foul, stale air hit her, and she staggered back half a step.

Now she was sure she could hear sounds from elsewhere on the floor. She had suspected this door would be alarmed. Her time was limited now. Forcing herself to ignore the musty, moldy smell that clawed at her lungs, Twila fled along the dark passageway.

The gloom of the place was complete, for utility lights had long since burned out, but Twila rushed on headlong. She almost tripped on the first step before she saw the stairs leading upward. Catching herself on the railing, she had time for a quick glance toward their destination, but all was black. Heedless, she launched herself up the metal treads, clanging with every step. At the top was a platform where another door awaited her, with seals like those below. It was equally resistive, but yielded to her adrenaline-inspired strength. Twila slipped through and found herself in a metal bubble so dark that she had to grope her way around the wall to locate the next door.

Twila knew from her elementary-class days that there were several such utility domes connected to Numex. Some were called lungs, for their flexible interiors accommodated the natural expansion and contraction of the biodome's air caused by temperature changes. Another was the exhaust vent for the crematorium, where the ashes of infected corpses and other infected materials were blown out. Still others held a variety of equipment that for some reason was better off beyond the perimeter of the main dome. All were accessible from the underground utility area of Numex—the "basement," it was called—but only a few had doors for human passage to the Outside.

This door should be the last physical barrier between Twila and freedom. On the other side was the air she had dreaded all her life. Now she sought it—craved it—for once she was known to have breathed it in, who would believe she was not infected? It would be impossible for Krell to have her dragged back in without giving away the secret of her immunity.

The latch here was a wheel like that on a valve. Twila tugged on it in a counterclockwise direction, but it would not budge. Another lockout situation? Groping her way back to the interior door, she found that it, too, had a valve-like closure. On a hunch she twisted this clockwise as far as it would go. As she did so, she could hear the hiss of pressure seals activating. Once more she turned her attention to the outside door. This time she was able to grind the wheel counterclockwise and feel the latches releasing. Now no one would be able to enter this chamber from below until a phase one decontamination had been completed.

But Twila held no illusion that that would buy her much time. There were other exits from the biodome, she knew. The success of her escape relied on speed and strategy. As the door finally swung free and Twila stepped out, she knew exactly where she needed to go.

But she could not. The vastness of the sky above overwhelmed her, and Twila sank to her knees, head reeling,

stomach churning. Jon's words came back to her as the
world began to spin: "It made me dizzy, not having a roof
over my head." Now Twila knew that same dizziness, felt
the empty space around her like a physical weight
crushing her into the ground.

"She's out," the Security officer reported, face pale.
"Get her back in!" Krell commanded.
Shock showed in the man's face. "But, sir, she's
breathed the air—"
"She's immune, goddamn it!" Krell thundered. "The
source of immunity for all Security personnel who go
Outside. Now, *get her back in here!*"

Stop it! Twila chastised herself, screwing her eyes shut
to block out the disorienting openness. *You can't let your
senses fool you like this. It's the same world you looked
out on from the Stargazing Room; it is no larger, no
heavier, than it was with a layer of glass between you and
it. Now you must conquer this feeling. You must open your
eyes and use your legs and run—run for your life, if it is
to be any kind of a life, run for your children's lives. You
can't let Krell go on. You must put an end to this obscene
practice.*
Gulping deep breaths of air, Twila forced herself to be
calm. The air was cold and fresh, quite dry compared to
the air of Numex. Something brushed her cheek—a draft
of some kind. How could there be a draft out here, with no
circulators blowing—Oh! Twila wanted to laugh at herself in near hysteria. Wind! That was wind. It blew
through her shirt and made her shiver. But it was a
bracing sensation; slowly she opened her eyes. Again the
sky seemed to loom over her, but she kept breathing
deeply, evenly, until the dizziness subsided.
It's all mental, after all, she told herself. *Like finding
your balance in dance. You imagine yourself suspended
on invisible strings, and it keeps you from falling.* So she
imagined herself rooted to the ground. She made the earth
a great weight on which she rested, a stronger, steadier
entity than the vaulted sky. It supported her, it held her up
like one dancer held another in the old flatscreen movies.
In a moment she was able to get slowly to her feet, and

then carefully, as though walking en pointe, she began to make her way to the south.

The moon had set; she had made certain of that in timing her escape. But the pale star shine was enough to delineate the edge of the mesa on which the biodome was built. The old road to Numex ran in from the northeast, Twila knew, but that she avoided. Her plan was to make her way down the steep south side of the mesa to the dam that contained the hydroelectric plant. Old vids showed a road across its top; this she would use to cross the river, out of sight of the biodome. Then she would stay off the roads, for if Dr. Krell sent Security teams out after her, that is where they would look first.

Approaching the edge of the mesa, Twila was again gripped by irrational fear. The world was so vast, and she felt she must go tumbling off the edge . . . She stopped short and again closed her eyes, this time imagining herself back in the holo room of her apartment. Yes, that was it. She was only in the holo room, pretending to climb down a steep embankment. It was a dance exercise, one to test her coordination and balance. Thus fortified, she forced herself to walk to the brink, and then take a first trembling step down.

Initially she tried going down the slope backward, as though it were a ladder, her face to the comforting soil; but the emptiness around her seemed to ride like a demon on her back. So she turned around and sat down, working her way downhill on hands and feet like a spider. Once the natural contours of the earth became less severe, she began to feel more confident and returned to an upright posture. In another ten minutes she reached the dam.

It was an earthen dam, with gravel slopes falling away on both sides. The lake stretched back to the west, disappearing amid the mesas. On the east, a concrete spillway roared with the flow of water that had been imprisoned and forced to turn the mighty turbines of the hydroelectric plant before escaping through this narrow channel, and on to join the Rio Grande. Like me, Twila thought. Finding the narrow passage to freedom.

Just to the north and east of the dam was a low concrete building that housed the controls for the spillway and the other components of the plant. Twila ignored it, trotting out onto the broad track that crossed the dam itself. Every step was easier now. The breeze was stronger here, and the night air was chill, but she kept her habit wadded up under her arm. Its pale color would give her away if anyone looked in this direction. The khaki pants and dark green shirt served as better camouflage. As long as she kept moving, she would stay warm.

Suddenly there was the whine of an engine, and Twila dropped instinctively to the ground. Craning around to look behind her, she saw a Security vehicle climbing out of the side of the mesa near its crest. So that was their entrance! But she stayed flat, her heart pounding, and the vehicle roared its way to the top of the mesa and off toward the east.

"Have they spotted her yet?" Krell demanded.

There was an older man on the monitor now, a higher ranking Security officer whom Krell had known for years, and who did not grow flustered under the chair of the governing board's raging. His name was Rochman, and he was a thickset veteran with graying hair and deceptively mild blue eyes. "They're on the road," he reported. "They swept that whole area with infrared; they haven't spotted her."

"There's only one road off this mesa!" Krell snapped.

"No, sir," Rochman pointed out. "Not on foot. There's the road across the dam."

"Then try that!"

"I know my job, Sam," Rochman chided. "My team is on its way now. I've only got one working infrared unit, and it's a helluva long way around this glasshouse. It'll take another ten minutes."

Krell paced while he waited. He should have taken that badge away from her as soon as he knew about it—or at the very least, deactivated it. But he hadn't wanted to spook her, not while she appeared to be cooperating—damn her! He'd underestimated her again. He'd underestimated her at every turn. He'd have to keep her confined now, and that was going to be ugly. That aunt of hers would raise a stink, and Jon—

He darted back to the console. "Where's my son?"

"Still in the Stargazing Room, I believe," Rochman replied calmly. "Do you want us to pick him up?"

"No." No, most likely she had duped him, too. "No, but when he comes down, have a guard waiting to give him the news—"

"They're back at the tunnel now," Rochman interrupted. "They'll take the jeep to the edge of the mesa with the infrared scope. Even if she's made it to the opposite side, we should be able to pick her up."

Twila was sprinting the last twenty meters when the Security jeep whined around the corner of the biodome, its lights shining far over her head. Panic struck her, and she whipped around to stare at it, missing her footing and sprawling headlong in the gravel. Her hands stung where the skin was ripped away, but she hardly noticed as she clawed her way back to her knees.

Did they see her? Did they know where she was? The jeep had stopped at the edge of the mesa with its headlight tilted down toward the dam, but not low enough to reach her. She could still run. If she could just get across the dam and up into the rolling terrain on the other side, she could lose herself in a brushy low spot—

The guard in the passenger's seat of the jeep shook his head inside the helmet of an SCE suit. "Nothing on the other side," he said to his companions, studying the infrared scope. "She's had plenty of time to—no, wait! There she is!" He tapped the monitor with a close-gloved finger, and then pointed to the corresponding point on the dam below. "She hasn't even made it across. Everybody out! I'll bring the scope. Now that we've got her on this, there's no chance we can lose her."

Inside the biodome Krell received the message and began to calm down a bit. His thoughts turned to how he would handle Twila when she came out of Decontamination. Maybe there was a better way than physical confinement. There were any number of addictive drugs; a chemical dependency might do the trick, and the fetuses shouldn't be affected if they were conceived in vitro and planted in host mothers, as he had been doing all along. Jon would take that straight to the governing board, of

course, but it wasn't likely that they would act. Every one
of them enjoyed the benefits of the immunization.

He'd have to give it serious thought.

Twila saw the Security team piling out of the jeep, and
all reason fled. In their bulky SCE suits, they seemed
more like automatons than usual: nameless, faceless, fea-
tureless enemies bent on her destruction. Scrambling to
her feet, she flung herself in the direction of the opposite
shore; but her confusion betrayed her. Her frantic steps
carried her not to safety, but over the eastern edge of the
dam. The slippery gravel gave her feet and hands no pur-
chase, no means by which to stop her momentum. With a
sharp cry she slid down the steep bank and into the cold,
turbulent waters of the rushing river.

The four Security guards stood atop the dam, staring
down. Marks showed in the gravel where Twila had rolled
and slid down the pitched slide. "Jesus," one suited figure
whispered.

"Can she swim?" asked another.

"Where would she learn to swim?" demanded their
leader. "Only the marine scientists are allowed in the
ocean, and they have special gear." He ran the infrared
over the sloping south bank, knowing it was futile. They
had tracked her unchecked fall over the dam and had seen
the heat image disappear below the roiling surface a good
ten meters from shore. Because of the season, large
amounts of water were being drained through the
spillway; the river was running high and fast. The current
would have sucked her even farther out.

"Come on, we'll take the infrared across and check the
shore below here," he said without enthusiasm. "Just in
case. But I'm afraid we'll have to tell Dr. Krell his pigeon
is gone for good."

"*We* don't have to tell him, do we?" asked the first
guard.

"Hell, no!" the leader swore. "That's Rochman's job."

Twila's first reaction was to claw frantically for the surface, but the current sucked her quickly under. Choking

on the water, she felt herself buffeted and dragged, and she knew she was drowning.

Despair overwhelmed her. *Not like this,* she sobbed inwardly. *Not like this, alone and helpless. Not when I'd almost won free . . .*

The tree was still rooted in the bank, undermined but not torn loose by the water that cut away the ground from its roots. Its branches, however, dipped far below the surface. One of them caught Twila full in the stomach. Reflexively, she wrapped her arms around it; then, even as the current sought to prize her loose, she realized what it was and began to drag herself upward.

She broke the surface sputtering and gasping, but she knew she could not stop there. She had to get clear of the river, had to get out of the cold water before hypothermia set in and robbed her muscles of the ability to keep their grip. So painfully, slowly, her diaphragm convulsing to expel water and her head throbbing from the ordeal, she hauled herself up the length of the trunk to the shore and out of the water. There she huddled at the base of her savior tree, knowing she ought to keep moving, to get clear of the place, but unable to take a single step.

A breeze whistled along the defile of the river, biting through Twila's wet clothes. With it came a whispering thought, that she must get herself up into the lee of the tree, out of the wind and out of sight. She told herself it didn't matter, that she didn't care, that she couldn't move another inch; but the thought nagged at her until finally she forced herself farther up and under the massive trunk. There she curled up in a tight, shivering ball until a feeling of warmth enveloped her. She did not even hear the Security patrol pass above her, sweeping their instrument along the bank. They followed the instrument sweep with a light, for at this point they had more expectation of finding a corpse than a person, and they let it play for a long time over the branches of the fallen tree. In her misery, Twila was only aware of an odd brightness for a few moments, but it seemed no different to her than the occasional brightening or dimming of lights in the biodome and did not penetrate her state of shock.

Finding what they expected—nothing—the Security patrol went on its way. A mile farther down they were met by a jeep that had come out via the road; it carried extra packs of compressed air for the searchers, but the team leader declined. There was no point in searching farther. It would be dawn in an hour, and he knew well enough what dangers lurked in the abandoned city to the south. With a weary sigh, he and his companions climbed into the jeep and returned to safety.

Twila knew she was in shock, knew the seeming security of the tree was as much an enemy as the patrol that had chased her. It seemed the hardest thing she had ever had to do, crawling out from under the sheltering vegetation, but a nagging in her subconscious told her she must do so or die. Forcing her cramped legs into motion, she staggered up the slope and across the rolling ground that lay south of the river. It was maybe a kilometer to the main road, and she had seen buildings along it from the Stargazing Room. It wouldn't be safe, of course, to stay there for long, for Security was undoubtedly sweeping the countryside looking for her. But she needed dry clothes, and needed them quickly. If she stayed cold and damp, her body temperature would continue to plummet, and she would go into convulsions. The simple act of moving would help stave that off; until she found dry clothes and blankets, she could not afford to rest.

When she reached the road, to her dismay she discovered most of the buildings were businesses. However, she spotted one mobile home parked behind a service station, and managed to coax the door open and let herself inside. Broken windows had kept the interior air fresh. In a back bedroom she found what she needed. Stripping off her wet clothes, she began to dry herself, then gave up and crawled naked into the bed. In the back of her mind she knew she should go farther to escape any Security net, but her exhausted body simply could not. Within seconds of pulling the covers up around her, Twila was asleep.

Jon stood staring blankly out of the Stargazing Room windows at the growing dawn, numb with shock and grief.

Krell stood behind him, having delivered the devastating news personally. "Jon," he said softly. "It's not your fault. You had no way of knowing—"

Jon rounded on his father, fury and incredulity boiling in his eyes. "*My* fault!" he echoed. "*My* fault! Of course it's not *my* fault!" Rage filled him, and he knew he had never hated his father as much as he did at this moment. "It's *your* fault! You drove her to this! For years you violated her body without her knowledge; and when she learned what you were doing and protested, did you stop? No! You kept on. You used her, you robbed her, without her consent—Jesus, man, you can't even remove a patient's tonsils without permission!—but you went into her month after month and stole something far more personal. And I know it wasn't life to you, but it was to her— *it was to her!*" He seized his father by the shirt, and shouted into his face. "It's you who's killed her, damn it! You've killed her the same as if you put a knife to her throat and backed her up to a cliff until she had no choice but to step off the edge."

Krell stood quivering, his face pale. "That's not true," he whispered. "I loved her. I promised Carlton I'd take care of her—"

Jon thrust his father away in disgust. "Save it," he snapped, stalking toward the stairs. "Use that as salve for your own conscience, if you have one. To me, every word is just another spadeful of compost. You're so busy trying to preserve your own little kingdom in here that you don't even see the enormity of what you've done." He paused at the head of the stairs and looked back. "If your research fails, and my research fails, what's left? Twila could have been the mother of the whole human race."

Chapter 9

From the great height of its western bank, Twila looked down on the Rio Grande. It was enormous, spreading for a quarter of a mile wide in places, swollen with the first spring runoff. She had spent an entire day in the abandoned trailer, afraid to venture out in daylight even after sleep and a meal from her soggy backpack had refreshed her. At nightfall she had slipped out and left the vicinity of the highway, heading not east toward the major thoroughfares but west, through a series of empty housing developments that crowded the brink of the highland on this side of the river. She had had to move slowly in the darkness, and she'd lost time rummaging through houses along the way to refurbish her supplies. There were no viable foodstuffs, unfortunately, but her knowledge of botany assured her that once she got down to the river's edge, she would be able to find enough edible plants to survive for a time.

Now another day was dawning, and Twila needed to move inside out of sight. It was her second day of freedom, but she was too hungry and too worried to enjoy it. This was a foreign and hostile world. Besides having Security hunting for her, there were the local hazards of poisonous snakes, poisonous spiders, and wild animals. She had no real plan for the future except to stay alive and maybe, just maybe, to look for her grandfather. But look where? She had no idea.

In the distance she could see a bridge that spanned the great river. *That's what I'll do,* she thought. *I'll cross the bridge to the other side, where the ground is lower, where there's more vegetation. If Grandfather came this way, he'd have settled over there somewhere, where he could raise a garden and fend for himself. Tomorrow—tonight—*

I'll go across and start searching the east bank. At the very least I should find something to eat.

That decided, she turned to a nearby house to take shelter for the daylight hours. Like other houses she had entered, the door was closed but not locked. When she'd collapsed the first night inside the mobile home, Twila had taken no time to examine her surroundings nor wonder about them, and her earlier forays into domiciles had been confined to kitchen and utility areas. But now she surveyed her chosen shelter, knowing if it was unsatisfactory, she could move on and find another.

All the windows in this particular house appeared to be intact; nevertheless, the furniture was coated with dust and grit. Twila wondered how long it took to accumulate a layer this thick. Nothing scurried out at her—no lizards or rodents seemed to be in residence—which was a definite plus. Carefully she moved through the house, peering into each room. In the small bedroom at the rear she found what she had dreaded to find: a skeleton was stretched out in the bed. Twila backed out of the room, heart pounding, fighting the urge to turn and flee. Remains of the dead would be everywhere—she'd better get used to them. This skeleton, she thought, looked long dead: there was no trace of flesh, nor were there any insects or other predators of the recently deceased.

Carefully Twila closed the door on the figure and went back to the living room. Although the dust was thick on the couch, there appeared to be a blanket of some kind beneath the grime. Carefully she peeled it back and found the surface underneath fairly clean. Daylight was streaming in through an eastern window now; warmth must soon follow. Exhausted, Twila curled up on the sofa and fell promptly asleep.

When she awoke in the early afternoon, Twila found that her hunger was nothing compared with her thirst. The stuff that came out of the faucets in the house was a sickening brownish color, and so when she moved on she first clambered down the steep bank and bushwhacked her way to the river. The water there didn't look much better, full of silt from runoff; but reason told her that water from a moving river stood less chance of being contaminated than that which had stood in metal pipes for years, so she dipped in with a water bottle she'd found the day before and managed to gag down enough to slake her thirst. Filling the bottle, she added it to her backpack and headed south.

When she reached the bridge toward evening, Twila hesitated. Would Security have it staked out? In truth, she hadn't seen any sign of Security since she'd crawled up the bank from the Numex river, where she'd nearly drowned. It didn't seen likely that they could stake out every bridge, every road into the old city. Besides, she needed food, and soon, to keep up her strength, and there simply was no food on this side of the Rio Grande. She checked the area as carefully as she could, waited for dusk, and then in the half-light of the waning day began to cross over.

It was fully dark by the time she reached the other edge, and Twila knew she would be able to rest, and begin again in the daylight, without fear. Here on the east bank, trees grew thick along the water, and houses crowded together to block the view. Finding her here would be like finding a needle in a haystack. Twila drank again from the river, and found a few greens that she boiled for a taste-less but filling meal. Deeming it pointless to wander any farther at night, she settled down in what had been an elegant residence on the river and waited until morning light revealed the remains of a garden. Under the dried mass of last year's foliage, she found one or two shriveled squash that had survived the winter and not yet begun to rot. Together with some cactus pads, they provided a recognizable breakfast, although Twila wished sincerely for some herb to season them, or a little goat cheese to add flavor.

Now fortified and feeling somewhat in control of her destiny, Twila decided she would walk downriver to the south first, looking for edibles or signs of human habitation. It was unlikely that her grandfather was still alive after sixteen years with CM, but it was possible. And there had to have been others who were put Outside after he was. This was the most logical area for one of them to have settled. And, of course, there was the fact of her mother and her own birth Outside. Somewhere out here, and not too far from Numex, there had to be survivors. No doubt they were primitive, given a life span of only fifteen to twenty years, but they must have some kind of village or community in which they lived. That community had to have a source of water, and the river was the only one Twila could think of. So she headed south.

She had gone no more than two kilometers when she heard screaming.

Trish didn't leave the goat pens until after Roxanne had gone. Normally she was put off by her sister's insistence that they observe proper form by not traveling together, but today it was a relief. Trish had had more than she could stand of Roxanne's whining complaint about her baby being gone. The loss had been overwhelming to both of them, but Roxanne could never conceive of anyone's pain being comparable to her own. It became almost a contest in which Roxanne had to grieve more ostentatiously to prove that she had loved Twila more.

If you had truly loved her more, Trish thought unkindly, *you wouldn't have to spend so much time trying to convince me you did.* With a sigh Trish pushed that thought away. There were just the two of them now, with no bright and vibrant Twila to relieve the monotony and the loneliness. Somehow, they would have to put pettiness and recriminations aside and comfort each other; and it was up to Trish to make that happen. It was always up to Trish.

Preoccupied with her sorrow, Trish was totally unprepared to find a solitary figure waiting when she came out of the enclosure.

He wore a habit, but the hood was pulled back away from his face, and she could see both his bristling beard and his gray eyes. She gasped in shock, even as her mind told her who it must be. Immediately he flashed a clean tag at her and confirmed her guess. "Please don't be afraid," he said quickly. "I'm Jon."

Jon. Trish stood for a moment, heart pounding, trying to get herself under control. She had not been face-to-face with a man since her father had gone Outside; in fact, she had not been face-to-face with anyone except Roxanne and Twila, and an occasional med tech. So she had to force her breathing back to a normal rate, had to consciously reassure herself that this was Twila's friend, and no threat to her.

"What do you want?" she asked finally, her voice breathless. Behind her, the bleating of the goats blended with the sound of clucking chickens and clicking crickets.

He stood a circumspect three meters off. "I wanted someone to know the truth," he said, making no move to come any closer. "I know they told you Twila went over the Edge, that she had a breakdown and overdosed on pills. That's not true."

It was confirmation for Trish. "I know," she said, her voice under better control but her knees still weak. "She's not the type. Roxanne bought it, but I don't. Tell me—" Tears welled up in her eyes. "What happened by my little girl?"

Moisture glinted in Jon's eyes as well, and he struggled a moment to control his own voice before he could reply. "She went Outside."

Relief flooded through Trish, and she almost took a step closer to this man, this angel, who brought her such good news. Outside! "Then, she's alive!"

"No." He wiped a sleeve across his face, and Trish knew it was not perspiration he blotted away. "No, she tried to escape across the dam and lost her footing. She . . . Security looked downstream for her body, but . . ." He could say no more.

All the strength went out of Trish, and she sank wearily to the ground, arms clasped around her knees. Her head drooped, and a single tear trickled down one cheek. For a moment she had hoped . . .

Long shadows stretched across the hard-packed dirt of the animal yards, cast by squat utility buildings and stubby browse. Two zones away a tall habited form finished pitching fresh straw into a birthing pen, locked the pitchfork in its secured rack, and headed for the transit stop. It cast one curious look at the two people obviously conversing outside the goat pens, then turned its back deliberately and continued on its way.

It was several minutes before Jon spoke again. "Do you know what my father was doing to Twila?" he asked.

Trish nodded. "She told me everything. The immunity, and the, uh, egg harvesting . . ." It all sounded so logical in a clinical sense, but Twila had been extremely distraught, which set Trish to considering how she herself would feel had she been the victim. When it became *her* child, the child she'd been forbidden to bear, it had struck her with heart-wrenching force. But was it worth this? The loss of the only child she had known? *Twila,* she wondered, *was it worth your life?*

"Thank you," she told Jon sincerely. "Thank you for coming to tell me."

"There's one more thing." Jon glanced over his shoulder, knowing an alarm had sounded the minute he crossed into her red zone. Security would arrive any minute now to break up this meeting, to take him back to Medical, perhaps to slap an electronic monitor on him so he could no longer wander freely about the biodome. To hell with it. He had to do something. "I need an ally," he said frankly.

Wary now, Trish raised her head and regarded the man before her. Twila's description of Jon had never painted him as very stable: a bitter young man who harbored an unnatural enmity for his father. Or was it unnatural? Perhaps he just knew Krell better than the rest of them. "For what?" she asked suspiciously.

"Somebody's got to stop my father," he said. *Maybe if I'd been willing to do this before, Twila would have stayed* . . . "I'm taking a couple of proposals to the board of governors, and they're going to get me in a lot of trouble. I have no doubt Security will squash them the minute I put them out on the net. I need them to leak."

Shaking her head, Trish rose slowly to her feet. "They'll squash me, too," she said. "And I don't mean just my files. They have less reason to deal charitably with me than they did with Twila."

"Deal in diskettes," he told her, drawing a plastic square from his sleeve by way of illustration. "Drop copies where people will find them. Ask questions on the conferences that will get people thinking. Hint at things. Plant seeds. Anything you can do will help."

The hum of an electric motor told them a Security scooter was approaching. Quickly he dropped the diskette and tugged his hood farther forward. "Don't carry it on you. Hide it now, pick it up later," he said, backing off.

"Stay cool with Security; you're not in any trouble at this point. When they ask, say I was just offering my condolences." Then he turned on his heel and strode off, into the arms of the approaching Security detail.

Trish did not try to pick up the diskette from the dirt, where it had fallen. Instead she walked toward it and casually caught it with the toe of her work shoe, skidding it under the fence and into a pile of loose straw in the goat pens. Jon was right; without damning evidence, it would be easy to convince Security the strange young man was only expressing his sympathy for Twila's death. They had no reason to search the area. The diskette would still be there next week, if she decided she wanted to look at it.

The screaming was intermittent now, punctuated by shouts and curses. The screams were feminine, but some of the shouting and cursing was not. Twila slowed as she neared the source of the sound—what was she, crazy? She ought to be running the other direction from such danger.

But she couldn't.

Still, she became more cautious as she drew closer. She kept in the shadow of buildings, glancing all around for hidden threats, and noting always the closest hiding place. The sounds were dying down now: no more screaming, but a terrified sobbing, and a few muttered expletives. Twila ducked into an alley, sure the commotion came from just around the corner of the building that sheltered her. Then there was a rumbling mechanical sound—a motor, she thought, but a very loud one, running very badly. It rose to a dreadful volume, then began to fade as its source moved farther and farther away, till it was only a pulsing in the distance.

Cautiously Twila peeked around the corner of the building. Silence hovered in the wake of the cacophonous engine, seeming to echo off the block and adobe structures that lined this avenue. They were commercial buildings here, packed close together, unlike the houses that dotted the nearby riverbank. Slowly she crept closer to the intersection.

A moan came from just beyond the corner, followed by a string of articulated sounds Twila did not recognize, heavily salted with curses she had only heard in old flatscreen vids. Heart pounding, Twila peered around the corner and saw a young woman lying on the sidewalk.

Her skin was darker than Twila's, her hair a flatter black but also curly, though now it was a mess of tangles. Her denim jacket hung open, and beneath it her blouse had been torn apart; her skirt was bunched up around her hips. Slowly she pushed herself into a sitting position, still swearing, and sat for a moment with her head drooping between her knees.

Quietly Twila stepped out from behind the building, wondering what she should do. It was obvious the woman had been attacked; should Twila approach her, offer assistance? What kind of assistance could she offer? Would it be better to just slip away, pretending not to have witnessed? Were there other people nearby? Spooked, Twila searched the surrounding buildings with her eyes.

Now the stranger struggled to her feet, adjusting her clothing, rubbed a knee, and took a few limping steps. Curses still bubbling from her lips, she straightened painfully—and saw Twila.

For a moment the two women stared at each other. Startlement registered in the stranger's eyes, but not fear. In that moment of surprise, Twila saw that the other was younger than she had first thought, only a teenager—but of course. No one on the Outside could live past their teenaged years, unless, like Twila and her mother, they were immune.

Now the girl spoke. "Who you?"

Twila's mouth was dry, and her voice cracked when she replied. "My name is Twila."

"You ain't no Hat," the girl accused.

It was a non sequitur to Twila. "I'm sorry?"

"Ain't no Barioso, neither," the girl decided. "Where from?"

"I'm—I'm—" Suddenly Twila wondered if it were a good idea to reveal her origin. "From up there," she finished lamely, waving a hand to the north.

"You Bubblehead?" the girl screeched.

Again the meaning escaped Twila. "I'm—I don't mean you any harm, really," she stammered. "I heard the screaming, and I came—are you all right?"

"All right?" The girl snorted. "Throwed on the ground

and filled up by Bariosos, ain't no picnic." There followed another string of unrecognizable sounds punctuated with vulgarities. "Hell, I been worse," the girl finished, limping over the where a canvas satchel had been dropped on the sidewalk. "I been filled up before. But Lacy—they got Lacy. I gotta get back to Spider, tell him."

"Who's Lacy?" Twila asked.

"Bobo's sister," the girl replied, bending over to pick up the satchel. "She thirteen, and she prize—Spider, he be hot, and China, too—he's next to blood. They try to get Lacy back before she cookin'."

"Cooking?" Twila echoed, following none of the conversation beyond the kidnapped girl's age.

The girl straightened up. "You be Bubblehead for sure. Cooking. A baby. Or don't they tell you Bubbleheads that what happens when you get filled up?"

Suddenly the meaning sprang clear, and Twila blushed furiously—first in embarrassment, then in hot anger at what was to be perpetrated on a thirteen-year-old girl. "We have to stop them," she blurted.

The girl regarded her haughtily. "We?"

"I mean—you. Your people. But believe me, I'd help if I could."

That brought a sharp laugh to the girl's lips. "Bubblehead, help!" She was checking the contents of her satchel. "Bubblehead, you can't help yourself, much less help the Hats spring Lacy from the Bariosos."

"What's your name?" Twila asked. Her mother's name, according to the cryptic file Dr. Krell had given her, had been of Hispanic origin: Lupe. Did all people Outside have Hispanic names? This girl certainly did not have what Twila thought of as Hispanic features, but who knew what kind of interbreeding had gone on among survivors?

"Starbright," the girl replied, fishing a piece of broken glass from her satchel. "Shit, look what they done! I was gonna give that to Reenie to make her smile." She cast the fragment aside in disgust. "Shakin' Bariosos."

"What are Bariosos?" Twila asked, postponing the more pertinent question of what Hats were. She already seemed ineffably stupid to this girl, and she was reluctant to risk offending any pride that might tie her to Hats.

"Enemies," Starbright replied succinctly, rubbing at her

knee again. Blood oozed from a cut on her left leg, making Twila shiver, but Starbright seemed not to notice. "You find out soon enough. They find Bubblehead strutting the streets, they take your head off."

"You mean kill me?" Twila asked in disbelief "Why? I haven't done anything—"

"You just is," Starbright interrupted. "They don't care. Only maybe, 'cause you chick, they just fill you up. Fill you up, see if Bubbleheads make babies same as us. As long as you make Barioso babies, maybe they keep you alive. Course, Hats might kill you in a raid—or Hats might keep you to make Hat babies. Either way, Bubblehead, you ain't no help to nobody." She tried to tug the pieces of her blouse together in front, gave up, and buttoned the jacket instead.

Twila's cheeks burned. She had never imagined rape would be a part of life Outside. She had not imagined violence by human beings to be a part of it at all. If she could panic at Jon's touch—"That will not happen to me," she vowed.

The younger woman regarded Twila with a worldly eye. "Girl, how you gonna stop it?"

How, indeed? Starbright was obviously a strong girl, with well-muscled arms and thighs, yet she had not been able to stop an assault. "I'll avoid them," Twila decided, not knowing what other option she had. "Where do they live, these Bariosos?"

Starbright shrugged, looking around on the ground for something. "Last we knew, over East Heights; so what they doing up here in Alameda? Looking for us, probably." Then, "Damn, they got her bag, too," she said in disgust, "and it was almost full."

Twila's heart thudded dully in her chest as the girl's speech made her realize how lost she was in this new world. When she was running from Security, at least she knew who she was avoiding. But who were the Bariosos, what were their habits and their weapons, and where was East Heights? And how could she hope to stay out of their way? "Where can I go to be safe from them?" she asked, bewildered.

Again the sharp, raucous laugh. "Only place safe from Bariosos is with twenty-five Hats around you. Then maybe not." Starbright had discovered the blood trickling down her leg now, and was using her sleeve to wipe it away.

"No, I think I'm better off getting away," Twila said, looking for the sun to get her bearings. It was mid-morning now. "I'll go back upriver. I'll just find a place and plant a garden and—" And what? Just what would she do, all by herself? No one to talk to, no holo room for entertainment—What had Grandfather done? And where? "Do you know an old man?" she asked suddenly. "Or did you? He may be dead now. Probably."

"Old man?" Starbright brushed hair back out of her face with a dirty hand. It was a round face, with hazel eyes and a broad nose. "Raunchy's close eighteen. Vic, he was same age but he got sick last year."

"No, I mean an old, old man," Twila qualified. "Older than me. From the biodome, like me."

"From Bubbleland?" Starbright shook her head. "Shit, girl, everybody—"

Suddenly she stopped short and held up a hand, listening. Her nostrils quivered as she focused every perception on some distant happening. Then Twila heard a loud pop with a rumbling echo from the direction of the river.

"Dance!" the girl exclaimed.

"What?"

"A fight, Bubblehead!" the girl shouted. "A war, a battle! Spider must have made those Bariosos who rode on us. Or maybe they found our digs. But there a dance going down, for sure." And she began to run in the direction of the noise.

Twila followed, asking herself why she did so. A battle! Why would she want to get anywhere near a battle? But Starbright hadn't finished her sentence. Had she known something about an old man, a Bubblehead? Twila couldn't be sure. She had to stay with Starbright until she could ask again. Could Grandfather actually be alive? "Wait!" she called as her quarry began to out-distance her. "Wait—!"

The commotion grew louder toward the river. There were two more pops that Twila interpreted as gunshots, then the rough roaring of a motor, and finally shouting. Still Starbright ran, with stamina even Twila could not match. When at last she slowed her steps and began to slink around buildings, Twila was gasping for breath and hardly able to catch up. "Wait," she called again. "The old man—"

Starbright waved her back. "Stay out the way till I see what going down," she commanded. She tucked her satchel into a doorway and disappeared around a corner. For several minutes Twila leaned up against the wall of what had been a stable, panting and trying to sort through things. This was crazy. So few people left in the world, and here they were *fighting* each other. How deadly was this battle? Did they, perhaps, only fight for sport, like the ancient Native American tribes, counting coup to prove bravery?

No. You didn't count coup with a gun.

The motor noise was fading again, and in a moment it stopped abruptly; but the shouting and scuffling sounds continued. Finally Twila's curiosity got the better of her judgment. Hunching close to the ground, she peered around the corner of the stable.

The battle was being fought on a street that followed the river, at a point where an irrigation channel watered a small orchard. Three or four rusted vehicles stood in the street, but they were obviously nonfunctional, with flattened tires and sagging tailpipes. Around and between them, eight youths engaged in hand-to-hand combat, some wielding knives, others using sticks or pipes or lengths of clinking chain. On the hood of one car stood a short, dark-skinned boy wearing a cap, and he held a handgun, which he tried to bring to bear on one of the combatants. But something stayed his hand; Twila learned later that he was reluctant to interfere with a "kill" or a "blooding" for one of his companions.

One casualty already lay stretched on the ground: a smallish youth with a bandanna tied in his dark, curling hair. Now Twila could see that four of the combatants wore bandannas and four wore caps. This, then, was the distinction between the Bariosos and the Hats. Beyond that, Twila could see little difference except that the Hats were a little taller and perhaps a bit darker than their enemies. All fought viciously, and several were bleeding.

One boy stood out from the others: a tall black youth in a sleeveless shirt whose biceps bulged as he swung a rusted iron bar at his shorter but heavier opponent. The stocky Barioso exhibited an unexpected agility in dodging these blows; he danced and flashed a long-bladed knife and made shrill, mocking sounds at the giant.

"Who's that?" Twila asked Starbright, who came back to her now. "The tall boy."

"That Spider," Starbright replied with obvious pride. "He the man. He take that Barioso down like nothing. Come on, we got to find Lacy." And she jerked Twila to her feet.

"Find Lacy? How?" Twila asked in surprise.

"This way," Starbright said, dragging her by an arm toward the south. "Other Bariosos got her stashed in their wheels, out of reach so they don't lose their prize. But they don't go far till they see how this dance go down. If we can find 'em, maybe we can spring Lacy when they ain't looking."

They were out in the open now, within easy sight of the fighters, but Starlight trotted quickly across the yards and parking lots as though there was no danger. Terrified, Twila followed, hoping by staying close to avoid drawing the fire of the young man with the gun. They had just made it past the irrigation ditch when a sharp cry caused them to turn and look back at the conflict.

One of the Hats was down, and the odds had shifted. The boy with the gun had been knocked off his perch—it was he who had cried out—and now struggled with his opponent for possession of the weapon while another Hat hovered nearby, clutching an arm in pain. Two Bariosos converged on Spider, who was backing slowly toward the swiftly flowing ditch.

Now Starbright was concerned. Thoughts of Lacy left her head as she was drawn back toward the ditch, watching Spider struggle on the opposite side. One of the Bariosos was wounded, and staying well out of Spider's reach, but he taunted and feinted, trying to throw the Hat leader off balance. The two were among the trees now, and there was much dodging and twisting, trying to use the thick trunks and low-hanging branches as both shield and ambush. Spider was clever and coolheaded, but he was definitely in trouble.

"I'm going back," Starbright announced unnecessarily,

then bolted back toward the road that had crossed the ditch. Twila was not too eager to get involved; but morbid curiosity drew her closer to the edge of the channel, and she stared, fascinated and horrified, as blade and bar leaped out to injure living beings. There was an air of unreality about it, as though she were watching a holo—after all, real people didn't act this way, did they? Wasn't it only make-believe?

Yet she knew it was real, and she knew that the blood tricking down one Barioso's face was real blood, and he would gladly draw its like from his enemy. *Edgewalker,* she thought. *Madness.* Yet it did not seem so to the participants, nor to Starbright, who was bursting through the trees toward them now. From the grim set of their faces, it seemed only a business, the business of survival.

"Yo, sucker, watch your back!" Starbright snarled. The wounded Barioso spun to face her, for she had been careful to come up behind him and in full view of Spider, whom she did not want to be distracted by her appearance. The ploy worked; finding himself with only one opponent, Spider lunged in a step and swung the metal bar with crushing force.

But he had miscalculated the height of the tree branches around him. The bar was deflected, the blow delayed, and the Barioso stepped in with his knife to take advantage of the opening. Spider leaped back in time, but the move cost him his footing. He fell to the ground and rolled—

—into the irrigation ditch four feet deep with fast-running water. He was downstream from Twila; without thinking she began to run toward him. At first he struggled to his feet, and she thought he would simply climb out again; but the Barioso on the other bank would not allow it. Picking up a fist-size rock, he launched it at Spider, striking the struggling youth square in the forehead.

Spider went down. Twila heard a shrill scream, but she could not take her eyes from the man in the water. A shot sounded, then another, but Twila only raced along the edge of the ditch, watching the thrashing body being swept down toward the river. *That was me,* her brain thrummed as she ran. *That was me, pulled along in the cold and choking water, fighting for breath, drowning, drowning . . .*

What could she do? How could she stop the headlong rush of the water's victim? Only a fallen tree had saved her. Only that . . .

Her eyes picked it out thirty meters downstream, a long branch hanging low across the channel. There were perhaps two meters between it and the surface of the water. Without a second thought Twila dashed toward it, trying to outrun the current. She was two meters ahead of Spider now, three . . . The branch looked sturdy, but it was only six or seven centimeters thick where it joined another branch. Four meters ahead now—was it enough? It had to be, just as her meager weight had to be enough—

Twila launched herself at the branch, caught it with both hands, and wrapped her feet up around it. It swayed, dipped, cracked . . .

"Grab on!" she shouted; but Spider did not need to be told. Strong hands clamped on the trailing branch. He pulled his head above water, coughed, and finally gained his feet. The water was deeper here, for they were almost at the river, but the water came no higher than his armpits. For a moment he coughed and panted and caught his breath; then slowly he hauled himself along the branch to the edge of the ditch and out.

Only then did Twila realize her own predicament, hanging out over the water on a branch that had cracked under her assault and could easily part from the mother tree to drop her in the swirling waters. Carefully she shifted her weight and shinnied back through the branches to safety. She dropped to the ground beside Spider.

Then Starbright was there, and two other boys. The Bariosos had taken to their heels, and now the sound of an engine could be heard as the group made good its escape. Two wounded Hats and one dead Barioso remained on the field; those with Starbright crowed over their victory. Twila watched in amazement as they slapped each others hands, traded cuffs, and swore in happy tones over the damage they had inflicted.

When they had done that for several minutes, and Spider had caught his breath, he turned to glare at Twila. "Who you?" he demanded.

Twila felt her hackles rise, but Starbright jumped in. "She Twila. I found her."

"She ain't Barioso," Spider observed, eyes dark with suspicion.

"She Bubblehead, Spider, but you be good to her. She save your ass."

Twila stared back at the muscular youth, determined not to show her fear. His eyes searched her, taking in every detail of her face and her dress, until finally he nodded. "I owe you," he acknowledged.

"I'll remember," Twila said brazenly.

"So will I," he promised. Then he turned back to Starbright. "They got Lacy," he said.

"They jump us up Alameda," Starbright elaborated. "Seven, eight of 'em, with wheels. Fill us up and then take her."

Spider clambered to his feet now, eyes flashing. "We get her back," he swore darkly. "And we take prize, and a whole handful of Barioso rings." Looking back across the ditch to the battlefield, he saw the fallen Barioso. "Who got a ring this time?"

The taller of the two boys with them, a sinewy lad of maybe fourteen, grinned and held up his trophy: a gold hoop earring, with a large piece of ear still attached.

Chapter 10

The Hats' stronghold, or "digs," as Starbright called it, was a once elegant home about two miles south of the battlefield, tucked back behind some trees near the river. It had a peculiar architecture with adobe walls rising above roof level, creating a functional parapet where the glint of metal in the sun told Twila a lookout was stationed with a rifle. No sooner had she spotted him than the boy—he could not have been more than ten or eleven—gave a shrill whistle and shouted down to the occupants, "Spider been to a dance!"

Those Hats who were not out foraging came tumbling out of the house to see for themselves the results of the battle, and half a dozen dogs barked and raced among the legs of the returning fighters. There were three or four teenage girls, all in the late stages of pregnancy, who stayed at home in charge of a dozen or more "babies"— children under four. They bore anxious faces as they came to inspect the injuries and bark curt instructions to older children, who were dancing around wanting to see the earring trophy that the boy Zit waved proudly. Spider swaggered nonchalantly in their midst, although Twila knew he was concealing a knee injury he had suffered in the fight, and he pushed away the young woman who wanted to clutch him in relief.

Twila found herself the subject of wary sidelong glances, so she took care to remain at Starbright's elbow despite her remaining unease at being so close to so many strangers. There were some cries of distress when it was announced that Lacy had been captured, but there was no sympathy for Starbright or the fate she had suffered. Whether that was because it was too common, or it was simply something no one spoke of, Twila could not tell.

Or perhaps, she thought as she watched the fighters with their girls, *it's because the way their own men take them is not much different.*

The house itself was a pigsty. The smell upon entering slammed against Twila's nostrils like a physical blow, and her empty stomach threatened to revolt. Diapers seemed an unknown concept, and the smell of sour urine predominated. Garbage accumulated in corners, dog feces dotted the floors—though not, Twila noted, in the room where the babies were kept—and a glance out the back door told her human waste was not taken far from the house before being dumped. "It's a wonder the Bariosos don't smell you out," she murmured.

The Hat men and their women—it seemed strange to call them men and women because they were so young, but here Outside that is what they were—settled into a large common room at the north end of the house. One of two fireplaces was located in this room—the other was in the "babies' room" to provide warmth for the small children—and on it two large pots steamed. One contained a stew of sorts, the other plain water. "You boil your water?" Twila asked in relief as she followed Starbright to the fire to dish up food for the men.

Starbright looked insulted. "Water ain't boiled make you sick, don't you know that, Bubblehead?"

"Oh, I know; I'm just glad you do."

Starbright made a disgusted noise and grabbed a bowl from the mantel, a ladle from the hearth. Twila cringed as the dirty utensil was plunged deep into the stew. But she was hungry, and the food smelled good. When all the men had been served, she did not hesitate to take the bowl of stew Starbright offered her.

From the number of blankets and similar articles scattered around the room, Twila guessed this was also the main sleeping room for the Hats. Totaling the numbers Starbright tossed around, she estimated there must be close to eighty individuals in the clan: a dozen adult males, fifteen "wannabes" ages six through eleven, maybe twenty childbearing females, another twenty young girls, and the babies. "And you all live in one house?" Twila marveled as they sat on the floor eating. "How do you fit?"

Starbright looked up from her bowl, surprised. "Easy. Wannabes upstairs, babies over there, Hats and their ladies here. No problem."

"But—you don't have any privacy," Twila protested.

"Privacy!" Starbright hooted. "Privacy! You mean like two alone? Hell, there's Spider's room upstairs, and house next door, and behind the shed—privacy! I been trying to avoid privacy." She poked at the food in her bowl with a tarnished spoon that was, Twila felt sure, real silver. "Least since Bariosos got Mako. Ain't the same with nobody else."

Twila heard the sadness in her voice and did not pursue it.

The stew was flavorful, laced with onion and peppers, although the meat was full of bones. "Rabbit," Starbright explained. "I like pig better, but they're ornery. Gotta watch yourself, getting close to a wounded one." Twila wondered if she meant actual pigs, or the piglike javelina she knew were native to the area. "Used to have cow sometimes, when Tudy was the man, but Jocko, he got killed by a mean one, so we don't go for cow no more. Too much work, too much waste, Spider say. Jocko was his ace kool when they's wannabes."

A new commotion rose now as a band of men and boys returned from checking traps, one of the favorite ways Hats collected game. It wasted no ammunition, which was scarce, and posed little threat to the trappers. Among this returning group was Bobo, Lacy's older brother. He was outraged at the turn of events and stormed around the room, kicking furniture and breaking dishes and demanding that they go out immediately in search of his sister.

"Chill, man," Spider told him. "We gotta find their set first. Then we make a plan. *Then* we get her out."

"If it was your sister," Bobo accused, "we wouldn't be sitting here."

"Well, it wasn't my sister, was it?" Spider snarled. "Nobody take Starbright 'cause they know better."

"Nobody take her 'cause she too old!" Bobo shot back.

In a flash Spider was on his feet, and the back of his hand caught Bobo full across the face. Twila jumped and dropped her empty stew bowl, and others in the room backed away from the two combatants. Bobo tried to come back from the reeling blow and attack Spider, but Spider was taller and stronger and older and more experienced. He simply threw Bobo up against the wall and pinned him there, nose bleeding on the plaster, arm bent painfully behind him.

"Don't nobody dis my sister," Spider hissed. "You got that, sucker?" He twisted Bobo's arm harder. *"You got that?"*

"Yeah, I got it!" Bobo growled through clenched teeth.

Tension eased off the arm, and in the room. "And who's the man?"

"You are, Spider," Bobo said.

Spider let him go and backed away. "We get Lacy back," Spider promised. "I the man, and I say it. But we do it smart, not stupid. First we find the Bariosos, then we make a plan. And we get new wheels." He looked around the room. "And a new house. In case the Bariosos made this one. Tomorrow."

"Yeah, tomorrow," Bobo grumbled, wiping the blood from his face and dropping onto a cushion on the floor. "Jens, get me some food."

It did not take Twila long to understand that the tie between siblings was stronger than that between mates, nor the reason for it. In addition to a general promiscuity among the adult Hats, their life spans allowed no more than five or six years of sexual activity before war or disease took them. It was barely enough time for courtship, Twila thought, let alone to develop a lasting relationship between two people. But siblings were together from early childhood, and they protected and nurtured each other in the absence of parents, who rarely saw a child's fifth birthday.

Twila did not allow such thoughts to distract her for long, though. Now that the hubbub had subsided and the Hats seemed to be settling in for the rest of the afternoon, she turned again to the question that had propelled her after Starbright in the first place. "Before the fight—the dance," she said to her new friend, "I asked you about an old man, and you started to say something. What was it?"

Starbright looked up from idly twirling her empty bowl

on her spoon. "The old man? Spider, you remember the old man, the crazy one up Bernalillo?"

"Some," Spider replied. "Why you wanna know?"

Twila's heart thudded, and she tried not to get her hopes up too much. An old man to a Hat was anyone over eighteen. If her own mother had lived to thirty Outside, there could be another mutant who seemed old to them. Or there could have been other people put Outside the biodome in the years before or since her grandfather's expulsion; those things were seldom publicized. "I'm looking for someone," she told Spider, "an old man, a Bubblehead. He would have arrived here—probably about the time you were born."

"Then, why you ask me?" Spider snapped. "Ask Raunchy."

"But he might be this old man you spoke of," she persisted. "A very old man, with white hair—tall and strong, and with great gentle hands . . ." Would his hands have stayed gentle in this place? Would he? "Please, will you take me to him?" she pleaded. "The man I'm looking for is my grandfather."

"Gran'father?" a wannabe piped up. "What kind of father is that, gran'father? Is that good or bad?"

"It's my mother's father," Twila explained.

"Like grampa grampa," Starbright added. To Twila she said, "Sometimes we talk about grampa grampa times, that being times before our mothers and fathers be born."

"Can you take me to him?" Twila asked again.

Spider scowled. "I don't know if it him. I don't know if that crazy man was a Bubblehead. Ask Raunchy when he get back." Twila wondered why his eyes carried hostility all the time. It was not just toward herself, she decided, for they looked the same when he spoke to anyone. Was that how he maintained his position in the clan? By keeping everyone a little frightened of him? His treatment of Bobo had been a study in power, both physical and psychological. Was that what made his eyes so hard and flinty? Or was it just life?

She thought of Jon, of the coldness his eyes so often held, and wondered.

* * *

Jon stared dispassionately up at his father, seated at his desk while the elder Krell towered over him in a thinly concealed rage. "I asked you what the hell this is!" Krell repeated, slapping a sheet of paper down in front of Jon.

"You should lay off your printer," Jon replied. "Paper's becoming scarcer all the time—unless you'd like to convert your lab into a paper mill." Pre-plague supplies of finished paper seemed boundless, but age had despoiled most of it.

"Don't be cute," Krell snapped. "I want an explanation."

Jon glanced down at the paper as though it were of no importance. "It's a proposal to the governing board," he said. "You're the chair; you got a copy like everyone else."

"It's a proposal to deceive the people of this biodome!" Krell flared.

"It's a proposal to tell them the truth," Jon countered. "You know the statistics as well as I; the chances of contracting CM for the population at large are point zero two. People don't have to live in fear of touching each other. It isn't necessary."

"But to offer them a—a *placebo*—"

"It was Twila's idea," Jon told him. "The more I thought about it, the more sense it made. For years they've been awaiting a miracle drug—let's give them one. It's the old half-full, half-empty gambit. Tell a man his glass is half empty, he feels cheated; tell him it's half full . . ."

"It's preposterous, and I won't have it!"

"You're welcome to debate me in the meeting Tuesday," Jon invited. "That's what board meetings are for."

"No, board meetings are for serious business," Krell informed him. "This proposal is not on the agenda. And this"—he slammed down another sheet of paper—"isn't, either."

Jon did not need to look at the paper to know what it was. It was his second proposal, the one entitled Patient Consent. "It's already in the Code of Ethics," he said calmly. "I'm just asking for an affirmation of it."

"Which is totally unnecessary and redundant."

"Really?" Jon had promised himself he wasn't going to

speak to his father about either of these before the
meeting, but the confrontation was upon him, and he
found it impossible to resist. "It seems to me there's been
a major infraction of it just lately."

"Jon—" Suddenly Krell's tone changed, and his face
changed, and Jon watched in concealed disgust the
chameleon act he had seen too often as Samuel Krell
became the rational man, the caring father. "Jon, I know
you're hurt. I know you cared for Twila, and her death has
wounded you terribly. But you should know me well
enough to know that I would never perform a medical
procedure without permission."

Now Jon stared at his father in amazement. What under
the dome was he talking about? "You didn't have Twila's
consent," he said dumbly.

"Not Twila's," Krell admitted. "But legal consent
nonetheless. When this process began, Twila was a minor
and we had the consent of her legal guardian."

"Roxanne may have signed something without reading
it," Jon agreed, "but when Twila was no longer a minor,
you continued the procedure."

"Roxanne was never her legal guardian," Krell replied.
"Carlton was that, until he"—his eyes dropped momentarily—"left us. So then the responsibility had to be transferred to someone else, someone more stable than
Roxanne."

"You," Jon breathed as he realized how it had all been
manipulated. "And when she turned twenty-one—"

"—because of the unusual nature of the situation, it was
deemed necessary for me to continue as her legal
guardian," Krell finished.

"To legalize the rape," Jon rasped. "And is the governing board aware of this 'unusual situation,' and the
conflict of interest involved?" But even as he asked the
question, he knew the answer. Of course they knew. They
were all receiving the injections.

Krell took back the sheets of paper and carefully tore
them up. "It's better if these don't circulate any farther,"
he said mildly. "It's better if we present a united front,
you and I. Father and son—that's what they want to see,
you know." He let the pieces flutter into Jon's trash
basket. "We're a small, closed community, Jon. Our sur-

vival depends on our cooperation with each other. We can't let internal strife tear us apart."

Jon closed his eyes as though that could shield him from the pain he felt. "And who will you sacrifice next?" he whispered tightly. "Which of Twila's children will take her place upon the altar? Are you legal guardian of them all?"

"Every one," Krell replied. "And the oldest is a girl of eleven; she should reach menarche sometime in the next year or so. But it may not be necessary to wait that long. There was a technique perfected in Europe before the plague, for using the eggs of fetuses to create new fetuses—unborn children of unborn children, so to speak. It was never practiced in this country because of laws against using fetal tissue, but it was successful overseas. I've been digging the information out of the literature. If we have the proper instruments and the proper chemicals, we might not need to trouble living children."

He laid a fatherly hand on his son's shoulder. "You could work with me on it," he suggested. "Take a break from this line of research; maybe you'll come back to it with a fresh perspective. And it might make you feel better to do something for Twila's children—something to help them avoid those constant medical procedures."

Jon felt suddenly overwhelmed, as though the very presence of his father in the room would suffocate him. So logical, so practical— As a doctor, the procedure made eminent sense to him. But Twila had thrown her life away to stop the theft of her eggs and destruction of fetuses that she could only think of as her children. Would it make any difference to her if the fetuses were one generation removed? If Krell were successful, was this new technique any more acceptable than the old?

He thought of Twila alive, here in this office. What would she say if she knew? And all that would come to him was a vision of her weeping hysterically in his arms.

Raunchy came in at sundown with two other Hats, one of the last to return from the day's activities. He was as tall as Spider, but less muscular, having a more sinewy appearance. He stared openly at the stranger among the Hats and did not have to ask the question.

"This is my friend Twila," Starbright said immediately. "She save Spider's life today."

"She look Barioso," Raunchy said bluntly. It was the first time anyone had said it, but Twila knew immediately that it was true. There had been much intermingling of Hat and Barioso blood over the years due to raids and rapes by opposing factions, but in their minds, at least, the warring factors saw a racial difference between themselves. What they were exactly, Twila's untrained eyes could not distinguish—a degree of skin tone, the shape of facial features—but she knew the others saw them. She knew every time they looked at her, and she knew now one more thing about herself: her mother had been a Barioso. The ragged, unkept woman in the old video footage had spent her life in a war zone, subject to rape and abuse, expecting death at an early age and not finding it, but having to endure the stigma of being *old*. No wonder she had tried to escape with her baby to the biodome.

"Twila a Bubblehead," Starbright explained quickly. "And she looking for someone. You remember the old man, the crazy man, up Bernalillo?"

"Yeah, maybe," Raunchy evaded, glancing at Spider to see how he was supposed to react to this line of questioning. Starbright was pushy for a woman, but she was the man's sister, and if Spider had sicced her on him with these questions, Raunchy had better answer.

"He'd have white hair and pale skin," Twila told the youth. "He was from the biodome—from Bubbleland. Does that sound like him?"

"I just see him once," Raunchy qualified.

"Could you take me to him?" Twila asked. "It's very important to me."

Raunchy snorted, glancing again at Spider and getting no clue what was expected of him. "I can maybe find the place again, but it won't do you no good. Crazy man bought it long time ago."

It was the answer she had feared but half expected. Even though Hat grammar was almost unrecognizable, Twila had gotten the feeling they were speaking of the crazy man in past tense.

"Can you at least tell me about him?" Twila asked. "What he was like? What you remember about him?"

Now Spider gave Raunchy a nod, so he flopped down on the floor and gestured at one of the girls to bring him food. "He was crazy," Raunchy said simply.

"In what way?"

"I was just wannabe then," he continued, settling down with the bowl of stew that was brought to him. "So I didn't see him but once, but I heard lots. All these eating plants growed up around his house, like magic, so he never had to go far for food. And if a Hat got cut bad, he could go to the crazy man, and the crazy man would sew him up."

Twila's eyes widened. "A doctor? The crazy man was a doctor?"

"Dok-ter?" The word was unknown to him. "I don't know, just if you was hurt, or a baby was sick, you could go to the crazy man and sometimes he could help you. But not just Hats—Bariosos, too. Didn't matter to him."

"Now, that's crazy," Road Dog put in.

"And what happened to him?" Twila pressed, speaking around a lump in her throat. "How did he die? Did he get sick?"

Raunchy made a rude noise. "Hell no, woman. Like the man say, that's a crazy thing to do, fix up Hats *and* Bariosos. You gonna make someone mad that way. And he did. Sewed up some Hat that would have died. Would have been first kill for this one Barioso, so he got mad. Went up there and shot the crazy man."

Her heart stopped. "Shot him?" A man who did nothing but good, who brought healing and hope into this place of pain and despair, and they shot him?

"I 'member that part," Starbright agreed, and several others nodded. "Hatchet was the man that year. He took a bunch of fighters, and they went and buried the crazy man, just like he was Hat. Only I never see, so I didn't know if he was a Bubblehead, like you ask. I thought maybe he a mountaineer."

Tears streamed down Twila's face. "It could have been. It sounds like him. Sounds like what he would do." She turned to Spider. "I know you need to go after Lacy. But could someone show me the place? Where he lived? If I could just see the place, see the things he kept there, I might know. I'd like to know if it was him."

Spider scowled and turned away from her. "I think about it," he said.

Starbright whispered in her ear, "I'll work on him."

It was several hours later before it occurred to her to wonder what a mountaineer was.

Twila spent that night and the subsequent two in the babies room. The smell was overpowering, and disruptions of sleep frequent, but she could not stand being in with the Hats and their ladies, or the wannabes upstairs. They seemed to have no sense of modesty as she knew it: the wannabes were always quarreling and wrestling, the teens sharing sexual caresses openly. Only among the small children and the pregnant girls did she feel some measure of security.

On her fourth day with the Hats, the entire camp packed up and moved to a new stronghold. It had taken some time to find just the right house, with fireplaces and large rooms, set in a defensible location with a ready supply of water nearby. There was dust and dirt everywhere, and some human bones in one of the bedrooms, so the first order of business was to clean out the place. It seemed strange to Twila that the women put so much energy into this initial cleaning when their previous residence showed such a disregard for continuing housekeeping, but she certainly did not object.

Maybe, she thought, *if I set the example, they'll take better care of this place than they did the last one.*

But she found she had little time for housekeeping in the weeks that followed. During the days she and Starbright ranged far afield, searching along wash beds and feeder streams for edible vegetation. Twila opened a scavenged package of bean seeds from her backpack and showed Starbright how to plant them in the yard of the Hats' stronghold. After ten days of patient watering and plucking away weeds, she was rewarded with the amazement on her young pupil's face as the first tiny sprouts pushed their curling stems through the caked earth.

For her part, Starbright imparted a wealth of knowledge about life Outside and gave Twila some insights into Hat culture. War was all they knew, all they lived for. A boy was not considered a man until he had first reached puberty—and Twila had blushed at the proof required in company of other males—and then "blooded," or wounded an enemy fighter with a knife. Guns were used to keep a battle from getting out of hand, or occasionally to perpetrate a massacre; but the scarcity of ammunition led to a reliance on other weapons for most fighting, and a manhood fight required prowess with a blade.

Once a boy had blooded, he was given a "prize"—a virgin girl—if one was available. If there was no prize available, he was given a girl of his choice; and thereafter all girls were available to him, except one that the leader might choose for his own.

Girls did not fight, except in self-defense; their function, as in ancient societies, was to give birth and care for children. The children were cared for communally, since mothers seldom lived five years past puberty. Even that was a testimony to the work of natural selection since the advent of CM—only those with a natural resistance to the disease lived long enough to reproduce, and the greater the resistance, the more children were born to carry on that trait.

Not surprisingly, Starbright could not give Twila a reason for the enmity between the Hats and the Bariosos. "Always been," she said. "From grampa grampa times. Bariosos kill our men, fill up our women, so the world be full of Barioso babies. We do the same to them, so someday we rule."

"And what do you do when a Hat girl has a Barioso baby?" Twila asked, afraid she did not want to know the answer.

"Ain't no Barioso babies born to Hats!" Starbright flared. "Only Hat babies. Girl gets filled up by a Barioso, she goes home and gets filled up by a Hat. That way, who can say? They ain't born with bandannas."

"What about Lacy?"

That was obviously a sore spot. "Bad news," Starbright said glumly. "They try to keep her till she cookin'. That what they do, if they think she prize, then dump her back when it too late for a Hat to fix it."

"And what happens to the Barioso baby?"

Starbright shrugged. "If it girl, don't matter, she have

Hat babies anyway. If it boy . . ." She shrugged again. "One less Barioso to fight when he grow up."

Twila felt the contents of her stomach rise in her throat.

"So we gotta get Lacy back," Starbright finished.

"And what about me?" Twila asked. "How long before one of the Hats decides to fill me up?"

Starbright shrugged. "When they do, they do. You ain't no prize or nothing. Are you?"

"No," Twila lied. "But I don't want to be filled up. Not by a Barioso, not by a Hat."

"You can say no," Starbright suggested without much hope, "but if he want to anyway, not much you can do. Sometime Spider say no, leave the woman alone, if she like sick or something, but mostly he stay out of it. Don't worry," she tried to comfort. "You too old, I don't think they bother you. They don't bother me much."

But Twila did not find that comforting. She had noticed Raunchy following her with his eyes since the day she had arrived, and she did not like the look in them. Like all the Hats, she had begun carrying a knife, just as a basic utensil for scavenging. She wondered if she would have the nerve to use it for anything else, and what the Hats would do to her if she did.

It was with mixed emotions, then, that she heard Spider announce two weeks later that Raunchy and Bobo would accompany her to Bernalillo to find the place where the crazy man used to live. "And Starbright?" she asked quickly.

" 'Course Starbright," Spider growled. "You too dumb to send out without another woman. You go tomorrow."

It was evening, and they were all in the common room eating and talking. Raunchy now stretched himself luxuriously and yawned hugely. "Look like you and me going to spend some time together, Bubblehead," he told Twila.

"Thank you for taking me up there," Twila responded. "It's very important to me."

"Oh, you can pay me back," he assured her, coming to sit beside her on the floor and draping both long arms around her. "You can start now. Might as well get used to each other."

Twila stiffened at his touch and fought down panic, for this was what she had most dreaded—that he would make his move in front of all his friends, where he could not afford to back down. *Dear God, what do I do?* she wailed inwardly. *There's no place to run, I'm cornered; and with legs like that, he'd overtake me in no time anyway. What do I do? Fight? Something tells me he'd like that. Acquiesce? I can't, I can't, I can't—Play for time? How? What do I say? What do I do? And what good would it be—*

A laugh penetrated her fear-numbed senses. "Raunchy, you not serious, are you?" Starbright asked, her eyes twinkling with merriment. "Do it with a Bubblehead?"

"What's wrong with that?" Raunchy demanded.

Starbright laughed again and swore disdainfully. "Everybody knows what happen if you fill up a Bubblehead."

Uncertain, Raunchy glanced back at the other boys in the room. They shifted uncomfortably and looked at one another. They did not know. "Suppose you tell us," he growled at Starbright.

"You ever see any Bubblehead babies?" she asked.

Again the look to confer with his friends. "No. I ain't seen a Bubblehead at all till this one." He looked down at Twila and cupped her breast roughly with one hand. "And she look deft to me."

"They don't get babies," Starbright told him. "They born old."

Raunchy looked at Spider for verification. "Can't be," he objected.

"They born in a *factory,*" Starbright went on, prevaricating grandly. "They born without mamas, they just made outta stuff by *doctors,* and then they go out to work right away." Twila recognized concepts she had tried to explain to her young friend as they had roamed the dead city together. "An they don't do it, like we do. They afraid to, and you know why? 'Cause it make them o-o-o-old," she finished, drawing out the word to frighten him with it.

"What you mean, woman?" Raunchy demanded, clearly nervous.

"I say righteous," she lied sincerely. "Twila here, she was made—what, five, six years ago? Ain't that right?"

"Six," Twila agreed, trying to play along.

"Six years ago, and look at her: look her face, how old it be, and you know why? 'Cause she did it. She sneaked off with some guy, and they did it, and that's why they threw her out, ain't that right?"

Twila nodded, too amazed by the story to dare adding to it.

"Threw her out 'cause she did it, and now she looks like this, and worse every day. She get almost a year older every weak, don't you notice? And the guy she did it with? Mm, mm." Starbright shook her head. "He got wrinkles all over his face, and he can hardly remember who he is, he's so stupid."

"They turn him out, too?" Raunchy wanted to know.

"What for?" she came back. "He can't do no harm; he can't never fill up no woman again, 'cause it don't work no more."

Raunchy jumped to his feet, aghast. "Now, that's a lie!"

"Do you see him standing here?" she challenged. "I'm telling you, these Bubbleheads is like black widow spiders—female uses up the male in one shot."

Now he turned his disbelieving eyes on Twila. "She say righteous?"

Twila's heart lurched as she stared up at him. He positively towered over her, and the smell of him lingered in her nostrils. She wet her lips and cleared her throat. "Why don't you find out?" she asked thinly, managing to put what she hoped was the right amount of disdain in her voice.

He drew back and considered a moment. Then, "Hell, I don't need this," he muttered. "They lots of good Hat women around. I don't need no Bubblehead." With that he grabbed another girl by the arm and pulled her off into the next room.

Twila felt relief wash over her, though she knew this was a temporary reprieve. But, then, this whole situation was temporary—it had to be. She couldn't continue to live among people whose primary occupation was murder and rape. She couldn't live in this squalor, with the threat of violence hanging over her daily. She would have to find another place.

But for now, she needed them. She needed their protection while she adjusted to life Outside. Somehow these children—these people—had survived as a culture for seventy-five years, despite the ravages of war and CM.

She had learned much from them already, but there was much more she needed to know. And if down the road there was a price to pay—

She would just have to get out before the bill was presented.

They set off the next morning with few supplies, for the two women were expected to forage along the way to keep them fed. The men, of course, were only expected to watch out for Bariosos and other dangers, and to set a fast pace so that the trip would not take more than a day each way.

It would have taken considerably less than that except that it had been ten years since Raunchy had been to Bernalillo, the northernmost of the suburbs, and it required some head scratching and a couple of false trails before he located what he sought. In a highly rural area along the river's edge was a small bungalow flanked by several outbuildings. The yard was overgrown with grass and weeds, but Twila recognized a square of ground that had probably been a garden plot at one time. All the glass in the windows was intact, and the roof showed evidence of having been patched in recent years. Someone had lived here, obviously, though not for some time. But had it been her grandfather?

They approached cautiously, not knowing what wild animals might have taken up residence in this pastoral setting so far from the warfare of the Hats and Bariosos. Snakes, skunks, and wildcats were among the possibilities, so Twila did not argue when Raunchy insisted on going inside first. After a few minutes he came back out and announced that it was safe to enter. "And I was right, this is the crazy man's place," he told them, "and that's righteous."

Twila entered with trepidation. The inside was cleaner than most of the houses she had been in, although dusty tracks showed that some small creatures had invaded recently. She moved through the front parlor, the kitchen, and then down the short hallway to a bedroom. Clothes hung neatly in the closet, among them a kapok habit; she opened a dresser drawer and found other clothes folded there: socks, underwear, shirts, handkerchiefs. Were they the right size? Twila did not know.

Across the way from the bedroom, the final room in the house gave more hope. It held not a bed, but two cots and a table covered with once white paper, now brittle and yellowed with age—an examining table, she thought. Boxes of bandages and bottles of medications lined shelves all around, and a stethoscope, blood pressure gauge, and other medical paraphernalia hung from hooks on the walls. There was no doubt this room had served as an infirmary. But served whom?

In the top drawer of a desk in the corner, she found the answer.

It was a journal, and although she was unaccustomed to the handwriting, Twila could easily make out the lettering on the first page: Carlton Grimm, 4 June 2082. There was no doubt about it anymore; this was where her grandfather had lived after his expulsion, and where he had died a victim of tribal violence. Hands trembling, Twila turned to the first entry.

> *To whomever may find this journal in years to come:*
> *My name is Carlton Grimm, and I am a physician. I was a resident of the Numex biodome until 27 May of this year, at which time I was expelled. No, let me be honest: until I was murdered.*

Chapter 11

Twila caught her breath. Murdered! She narrowed her eyes and read on.

> *I cannot call it anything else, for I know that my poisoning with the CM virus was no accident. There was a spill in the laboratory where I was working, the accidental release—so it was claimed—of live CM virus into the air. My colleague Samuel Krell and I were both exposed, and although they rushed us through decontamination procedures, I had already contracted the infection. Krell was wearing a filtration mask and escaped. That's the official story.*
>
> *But the med tech who did the lab work on my blood came to me as I sat in isolation, waiting the results, and told me herself what she had found. Indeed I was infected, but not with the airborne CM-B virus. It was CM-A she found in my blood.*

Twila's eyes opened wide. CM-A! Then Grandfather could not have gotten it from the spill in the lab, as Dr. Krell had told her. A lie? Or did Krell not know the truth himself? She read on.

> *She assumed that I had contracted it from a woman, and I did not bother to correct her because I did not see the point. But there has been no one since Sharee died. Besides, I had gone through a routine blood check that morning and tested clean. The level of the virus in my blood was too high to have sprung up in twelve hours. The exposure had to have been massive.*
>
> *There was only one time that day I was at risk of such an exposure: after the supposed spill in the lab,*

*Krell and I drew blood from each other for testing. I
can hardly believe it yet, but there is no other answer.
The needle that penetrated my arm must have been
loaded with the virus. Samuel Krell, my colleague, my
friend, has murdered me.*

Deep, bitter anger rose in Twila. Krell! Jon was right,
but not right enough. He hadn't believed his father
capable of intentionally infecting Carlton. But Carlton
believed it—and Twila did, too.

She read on—Carlton's explanation of why he told no
one in Numex his suspicions of Krell. Next to himself,
Krell was the most experienced and capable person
fighting CM. To take them both out of the picture would
have set the research back a decade, and he had so much
hope now that they'd isolated the immunizing agent in
Twila's blood. So Carlton had borne his secret quietly,
angrily, out of the biodome. He'd left a megalomaniac in
charge of Numex, believing that to do anything else
would have been a greater crime.

But did you know, Grandfather, Twila wondered, what
he would do to me? And if you did, would you have made
the same decision?

"How long you got to stay here?" Raunchy interrupted
her reflection.

Twila discovered it had grown late; the sun was setting
and soon there would be no daylight left to read by. "A
little longer," Twila told him. "A little while, please. We
can stay the night here, can't we?"

"I start a fire," Starbright volunteered. "Outside—ain't
no fireplace in here. But they's greens to cook, and lots of
pans here pretty clean. We be fine till morning."

"Hey, Bubblehead," Raunchy prodded. "You know how
to turn on the juice in this place?"

Twila stared blankly at him. "Juice?"

"Yeah, juice," he repeated. "The crazy man, he had
juice at this place. Made things run, you know."

"Electricity?" she guessed.

"I don't know. He could make, like, lights come on,
and things get hot without fire, and stuff like that. You
know how to get that working?"

Twila shrugged. "I don't know much about elec—about juice. Let me keep reading his book, maybe I'll find out."

"How can staring at some stupid hunk of paper tell you about juice?" he demanded.

It dawned on Twila then that not only did Raunchy not know how to read, he had no concept of obtaining information from written symbols. She shook her head in bewilderment at how to explain. "I just—these marks on the page." she said, showing them to him, "they mean something to me. They tell me things, like—like the marks on the ground tell you what kind of animals have been here, and the different leaves on the trees tell you what kind of tree it is. Let me study the marks, maybe they'll tell me about the juice."

Raunchy made a rude comment and turned away. "Crazy man your grampa grampa for sure," he muttered as he walked away. "You just as crazy as he was."

Several miles to the northwest, a band of four travelers was preparing to set out under shelter of the coming darkness. They had come across a wide, rolling expanse of land that morning but rested through the late afternoon and evening, for although the hostile city dwellers rarely came this far north, they took no chances. They would make their final approach in darkness. Once across the river and into the town of Bernalillo, they would stop again for the night; then with the daylight, they would venture through the maze of empty streets in search of badly needed wire cabling. They needed the daylight to find it; they needed the darkness again to make good their escape.

"Len, check that lead mare's right foreleg," a young woman instructed. "Looks to me like she's favoring it. Tim, you've got the saddle mount, we need you to ride ahead—you know that, don't you?" It was plain she did not like sending him into danger.

The rangy youth nodded absently, clucking to his mare and starting off down the winding road between the hills. He carried no weapon; none of the party did, except for the utility knives that were as much a part of them as their leather footwear and broad-brimmed hats. Only a fool ventured out without all three.

But as Tim cast his gaze eastward into the growing gloom, it was not danger he was searching for. It was her. He had felt her for days, known that she was coming . . .

Where are you? his thoughts went out. *And who are you? And what is it about you that has drawn Melinda's mind to you so many times?*

By the time Twila found her grandfather's journal entry dealing with the generator, it was too dark to hope to do anything about it. When morning arrived, though, she was eager to try. They found the generator in a shed near the house with plenty of fuel in the tank. Grandfather had written about shutting it down during the summer months, about cleaning and priming it again in the fall, and between his sketchy accounts and Bobo's knowledge of car engines, they managed to get the ancient piece of machinery started up.

Its throaty rumble was music to Twila's ears, for she had a plan. She wandered through the bungalow with a secret smile on her face, turning on lights and testing small appliances, feeling sure that now she had a solution to her problem with the Hats. It was so simple! She would stay here. When it was time to go back, she would send Starbright and the two young men on their way with thanks, and she would stay. There were plenty of places to forage from nearby, for the Hats and the Bariosos seldom wandered so far north; and she could clear the old garden plot for new planting in no time. Now, with electricity to power a stove and even a refrigerator, she would be quite comfortable. Her grandfather's journal was like a copy of *Robinson Crusoe,* filled with his account of how he had survived in this very place.

She hummed a little as she looked over the tiny infirmary set up in one room. She would not know how to use most of it, of course, but at least there were first-aid supplies if she needed them. A good medical text would help; surely Grandfather had one here somewhere—

Her eyes drifted to the computer terminal on his desk. She had passed so many dead terminals in so many dead houses that it had not occurred to her until this moment that, with electricity, she might be able to make this one work. Why would Grandfather have had it here, if he couldn't make it work? Quickly she crossed into the room and snapped on the power switches.

It crackled and hummed, just like her terminal at home, and Twila wondered how badly the components would corrode out in the open like this for so many years. Perhaps Grandfather had known about rebuilding computers, as he seemed to know about so many things. If she read further in his journal, she might find something about it. But for now, the silent monitor seemed to be coming to life.

Twila did not recognize the screen that appeared first. She had assumed the PubInfo shell would appear—but, of course, that was only for Numex residents. Supposedly each biodome's residents got something different. But could she get to PubInfo from this machine? If so . . . she could call Jon. She could call him and tell him she was all right, and make sure there had been no repercussions for him . . . How to avoid alerting Krell, though? She wasn't sure if he could get a fix on her location from a computer transmission, but she wouldn't take any chances. She'd use the id Jon had given her, the secret system he knew—Yes, that was it. If only she could get to the PubInfo shell . . .

It took her twenty minutes of hacking to find the right access combination, and then there it was—the familiar blue-and-white background with its colorful icons. There was no video capability on this system, so after she had keyed in the codes he'd made her memorize—how long ago was it? Six weeks? Eight?—she composed a simple message: SAFE AND SOUND AND MAKING NEW FRIENDS. TWILA. Then she sat back to wait.

The minutes ticked by. Jon must be in the lab, involved in some experiment. Or perhaps with Dr. Mintz. Somehow, the thought did not make her jealous. Let him have a happy life.

She got up and strolled around the room. She thought about going to find Starbright, of showing her the computer—but it would be only a toy to the Hats. Time enough for toys later. She wanted to wait a little longer and see if Jon responded . . .

Then it came, blasting across the screen like a shout. WHERE ARE YOU?

Twila laughed as she sat down at the terminal and typed back. IN A SAFE PLACE. I PUT ON MY MECHANIC'S HAT AND FIRED UP AN OLD GENERATOR. AM I CLEVER, OR WHAT?

There was a brief pause, and Twila wondered if something was causing a lag in transmission time. Hadn't Jon said he would set up this system as a multiuser domain, operating in real time? Why should there be a delay?

When his response appeared, one word at a time, she understood. WE THOUGHT YOU WERE DEAD.

Dead! Well, they were almost right, Twila remembered. Had they seen her fall in? They were that close behind her. Yes, they must have seen her fall in and assumed—Oh, poor Jon! she thought suddenly. And her mother—her mother must have been hysterical. And Trish—

Twila realized she needed to respond to Jon's message. I CAME CLOSE, she typed, BUT I SURVIVED.

She should not have been surprised at his next message, knowing Krell, knowing how Jon distrusted him.

PROVE YOU ARE TWILA.

What could she tell him that she knew and Krell did not? What intimate secret did they share that Krell could not have penetrated. Those fumbling moments in the Stargazing Room . . . the tune he had whistled when they met on the transit . . . but even these, she realized, were suspect, for they could have been overheard or guessed at. If she were Krell, perpetrating a hoax on Jon, what is the one thing she could not—or would not—tell him?

And then she knew.

I FOUND MY GRANDFATHER'S JOURNAL OUT HERE, she typed. IT SAYS HE WAS INFECTED WITH CM-A, NOT B. IT SAYS HE WAS CLEAN AT BLOOD CHECK THAT MORNING AND THE ONLY WAY HE COULD HAVE BEEN INFECTED WAS FROM THE NEEDLE USED TO DRAW HIS BLOOD FOR THE SAMPLE AFTER THE SPILL. IT SAYS YOUR FATHER DREW THE BLOOD.

Then she sat back to wait.

Jon stared stupefied at the computer screen. Then his hands flew to his face, and he doubled up in physical pain as the truth sawed through his gut like a dull scalpel. He could verify it, of course, and would later: though Carlton's medical records were sealed and beyond his reach, the record of who had run the lab work that day would be open to him, and he could find the tech who undoubtedly thought he or she was protecting Carlton's reputation with silence. But he knew already what he would find, for it all locked into place. Carlton had been the most powerful man in Numex, although he had used such a light hand on the reins that few knew his authority except as a guiding light. Krell was a kingdom builder, and both Carlton's policies and his presence blocked the ambitious young doctor's progress. Removing Carlton was the logical thing to do.

Even as he knew this was true of his father, Jon knew that the sender of these messages could not be one of his father's minions. It truly was Twila; she truly was alive. His hands trembled as he put them back to the keys.

COME BACK INSIDE, he pleaded. YOU'LL DIE OUT THERE.

I CAN'T, came her reply. YOUR FATHER WILL KEEP STEALING MY BABIES AND KILLING THEM.

He hesitated, wondering if he should tell her. The efforts to create new fetuses from the eggs of those in cold storage was not going well; the obstacles were many, and if Krell were able to surmount them at all, it would take him years. But there were the other children. Anguish welled up in him. He wanted her to come home. They could work on the problem together, once she was Inside. And she would reason it out anyway, once she had time to think about it, for she knew there were children of hers Inside. So he wrote, YOU HAVEN'T STOPPED HIM, MY INNOCENT. YOUR OLDEST DAUGHTER IS ALMOST ELEVEN. AS SOON AS SHE REACHES PUBERTY, HE WILL START ALL OVER WITH HER.

It was several moments before her answer came. It appeared slowly, word by word, and he could almost see her tapping it out on her keyboard: I . . . WILL . . . SEE . . . HIM . . . STOPPED.

Then the connection dropped.

Twila powered off the terminal, not bothering to exit the system but crashing ungracefully out of it.

Goddamn him to hell.

Goddamn him to hell.

GODDAMN HIM TO HELL!

Mind churning, stomach churning, she left the bungalow and wandered aimlessly through the yard surrounding it, back to a main road, into the town. Goddamn him to hell, he was going to do it to another child—*her* child, the child he had not let her bear in her own body. The child he had stolen from her and given to another woman to raise. *Is that what he did with me?* she wondered. *What really happened to my birth mother? Was she uncooperative, and did he dispose of her? As he disposed of Grandfather? Now that I am uncooperative, does he even want me back? Won't it be easier for him to prey on this new child, and another after that, and another after that?*

God damn him to hell!

She was shaking now. *I won't allow it,* she vowed. *I won't allow him to perpetrate this crime on another human being, on* my *child, without her knowledge or consent. I will stop him. I* must *stop him.*

But what could she do? Send a message to someone Inside, exposing Krell as her grandfather's murderer? Who would believe it? Could she spread scandal by revealing that he allowed—and participated in—sexual intercourse and promiscuity among the MA staff? That he was granting temporary immunity to an elite few who were in his favor? And the grisly means by which that immunity was achieved? She doubted her message would get through. And who would she send it to? What authority was there, except the Medical Authority? Besides, if she sent some highly placed individual a full report, what was to say he wouldn't just use it to blackmail Krell into giving him the immunity, too?

A daughter almost eleven. Could I smuggled her out, too? Who would help me find her? And what kind of life would she have out here? Even staying at Grandfather's place, the Hats would know where we were, and in time the Bariosos, too. In a year or so my daughter would become prize for these hoodlums, and no tall tales would stop that. Prize? A rape victim, no more, no less. And then over and over, a life of forced intercourse, and too many babies, and although CM wouldn't kill her, overwork and childbearing would.

I have to find somewhere else, she decided, knowing

her grandfather's clinic could be only a temporary sanctuary. There must be some other place, some other people. They spoke of mountaineers—I'll find out where they are, and go there. Or I'll head up the old highway for Santa Fe, see what's there. There has to be something better than this. Then, when I've found it, I'll figure out how to get my daughter out. Aunt Trish will help. Jon, too, if I'm careful and don't tell him too much. But I mustn't endanger his position, because in the long run he may be right—he may be the only one who can break his father's power. I will let him have the chance.

But I will not let that monster touch my daughter. I will not allow his clinical rape and murder to continue.

So absorbed was Twila in her thoughts that she did not see the curly-haired child with his bandanna stealing from building to building on her right, nor how he slipped away to find the older boys nearby.

"Trish." Jon called from the nearest zone, not daring to cross over into the barnyard, where Trish was working. Her head jerked up, and he tugged back his hood so she could see who it was. "Trish, she's alive. I had a message from her. She's Outside, but she's safe."

Hope and terror warred in Trish's face. Then, "Get out of here!" she hissed.

He began to back away, unable to keep a beaming smile off his face. "By the way, you're doing great. Keep up the good work." Strange rumors had been circulating on the conferences for a week; Security was in an uproar, trying to locate the source, but although they had confiscated several diskettes, they were unable to tell who had made them. Jon threw her a quick salute, then turned and trotted back toward the road.

He had not gone a hundred yards when the Security scooter overtook him. "Dr. Krell?"

He nodded.

"Please come with me. Your father wants to see you."

"Jon, there's old and fragile data in those files" was Krell's excuse. "I cannot have you mucking around in them."

Jon knew then that Security still hadn't been able to

break into his files on Carlton's old id. His father did not know that he'd gotten a message from Twila. They were having this discussion in his father's office, with Krell in his favorite power position behind his desk, in front of the windows. "I didn't touch the data," Jon stonewalled. "I like to keep some files on that system, that's all. What's wrong with keeping a few files on it?"

Krell was employing his calm, firm, no-nonsense tone. "You're going to use up space, and you'll jeopardize our ability to get to those old files if we need them. Now, just stop."

"That's a piece of crap," Jon flared. "You don't want me keeping files where you can't see them, and that's the crux of it."

Krell's eyes narrowed. "What kind of files do you keep that you wouldn't want another researcher to see? We're all in this together; we're all working toward the same end."

"Personal files," Jon retorted. "Do you know what that means, personal? I can't take a leak or kiss a woman but what you and half Security knows about it. Can't you allow me one or two *personal* files?"

Krell leaned back in his chair now, looking levelly across at his son, who was seated opposite him. Behind him the early May sky was clear and cloudless and startling blue through the window of his office. *This used to be Carlton's office,* Jon remembered. *We used to sit here and talk for hours. He was more father to me in just one of those sessions than this man has been in twenty-two years.*

And he wondered about Twila, out there somewhere, in the company of savages . . .

"There's a rumor going around the conferences that the MA has a cure of CM and won't release it to the public," Krell said gravely.

Jon said nothing.

"There's an interesting figure being quoted in the rumors," Krell continued. "They say this mythical cure leaves you with a point zero two percent risk of contracting the virus." He leaned forward again. "That's the same figure you quoted in your proposal to the governing board."

"It's a figure every medical student knows."

Krell sighed. "Anyway, the board is meeting next Tuesday to discuss how to deal with this rash of rumors. Similar ones crop up from time to time; we've always managed to quell them before, I imagine we can do so again."

"I'll look forward to the meeting," Jon promised, rising and starting for the door.

"You won't be at the meeting."

Jon turned slowly and looked back at his father.

"I'm removing you from the board," Krell told him.

Jon's heart lurched. Removing him—But the board was his forum, his vehicle for bringing pressure to bear on his father. Without his seat on the board—

"And I think perhaps," Krell went on, "you've been working too hard. Twila's death has upset you; you're not thinking straight, and your work is suffering. I think you ought to take a vacation, do something else for a while. Renea can keep the lab running for a few weeks without you."

Vacation! It was no vacation; it was an exile. An exile and a threat—his father was threatening to take his lab away from him.

"I've put you on the Required Labor lists," Krell told him. "It will be good for you to do some physical labor, work out your grief and your frustration. I thought maybe the rain forest; but you can pick something else if you'd rather."

"No, rain forest is fine," Jon said numbly. Time to agree. At least the rainforest would put him out of range of his father for a while, though not out from under the scrutiny of Security, who watched the machete-wielding foresters very closely, indeed. "That sounds good. Maybe you're right."

And he knew as he walked away that he had conceded both too much and too little. He should not have surrendered his lab without a fight; but he should not have pushed his father to this point. What good was he to anyone without his lab, without his seat on the governing board? How could he work any changes from the depths of the rain forest? No, he would have to be cooperative now, very, very cooperative in order to keep his place near the seat of power. He would have to make a show of conciliation; he would have to adopt his father's methods of deceit and guile to accomplish his ends. It stuck in his throat, and the ulcer in his stomach twisted.

But Twila was alive. And somehow, he would get through this.

"It's enough to last us for ten years," Len said with satisfaction when they had loaded the spool of cabling onto their wagon. It was high noon, and all four of them were perspiring freely from the effort and the warmth of the early May sun. Sally lashed the spool to the side of the wagon as Delia tossed the crowbar and other tools in beside it.

"Want to look for anything else?" Sally asked the younger girl.

"Not me," said Delia, who shot a coy glance at the fourth member of their party. "But Tim does."

Tim's eyes were fastened on the streets and buildings to the south of them, separated from their position by a dry wash and a modest block wall. Sally rested a moment and watched him. "Tim."

"Hm?" His eyes never stopped searching.

"We're starting back."

"Good." Tim untied his saddle horse slowly. "I'm going to linger a bit. I won't be long."

"Tim—"

"I told Melinda I would."

Sally sighed and hauled herself into the wagon. A promise to Melinda was not something anyone would ask him to break. "Suit yourself. Come on, Len, Delia."

They joined her in the wagon. Sally chucked to the horses, and they started east down the broken paving of the street. They were a quarter of a mile in on a dead-end road, and it made Sally nervous. Too easy to get cornered here. She'd be happier when their noses were pointed north again. Silently she debated whether she wanted to wait for cover of darkness to leave the ruins, or chance going on in the daylight. They had seen no sign of the hostiles who dwelt here.

Tim mounted his horse, still gazing south across the small wash. The horse's ears twitched, cocking in the direction its master looked. "What is it?" he whispered softly. "Do you hear something? Is it her?"

It was a sound that caught Twila's attention. A cat yowled, and although it was a perfectly natural noise in this new world, it was still strange and disquieting to Twila and so she looked up from her aimless walk, turning back toward the sound.

There were four Bariosos following her.

She knew they were Bariosos from the headbands, and she knew they must have been following her for some time because of the smug looks on their faces as they strolled out in the open, waiting for their stupid quarry to notice their pursuit. Twila froze like a startled deer and stared at them, two wannabes and two warriors, and she knew what her fate would be if they caught up with her. For a moment they stared back, until one of them made a mocking comment in some language Twila did not understand. But she understood the tone, and the gesture the boy made. Twila turned tail and ran.

She fled headlong through streets with only a block head start on them. The older boys were longer legged than she, and began to gain ground quickly. Twila tried desperately to think where she could go that they couldn't follow, what kind of obstacle she might put between herself and her pursuers to slow them down. Too late she realized she was running in the wrong direction; she should have headed west, back toward her companions and the assistance of two Hat fighters. Instead, her blind flight was taking her north.

Cutting to the left, Twila dodged down an alley and jumped a fence, hoping that she was nimbler than they, that her dancer's reflexes would give her an edge. But they stayed with her, and by the time she scrabbled over another fence and back into the street, they were only twenty yards behind her. Spotting a block wall separating two houses, Twila vaulted to its top and began to run along it to another alley, trusting her balance-beam work would give her an edge—but it didn't. She could hear the boys behind her. To make matters worse, she heard in the distance the raucous clamor of a car engine drawing nearer.

Twila dropped to the ground in the alley, and ran again. Her only hope was to slip out of sight somewhere and try to duck into one of the abandoned buildings before they saw where she went. But as she ducked around corners and through yards, she could never get far enough ahead to try it; and she was afraid to enter a building while they could see her, for fear of being cornered inside.

Bailing over a crumbling block wall, Twila suddenly found herself, not in an alley as she expected, but on the edge of a small wash. Blood! A hundred yards or more of open space! They'd catch her for sure. The sound of the car engine was growing louder, much louder. No sense running laterally; the best to hope was to get across the wash as quickly as possible and try to disappear in one of the warehouse structures beyond. But they were set far apart. Too open, too open, she'd come to the end—

Movement caught her eyes. Had they gotten in front of her? Or was it some wild animal, a deer perhaps, startled by her arrival?

"Hurry!" a voice called to her. "Hurry!"

It was a horse. A person, riding on a horse. It was too strange to even wonder at. Twila made a beeline for the pair.

Behind her the car engine cut out, and she could hear more voices as additional Bariosos joined the chase. They must be just on the other side of the wall, and the first four were now less than ten yards behind her and closing fast . . .

The wash was dry, though it hardly mattered to Twila except that water might have slowed her down. She stooped while going up the other side and snatched up a fist-size stone, but she was afraid to stop long enough to throw it. The horse was charging toward her, hooves thudding against the rock-hard ground. As it drew near, Twila saw its eyes flashing wildly, and for a moment she was afraid it would trample her; but the rider was shouting again. "Take my hand!" he cried, reaching out to her with his right arm as he thundered nearer.

They were reaching out for her now, almost close enough to grab her, but the two younger ones were slowing down as the horse pounded straight at them. Twila flipped the rock over her shoulder without looking;

she heard a grunt and gave a last spurt of speed, reaching out as the horseman drew near. He slowed just the slightest bit; his hand caught hers. With agility born of desperation and the dance, she jumped and let the rider haul her up behind him. "Hang on!" he shouted as the horse bolted forward.

Then they were flying, Twila clinging for dear life to the stranger. The thrumming cadence of the horse's gait reverberated through her body and her brain, blotting out every other sensation but fear. She expected at any moment to be bounced from her precarious seat, but she was not. Slowly, slowly, she began to trust, to feel herself flowing with the smooth rhythm of the horse and rider.

Behind her, the shouting and cursing grew fainter. The horse was faster than any human could be, and it was rested. Hearing an engine, Twila knew the car was trying to find an alternate route to reach her, but horse and rider turned north and galloped on. A mile passed, two. No one followed. They overtook a horse-drawn wagon, and the horse slowed. "Gangsters behind us," the rider shouted to its driver. Then to Twila, "Climb in the back of the wagon." With a hand from him she slid to the ground, then rolled over the side of the wagon to relative safety. As soon as she had, the wagoner whipped up the dray team, and the wagon began to bounce and rattle across the country at breakneck speed, the lone rider following closely.

For a long time Twila lay on her back in the jouncing conveyance, eyes shut tight, listening intently for the sound of the car engine following. But all she heard was the creaking of the wagon and the pounding of the horses' hooves on the broken asphalt.

The horses plodded slowly now, their breathing slowed, their flanks no longer heaving. For five miles they had been walking, sure that no one pursued them.

Twila's head pounded as she looked off to the northeast, seeing the glistening shape of the biodome perched on its mesa not far away. The setting sun reflected sharply off its many glass panels. It looked so strange from the outside, like a city wrapped in spiderwebs, shielded, shrouded, isolated from the landscape and the world in which it dwelt. How many people Inside even knew the Hats and Bariosos existed? How many cared?

"Feeling better?" the young man called Tim asked solicitously, having joined her in the back of the wagon. He was, she thought, somewhat older than the Hats, maybe nineteen or even twenty. Was that possible? His skin was tanned and his hair, where it showed beneath his gray felt hat, was a dusty blond. He was lank and tall, though not as tall as Spider. Blue eyes smiled out of a friendly face with high cheekbones and a pointed chin.

"Much, thank you," she replied, sipping again from the canteen he had given her. His horse was now tied behind the wagon, looking tired. Tim did not look tired, but rather a quiet elation characterized his expression, as though he had just won some great victory. In a way, he had. There was no sign of the Bariosos following them. "You wouldn't happen to have any food, would you?" she asked him.

The smile he'd been wearing for the last five miles broke into a grin as he rummaged in a nearby pack. Shortly he produced fresh bread spread with soft cheese. "Your wish is my command!"

Twila returned his smile wanly. Maybe when her head quit throbbing, when she had assimilated what had happened to her, she could muster more enthusiasm. For now she contented herself with tearing into the bread and cheese. To her, it was a feast.

They lived, she had learned, in the mountains northwest of here—probably those people the Hats called mountaineers. "We don't call ourselves anything," Tim had laughed when she'd asked. "We're just people. From the Springs. Springites, I guess."

"How long will it take us to get to your village?" she'd wanted to know. She couldn't see the mountains yet, only miles of rolling hills stretching out beyond them.

"We won't make it to the junction before dark," he told her, "so we'll probably stop and make camp before then. Depending on how far we make it tonight, it will probably be noon tomorrow before we turn and start up into the mountains. Hauling this heavy spool, I'd say it'll be close to nightfall before we get there."

Delia, the youngest of the group, looked back at them

now from her place on the wagon seat. She was thirteen, a tall, freckle-faced girl with brown braids. "You don't think those, um, those gangsters will follow us, do you?"

Twila found the term odd; the Hats and Bariosos were nothing like gangsters she'd seen in old flatscreen vids. For a response, she only shrugged helplessly. There was only one road going into the mountains; surely the Bariosos could find it if they wanted to.

"They've never followed us out of the city before," Len chimed in. He was about Tim's age, but huskier, sporting a full brown beard. He sat on one side of Delia. "Not that I know of, and I've read most of the Chronicles."

Tim reached out a hand and patted Twila's knee reassuringly, still smiling. "Don't worry, you're safe. I just know it."

Twila was inclined to believe him. It made her head hurt less to do so.

The other girl, Sally, was quiet. Twila would have guessed Sally to be her own age, except that that was not possible. More likely responsibility had aged Sally. Like the others, her face was tanned beneath her broad-brimmed hat, but there were shadows there that were absent on the others. Dark blond hair hung limply to her shoulders, and eyes of an indistinct light color seemed tired and too serious. There was an air about her that said she was more than just the wagoner in this group. Twila never doubted for an instant that Sally was in charge of it.

Miles passed; the sun slid toward the mountain peaks even as the moon rose to make its way westward, as though trying to catch the brighter orb. Twila dozed off and on, tired enough not to fret when her head made a cushion out of Tim's muscular thigh. During her waking periods, she explained about leaving the biodome and living with the Hats briefly, about finding her grandfather's clinic. She told her rescuers abut Dr. Krell, and that he had conducted research on her without her knowledge; but she did to tell them what kind of research. It seemed too sordid to speak of to strangers just now. Instead she spoke of his power to make or break careers, to access private holographic programs, to spy electronically on whomever he pleased. "I had to get away from him," she told them. "I couldn't let him have that kind of power over me."

As night began to fall, they pulled off into a copse of trees at the edge of the broad, slow-moving river, which farther downstream provided the domizens with power. Sally assigned duties, and the four began settling in for the night. Twila was fascinated to see young Delia unhitch the horses and lead them away toward the water's edge. The lanky adolescent seemed dwarfed by the dray animals.

Twila saw Tim watching her as he unsaddled his own mount, and his expression was bemused. "I guess I never realized horses were so—big," she explained.

Tim's ready grin spread across his lean face. "I guess they are kind of intimidating if you haven't grown up around them," he agreed, tossing the saddle onto a nearby rock. "At least, that seems to be a common reaction among refugees from the biodome."

"Refugees?" Twila was surprised. "You've encountered other people who left the dome?"

"Oh, we've been picking them up for generations," he replied, beginning to rub down the horse with a brush taken from his saddlebags. "But there haven't been many lately—and never one who's come out voluntarily." Admiration shone in his eyes. "It took a lot of courage to do that."

Twila didn't know how to respond to that. She knew Tim thought she had chosen death when she left Numex, and she hadn't—but it had taken courage, anyway. The unknown of life outside the dome was little less frightening to its inhabitants than the unknown of death. So instead of responding, she said what she'd thought when he spoke of refugees. "I wish you'd found my grandfather," she said, "when he was forced out sixteen years ago. He might still be alive."

Tim shrugged. "It wouldn't have been me, I was only five back then, but it was our loss, too. We could use a good doctor."

Twila did some quick addition in her head. "But—if you were five, sixteen years ago, then you're—"

"Twenty-one."

Twenty-one! Then, was it possible—could it be—

"I know, you're wondering why I'm not dead," he interpreted. "We live longer at the Springs—longer than the gangsters, longer than refugees. The usual age for manifesting is twenty; the usual age to cross over is twenty-three, twenty-four."

Manifesting Twila understood, but "cross over" puzzled her until she realized it must be a euphemism for death. A chill ran through her.

Tim was brushing the horse's legs now, squatting near the ground. "It's a process of natural selection as much as anything else," he continued. "Those who live longer produce more children, so those children are more likely to live longer, etc. But we like to think our lifestyle contributes to the longevity of our people."

"Your lifestyle?"

The sun had gone, and the twilight deepened quickly; Tim stopped currying his mount to look at her in the fading light. It was an open, even gaze. "Caring," he said. "Looking after each other. Loving those who manifest, instead of shunning them."

Twila nodded. As a botanist, she had read the literature on the effects of attention and affection on plants—it only made sense that that would apply to human beings, as well. Only they didn't teach you that in Numex. They probably went out of their way to bury that knowledge. Elizabeth Modecko's influence—or Samuel Krell's? Certainly the isolationist philosophy helped keep his empire in place. She thought of all the things he had hidden from her, information he had deliberately denied her access to—

"Would you like to meet Rex?" Tim was asking.

Pulled from her thoughts, it was a moment before Twila realized he meant the horse. "Oh. I suppose it's only proper, seeing how he helped rescue me from the Bariosos." She forced herself to take a few steps closer to the animal. It really was big, even if not as big as the dray horses. "Hello, Rex."

"You can pet his neck," Tim invited, patting the long, arching neck himself. "Not his head, though, he doesn't like that."

Tentatively Twila reached out a hand to touch the horse. It had a warm, solid feel, and a smell that was pungent but earthy. As she slid her palm along the curve of its neck, the horse turned his head slightly toward her, and she felt the puff of warm breath from its nostrils.

But it was so big!

"Come on, I have to take him down to the stream," Tim told her, tucking the brush back in his saddlebags. "He deserves a good drink after the run we gave him."

Delia had brought the drays back up and was tethering them among the trees as Twila tagged along with Tim down a gentle slope to the creek's edge. She could hardly see it in the dark, but she could hear the water bubbling over the sand. The ground was fairly flat here, so the channel was not deep. Rex waded out into it while they watched from the bank.

"I really do owe you and Rex a great debt," Twila said. "I don't know if you know that, ah . . . what the Bariosos would have done . . . to me, I mean, what they do to women they capture . . ."

"Rape," Tim guessed.

A shiver ran through Twila. "The Hats are no better, really. They're so violent, even to their own women, and they just seem to—they seem to think nothing of it, as though it were just the natural order of things—" Away from the Hats, she was finally able to vocalize her feelings on what she had witnessed, but the words did not come easily.

"*Sex* is the natural order of things," Tim said with conviction. "Rape is something else. If you watch animals in the wild, the male has to woo the female, to entice her, to win her. He doesn't take her by force." They could hear the horse drinking noisily. "Forcefully, maybe, but not by force. Take horses, for example. During mating, a stallion is an amazing thing to watch; but if a mare's not in season, if she's not ready for him, he's out of luck."

Twila felt herself burning a bright crimson at the thought of watching horses mate. The daylight was gone now, but the moon was almost directly overhead to illuminate her discomfiture, and Tim grinned at her reaction. Then the grin quickly softened to an understanding smile. "Sex is a good thing," he told her. "When there's mutual desire, and mutual pleasure. I know they don't teach you that in the biodome, but it's true."

"Some people are well aware of that," she told him

dryly, thinking of Jon and Dr. Mintz. "But most of us—
it's not that we don't have any sexual release," she
blurted, still blushing furiously, though she wasn't sure
quite why. "It's just—not with other people. Not touching
other people."

Now it was his turn to look a trifle embarrassed. "Well,
that has its virtues, but . . . it really can't compare. You'll
see."

Twila stiffened.

"I mean, when you're ready," Tim stammered quickly,
seeing her reaction. "Only when you're ready. No one
here will touch you until you want. I'm sorry, I didn't
mean—sometimes refugees don't, uh, participate for
years. And Melinda says sometimes they never do. That's
your choice. It's always your choice."

He looked so anxious and apologetic that Twila's fears
melted, but she knew living with the mountaineers would
be an adjustment for her. Caring and loving as they might
be, their value system was still very different from hers,
and they would have different expectations of her. As
understanding as Tim was trying to be, she suspected he
had some expectations as well. Or hopes, anyway.

Rex nickered softly from the water. Tim started to turn
away, but Twila reached out and put a hand on his arm. It
was a conscious action, though not an uncomfortable one.
She had touched her Aunt Trish, after all; that had always
been a comfort to her. And, of course, she had touched
Jon, but that had been different—so very, very different!
This was just to reassure Tim—and herself—that things
were going to be all right. "It's okay," she told him. "No
offense taken. But I have some reflexes that aren't going
to go away overnight." The evening she'd spent with Jon
up in the Stargazing Room was fresh in her mind.

"I understand. I just—" He still looked miserable. "I
have this habit of putting my foot in my mouth—"

"Stop," she bade him gently. "You've been nothing but
wonderful. I need time, that's all. And I need you to do
one more thing for me."

His face grew eager. "Anything," he vowed.

Twila smiled, amused and flattered by his transparency.
"I was just thinking about some people I left behind," she
confessed, "and the people I'm going to meet tomorrow,

and I think—" She tilted her head upward to gaze into his shadowed face. "Would you just hold me for a minute?"

Tim's mouth fell open and for an instant Twila was afraid she'd misjudged him. But then his arms slid quickly around her and gently, gently, he pulled her close.

It was strange at first, the firmness of his chest and the scent of him foreign to her senses. And he was so tall, taller than Jon by several inches. But she rested her cheek on his shirt and let herself relax against him as he bent over her and continued to cradle her in his long, sinewy arms. Warmth and comfort seeped into her.

Yes, life among the mountaineers would be an adjustment. But she thought that it was going to be a good place to live.

Chapter 12

Several miles before they reached the town, Twila began to see the signs of habitation. Cultivated fields lined the stream on their left, and an occasional horse-drawn machine worked the land. The driver of the rig always waved to them, and the entire party waved back. In some places the land was carefully terraced to counter-act its sloping nature, and other places were simply given over to pastureland. There were no animals evident, for they were all farther up the mountain in summer pastures, but Tim told her that cattle and sheep were plentiful.

Twila rode horseback behind Tim, and when the eleva-tion began to climb sharply, Len and Sally walked as much as they rode to lighten the load for the horses. Delia drove the team, comfortable and competent in handling the animals. A slight breeze sighed through the canyon, although they felt little of it on the floor.

As they worked their way slowly up the steep road, the canyon walls grew dramatically higher on either side. Conifers mixed with the cottonwood and oak trees, stretching high overhead to reach the sun as the distance between the walls grew narrower. Here and there a farm-house appeared to be occupied, with chickens and pigs in the yard and an occasional small child staring at them as they passed. But they found no dwellings near the road until the sun was high overhead and they finally reached the town itself.

It spread for some three miles along the banks of the Jemez River, never more than two hundred yards wide on either side of the watercourse. To Twila, who was accus-tomed to boxlike, compressed living Quads, it seemed to ramble on forever. Construction was mostly wood, with some adobe and an occasional steel building dating back a century, but the architecture was as unfettered as the layout. Twila recognized examples of ranch and saltbox and A-frame and Cape Cod, rustic and modern, aesthetic and utilitarian. Most of it was old, having existed before the onslaught of CM, but some bore witness to the recent industry of the residents.

As they neared the town's center, children swarmed out to the road to greet them. Twila was sure there were not so many children in all of Numex, although that couldn't be possible. But here they were happily, joyously thronging together, pushing and shoving, laughing and shouting. Their clothes were rough, but their faces shone, and like their elders nearly every one wore a broad-brimmed hat. They pressed in toward the wagon, and Twila was afraid some would get run over, but they were all nimble in their antics. Len gave a shout as two small boys broke through the crowd and launched themselves into his arms. The youngest looked to be three. Although tired from the journey, Len grinned proudly and his step took on a new bounce as he carried them, one in each arm, through the town.

They stopped in front of a barnlike structure, which Tim explained was the town's warehouse. Here they dismounted, and Tim left Twila holding the reins while he helped several other strapping youths to unload the spool of cabling. The children were drifting off now, mostly in the direction of a large, spreading building just up the canyon from the warehouse. Some scampered off toward houses, others to the grassy area across the road where playground equipment beckoned. Only a handful stayed to prowl through the dim warehouse, or to beg a ride as Delia and Sally took the team back down the hill to unhitch the wagon and put the horses to pasture.

Now Twila became aware of the curious glances thrown her way. The young men especially were giving her a discreet, but thorough, looking over. Tim noticed it, too. "This is Twila," he said to the group in general as he came back to her. "She's from the biodome; we found her being chased out of the city by a group of gangsters." They all smiled and murmured greetings. "We're going to see Melinda now, but don't worry—I'm sure she'll be at the dance tomorrow night."

"Dance?" Twila's ears pricked up.

"Every Saturday night," Tim told her as they walked away from the warehouse, "we have a dance at the school. There's a small generator there, enough to keep lights going after dark and power the sound equipment. The first survivors who settled here promised themselves that no matter how bad things got, they'd get together every Saturday night to dance and make merry. So no matter what the harvest is like, or how many calves have been lost in a snowstorm, or who's died before they manifest, each and every Saturday night we put aside our work and come together as a community to relax and rejoice. And"—he laid an arm casually around her shoulders—"meet girls. So every one of those yah-hoo's will be there tomorrow night to make his play for you. Just remember, you don't have to do anything you don't want; you don't have to dance, you don't have to take a walk outside—"

"Oh, I'll dance," she assured him. "I love to dance, and I'm very good at it. But"—her heart pounded—"I suppose you dance touching here."

"Every chance I get!" he grinned. "But we dance not touching, too, so don't worry. If you don't want to slow dance, just say so. People will understand."

They turned off the main road onto a well-beaten dirt track that led toward the river. "Who is Melinda?" Twila asked.

"My wi—" Tim stopped short, then continued. "My wife. She manifested two years ago, you see," he rushed on, "and even though I'm allowed to take a second wife, I haven't done that yet. I've, I've, had one or two relationships, just passing things, and I've opened a few virgins, but nothing that's developed into anything serious. It's been okay, Melinda's not hard to take care of yet, but soon—Well, anyway." He took a deep breath. "You'll like Melinda, I know you will."

Twila's head reeled as she tried to sort that through. "I'm sorry," she apologized, "but if I'm going to live here, I need to understand all of this. You're married—"

"Yes, but Melinda manifested two years ago," he interrupted.

"But you don't divorce her because of that, you just take another wife."

He looked shocked. "I wouldn't divorce her! I love her. Even if I didn't, I'm dedicated to her; I'll take care of her till she crosses over. That's the way things are done here."

"You love her, but you've—had affairs—with other women?"

"Once a woman manifests," he explained, "it's not advisable for her to have any more children. Pregnancy shortens the mother's time, and the baby usually dies when the mother crosses over early. But we all have an obligation to propagate, so when a man's wife is unable to bear, he ought to find other women who can."

It sounded so practical; yet somehow it seemed unfair, and Twila wasn't sure why. "Do women ever have two husbands?" she asked.

"Of course." They were entering a fenced-in yard near the river's edge. "When manifestation becomes intense, a man's body becomes so weak that he's often not able to satisfy his wife. Then she's encouraged to look elsewhere. If she takes a second husband, there's someone around to help look after the first—just like a second wife looks after the first."

Twila shook her head. "This will take me a while to get used to."

They were just outside the house, and Tim tossed the reins over a porch railing. "I'll tend to Rex later. Sally will be along in no time to find you living quarters, and I want you to meet Melinda first. Provided she's awake." He clomped up the wooden steps to the porch, leading Twila by the hand. "With any luck everyone else will be out working, and we can have some time alone with her."

"Everyone else?"

"We share the house with six other people," he explained. "The kids all think of Melinda as their mom, even though two belong to Tanya." He opened the door and called out. "Melinda?"

A thin voice answered from the other room. "I'm here."

A glow lit Tim's face as he led Twila into a bedroom off the living room. Sitting in bed was a pale blond woman, thin to the point of emaciation but smiling radiantly. "Oh, Tim!" she cried. "You found her."

Tim left Twila to sit on the edge of the bed and kiss his wife hello. "Are you so surprised? Melinda, this is Twila

Grimm, and we narrowly got her out of the clutches of the
gangsters in the city. Twila, this is Melinda."

Melinda's smile disappeared. "Oh, was anyone hurt?"
she asked anxiously.

Tim waved a hand to dismiss the notion. "Not even a
gangster."

"I'm so glad." Melinda held out her hands to Twila.
"I'm so pleased Tim found you. I was worried about you,
and with just cause, it seems."

"I don't understand," Twila stammered, reflexively
taking the hands Melinda offered. "How could you—did
you know that—"

"I saw you come out of the dome," Melinda told her,
"and all those people come chasing after you. You were
so frightened! And then I saw you fall in the river and
nearly drown; and when you crawled out, I was afraid you
wouldn't think to get under that tree to hide. But you did,
almost as though you could hear me. It's a good thing,
too—those men came right by you and shone their light
on your tree—But you couldn't hear me when I tried to
warn you not to go into the city, to wait for Tim, and I
was afraid we'd lost you after all. By the time Sally
needed to make that trip for cable, I was afraid it was too
late." She smiled. "But Tim said he could feel you there,
coming back toward us. And it seems he was right—
again." With a sigh of contentment Melinda leaned back
against the pillows. "Tim is very gifted that way."

With the last word, Melinda's jaw fell slack and her
eyes glazed over. "Ah," Tim said, closing her eyelids and
easing her into a prone position on the bed. "Just in time.
Fly well, love." He kissed her lightly and turned back to
Twila. "She'll be gone till tomorrow evening, at least—
maybe longer. Come on, I'll get you something to eat
while we wait for Sally. I don't know about you, but I'm
starved."

Dumbfounded, Twila could hardly move. Melinda had
described in detail Twila's flight from the biodome, as
though she had been standing there watching the whole
episode. And the tree . . . Twila tried to remember what
prompted her to crawl under the tree, when she didn't
even know Security was still searching for her. How
could Melinda know those things? She had to have been

there! Yet Twila knew from the woman's condition that Melinda had not left this sickbed for a very long time.

Tim tugged on her hand, and she stumbled after him into the kitchen. The only thing that had made sense to her since she set foot in the house was that Melinda had just slipped into catatonia, which might last for days— one of the symptoms of advanced CM. One day, she would slip into such a coma and not awaken. But that did not jibe with her being able to tell Twila about the escape . . .

Her voice returned, and Twila demanded, "How could she see me? How did she know these things happened to me?"

Tim turned from the counter where he was slicing into a fresh loaf of brown bread. A secretive smile sparkled on his face. "Because she's special," he replied cryptically. "We're all special, we survivors. You're special now, too." He dipped a knife into a crockery jar and globbed creamy yellow butter onto the slices of bread. "They don't know about it in your biodome, because you eject all the special ones. The gangsters don't know about it, either, because they kill each other off before anyone can find out. But the founders of this community took a different approach, and so we learned." He set the buttered bread on the table along with a large jar of fruit preserves, then sat down and indicated Twila should do likewise. Still stunned, she obeyed.

"About eighteen months after manifestation," he explained, "people begin to lapse into periods of unconsciousness. At first, there's nothing to them, but then— you start to fly."

"Fly?" she echoed dumbly.

"That's really a poor way to describe it," he admitted. "I guess you could call it psychoporting. What happens is, your mind leaves your body and is able to travel on its own."

"Out-of-body experiences," Twila said. "I've heard of that, yes. A person feels like they've left their body lying in bed while their mind wanders the planet. I didn't know that was a symptom of CM."

"You don't just feel it," Tim corrected, "it really happens. Flyers see things. They can see our herds of cattle up in the summer pastures. They can see when a wolf comes marauding, and sometimes even follow it to its lair. They can prowl the city looking for salvage. They can even peer into your biodome, although not many do. They say that's a very disquieting experience."

"The whole thing sounds disquieting to me," Twila managed.

Tim laughed. "But it's not. You should see the rapture on the faces of the flyers when they come back. Flying—psychoporting—is absolutely exhilarating. So they say. I haven't done it yet."

Yet? Twila's eyes strayed unconsciously to Tim's hands. He smiled and held one out; it trembled slightly. "Yes," he told her. "I manifested about a year ago. I'm on my way now."

"You sound almost glad," she breathed incredulously.

"Why not?" He took a huge bite of bread laden with preserves, chewed a moment, then talked around it. "In the biodome they teach you that physical contact is bad, and they're wrong about that. Dead wrong. Why shouldn't they be wrong about CM, too?"

"But you *die*!" Twila blurted.

"Do we?" Tim swallowed. "A flyer goes on longer and longer trips. Eventually the body ceases to function. But what of the mind? Isn't it still out there, somewhere, traveling? Forever rapturous?"

Sally took Twila to a small cottage near the school. "Meghan and Justine have agreed to take you in," Sally told her. "They each have a daughter, plus Meghan's sister Tina lives with them. We find that refugees adapt better if they have living arrangements similar to what they had in the dome, at least to begin with. Since you lived with other women, I looked for a house with all girls for you. But anytime you find living arrangements you prefer, you're free to move in."

"Thank you," Twila said. "I appreciate your thoughtfulness." No such consideration had been given her with the Hats. Sally struck her as a bit remote, but her intentions seemed good.

"Everyone works here," Sally continued as she banged on the door—loudly, trying to override the sound of happy childish shrieking inside. "Meghan and her sister look after half a dozen small children while their parents work; but Kent, next door"—she waved a hand to the north—"goes out to the vegetable gardens. I thought that might be a good place for you to start. You did say you're a plant specialist?"

"Yes," Twila replied, "but I hope to learn other skills as well."

"You will," Sally promised, pounding on the door again. "And teach us some, I suspect. But we know how to play, as well; every Saturday there's a social, a dance, and Sunday is a rest day. Some worship; most just take time for things they enjoy—games, art, visiting, etc. Our ancestors found that one day of rest every week was good for the spirit. Are you a worshiper, Twila?"

Twila blinked. "Uh . . . no." There was little of organized religion left in the biodome. A couple of conferences were dedicated to theology, and several holographic programs offered people an opportunity to worship, but even those were largely unstructured, offering surroundings for meditation more than inspirational teachings. Twila had never known anyone who practiced religion.

"This town originally had a couple of religious orders in it," Sally went on; "so we've always felt a bond with spirituality. But there are a few people here . . ." She hesitated, which surprised Twila. She had found Sally to be forthright and unshakably sure of herself to this point. "They're pretty adamant about their beliefs," Sally went on. "You're bound to run into one of them, probably very soon, and I just want you to know we don't all believe that way. To most of us, religion is a personal thing, and we don't tell others what to believe. So these people—just be patient with them," she finished, as the sound of someone hushing the children within reached them. "And don't be frightened by them."

Long after Sally had gone, Twila continued to puzzle over this obscure warning.

The dance hall was crowded and noisy and absolutely huge. Accustomed to her computer-generated dance hall, which even in appearance was only an eighth the size of this place, Twila found herself feeling slightly overwhelmed by the mass of talking, moving people she faced. She'd been told the inhabitants of the Springs numbered nearly three hundred, and she was sure every one of them was here.

At her side, Tim saw the worried look on her face and squeezed her hand reassuringly. "Don't be afraid," he shouted into her ear, which was necessary to be heard above the general din. "They're all very nice people, and by now they've all heard about you. They'll try to be considerate."

The music blasting through the room was late-twentieth-century rock and roll. People of all ages jigged and bounced to the throbbing rhythm, some in pairs, some in groups, some individually. None of them performed artistically, to Twila's eye; their movement seemed epitomized by an energetic two-year-old who stood boldly in the center of the dance floor, stomping his feet and waving his arms with great joy and little regard for the beat.

When Tim led her onto the dance floor, however, Twila rapidly forgot her uneasiness. Caught by the driving rhythm, she was soon lost in her own inventive steps, twirling and twitching and twisting. She was aware of people watching her, but that was only natural. People always watched Twila when she began to dance.

Neither was she surprised when her partners changed often. They all seemed young to her, in their early teens, but she surmised that most of the older teens were married. A few men Tim's age asked her to dance; no doubt they were looking for a second wife. Twila danced with everyone who asked; and when no one was quick enough with an offer, she would join a group of women dancing together.

The slow dances were strange at first. She had promised herself she would not shy away from them, but learn to touch her partner as she had seen in old flatscreen vids. What was awkward, however, was not the touching, but learning to follow her partner's steps. For years she had relied on visual cues in matching steps for holographic dancing; with touch dancing, she discovered that cues were mostly tactile. So close to her partner she could not see his feet, she had to learn to anticipate his movements by the tension in his limbs, the gentle pressure of his hands. At first she stumbled, and was terribly embarrassed; but after a few dances she got the sense of it, and moved more smoothly.

After an hour or so of continuous dancing, she found Tim once more at her elbow. "It's warm in here," he shouted, bending close to her ear. "Let's go outside for a minute."

The night air was a relief, as much for the absence of sound as for the coolness. Twila's ears rang as they walked away from the people clustered outside the building and onto the thick, spongy grass of the school yard. "You really are something," Tim commented as the music and noise receded behind them. "How did you learn to dance like that?"

Twila laughed. "Years of practice. Botany was my career, but dance was my passion."

"And still can be. I hope you'll give lessons to some of our children."

"I'd love to!" Twila exclaimed.

"But next winter," Tim added hastily, "when things aren't quite so busy. Winter is a time for study and lessons; summer is a time for work, for growing things."

"It's the same in the biodome," she agreed. "Summer is physical work; winter is paperwork."

He laughed, and Twila thought his face in the moonlight was almost handsome. "I always hated paperwork," he admitted ruefully. "I'm happiest with the cattle and horses, or riding up into the mountains to cut firewood. Let Len and others like him learn how to keep the generators running, or how to improve the water system."

"I've been meaning to ask," Twila put in, "how do you get running water without electricity?"

"Magic!" he teased. "Actually, we do have some electricity, enough to run pumps. It's generated by a waterwheel in the river. Cold water is piped up from the river, hot water from the springs."

"The springs?" she asked. "Is springwater hot?"

They had stopped under a tree on the far end of the school yard. He grinned down at her, enjoying his role of teacher. "*Our* springwater is. That's how the town got started here, a couple centuries ago. There's a natural hot spring that bubbles to the surface here. There used to be public bathhouses, although they fell into ruin sometime ago, and we haven't bothered to rebuild them. We just pipe the water into our water system, so we don't have to waste fuel heating water for washing. In the winter, we use it for heating, too, although we can't heat the whole town that way. People still use wood."

"Is it really hot enough to warm a house?" she marveled.

"A hundred and six degrees, out of the ground," he replied. "Here, that is. Other places where it comes to the surface, it varies from a hundred and two to a hundred and eight. Or so I'm told. I don't carry a thermometer with me."

"What other places?"

"Well," he drawled, and a nostalgic look stole over his features. "There's a spot up the canyon several miles, up in the woods, where there are some rock pools—part natural, part built up. The hot water flows out of the ground and fills up these pools like a steaming bathtub. People like to go up there and bathe in the pools."

The only bathing Twila had ever done was in a shower stall. "You mean they take soap and—"

"No, no!" he laughed. "We wouldn't pollute the place with soap! No, this is a place for soaking; just sitting in the hot water, feeling it relax all your muscles, warming you so deep that you can get out and walk around naked for hours without feeling chilled."

The thought sent a shiver through Twila. "And people go there together."

"Always together." He leaned back against the trunk of the tree, holding her hands in both of his. "Couples, especially. It's a special place, a place to . . . learn about each other. To be private, and close to the woods and the mountains. All of nature, and only two people. I don't think I'm saying it right."

"Oh, you're saying it right," Twila told him, her heart thudding. The image was a vivid one, something she might expect to find in a holographic program designed for a private link. It had an effect on her that was not surprising. Or perhaps it was Tim who was having the effect on her. He spread his arms wide, still clasping her hands, which drew her closer to him.

"Does the idea frighten you?" he asked softly.

"You frighten me," she whispered. "I don't know why I trust you so."

He dropped her hands and slid his arms quickly around her waist, pulling her slowly, inexorably closer. "How much do you trust me?" he asked.

"Enough, I think," she breathed. "But you must go slowly, oh, so slowly."

"As slowly as you like," he promised, pressing his lips against her forehead. They were warm and soft, and Twila was aware of nothing but their touch. "We'll just start tonight and go step by gentle step." His lips brushed her eyes now, a cheek, the top of her nose. "Just as slowly and carefully as you like." And then they were on her mouth, teasing, coaxing, until her response was as eager as his.

It was late May, and even at this elevation the afternoon sun was hot. Twila toiled between the rows of squash plants, clawing persistent weeds from the ground with her tri-pronged cultivator. Labor here had a different feel to it than in the biodome. Part of that, she realized, was because it went from sunup to sundown, as opposed to the four-hour shift of Required Labor she, as a student, had been accustomed to. Each morning she and Kent walked three miles to the fields, worked till mid-morning when Kent's very pregnant wife Judy showed up with lunch, then worked till noon when they ate what remained of the morning lunch and flopped in the shade for an hour's nap—a "siesta," they called it. After their siesta, they went back to work until about four, when Judy again brought them a lunch. Then it was more labor until the sunlight on the eastern canyon wall disappeared and they trudged their weary way homeward. There, ravenous, Twila managed to consume more food than she'd thought humanly possible before falling into exhausted slumber, only to rise again the next day and repeat the cycle.

But labor here felt different for other reasons, too. One of them was the companionship of Kent and other workers. There was little idle chatter as they worked—no one had breath to spare—but there were discussions of the plants and the seasons and other "shoptalk," which Twila had previously known only through flatscreen connections. And in the shade of the cottonwood and oak trees, as they ate and rested, there was socialization of the kind she had formerly experienced via computer terminal. Community laughter, practical jokes, and horseplay were new to her.

What gave this labor its distinctive feel, however, was the absence of a ceiling over her head, or artificial walls within view. Though stone enclosed them on two sides, the canyon walls here soaring high over their heads, the ambience was one of openness and unfettered space. She had seen birds overhead while living with the Hats; she had felt the breeze rushing between buildings of the city. But here, birds were the lords of the realm, not intruders on man-made ruins. The breeze that cooled her sweat-soaked body and tossed grit in her eyes was master of the canyon, not a sly vagabond stealing through another's domain. Sometimes Twila would pause to look upward at the azure sky, at the limitless space above her, and once again vertigo would strike her. Then she would have to bury the blade of her hoe in the earth, binding herself to the land, until the feeling passed.

This was her third week with the mountaineers, and the first in which Twila felt she was beginning to find her place in this society. The irritation she had originally known at living in a household with small children had vanished; for six days a week she didn't spend enough time in the house to notice them, since they were asleep when she left in the morning, and fed and out of the way before she returned. She had been distressed to discover that on Saturday nights she was too tired to enjoy dancing; but this week she thought her improved stamina would help her hold up longer. Meghan had suggested she teach some of the Springites one or two of the Latin dances she knew, things they had seen her perform, and Twila was looking forward to that. Tim had come calling each Sunday, but he never had more than a few hours to spare because of Melinda; and Twila found visiting with Melinda a disquieting experience. She understood that Melinda knew about, and did not object to, the caresses she and Tim shared on Saturday evenings, but it still made Twila uncomfortable in the other woman's presence. Furthermore, there was something eerie about Melinda, with her pinched, hollow face radiant from visions, eyes bright with the virus that was slowly killing her brain. It was not just looking upon the face of death; it was Melinda's quiet, unspoken assumption that her disease was not an affliction, but a blessing.

But Tim had asked last weekend if Twila would plan to spend the entire day with him this Sunday. Just the two of them, on a horseback ride up the canyon. It set her nerves thrumming to think what might come of a day alone with him; yet mingled with the apprehension was an undeniable sense of excitement.

The jingling of a bridle caused Twila to look up. Tim was riding down the canyon road, wicker basket in hand. He reined in under a cottonwood at the edge of the field, and all the workers there converged upon him. "I told Judy I'd bring the lunch today," Tim called to Kent. "As a matter of fact, we should find someone else to carry it out to you now until the baby comes. Maybe Ronnie can put it on a wagon and pull it. He's what, seven now? He should be able to handle that." Ronnie was Judy's stepson from her first marriage.

"Good idea," chimed Sylvia, taking the basket from Tim and beginning to spread its contents in the shade. "Maybe it will keep him from using the oil can on the petunias." Earlier that week Kent had regaled them all with the story of the little boy's attempt to "fertilize" Judy's flower garden with axle grease.

"I'll talk to Judy about it." Kent flopped down in the thick grass and shoved an entire hard-boiled egg into his mouth. "I imagine she can be persuaded." Kent was a lank, red-haired boy of fifteen with more freckles than Twila thought could fit on a human face. Judy was seventeen, with two children of her own in addition to Ronnie, and a proud determination to share in the community's workload, in spite of her advanced pregnancy.

"Tell her she has to keep cooking, though," Raul admonished as he tore into a cold leg of turkey. "No one roasts a bird to perfection like Judy."

Twila smiled, knowing the compliment would go a long way toward placating Judy's pride when her husband put forth his suggestion.

Twila helped herself to a sandwich and an apple before dropping into the grass and leaning back against the bole of the cottonwood. Tim joined her, leaving Rex to crop the sweet green blades nearby. "Tired?" he asked.

"As usual—although it's getting better," she told him. "I no longer fall asleep while I'm eating." Then she laughed. "I think I might make it through the entire dance this Saturday."

"I may not come," he told her. "Since we're going up the canyon on Sunday, I might spend the evening with Melinda. If she's awake."

"Of course," Twila forced herself to say, though the sandwich felt suddenly very dry in her throat.

Then Tim cast a glance around at the other workers. "I might steal Twila away from you next Monday," he announced casually to the group in general. "Be sure you work her twice as hard when she gets back."

"Don't worry," Sylvia quipped, "we'll send her down to Lorraine to pull the mower when Bonnie goes lame." Everyone laughed. Bonnie was a worn-out workhorse who daily plodded along the various roads in the canyon pulling a small-swathed mower that kept the weeds from encroaching too badly on the dirt trails.

Twila laughed, too, but gave Tim an inquiring look. "I thought we might camp overnight," he said quietly. "If we want to. Have the option, anyway. We'll see."

Twila flushed, for the idea of spending a night alone with Tim, resting in each other's arms, frightened her. And excited her. She reached for her canteen and took a drink to cover her embarrassment; but her friends were still joking about Lorraine's mare and had either not heard, or not cared about, the exchange.

"Is that okay with you?" Tim asked.

"An option is just that, an option," Twila replied. "I'll know better when we get there."

He grinned in response and struggled to his feet. "Well, I'd better get back to work. I'm breaking a new team to harness this afternoon. I'll take that basket back to Judy, if it's empty."

But Kent waved him off. "I'll take it to her when we quit for the day."

"Hey, Tim," Raul called. "You going up the canyon anytime soon?"

Tim hesitated. "Maybe."

"Take a look around, will you?" Raul asked. "Someone said they saw my sister Gloria up there last week."

A shadow of concern passed over Tim's face. "I'll keep an eye out," he promised dubiously, "but even if she's there . . ." His voice trailed off.

"I'd just like to know," Raul mumbled into the turkey leg.

Tim nodded, then mounted his horse and started back up the road.

Twila looked around the group sprawled in the shade, hoping someone would tell her who Gloria was, but they seemed intent on eating in silence. She got the distinct impression it would not be wise to ask.

Chapter 13

Twila's first trip up the canyon was breathtaking. Mounted on a gentle mare named Sugar, she let the animal follow Tim's gelding while her senses drank in the beauty all around her. Tall, sweeping pines brushed skies that were edged by the canyon walls, like a startling blue canvas stretched in a rustic frame of pinkish-red and buff. Birds called to each other, insects chittered, and the creek rushed its way over stones and logs, eager to reach its destination. The air was still cool and moist when they started out in the early morning, but soon enough they would be peeling off their jackets as the sun made its warmth felt on the canyon floor.

Everything was green and lush from the spring runoff. Wildflowers breathed gentle colors among the emerald grasses and weeds. A mile up the road from the town, orchards were planted—apple and cherry—and they stopped so Twila could inspect them. Among the trees were the remains of numerous buildings. "Another town?" Twila asked.

"No, the rectory and so forth for a religious order," Tim replied. "This canyon has a very spiritual heritage: first the Anasazi with their kivas, then the Jemez, the Spanish and their churches, and the Europeans. And us. But no one wanted to live this far north of town, so we stripped the buildings for materials generations ago."

They rode on, past a peculiar rock formation, a white and crusted arch that looked to be formed by calcium deposits. The creek foamed out from under it like carbonated water. Small puddles dampened the roadside, though it had not rained in weeks. Twila thought she saw steam rising from them; and sure enough, when she touched the puddles they were warm, their water seeping up from deep within the volcanic rock.

Around mid-morning, Tim turned his horse off the road and into a flat, grassy area overlooking the creek to the east. They had crossed the snaking watercourse several times on their journey, the bridges built a century ago standing as solid testimony to the engineering technology of the past. Dismounting, Tim picketed the horses in the lush greenery, then helped Twila unload their gear. "This is a beautiful spot," she commented, thinking that the ground would not be too lumpy to sleep on here.

"Not as beautiful as the place we're going," Tim told her with a grin. "It's on the other side of the river, up there." He pointed east and slightly north. "It's a bit of a climb; the horses can't cross the river here, let alone navigate the steep slope on the other side, so we'll have to be our own pack animals. Come on!" Shouldering their camping gear, he stepped off the edge of the miniature meadow and crab-walked his way down the nearly vertical bank to the river's edge.

Twila followed cautiously, a knapsack with their food slung on her back. She was tempted to sit down and slide on the slippery grass to the bottom, but she had already encountered enough of the native vegetation to know that stickers were everywhere. So she did her best to pick her way down the slope, using her heavy canvas shoes and gloved hands.

Huge boulders lined the creek at this point, and the water between them ran fast and deep. Thornbushes and desert broom clawed at them as they followed the footpath, which, for all the encroaching creepers, gave evidence of being well-used. The rocky, gravelly ground underfoot was the same reddish hue as the bluffs rearing their regal heads beyond the creek, but it bore a carpet of golden pine needles. Red and gold and vivid green—a feast for the senses, Twila thought. "By the way," Twila asked as she followed Tim panting upstream. "How are *we* going to get across the creek?"

"Tree," Tim called back over his shoulder.

Twila balked, gave her head a shake, then repeated, "No, I asked, how are we going to get across the creek?"

Now he laughed. "I heard you," he replied. "And I said,

tree. See, there it is!" He pointed to where a huge log stretched from one rocky bank to another. It was a good three feet in diameter and had been stripped of its bark, but the surface looked round and slippery to Twila. "I was about ten when we brought this one down," Tim continued. "It stood on the far side, and we threw ropes across to this side and hitched it to a team of horses up there on the road to drag it into place." He pointed behind them, where the road was now a good forty feet over their heads. "But it's much better than the old bridge. There were two logs to that, each one resting on boulders only partway across, and you had to transfer from one to the other midstream."

As they came to the head of that makeshift bridge, Twila lowered her knapsack and stood staring at the large, round trunk. It rested on chunks of gray stone some four to eight feet in diameter; they were strewn down the opposite bank as well, looking like giant building blocks that had tumbled down the precipitous slope from the nearby bluffs. Moss and lichens crusted the ancient boulders, but the log looked yellow and firm and new. Both rocks and log were damp with the spray of the muddy creek water, which swirled madly around these obstacles as though it knew that, given the millennia, it would inevitably grind them to dust.

Tim was climbing up onto the felled tree, and it neither rocked nor sagged as he stepped out on it. But the water crashed over stones with deadly force only a few feet beneath. "Come on," Tim called gaily. "It'll hold us both."

Her stomach churning, Twila reshouldered her pack and climbed up the rocks to mount the treacherous bridge. *It's all a matter of balance,* she told herself, *and you've got great balance. It'll be just like walking along the top of those block walls in the city.*

But the block walls were not round and damp, and they did not have certain death sweeping past beneath them.

Tim was two thirds of the way across now. "Don't look down," he called back sharply, seeing the fear in her face. "The movement of the water will throw you. Just look across, here, at me."

Obediently Twila raised her eyes and found that her

stomach settled. "Cone on," Tim coaxed. "I'll wait here till you catch up."

Slowly she inched her way out onto the great tree. Her footing was uneven, and she wanted to look down to see where the knots and boles were, but Tim was right; better to keep looking straight ahead. Carefully, sliding her feet and testing each step before shifting her weight, she began to make her way across.

By the time she reached Tim, she had grown more confident, and when he turned to walk blithely to the far shore, she lagged only a little behind him. When she scrambled off the log and back onto solid ground, her heart was pounding, but it was more from natural exertion than from fear. "Good girl!" Tim praised. "I'd forgotten how scary that is the first time. I've been doing it since I was six. You have great strength of character, doing things that frighten you."

"Or great lack of common sense," she panted. "I've never been sure which."

"Well, come on," he encouraged, "it's all uphill from here."

And indeed it was. The trail was marked by splashes of paint on the boulders, and it zigged and zagged up the steep slope among the dense pines. Here and there large stones or small pieces of timber had been set into the ground to give firmer footing, but it was still an arduous climb. After several minutes Twila could hear water running on her left, but the thick foliage and boulders blocked any view of the stream until, quite suddenly, they were at the pools.

There were three of them. Water from the highest one sluiced over smooth stones to fill one directly below, while a third was off to the left and fed by water gushing from a corroded pipe. Some of the stones that rimmed the pools had obviously been set, but no masonry was evident. Nature supplied the grouting of red volcanic dirt and grass roots, which kept the water from slipping away too rapidly. Below the lowest pool, however, it splashed and tumbled away over timeworn rocks in a noisy cascade to the cold mountain stream below.

Tim did not stop by the first pool, but kept climbing upward. "Almost there," he told her. "We'll dump our gear at the top, then come back. I don't know about you, but I'm ready for a long, hot soak."

Above the highest pool the ground was bare and rocky, but there was a small open patch where all the stones had been cleared away, and here Tim stopped and began to deposit his gear. On all sides the pines stretched gracefully upward, their tops waving slightly in a breeze that never touched the forest floor. Gratefully Twila dropped her knapsack beside the rest of the camping gear, and reached for her canteen. "It's beautiful!" she breathed. "Oh, Tim, it's just the right amount of sky!"

He laughed. "To tell the truth, that's the way I feel, too. I don't care much for open country. Give me the tall trees and some mountain peaks, and just about that much blue sky." He drank long and deeply from his canteen, then tossed it aside and began to tug off his sturdy leather boots.

It looked like a good idea. Twila pulled off her stiff-soled canvas shoes and heavy socks, wriggling her toes deliciously in the open air. The shoes had been obtained in the city, necessary for tramping the asphalt streets and brushy yards of that place. They had been useful in the fields, too, protecting her feet from thorny weeds and sharp stones. But like most domizens, she was accustomed to going barefoot or wearing only light slippers while indoors, or riding the transit from one building to another. Even when she worked in the orchards, Twila wore only light canvas shoes with thin leather soles. Now she rubbed at the calluses that were forming on the balls of her feet. How nice to walk barefoot on the smooth, powdery earth!

Tim had not stopped with his boots, however. He had shed his cotton shirt, and now he was climbing out of his denim trousers. Twila flushed and looked away. It was not that she had never seen a man undress before; but she had never been physically present.

Tim saw her discomfiture and stopped with his underwear still in place. "Well, I'm going down to the pool," he announced. "You come when you're ready. You can cover up with one of the blankets and just sit on the edge for a while, if you're uncomfortable." Then he stripped off the last of his clothing and walked away.

For several moments Twila sat, cheeks burning, cursing herself. Simpleton! He said they bathed in the pools. Did you think they did it with clothes on? And what's the big deal? You've displayed yourself to men before, and in more tantalizing fashion than this. Just take your clothes off and follow him down.

Angrily she peeled out of her shirt and trousers, demanding that her hands not shake, and being refused. Parting with her underwear was more unnerving. She debated about untying a bedroll and using the blanket as he had suggested, but she was embarrassed by the foolishness of it. Finally she compromised by pulling her shirt back on, but fastening only one button at her waist to keep it from flopping open. Somewhat comforted, she picked her way delicately to the upper pool.

Tim was sitting at the edge, kicking his feet lazily in the steaming water. He smiled up at her as she joined him, and made no comment about the shirt. "This pool's a little hot for me," he told her. "Let's move down to the lower one."

Twila could not help watching him as he climbed to his feet and made his way down the steep bit of trail to the next pool. For all his lankiness, he was quite graceful, and his bones were well covered with muscle. Not as beautiful as a dancer, nor as muscular as an athlete, but there was an easy rhythm to his movements that spoke of strength and daily labor.

This lower pool was far shallower than the one above, no more than eighteen inches, but it was nearly eight feet in diameter. Tim stretched himself out on the dirt bottom, sending bits of soil and plant material swirling and clouding the water, gradually to settle on his pale skin. "Ahhh!" he sighed as the water enveloped him. "I can feel the heat seeping into my bones."

Tentatively, Twila stepped into the pool. She gave a short gasp, for it was much hotter than she had imagined, raising gooseflesh on her legs at the sudden change in temperature. After a moment, though, her skin stopped tingling, and she sat down on the mossy stones that rimmed the pool.

Tim sat across from her, eyes closed in contentment, his head and shoulders propped on the stones as he slouched his torso under the water. "When I was a little boy," he said, "we used to sneak up here, my friends and I, to peek at the girls when they came bathing. It was the beginning of my sexual education."

"Will anyone come and peek at us?" Twila wanted to know.

"No." He smiled. "They'll see our horses across the creek, and they know Rex; they know what I'll do to them if they wander over here."

It seemed an idle threat to Twila, but she chose to believe him. It was more comfortable that way. A breeze stirred her hair and her shirt. She undid the sole button and let the garment slip off; then she slid quickly into the tinglingly hot water.

The particles of dirt in the pool felt gritty on her skin, and she tried vainly to brush them away; but every movement of her hands stirred up more dirt from the bottom. Finally she gave up and settled back into the water, mimicking Tim's slouching position. The view down over the canyon was spectacular; the brick red of the soil, the verdant green of the foliage, the deep brown of the tree trunks. Truly magnificent! she thought. This is what the word *breathtaking* was coined to describe.

When she looked back, Tim's eyes were open, and he was watching her. "It's magnificent," she told him.

"Yes, you are," he replied.

Heat crept into her cheeks that had nothing to do with the water, and she looked back over the canyon. "Do you intend to make love to me?" she asked.

"Eventually. When you want me to." He stirred a little in the water, and she could feel the ripples it made under the surface. "But I intend to soak for a while first. And to watch you. You truly are magnificent."

Twila didn't quite know how to reply to that. "Perhaps only different," she said after a moment. She had noticed very few dark-complected people among the mountaineers, and no women with her compliment of thick black curls.

"I guess exotic is the word," he admitted, struggling to sit up a little straighter. Twila could feel his eyes on her, traveling slowly from her face to her toes and back. "So tiny, and dark."

"And you so tall," she said quietly.

The simple remark evoked a visible reaction, despite the temperature of the water.

"You do want to, don't you?" he asked. "Make love with me. Eventually."

"Well, my mind wants to," she confided, "but I'm not quite sure how my body is going to react."

"Oh, is that all!" He laughed an easy laugh, and Twila glanced up to see his blue eyes sparkling in the deeply tanned face. His foot stretched out to brush against her leg. "As long as your mind is willing, and your heart, I know I can convince your body to tag along."

He was true to his word, and to all the promises he had made her. By the time he entered her, she was aching for him, willing to bear the initial discomfort in order to be satisfied—and satisfied she was. When they left the pools to return to the clearing, neither bothered to dry or dress, letting the sun bake the moisture from their skin. They ate ravenously, dozed in the sun, and before the light slipped away, they made love again.

Night fell quickly, and the warmth of the day disappeared with it, but Tim and Twila cuddled together in their blankets, gazing up at the myriad stars, whispering and laughing and sharing kisses. A small campfire warmed stones whose radiant heat lasted into the night, and in the morning they fled quickly from the meadow to the pools to warm themselves once more.

"I have to go up the mountain next week to check the cattle in the summer pastures," Tim told her as they soaked up to their chins in the steaming water. "I'll be gone for a couple of weeks, maybe more, depending on what I find up there."

Twila felt a crushing disappointment, along with a strange sense of relief. She wanted to make love with Tim again, and soon; but she was not ready to move into his house with his strange first wife, and she'd been afraid he would ask.

"You could come with me," Tim suggested.

Twila thought about that. It would be nice, having Tim all to herself for a couple of weeks; but what would he expect following that? And there was the unspoken work code; how would her comrades in the vegetable gardens feel if she disappeared for several weeks, for no other reason than that she wanted to tag along with Tim in the mountains?

His hand stroked her smooth, flat belly. "It would increase our chances, you know."

"Chances?"

"Of having a baby."

Twila bolted upright, sloshing water over the stones, and stared at Tim.

"Well, that is what happens, you know," he observed dryly. "A natural consequence of making love."

Twila's jaw worked, but for a moment no sound would come out. "I know that's what happens," she stammered finally. "It's just—I hadn't thought of it in those terms. Domizens don't have babies that way."

Now it was his turn to look startled. "How *do* they have babies?"

"By artificial insemination," she replied. "Look, I know what—I mean, I realize that—I just didn't stop to think about it, that's all. Babies and sex have never been connected for me."

Now he sat up and looked at her seriously. "You do want babies, don't you, Twila?" he asked anxiously.

Want them! "Of course I want babies, Tim. You might say my leaving the biodome had something to do with wanting babies, but—I'm not sure now is the right time for me to add yet another change to my life. I'm just getting my feet, Tim, trying to figure out where I belong, how I fit. A baby—" She shook her head.

"A baby will help you fit," he encouraged.

"In your eyes, in the eyes of your community," she agreed. "But I need to fit in *my* eyes. And until I'm a little more comfortable with that . . ."

He looked gravely disappointed, but he nodded his head. "I can understand that, I guess."

"We can still make love, can't we?" she asked, suddenly afraid that he would avoid touching her in order to honor her request.

In answer he wrapped her in his arms and planted a long, demanding kiss on her lips. "I'll make love to you whenever you want," he whispered huskily. "I care for you, Twila, and I want to be with you. But I have certain obligations . . .”

Of course. The obligation to propagate. When a man's wife could no longer bear him children, he was expected to find someone else who could. If Twila was not willing, he must find another.

“Just give me a couple of months,” she pleaded. “Can you do that? Can we wait just a couple of months before we—before we deliberately try to make a baby?”

He smiled softly at her. “Sure we can,” he agreed. “Hell, when I first met you, I was sure it would take a couple of months before you'd even want to make love. A baby can wait that long.”

They had packed up their gear and were getting ready to start back down to the tree bridge when the girl came walking out of the trees to the north. Tim let the bedroll he was hoisting to his shoulder drop back to the ground and watched her approach, but she did not return his gaze. Clad in a heavy wool serape, her hair a disheveled mass of chestnut brown, she ignored them in her singleminded trek across the clearing.

“Good morning, Gloria,” Tim called as she passed them by.

“Morning, Tim,” she muttered, never taking her eyes from her destination.

It was hard for Twila to tell how old she was. With sunburned face and wild, uncombed hair, she could have been anywhere from fifteen to thirty-five. “Who is that?” Twila whispered, but Tim waved her to silence. He watched the girl disappear down the trail; then slowly he followed her. Twila tagged along behind him.

At the edge of the clearing, they stopped, looking down on the upper pool. Gloria had thrown her serape aside, along with some other indeterminate garment, and was submerged in the steaming hot water with only her head protruding. Her ruddy face was turned upward, eyes closed. Unclothed, she looked younger—fifteen or sixteen, Twila thought. For these people, middle-aged.

“Your brother was asking about you,” Tim called down to her.

“The wind is my brother” was her cryptic reply.

"He worries about you, you know."

Now her eyes snapped open, and they burned like dark embers in her face. "Tell him to worry about his soul!" she snarled. "All of you, if you want to worry, worry about your souls! It's a dark god you worship, a dark and seductive god that eats you alive, and I'll not be part of it!"

Tim turned away in disgust, going back for their gear. Twila followed him, as the girl's voice carried through the clearing after them. "I'll never be part of it!" she howled. "I'll never offer children to the demon, never teach them to bow down to its bitter command, to offer themselves as willing sacrifice at its bloody maw! Never! And all you who do will burn in hell for it, do you hear me? Fight it! Fight the evil, don't make love to it! Reject the spirit that steals upon you, that fills your head with sweet lies and false euphoria!"

Tim had shouldered his burden and began grimly down the trail. Gloria rose from the water as they passed, her pale skin pink from its heat. "Cry out against it!" she shouted at Tim. "Abandon those who have succumbed to it, and flee to the woods! None can save your bodies, not even these ancient mountains, but God can save your immortal soul. Make sacrifice to him, not to the demon! Offer your life to his service, not the service of this evil thing you worship! He gives life; the demon only cheats you. You think it gives life, but it gives only death. Do you hear me, Tim? Tell my brother . . ."

Her words floated after them as they descended the steep slope to the river, until finally the rush of its waters drowned them out.

"Gloria's crazy," Tim explained bluntly as they rode down the mountain toward the Springs. "She went off the deep end a couple years ago, and she's been living out in the wilderness since then. God knows what she eats, or where she sleeps; I don't even want to think about it."

"What demon was she talking about?" Twila asked, still shaken by the encounter. "What sacrifices?"

"She means CM," he replied, his disgust with Gloria ill concealed.

"It's not a demon, it's a disease!" Twila protested. "It's

not like you're intentionally contracting it. You're not purposely giving it to your children. There's nothing you can do about it!"

"Gloria's beyond reason," he said. "She was always into mysticism, wanted to revive the religious order that built the school—nuns, I think they were called. Celibate, if you can imagine. Well, everyone's entitled to their beliefs, I guess. But Gloria was obnoxious about it. Brayed all over town that she was going to be celibate, as though that made her better than everyone else. And then—" He broke off.

"What?" Twila prompted.

"She was raped."

Twila gasped. "I thought you didn't have rape here."

"We're not perfect," he protested. "There have been thievery and assault and other crimes at the Springs—even a murder once, in the early days—but they're considered just that, crimes, and they get punished. Nobody condoned what the boy did. He was sorry himself, afterward—it started out as a joke, a bad joke, and it just went too far. Way too far. But Gloria,"—Tim took a deep breath and blew it out loudly—"she was unstable to begin with, that's what I think, and it just sent her over the edge. She'll never be sane again."

Edgewalker, Twila thought. *My grandmother was killed by an Edgewalker. But poor Gloria . . . poor Gloria . . .*

Tim reached out and stroked Twila's cheek, a wry smile on his face. "Don't let her scare you," he soothed. "She's not dangerous, just . . . annoying. Mostly she stays out in the woods, anyway. Hardly ever comes to town to preach at us anymore."

"Preach at you?"

"Not to have children who are born to die."

Born to die . . . That had been the fate of Twila's children, of the countless fetuses created to be destroyed, so that people like Krell could be safe from CM. Safe to do their jobs; safe to touch each other, to kiss and fondle and have intercourse—oh, it was seductive indeed, the demon that Dr. Krell served. And it was her children who had been sacrificed on its altar—

"Hey—you're not worried about that, are you?" Tim asked gently, searching her face.

Twila looked up, startled, and realized what emotions must have been playing across her face, but she had forgotten what Tim had been speaking of. "Worried about what?" she asked guardedly.

"Having children who will die of CM."

"Oh, that." Twila felt relief swirl through her like a summer breeze. "No, one thing I can say categorically is that I'm not afraid of having children who will die of CM."

"Good." Tim smiled. "Because it's not as frightening as they teach you in the biodome. Look at Melinda—does she seem frightened to you? Or unhappy?"

Twila forced a smile. "Not at all."

But that's what Gloria really meant, she realized. *When she talked about worshiping the demon—she meant the way you almost look forward to manifesting the symptoms of the disease, to having the out-of-body experiences you told me about. She thinks you've been seduced into loving the thing that's killing you.*

Have you? What would you say if you knew that I am immune to CM, that I will never "fly," as you say? Would I still be welcome at the Springs? Would all the boys still want to dance with me on Saturday nights? And you, Tim—if you knew my immunity is hereditary, would you still want me to have your babies?

Chapter 14

Twila woke sweating from a dream in which Gloria raved while townspeople dragged her off. "Cast out the evil!" she screamed at them. "Fight the demon! Drive it from your midst!" And then suddenly she fixed plaintive eyes on Twila and cried pitifully, "But you have to help me, you're my mother!"

Sitting alone in her sweat-soaked sheets, Twila stared hard at the window of her room and willed the dawn to come. It was Sunday, and there was nothing in particular to get up for, except to escape the dream. She had grown to cherish Sundays for many reasons, the luxury of lying in bed being one of them. But there were many things she could do if she got up early, things for which there was no time during the rest of the week. Even though she had grown stronger over the two months and found physical labor less taxing, she missed the five-day work/school week she had known in the biodome. And she missed Papa Joe's.

Maybe I'll go to the school gym and dance, she thought. Yes, that was what she needed to do, dance the nightmare out of her system. She wouldn't have any music to dance to, of course; the generator couldn't be cranked up to provide electricity just for her dance session. What would happen when she began to teach in the fall? Dance steps could be taught to a count, of course, but they never really came to life until there was music. Maybe someone who played an instrument could—

Whoa, she told herself. Best not make too many plans for the fall. Because the nightmare was rooted in fact: inside the biodome, a young girl needed her help. Somehow, and sometime soon, she needed to do something to stop Krell. But she needed a plan, a *plan*, how could she fight Krell? What kind of threat could she make, what kind of leverage could she apply?

Let Jon do it, one part of her said. *Jon knows him; Jon will change things in the biodome; he promised he would.* But when? Soon enough for my oldest daughter? My youngest? Their children?

I can't wait for other people to save me and mine, she decided in the darkness. I had a hard time trusting Jon then, when the nearness of him set my heart pounding and my head swimming—and now he seems so distant. Did I love him? Is that what I felt? It was intense, but was it love? It was so different from what I feel for Tim . . .

Tim. With a great sigh Twila threw her legs over the edge of the bed and struggled upright. She'd better do her dancing early, if that's what she wanted to do; by noon Tim would be expecting her at his house. She looked forward to seeing Tim, of course. But going to his home . . .

Melinda was deteriorating rapidly. She had fewer and fewer wakeful spells, so Tim spent what time he could at home in case she should rouse. But he particularly wanted Twila to be there when Melinda came back from "flying." It still seemed bizarre to Twila, that he should want to present his current lover to his wife; but there was no denying that Melinda seemed to take great pleasure in the relationship between Twila and Tim. *She wants him to be happy, that's all,* Twila told herself.

But there was more to it than that, somehow. It was as though Melinda had chosen Twila for Tim, and was now waiting to see the match borne out. *But you can't predict who will love whom,* Twila thought testily. *Even if Melinda really does psychoport, even if she really did see me making my escape from the biodome, even if it was her voice that whispered to me to crawl under that tree, that doesn't mean she can predict whom Tim will love, or whom I will. And it certainly doesn't mean she knows who should marry whom.*

And if psychoporting is a part of CM, why is there no record of it happening anywhere but this village?

Other things about this village bothered Twila. Melinda had spoken of Tim "feeling" that Twila was in the city, that she was headed north. Because Tim had not yet experienced the catatonic episodes of CM, he did not psychoport; so what was this "feeling"? "He has a gift that way," Melinda had said. Once such gifts had been called extrasensory perception, parapsychology, psychic. Was that what was at work here? Did the changes CM wrought in the brain enhance such abilities? Or did they exist in this particular community unconnected with CM?

Did they exist at all?

Feeling disgruntled, Twila dressed rapidly and then gingerly opened her bedroom door, knowing it would creak and praying it would not waken the babies down the hall. She still felt like a stranger in this house, because it seemed she only ate and slept here. Nearly all her spare time was spent with Tim. She was getting to know his two daughters, and his stepdaughter; but she always got the feeling they thought of her as an oddity. *What if I did marry Tim?* she thought. *Would they ever think of me as their mother? And in a couple of years, when Tim dies . . .*

She had wrestled much with that thought. Now as she padded quietly to the bathroom to answer a call of nature, she tried to shove it away. First things first. She needed to do something for her children in the biodome; then she'd answer the question of whether or not she'd marry Tim. She couldn't resolve the second issue until she had resolved the first.

Two hours of dance were both encouraging and discouraging. Twila was encouraged that not only had she not lost any agility in her art, but she had gained a great deal of strength and stamina from her daily toiling in the fields. But she was discouraged because it did not free her mind and let a solution to her dilemma shine through as she had hoped. Drenched with sweat, she made her way to the river and waded in cautiously, for even at this time of year the current was swift, and Twila had never learned to swim. Just upstream a paddle wheel turned in its endless motion, generating the precious electrical power that drove the pumps supplying both hot and cold water to the village. The icy river water was a shock to Twila's senses, but it did not shock an answer to her beleaguered brain.

After changing clothes and drying her thick black curls in the sun, Twila started for Tim's house. It was nearly noon, and the August sun was hot even here in the sheltered canyon. Her warm brown skin had grown darker

from fieldwork, and she thought sometimes that she would
soon be as dark as a Hat. Still, she loved the feel of the
unfiltered sun and the sweet kiss of the canyon breeze. She
was Outside. On days like this, it still amazed her.

Shading her eyes against the sun, Twila could make out
two figures on Tim's porch. One was unmistakable, the
tall, lank form that quickened her heart and her step. But
who was the other? A long-legged girl in the first blush of
womanhood, with dark brown hair—Delia. It had taken a
moment to recognize her, for her hair was not braided but
worn long and rippling around her shoulders. Twila was
about to call out to them when Tim bent down and kissed
Delia. It was not a long or passionate kiss, but it was definitely a kiss.

A new set of emotions swirled through Twila. Why
should he kiss Delia? Well, why *shouldn't* he? Surely
Twila and Tim had "a relationship," but it was not a
formal one, not yet. Still, it was special—wasn't it special
to him, too? How would he feel if she kissed someone
else? Or was kissing a more casual gesture than she had
thought? This society was very open about touching, and
they shared food and drink in a thoughtless manner that
still made Twila cringe—maybe a kiss was no more than a
wink. Maybe it was a way to say, *you're sweet,* or *thank
you.* Maybe it was considered a "fatherly" gesture.

But Delia was too old to be accepting fatherly gestures
from Tim. She was, in the context of her society, ripe for
marriage.

Confused, Twila considered turning around and going
back home. But then Delia turned and ran from the porch,
and Tim looked after her and saw Twila.

He waved, smiling broadly. Whatever the exchange
between him and Delia, he felt no guilt about it. But Delia
missed a stride when she saw Twila, then smiled in a shy,
almost embarrassed way and slowed her run. "Hi, Twila,"
she said, and Twila thought the flush on her cheeks was
not from running.

"Hi, Delia."

And then the girl brushed past and ran on up the road
toward the town.

As Twila approached the porch, Tim sauntered down
the stairs and lifted her casually off the ground wrapping

long arms around her in a sturdy embrace. "Hi, darlin'," he greeted, placing a firm kiss on her lips.

"Hi, yourself," she replied, feeling odd about the embrace, and awkward.

He sensed it and put her down. "What's wrong?"

"Nothing," she lied, embarrassed by her jealously and suspicion over something that he apparently did not feel worth commenting on. "I had a nightmare last night; it's still hanging with me."

He slid his fingers into her thick, dark hair and tilted her face up to his. "I wish you'd been here with me. Then I could have held you and whispered to you and chased the demons away."

But Twila could not cast off the thought of Delia. "What was Delia doing here?" she asked, in a tone she hoped was simply curious and not accusatory.

Now Tim hesitated. "She asked a favor of me," he said.

What kind of a favor? Twila's brain screamed, but she did not dare ask. There were many possibilities, of course, but Twila knew that a virgin would often ask an older, experienced adult to be his or her first lover. "Opening a virgin," Tim had called it. She knew he had done it before, since Melinda manifested.

But not since he met me, Twila thought doggedly. Monogamy was still ingrained in her, the product of the biodome's disease-conscious society and hundreds of flatscreen movies from a bygone age. It still seemed to her that an intimate relationship excluded sexual encounters with outside partners. That's why she felt so guilty in front of Melinda. That's why she felt so angry now.

"How's Melinda?" she asked, determined to throw the conversation in a new direction.

"Still flying," he replied easily. "It takes her longer and longer to find her way back to her body. I think she'll probably cross over before the end of summer."

Twila knew she would be relieved, and hated herself for feeling that way.

"When are you going to move in with us?" Tim asked, as though it were part of the same thought. "I'd like you here in the last weeks. The girls would, too."

Now it was Twila's turn to hesitate. "I don't know," she admitted. "It just seems like such a big commitment, and—" *And I haven't been honest with you,* she thought. *You don't know about my children, about the battle I must do with Dr. Krell. You don't know that I am immune.* "I want to think about it a little longer."

She knew he was disappointed, but he didn't press her. Instead he switched to a related topic. "Time to start cooking something soon," he hinted, rubbing her flat belly.

There, too, I have not been honest with you, she thought. She covered the thought with a sly smile and a flirtatious look from under thick lashes. "Is that an invitation?" she asked coyly. As long as his libido was fed, she reasoned, it would be easier to stall the question of marriage.

As she expected, his grin reappeared. "Shall I show you the hayloft in the stable?" he suggested.

"Only if there's a blanket between me and the stickers," she pouted. Tim laughed and disappeared into the house, to emerge a moment later with a soft woven rug. Catching her hand, he started off down the path to the stable.

Immediately following their visit to the hot spring pools, Twila had asked her host family if the school might have some textbooks on biology. They obliged by pointing out the local font of knowledge for adults in the community, a small building of corrugated aluminum that housed the Springs' library. Dealing with the printed word was new to Twila, whose entire education had been on-line; however, a helpful schoolchild had shown her the system of paper cards, which told what kind of books were located where, and Twila had delved into research on human reproduction.

She had, of course, studied the subject before, in her schooling and on her own, but never with an eye to contraception; it was not something for which people in the biodome had a need. But now she needed to know when in her monthly cycle the chances of conception were greatest, and how she could decrease those chances further. Oh, she still wanted to bear a child in her own body, and the thought of carrying one of Tim's was far from repugnant—but not now. Not when she had other children, already born, who needed her. So she was very careful about when she made love with Tim, and when she pleaded exhaustion. Thus far, it had worked.

Once she had found and mastered the library, Twila's curiosity pushed her into other reading as well. The Chronicles, a history of the present settlement at the hot springs, answered many questions she'd had about who these people were and how they had managed to survive in such a different state than the Hats and Bariosos. She had also investigated what information they had on immunology, hematology, the history of CM, and fetal tissue research of the late twentieth and early twenty-first centuries. Though it had helped her understand what Dr. Krell and Jon were doing, it did not give her the answer she truly needed—how to convince Krell to stop.

Even now as she followed Tim toward the stable, she knew she ought to tell him, tell him everything. But she was afraid what his reaction might be. Perhaps he would forgo her company for that of someone like Delia, who could give him the children he wanted, and who was probably not afraid to commit herself to raising his other children as well. Someone who knew how to live in a houseful of people as part of a family, and not as the eternal outsider.

It's what you deserve, Twila thought as she looked up at him. If I were a better person, I'd get out of the picture so you could find someone like Delia for your last days. But I'm not that strong, not yet. You are my only anchor in this foreign place.

They were only halfway to the stable when a boy of about six scampered through the front gate and called after them. "Dad?"

Tim stopped reluctantly and turned back to the boy. "Hi, Alan," he greeted. "What's up?"

Twila watched the tyke approach them solemnly. He had Tim's sandy hair and blue eyes, but his face was broader and the mouth very different. Or perhaps, Twila thought, it's just that I've never seen Alan smile.

"My mom wants to know, can you come by this morning," the boy repeated dutifully.

Tim squatted down so that his eyes were on a level with his son's. Alan was his child by his very first lover, a woman named Sybil: Alan Sybil-Tim, in the nomenclature of the Springs. He had been raised by his mother and stepfather, and though he called Tim "Dad," the word always sounded awkward on his lips. "How is your mom?" Tim asked him.

"Not so good," the boy answered, and a small frown puckered his sober face. "Even when she's awake, she don't eat much, and she seems sort-a unhappy a lot."

Tim's good humor evaporated. "Well, if she's awake now, I'd better come right away." He turned back to Twila. "Why don't you go on inside and—"

"Please, sir," the boy interrupted. "Mom said you should bring the lady."

Twila's eyes widened in surprise. "Me?"

"You're the lady from that dome place, aren't you?" Alan asked.

"Yes, but—I didn't think your mother even knew me." Twila was sure she had never met Sybil.

"But you're the one she really wants to see," the boy insisted. "She said I should find my dad, and you'd be with him, and to ask you both to come."

Tim stood up and smiled at her. "It'll be fine," he assured her. "Sybil has some odd ideas, but she's really very nice. You'll like her."

Twila wondered if there was anyone Tim didn't think she'd like.

Sybil's house was on the school grounds, for she had been a teacher until her illness prevented her continuing. Sounds of childish laughter came from the house; Tim and Twila followed Alan in to find a boy of thirteen playing with two smaller children on the floor near a bed that occupied the front room. In the bed lay a waxen-looking young woman with dull brown hair and haggard, sunken eyes. Twila caught her breath; the faces of those in the final stages of CM always startled her. The boy looked up as they entered. "Hi, Tim," he greeted.

"Hi, Carson. Where's Louisa?"

"Went to church," the boy replied. "I watch the kids for them every Sunday morning."

"Carson" came a whispering, rasping voice from the wraith on the bed. "Take the children outside, please. It's a lovely day."

Carson looked surprised, but realized that they were

being dismissed so the others could talk. "Come on, Alan," he said, scooping up one child with an arm around his middle and taking the other by the hand. "Let's go out and swing with the babies." They all disappeared through the front door of the bungalow.

Tim seated himself on the bed near Sybil. "Happy dreams?" he asked, brushing a strand of hair back from her cheek.

"No dreams, Tim," she said hoarsely. "I don't dream at all."

There was an awkward pause. "I didn't mean dreams, of course," Tim corrected, "I meant—"

"I know what you meant. I don't dream, Tim. I don't fly."

Shock wrote itself across Tim's face. Twila saw it there, saw the war waging within him. Then from the bed came a gasping, choking sound, and Twila looked back in alarm, sure that Sybil was about to expire in their very presence. But the sound turned out to be laughter: bitter, breathless laughter.

"Quite the joke, don't you think?" Sybil cackled. "All these years, waiting to fly, and all I am is sick."

"Oh, Sybil, you must fly," Tim contradicted, "you just don't remember it."

"Don't remember? Is that it?" The sarcasm was thick, though the voice was thin. "That's what I told myself, too, the first few times. It doesn't happen right away, I said. You have to grow into it. You have to become accustomed to the sensation. Some people don't fly till their third or fourth episode." The mouth grew grim. "Well, Tim, some people don't fly at all."

Still he was incredulous. "*Everyone* flies."

"Everyone claims to."

Now Tim set his jaw. "Melinda flies."

That seemed even funnier to Sybil. "Oh, God, yes, she probably does. But I don't, Tim. I lie here in this bed, too weak to get up, trying to choke down the nourishment my body needs to stay alive, and I ask myself, for what? Why live, if you can call this living? What good am I? What good am I, to myself or anyone else?"

"Your children need you," he said, his voice low and almost accusing.

"They need a mother," Sybil countered, "not a corn-husk doll."

Tim did not know how to answer that immediately, and Sybil turned to Twila. "I had the misfortune, you see," she rasped, "of marrying a man who didn't cross over until I had begun to manifest. It was a little hard to find a second husband after that."

Tim spoke up. "Louisa has been—"

"—a true friend," Sybil finished. "But she will marry John Tierza-Lee before their baby is born, and join that happy brood. Provided I die quickly."

"Sybil—!"

But she waved off his objection. "No, she's not said it like that. And she'd be happy enough to take my children with her when she goes. But I have another idea. One I like better."

Now she turned to Twila. "You're the lady from the biodome?"

"Twila Grimm," she responded, her heart fluttering a bit.

"Grimm! Like the fairy-tale brothers? How appropriate." Twila wasn't sure how to take that remark; she kept silent. "And you just came out of your domed city last spring?" Sybil asked.

The back of Twila's neck began to prickle. "In April."

"Then, you won't manifest for ten or fifteen years, even with your lower resistance." Twila felt gooseflesh rise on her arms, knew the question even before Sybil asked it. "Will you take care of my children?"

Twila's head spun. She didn't even feel comfortable with Tim's children, how could she—"You don't even know me!" she gasped.

"I know enough. You're a good person, or Tim wouldn't be interested in you. And you can be there for my children longer than anyone else in this town."

Yes, longer than anyone else, Twila realized with a start. Not only longer than Tim, but longer than his children, and quite possibly longer than *their* children.

"I was three when my mother died," Sybil went on. "And five when Zerbie died, and eight when Tony crossed over, and after that they all began to blend together. It didn't matter who I loved, they all went away.

I was damn near twelve before I figured out it wasn't my fault for loving them. I want something better for my children, Ms. Grimm. Can you blame me for that?"

Tim's jaw had dropped when Sybil first asked her question, and he had been too stunned to respond. But now he found his voice and began to object. "Oh, Sybil, you can't ask that of Twila!" he chastened. "The children don't know her, and she doesn't know children. Not really, not how to care for them. She needs time, and children of her own, and—"

"And then what?" Twila asked, her face burning. "Then I can look after everyone else? Then I can be the oldest surviving person in this community? Granny Grimm, the wise old woman who lives on the edge of town. No, better yet, Mother Grimm. Mother Grimm, the one constant thing in everyone's life, the one person who will outlive all of you. Don't tell me you haven't thought of it, Tim. Is that what you were thinking when Melinda sent you to find me? Were you thinking, here is someone who can care for my children, not just for a few years, but for a lifetime? *Their* lifetime? Is that why you're so anxious to marry me?"

Tim's face was frozen in pain, his body quivering with the need to speak words he could not articulate. Twila turned and stalked from the bungalow.

Twila found Tim sitting in the darkness in Melinda's room, staring down at his comatose wife. He didn't look up when Twila came in. "I'm sorry," she whispered.

For a moment he did not move, and she wondered if he had lapsed into unconsciousness as well. Then he spoke. "How could you believe that of me?"

"I don't believe it of you." She came and knelt beside him, took his hand and pressed it to her cheek. "I've known too many selfish and unkind people; sometimes I forget that not everyone I trust will betray me."

His head turned ever so slightly to look down at her. "It's Sybil," he whispered. "She caught you by surprise. She does that."

"Forgive me?"

Now he leaned over to put his arms around her and kiss her tenderly. "Of course."

"Good. Because the next part is going to be harder. Tim, I have more than just ten or fifteen years to live. I could live fifty, sixty—eighty years more. And I'll never fly, in all that time. However I die, Tim, it won't be of CM because I am immune to the virus."

She told him, then—the whole story of her immunity, of Dr. Krell's deception, of what had been done to the vast majority of her fetuses, of what lay in store for her children who remained. "Tim, I can't marry you until I figure out what to do about my children. I can't leave them to Krell's tender mercies, I just can't."

His hand trembled in hers. "If I can help . . ."

"Thank you."

For a long time they sat in silence, hands clasped. Finally he reached over and stroked her arm. "And if we have children, you and I, will they be immune also?"

"Yes."

"And they'll never fly."

Twila hesitated. "I don't know how to answer that. After what Sybil said today—"

"We do fly," he interrupted. "Sybil's wrong. Melinda flies, I know she does."

"I believe that, too," Twila assured him. "She couldn't have known what she knew about my escape from the biodome if she didn't see it. And I don't believe the people in this community are victims of a mass delusion. I'm just not sure the CM virus has everything to do with the psychoporting."

"What do you mean?"

"I've been reading your Chronicles at the library," she told him. "You were right about this being a very spiritual place. The people who fled here at the onslaught of the CM epidemic were—very mystic, I guess. People with—with a strong affinity for the paranormal. They wrote about psychic vibrations and esper abilities and high psionic ratings. The tendency for out-of-body experiences may have been present in those settlers, and passed on and intensified through generations of interbreeding. Or maybe the CM amplifies it—I know CM affects the brain cells, and it could very well alter portions of the brain to enhance those natural tendencies. It could be that your children will fly, even if they don't have CM. But it could be that they won't."

Tim was quiet a moment. "I guess that depends on whether I fly or not."

Her heart ached, and she leaned her face against his arm. "Oh, Tim . . ."

"I've been sitting here thinking," Tim went on. "What if I don't fly? What if, like Sybil, all I get is—sick? I'll have to stop riding horseback soon, you know." Twila knew how he loved riding, loved going up into the canyon to check on the cattle. "And crossing the log bridge to the hot spring pools. Once I start to fl—" He stopped mid-word and corrected himself. "Once I start to lose consciousness, I have to be careful not to be somewhere that a fall could hurt me. I can still drive a team, help with the calving, lots of other things, but—only for a while. I'll grow too weak for the work. I'll have to take up leather working, or carving, or—something. Something safe. I'll have to stay at home. And eventually I'll have to stay in bed. I've known that all my life, but I've been able to put it off and not worry about it because I'd be able to fly. I'd go places even a horse couldn't take me, see things that were only pictures from books, and I'd be so *free*—"

Her arms went around him, and clutched him tightly. "You'll fly, Tim. You already have 'feelings,' and the two have to be connected, they just have to."

"You don't know that," he said softly. "And now neither do I."

Just then there was a rustling from the bed, and Tim gave a start. "Melinda?"

Twila could see the sheets moving slightly in the moonlight. "Oh, Tim . . ." The voice always sounded so distant, as though Melinda spoke from another plane. "And . . . Twila? Is that you? I'm so glad you're here."

And for once, Twila thought, *I'm glad you are. Tim needs you now. He needs a reassurance I can't give him.* "How was your journey?" she asked.

"Exhilarating," Melinda replied. "I flew to so many places this time . . . is it night?"

"Yes, Melinda," Tim soothed, automatically filling a glass with water from a nearby pitcher and holding it to her lips. "The children are asleep. But we're here, Twila and I. Tell us where you've been."

"On the other side of the mountain," she answered. "In the old Indian ruins. There are so many spirits lingering there . . . But before that, I was in the city. Who is Lacy?"

Twila was startled. "Lacy? She was a young Hat girl who had been kidnapped by the Bariosos. Did you see her?"

"She's back with her own people. But she looked so sad . . ."

Tears smarted in Twila's eyes. "They're all sad, Melinda. It's a sad life." No doubt Lacy was pregnant, and now had been returned to the Hats carrying a Barioso child. And her brother would demand vengeance, and the cycle of violence would continue . . .

"And I saw Gloria."

Tim snorted derisively.

"Oh, be kind, Tim," Melinda admonished. "She's a troubled child. And she's sick. She's eaten something that's made her sick."

"Will she be all right?"

"I don't know. She's . . . in a shed of some kind. Not far from the summer pastures—northeast, I think. Just past the junction. Someone should look for her."

"I'll tell Raul," Tim promised. "Melinda, you should eat something while you're awake. Let me—"

"No," Her thin hand reached out to stay his departure. "No, let me tell you about my flight. I have to tell someone, or what's the point? Let's see, there was Gloria, and—oh, there's a huge buck with a rack of antlers you wouldn't believe—ten or twelve points. Young and strong, though. I hope no one is foolish enough to shoot him this season. There's an older buck—he's lost his herd to this young one—he has a grizzled white snout. Tell any hunters to look for a grizzled white snout . . ."

And Melinda was gone again.

"She didn't eat," Tim whispered.

"She'll be back," Twila assured him. But she wondered.

Chapter 15

Melinda crossed over twenty-one days later, without ever having regained consciousness. Tim spoke of the beautiful flight she must be on, now that she was eternally free of her physical body; but at night he wept in Twila's arms. She almost relented and moved into his house, because he needed the comfort; however, she was afraid it would become too awkward to avoid his advances during the time in her monthly cycle when she was most susceptible to impregnation. That was still something she wanted to postpone, so she never stayed more than one night at a time.

Raul found his sister Gloria up in the canyon in the remains of a ranger station. He brought her home, but the toxin she had ingested was beyond anyone's ability to treat. Not surprisingly, Raul and Sally approached Twila to ask if she knew of any remedy, since medicine was so far advanced in the biodome. Twila could only shake her head and say she was sorry.

The grizzled buck became the quarry in a contest between bow and rifle hunters, each group going out on alternate days. Mostly by luck, it was the latter bunch that found him, and fourteen-year-old Suzanne Bonnie-Martin fired the fatal shot. He became the main course at her wedding feast later that week—in the form of ground meat, of course, since he was too old and tough for roasting.

Of Lacy, Twila could know nothing; but she often wondered how the child fared, and whether Starbright was sad that Twila had not returned to her grandfather's bungalow.

Twila found herself taking more notice of Delia, though when or where Tim might have done Delia the favor she requested, Twila never knew and tried not to think about. But Delia herself began to intrigue Twila. She was always at the Saturday night socials, but rarely danced and seemed awkward when she did. The boys did not avoid her, but they did not seek her out despite the fact that she was growing into a tall and well-shaped girl. Delia herself seemed unconcerned by their attention or lack of it. In fact, she spent as much time entertaining the toddlers at these gatherings as she did with young people her own age. Shy, but not painfully so, Twila decided. A young woman with more confidence in her practical skills than her social graces.

I wouldn't mind a daughter like her, Twila thought. I wouldn't mind having a child of mine grow up here, in this village, with these people. It's a better life than she would have in the biodome with Krell. If I only knew who she was, my oldest daughter . . . and where she was . . . and how to get her out . . . how to get them all out.

It was Sunday afternoon in September when the answer finally occurred to Twila. She and Tim were walking beside the stream with his children, enjoying the late summer sunshine, which was tempered by a cool breeze rushing down the canyon. Sounds wove a symphony around them: birds for woodwinds, insects for strings, the splashing of water over stones for muted brass, punctuated by the rumbling and creaking percussion of the nearby waterwheel. Overhead the sky was as blue as Twila had ever seen it, untouched by a single cloud.

"I'm looking forward to the wintertime," Twila confessed examining the calluses on her left palm while holding little Emily's hand with her right. They had been putting up a second crop of hay this week, and soon it would be time to chop the corn. Though Twila could not drive a team of horses, there was plenty of hauling and stacking to be done. "Your girls will be in my dance classes, won't they?"

"Of course," Tim replied, plucking a foxtail from among the other grasses and using it to tickle Miriam's ear. The four-year-old turned and swatted at it, and Tim laughed. "Wouldn't you girls like Twila to teach you to dance?"

"You mean like a ballerina?" Yvonne asked, eyes

alight. "Oh, would you Twila? I saw a ballerina in a picture book, and she was soooo lovely!" Her seven-year-old
face gleamed, and she raised her hands over her head and
tried to pirouette on her toes.

Twila laughed, remembering a similar response when
Roxanne had asked if she would like to take dance
lessons. And how disappointed she had been in those first
lessons! Not to be able to dance on her toes from the very
beginning! "It takes a long time to become a ballerina,"
Twila cautioned Yvonne. "But, yes, I can teach you. First
you will need to learn the standard positions, and then
we'll put some of them together with some music. Only
we'll have to find some music—"

Suddenly she stopped short and stared across the river
at the rumbling waterwheel.

Tim shuffled to a stop a few steps beyond her. "Michael
Sue-Jason plays the piano," he offered. "Maybe he
wouldn't mind providing some music for you. Sometimes, when we run short of power in the winter, he plays
for our dances instead of using the generator to run the
boom box." He looked at Twila, who stood staring gape-
mouthed across the river. "Twila?"

"Hm? Oh, yes, that would be great," she responded
absently. "When you run short—why do you run short of
power? You don't use solar batteries, do you?"

He chuckled. "No, it's the river. When the water level
is down, sometimes we can't use the waterwheel, so then
we have to use the generator to power the pumps. So
there's no generator for the dance. Twila?" She was still
staring across the water. "What is it?"

"I'm not sure," she murmured, watching the ceaseless
turning of the waterwheel. "I think— I think I know how
to get to Krell."

She did not see him stiffen, nor hear his quick intake of
breath. "How?"

"I'm not sure," she repeated. "It's just a thought . . .
just the kernel of a thought . . ." Suddenly she disengaged
herself from Emily and turned on her heel.

The little girl began to wimper. "Where are you
going?" Tim called out as Twila bolted up the slope
toward the town.

"To the library," she shouted back. "I'll see you later."

* * *

Tanya, one of the other adults who shared Tim's house, looked peevish that night when Twila pounded up the porch steps and burst into the front room with a sheaf of papers in her hand. "He's putting the children to bed," Tanya snipped, without waiting to be asked.

But Twila noticed neither her tone nor her look. "I'll wait outside," she said, and exited without ceremony. Moments later Tim came out to find her seated on the porch, pouring over a series of hand sketches in the pale light offered by a hunter's moon.

"You'll ruin your eyes," he admonished.

"No, I won't, that's a fallacy," she replied absently. "Tim, I really think it can be done."

"Ruining your eyes?" he teased.

"No, Krell," she replied, missing his humor entirely. "I think I can do it. I think I can take away his power."

"Oh? You have a small army in your back pocket?" he asked dryly.

"Don't need one. Although, maybe . . ." Her eyes grew unfocused.

"Twila, will you please explain what you're talking about?" Tim urged impatiently.

She came back. "Power. Electric power. Everything in the biodome relies on it: computers that provide communications, education, information, food delivery—filtration. Water. The alarm system. You name it, it can't be done without electrical power." Excitement glittered in her eyes as she looked to him for a response.

"So?" he prompted.

"We take away Krell's power. That is, we threaten to." She pointed to a drawing she had traced from something in the library. "Look. This is the hydroelectric plant. It's on the river *outside* the biodome. It's vulnerable."

Tim glanced at the drawing. "Do you plan to stop up the river?" he asked.

"I haven't got time," she replied, unphased by the engineering feat that would entail. "I'm going for the controls, and they're in this building, here."

Tim looked patiently at the drawing in her hand. "It's a concrete and steel bunker," he pointed out.

"But the bunker has a door," she insisted. "Two of

them: one from a tunnel that runs out from the dome, one from the outside. Here." She shuffled through her papers and found a sketch of the bunker, which showed the metal door.

He was simply not being swept up in her enthusiasm. "How are you going to get through the door?"

"Cutting torch."

Tim nodded slowly. "We don't have one at the moment, but they can be found in the city. That part could be done. And then what?"

She seemed surprised that he couldn't understand. "Then I go to the main control panel, here . . ." She shuffled more papers until she found the drawing she wanted. "Here, see? And I tell Krell he has to stop his research or I turn off the power."

"You turn off the power and cause mass panic and let the virus in and indirectly kill everyone in the city, including your mother and your aunt."

"No!" Twila was horrified. "I wouldn't actually do it. But Krell doesn't know that."

Tim rose slowly to his feet. "Yes, Twila," he said quietly, "he does." Then he turned and went inside.

Twila sat on the porch staring into the darkness for half the night.

Twila did not go out to the fields to help with the harvest the next day, nor the day after that, nor the day after that. She spent most of her time in the library, although she spent many hours of that just staring into space. Finally on Wednesday evening she came back to Tim's house, much subdued. She played with the younger children while the older ones washed the supper dishes, and she visited politely with the adults until, exhausted from the day's labor, they followed their children to bed. Only she and Tim were left in the candlelit front room.

"You must be tired," she said.

"Not too." He was seated in a straight-backed rocking chair with colorful flowered cushions on the back and seat. "I was down in the winter pastures today, making sure everything is ready. We'll be moving the flocks and herds down next week. It was kind of an easy day."

Beside him, Twila leaned forward in her easy chair and

looked down at her clasped hands. "You were right: Krell knows me too well. I can't make a threat I'm not willing to carry out. So I thought of something I am willing to carry out. I need to verify some information, but if I'm right, this is what I'll do." Quietly, carefully, she laid out her plan.

When she had finished, he nodded. "You'll still need a small army," he pointed out. "And equipment, and supplies. They'll try to gas you out in that confined space. And they'll have no compunction about shooting."

"I thought of that," she admitted. "I think if I carry a grenade, or something like that, with the triggering pin pulled—you know, so that if something happens to me it goes off and blasts the controls anyway—I think that should keep them at bay long enough."

Again he nodded. "We can rig something. And your small army? You're not likely to get them from here."

"No?" she asked, searching his face.

"The plan includes violence," he said simply, "and you won't find many here who are willing to be a part of it." He shifted uneasily in his rocker. "I'll help you," he said quietly. "As long as you don't ask *me* to hurt anyone. And you might get some supplies from Sally, but not people. We're just not warriors," he concluded.

Twila chewed on her lip and leaned back in the chair, gripping the arms unconsciously. "I need the Hats," she said after a moment.

Tim's eyebrows flew up. "The Hats? Why would they help you?"

"I don't know that they will," she admitted. "But they love violence; they're warriors, and they might fight just for the sake of fighting. Besides, Spider owes me a debt. He might do this to pay it off. I'll have to ask him, anyway. The Hats are the only chance I've got." She took a deep breath and blew it out slowly. "I'll have to go back into the city and look for them."

Tim sighed. "Well, we'll need supplies for about a week," he said, "if you don't know exactly where to find your friends. Saddle horses would be my preference, but I guess we'd better try to get a wagon or buggy."

Twila turned to look at him, rocking slowly in the chair beside her. "I can't take you away from the Springs," she said. "Not now with the harvest underway and the animals being moved—"

"Most likely we can get a buggy," he continued as though she hadn't spoken. "They won't need a buggy for the work around here, and a small quick team won't be missed, either—it's the cow ponies and the dray horses they'll want now. I'll let them use Rex; I don't think anyone will complain."

For a moment she continued to stare at him, knowing she was missing something in all this but unable to imagine what it was. Why would Tim take a buggy when he could take Rex and— Then it clicked; her hand went out to rest on his arm. "You had your first episode, didn't you?"

He stopped rocking. "Episode. Yes, my first episode." A pause. "I didn't fly."

"It was only the first time," she encouraged. "They say you hardly ever fly the first time. It takes awhile to, to get accustomed to it, I guess. You will fly, Tim. I know you will."

The hand he placed on top of hers trembled. It startled her; she hadn't noticed how pronounced the trembling had become. How long now? How long for Tim? Two years? One?

Twila fought back tears. "Tim," she began, trying not to let her voice choke up, "when this is over—"

But he hushed her quickly. "Don't make me any promises," he whispered. "You make the plans you need to make for the rest of your life, but I'll make no more plans. From here on I'll take whatever the day brings, and I will cherish it." He raised her hand to his lips. "Indeed, I will cherish it."

The "buggy" they took was of typical Springs construction: a chassis reclaimed from an old sports car, complete with composite wheels, a lightweight molded plastic seat, a plastic bin for cargo, and a metal tongue welded to the frame. The result was a useful vehicle that could carry two to three adults and some gear with only two horses pulling. It had none of the charm of the buggies Twila had seen in flatscreen vids, with their upholstered seats and their bonnets to shade the passengers. It looked instead like a framework with skeletal appendages, like a half-finished product still waiting for its shell.

In the late afternoon they stopped near a dilapidated building half a mile upstream from the biodome and waited for nightfall. Under cover of darkness the two of them made a reconnaissance excursion to the utility bunker at the hydroelectric plant. Ostensibly they studied the lay of the land, sight lines from the biodome to the bunker, the composition and dimensions of the door. But time and again Twila found herself simply staring up at the glass and steel behemoth sprawled atop the mesa behind them. Here was her city, her country, the limits of her world until a few months ago. It stretched for miles to the north and east, seeming to glow with its own artificial light. Only the human habitations were lit, of course, and they were hidden from view by the rim of the mesa; however, the glass panels of the upper structure caught and dispersed the light until the whole of Numex seemed a giant jewel in the darkness.

And above it all, like the headpiece on a crystal coiffure, rose the Stargazing Room. From her position downhill Twila could see only the rounded top, but she could not help wondering who was up there tonight. Dr. Krell and some young med tech, as Jon had insinuated was often the case? Some other doctor who had done Krell a favor and now enjoyed the privilege of taking his or her consort there? Or was Jon there, gazing out, wondering where she was? And was he alone?

"Twila," Tim whispered, although there was no one around to hear them. "Time to go."

Reluctantly Twila turned and followed him back to the dam, then across it to find their way back to the horses. How simple it seemed now, compared to that night last spring when she had struggled, heart pounding, to overcome the feeling that the world was spinning wildly and that she would fly off into space. It seemed impossible to her that she had lost her balance and managed to fall down the side—the road was so broad here, at least four meters across! Living Outside had made her so much stronger, psychologically as well as physically. The care and nurture of the Springites were largely responsible for that—especially Tim. Oh, yes, especially Tim . . .

Yet there was something oddly compelling about the glass colossus on the mesa behind them. As alien as it looked from the Outside, it seemed to draw her. Within its walls an entire civilization lived out its existence, like ants in an ant farm, scurrying here and there, building, maintaining, creating, expending, living, dying . . .

And being controlled by Krell, she reminded herself. Whether they realized it or not.

Later, as they rolled into their blankets for the night, Twila could not keep her eyes or her thoughts away from the Stargazing Room. For the first time she told Tim about Jon, and about lying in the Stargazing Room looking up at the heavens on the night of her escape. It did nothing to alleviate the somber mood he had been in all week.

"Did you love him?" Tim asked gloomily.

Twila considered the questions anew. "I still don't know," she decided. "I never had time to find out, really."

"Do you love me?"

She snuggled up next to him, feeling the comfort of his warmth and physical presence. "I love being with you," she told him. "And I love making love with you. Right now you're the best friend I have, maybe the best friend I've ever had. I think that's what love really is, don't you? Wasn't Melinda your best friend?"

He was quiet for a moment. "I guess she was," he confessed. "I was just always so heart-stopping crazy about her that—" He sighed softly. "I guess I just can't imagine now knowing what love is when you feel it. But that's all right," he added quickly. "Whatever it is you feel, or think you feel, that's good enough for me."

Twila sighed. "If I had more to give—to anyone—"

"I know," he interrupted. "When I first met you, I thought it was just the things that had happened to you that made you so—removed. That after you got used to us, got used to people touching you, you'd relax and feel more normal. But this thing with your children—it's like part of you is still trapped inside there." He gestured toward the glass city. "You can't be a whole person until you've set it free."

"Yes," she agreed, clutching the arm he had draped

around her without taking her eyes off the luminous enclave. "Yes."

They crossed the Rio Grande before dawn and slipped into the ruins stretching up its eastern bank, headed for the last place Twila had seen the Hats. She wasn't sure how far she'd run in her mad flight from the Bariosos, but she knew that if she kept to the river, she would eventually run into the bungalow that had served Carlton Grimm as home and clinic. There were some items she wanted to retrieve, as well as something she needed to do there before she went looking for Starbright and Spider.

Following the river was more difficult than she had supposed, for numerous branches and channels fed into the Rio from the east, forcing them to do much backtracking to find suitable crossing places and continue their trek. Nevertheless, by mid-afternoon they had found the place they sought, and Twila was relieved to find it relatively untouched since her last visit. If the Hats had encountered any trouble with the Bariosos who'd chased Twila, it had not been here.

Twila found the items she sought easily—her grandfather's diary, some personal items she recognized, and the kapok habit she had last seen him wearing. The next part was more difficult, for the generator had shut down when it ran out of fuel. Twila knew some anxious moments, for she needed to contact Jon in the biodome, and she needed the generator to do that. But Tim had experience with generators and fuel and numerous mechanical things that eluded her. Carlton's reserve of fuel was soon discovered and tapped into, and by nightfall the generator was humming again. Then it was Twila's turn to play mentor as she demonstrated the electric lights and small appliances in the bungalow. Tim found most of them more curious than useful, but he hovered at her elbow in ill-concealed excitement when she turned on the computer.

To the mountaineers, the word computer was almost synonymous with magic. They learned in school of all the tasks that had once been done by computer, which must now be accomplished manually, and Tim wanted to see some of them. Twila obligingly showed him a few of the programs installed on the workstation's hard drive: a spreadsheet, a word processor, a database. Then she accessed the network and got to the PubInfo shell and gave him a quick tour of the tools there. Before long he backed away from the monitor, shaking his head. "Too much for me," he said, dazzled. "You go ahead and call your friend. I'll, uh—" He headed for the door. "I'll wait in the other room."

"You don't have to do that," she called after him.

He stopped in the doorway and looked back, and Twila thought his face looked shadowed in a way it had not just a few days ago. Or had it been darkening for months, but so gradually that she had simply not noticed? "I think I'd rather," he said softly.

Twila turned sadly back to the terminal, wondering if she would be able to watch him slip away from her bit by bit, first monthly, then weekly, then hourly— She shook her head to clear it. No point in thinking of that now. No point in thinking of it ever; what happened, happened. Right now, she needed to contact Jon.

Jon looked down at his hands, still callused from wielding a machete, although the blisters he'd endured at the beginning had all healed. Then he looked through the doorway of his office out into the lab with a grateful heart. God, it was good to be back here.

Through the sweltering months of summer, he had served his sentence, his "Required Labor" in the rain forest, hacking back the overabundant growth, harvesting the fruits, spreading the residue on compost heaps. Sometimes he would wake in the night and feel his skin crawling as though the grit and dirt of the place were still upon him, find the cloying smell of the compost heaps still in his nostrils. He'd endured for two months before his father contacted him, asking if he was ready to come back to work.

"If you want me," he'd said humbly.

"Of course, I want you," Krell had replied fervently, "but I want you well. How's your ulcer, any better?"

"Some," he'd lied.

Then, "Say, how's my granddaughter?" his father

asked, and Jon understood there was another price being added to his account—one Jon was not willing to pay.

So he gritted his teeth and went back to the rain forest. July, August . . . Rumors flew on the conferences, discussions were censored right and left, Security was visible in every section of the biodome. To his surprise, he found the seeds of dissention he and Trish had planted growing quickly, fed by the very censorship that tried to repress them. Still ensconced in MA housing, Jon also discovered a number of his colleagues would "stop by" to see him, asking him to come take a walk. For years he'd believed he was fighting a lonely battle; now that his father's retribution had struck him from power, he discovered there were people very interested in what he had to say.

But he declined every invitation for private conversation, refrained from any activity that might aggravate his father. He continued his research as best he could without a lab, searching old literature, running simulations on the computer. He bent to Krell's will in every way he could, except one: he would not allow contact between his father and his daughter.

Finally in September Krell had called again. "How are you Jon?"

"Wiser," he promised.

"I can't spare you any longer," Krell told him. "I'm taking you out of the rain forest today; use the rest of the week to recuperate a bit and be back in the lab Monday. Give Desirée my love."

The "no" had been on his lips, but he bit it back. "I will." It was a lie, but it was a compromise.

That had been two weeks ago. Now he was back in the familiar routine, back in the clean and filtered air of Medical, back in his comfortable chair and his white lab coat. His father stopped by frequently and Jon was polite, if subdued. They talked about Jon's work, and how slowly things had progressed in his absence; then they talked about Krell's research, and Jon forced himself to be clinical and not criticize the ethics of it. Experimentation was essentially stalled, he learned, until "the next donor," as Krell called Twila's oldest daughter, matured. "It should be any day now," Krell predicted. "Let's hope so, anyway. I don't dare send Security teams out very far because I can't immunize them. Even the techs in your lab are going without, Jon."

"We'll manage," Jon replied.

Of Twila they did not speak, nor of the governing board, nor of all the rumblings throughout the dome of a cure, or an immunization, or the possibility that the virus had burned itself out and no longer existed Outside. Jon wanted badly to talk to Trish, but he knew he didn't dare make contact. It would be risky for him; it could be deadly for her.

But although Twila's name never passed his lips, she was never far from his thoughts. Where was she Outside? Was she well? Was she safe? Who were the "friends" she had made, and were they taking care of her?

And what *kind* of care were they taking?

Every day he checked his mail, hoping there would be a message from her. He monitored his workstation almost constantly, thinking she was more likely to send a real-time message than a note, but nothing came. Had her friends turned unfriendly? Had her generator failed? Where was she?

A callus was starting to peel away from the pad of his middle index finger. He worried it with the thumbnail of his left hand but stopped short as a single line of print scrolled across his screen.

COME PLAY IN THE MUD.

It jolted him upright in his chair, and his fingers flew as he logged onto the multiuser domain he'd set up last spring. The system was old and clunky; it balked and hesitated, and Jon swore under his breath, and then finally he was in. I'M HERE, he typed. ARE YOU ALL RIGHT?

SAFE AND WELL came the answer. IS THIS PLAYGROUND STILL SECURE?

YES, he wrote back. I KEEP CHANGING THE LOCKS.

I WANT TO PAY YOUR FATHER A VISIT, she told him, BUT IT MUST BE A SURPRISE.

COME VISIT ME, he begged.

I WILL COME NEAR, she promised. NEAR ENOUGH FOR YOU TO SEE. BUT I NEED SOME INFORMATION. WILL YOU HELP ME?

ANY WAY I CAN, he vowed.

Her questions were concrete, with most of the information available to him through the MA systems. They also painted a sketchy picture of what she was planning to do: contact Krell from the power plant, lure him out of the biodome, divert Security—but then what?

I'LL TALK TO HIM was Twila's cryptic reply to that question. I THINK I CAN CONVINCE HIM TO SEE THINGS MY WAY. I'VE ARRANGED SOME LEVERAGE.

HE'LL TELL YOU WHAT YOU WANT TO HEAR AND BACK OUT OF IT LATER, Jon warned.

NOT THIS TIME, she said. TRUST ME.

Trust her. How could he trust her when she wouldn't tell him everything?

What choice did he have? And who was he to demand the truth from her?

I'LL NEED TIME TO ARRANGE THE THINGS YOU'VE ASKED FOR, he told her. GIVE ME TWO WEEKS.

GIVE ME DARK OF THE MOON, she responded.

DONE.

Jon put his hand on the computer screen, wanting badly to touch her through it, wishing he could at least see her and know that she was well, that she was *real.* So much of the world inside Numex was not.

ARE YOU STILL THE CROWN PRINCE? she asked him.

Jon drew a sharp breath. THE PRINCE IS A PAUPER, he typed back. THAT'S WHAT HAPPENS WHEN YOU FOMENT REBELLION. BUT I HAVE SURRENDERED. I BEND THE KNEE AND MOUTH THE LOYALTY OATH, AND HE BEGINS TO FORGIVE.

Her next remark startled him. BEND FURTHER.

I DON'T KNOW HOW, he told her.

LIE, STEAL, CHEAT, DO ANYTHING YOU MUST, she commanded, BUT GET YOURSELF BACK IN A POSITION TO TAKE OVER. THE KING WILL NOT ABDICATE IF HE FEARS CHAOS WILL FOLLOW.

A cold chill touched the back of Jon's neck. Abdicate? Was Twila's plan, then, not simply to stop Krell's research, but to remove Krell himself? A quick shiver ran through him. I'LL DO WHAT I CAN.

TELL HIM WHAT HE WANTS MOST TO HEAR, she advised.

AND WHAT IS THAT? he wondered, for he truly did not know.

TELL HIM YOU LOVE HIM.

Chapter 16

Tracing her way back to the Hats' stronghold was even more time-consuming than finding the clinic had been. Again Twila relied on proximity to the river for guidance; that and her memory of the territory around the digs were all she had to go on. There were some landmarks she recalled seeing along the way, and eventually they wandered into places she recognized from foraging with Starbright.

Tim was very nervous about being this deep in the city, and with good reason. This was the feeding ground of the two warring gangs, and a couple of mountaineers in a horse-drawn rig were tempting fish. If either gang still had working "wheels," the horses could not hope to outrun pursuit. If Tim and Twila were caught by Bariosos, they might be tortured for the gang's entertainment before they were killed. Even the Hats could pose a threat; not knowing Tim, they might shoot him before asking Twila why she'd brought him along.

Once she felt they were near the digs, Twila suggested they leave the horses and rig concealed in a dilapidated stable near the river. Tim readily agreed, eager to have the horses out of sight and presumably out of harm's way, and more comfortable about proceeding on silent feet than clomping hooves. Twila filled a backpack with food and water and a few odds and ends, but they left Tim's rifle and the rest of their supplies, including the items she had picked up at her grandfather's bungalow. It would not do to greet the Hats armed.

One of the first things Starbright had taught Twila was how to find her way back to the digs—via any number of circuitous routes, of course—so from this stable they proceeded confidently to the house that served as headquarters for the Hats. It was late in the day when they approached, and as soon as the lookout spotted them, he signaled to people in the house and out came five strapping Hat fighters to intercept them. Twila recognized Bobo, Road Dog, Zit, Gunner, and Echo; and she knew they recognized her, or she would never have gotten this close.

"Look what come home to roost," sneered Bobo. "We thought you was stretched in the street somewhere popping out Barioso babies right and left."

"Where's Spider?" Twila asked, ignoring the remark.

"That pussy?" Bobo spat in the street. "I cut off his nuts and had them for breakfast. I'm the man now."

For a moment Twila felt panic claw through her; then she realized that Road Dog would never have let Bobo take over the gang; he was Spider's "ace kool," his lieutenant. Even now Road Dog was giving Bobo a sharp sidelong glance. "I don't listen to dog droppings like you," Twila told the cocky Bobo, and she turned to Road Dog. "Road Dog, where's the man?"

Road Dog did not answer right away, but glared at her a moment and then spat in the street as well. "Out," he said.

"And Starbright?"

"I don't keep track of the bitch."

"Then, I'll wait under a tree until one of them shows up," Twila announced, turning her back on the five and marching toward a cottonwood nearby. Tim tagged behind her, with more than one wary backward glance.

"Who your friend?" Bobo demanded.

"Just that," Twila replied as she sat down on the dusty ground under the tree.

"He some Bubblehead reject, too?"

Twila took off the pack she was carrying and opened it up, reaching for the water bottle inside. "I'll explain to Spider; that way I only have to say things once," she informed Bobo.

Now the boys began to shuffle their feet and look at one another. Twila drank sparingly from the water bottle and fished out a small apple to eat. Beside her, Tim was also digging in his pack for some food. "I assume this is all a psychological ploy," he whispered to her. "I'm too scared to be hungry."

"It's like facing a wild animal," Twila murmured back. "You can't show fear."

Now Road Dog, Bobo, and Gunner turned away and headed back into the house. Zit and Echo, both younger fighters with lower status in the gang, approached the pair under the tree. "Spider, he out somewhere," Zit told Twila. "Starbright, she inside with Lacy, but Bobo don't want Lacy coming out where no stranger be." He gave Tim a scathing look.

"Why can't Starbright come out to me alone?" Twila asked.

Zit shifted uncomfortably. "Lacy, she don't leave Starbright for nothing no more," he mumbled. "She a little soft since Bariosos dump her back here."

Twila considered that as she munched her apple. Then she asked, "If my friend leaves, will Starbright and Lacy come out?"

"Maybe," Zit allowed.

Tim started to rise, but Twila snatched his arm and pulled him back down. "You give my friend a safe conduct," she demanded.

Zit looked unhappy. "I go ask Bobo—"

"I don't want a safe conduct from Bobo," Twila told him, "I want one from you. You stay with him; you be his safe."

Zit looked at Echo for help.

"Don't look to your ace kool," Twila advised him. "You're a man, act like one. Give me your promise, you'll be his safe."

Zit gave Echo one more sideways glance, then he straightened himself up. "I be his safe," he said. "Spider owe you, from the dance last spring. He rode Bobo hard when he and Raunchy lost you. He prob'ly give us all shit if we dis you or your friend, so I guess it righteous." He turned to Tim. "Come on, Bubblehead, we take a walk."

Tim got to his feet slowly, brushed himself off deliberately, and stared Zit straight in the eye. They were the same height and similarly built, and each took the other's measure with a careful eye. Finally Zit nodded toward the river, and the two of them started away.

"I tell Bobo," Echo offered.

"You tell Starbright," Twila challenged.

But Echo shook his head. "I tell Bobo. He the one let them out the door, or not."

It was several minutes before the front door of the house opened again, and two young women emerged. Twila heard harsh voices behind them, and Starbright's colorful reply as she stepped off the porch and came down the sidewalk with Lacy clinging to her arm. They walked slowly and steadily to where Twila waited.

As they approached, Twila could see more detail in their faces and bodies. Starbright looked weary, as though she had not slept well in some time. Lacy clutched her arm like a frightened child. Like? She *was* a frightened child, looking younger than her thirteen years with her hair tightly braided and tied in colorful ribbons. Her swollen abdomen was a profane mockery of that child-ishly slender body, and Twila's stomach churned to think of what Lacy had endured at the hands of the Bariosos. Then she thought of her own daughter, and the profanity of Krell's clinical version of a similar abuse.

"Will you sit down?" Twila invited them.

"No," Starbright said simply. "Too hard to get up again."

Twila came to her feet so she could face them as an equal. "How have you been?" she asked.

Starbright shrugged. "So-so."

Her face looked a little puffy—and, Twila noticed, she was growing thick through the middle. Lacy was not the only one who was expecting. "When is your baby due?" Twila asked.

Again the shrug. "Spring, I guess."

"And Lacy?" She turned to the youngster. "When is yours due?"

Lacy said nothing, only stared at Twila with wary eyes.

"She due in winter," Starbright replied for her. "Winter babies are hard." Then she said, "We thought Bariosos got you."

Twila could hear the concern behind Starbright's even tone, and she knew the girl had worried about her. It touched her that Starbright had cared enough to worry; but she knew that behind her tough exterior, Starbright cared about many things. "They tried," Twila said gently.

"But my friend Tim rescued me. He's a mountaineer. I've been living with them ever since."

Now Starbright looked Twila up and down. "You look good," she observed. "Strong."

"I've been working in the fields," Twila told her. "The mountaineers have a good life. They work hard, but they eat well, and they don't have any war." She saw the look of disbelief cross Starbright's face, and she continued, "They grow all their food in gardens, huge gardens, and they raise animals for meat, and they stay in one place and take care of the plants and the animals and each other."

Starbright snorted. "They mountaineers," she said simply. "We Hats. But I'm glad they got you, and not Bariosos." She took another look at Twila's flat stomach. "You not cookin' mountaineer babies?"

"No," Twila replied. "Mountaineer men don't fill you up unless you want them to."

Starbright's eyes grew wide, and her nostrils flared. "Not even Bubbleheads?" she demanded.

"Everyone is treated kindly by the mountaineers," Twila insisted. "Even Bubbleheads."

Starbright could only shake her head and mutter curses under her breath.

Twila tried once again to speak to the adolescent clutching Starbright's arm. "Are you hungry, Lacy? I have some cookies in my pack. Do you know what a cookie is?"

Lacy did not answer.

"She don't talk," Starbright told her friend. "'Cept to me, sometimes. Bariosos give her a bad time, and then when she come back—Bobo, he smack her around a little for being so stupid. Then he say some Hat got to do her, like that gonna make this baby a Hat baby. Shit. So Gunner, he do it to keep Bobo happy, but it don't make Lacy happy. She didn't want no one to touch her, and it went down real bad. Now she don't talk."

The depth of the young girl's trauma twisted at Twila's heart. She didn't know what to say. Instead she rummaged in her pack and found the promised oatmeal cookies. She gave one to each of the Hat girls and took one herself, then watched as they sniffed suspiciously at the offering. When they looked to her to see what to do with it, she bit into her cookie and began to chew. "Mm," she said. "Good."

Starbright bit into hers next, and her eyes widened a little. She nodded to Lacy, who followed suit. "Sweet," Starbright said through a mouthful of crumbs. "Where you find these?"

"They make them on the mountain," Twila explained. "With crushed grain, and honey, and spices. We had them in the biodome—in Bubbleland, too."

"Is there more?"

Twila smiled and fished the bag of cookies back out of her pack. She gave each girl two more, and then asked again, "Are you sure you won't sit down?"

This time Starbright nodded, and the two girls dropped awkwardly to the ground in the shade. Twila seated herself across from them and pulled out her water bottle.

"I need some help," Twila began.

Starbright looked at her cautiously, but she was listening.

"I need it from Spider, but I know he listens to you."

"Sometimes," Starbright agreed. "Sometimes I just make him mad, and he do the opposite of what I say. So what you want?"

Twila took a deep breath. "You remember the man I told you about, Dr. Krell? The one who did bad things to me in Bubbleland? The one I ran away from?"

"He out?" Starbright demanded.

"No." Twila said. "He's still Inside. But he has my daughter."

"Your daughter!" Starbright exclaimed, and cookie crumbs flew from her mouth. "You didn't say you had no daughter."

"Dr. Krell took her away from me," Twila tried to explain, "and I didn't know—well, let's say I thought she was dead." She couldn't begin to tell Starbright about the harvesting of ripened eggs from her ovaries, about artificial insemination and host mothers, and how there could be a child of her seed that Twila had not known existed. "Anyway, as soon as she's old enough—which will be very soon—he'll want to fill her up; but he won't let her keep her babies. He'll take them away, like he took her away from me, and he'll keep filling her up, like the

Bariosos did to Lacy." Twila sipped from her water bottle. "I can't let him do that."

It was clear that she had Starbright's sympathy. "How you stop him?" the younger girl asked.

"I have a plan," Twila told her. "But I need help to carry it off. My friend Tim from the mountain will help me, but I need more than that. I need to break into a building near Bubbleland and scare some people; that's why I need the Hats. The Hats are very scary, and the Hats are very strong." Starbright murmured a colorful ascent. "So I'm going to ask Spider to help, and I'm going to remind him that he owes me. You said last spring that he owes me, and I've come to collect." Twila searched the younger girl's face. "Will you help me convince him?"

Starbright wiped the cookie crumbs from her fingers on the front of her blouse and struggled to her feet. "Shit, you don't need my help," she told Twila. "You callin' in a paper. Just tell him that. Say, 'Spider, I callin' in a paper,' and then he got to do it."

"And will the other Hats come with him?" Twila asked.

"He the man." Starbright gave Lacy both her hands and pulled the adolescent to her feet. "Me and Lacy, I think we come, too."

Twila rose to her feet protesting. "No, Starbright, it's going to be very dangerous, and it's such a long way for you to walk—"

"I ain't never seen Bubbleland," Starbright continued, "and I ain't never seen a mountaineer up close. Lacy and me, we stay back out of the way, we good at that. But I getting old, I ain't got much time left before I get the shakes. When that happen, Lacy can't stay with me no more. It take some strong men to keep her off me, so I don't ever want to be too far from Spider and Bobo—they take care of her."

The thought stunned Twila. "Why can't she stay with you after you start to shake?" she asked.

"Shakes mean you sick," Starbright told her patiently. "You sick, you got to get away from other people or they get sick, too. I don't want Lacy to get sick."

But she's already sick! Twila wanted to shout. *Every one of you is sick, sick from birth, infected by the blood in your mother's body, by the air you breathe, by the water you drink.* But how could she explain that to Starbright? A microscopic animal, a "something" in the air? It would never fly. So she said, "Starbright, being around sick people who've started to shake won't make you get sick any faster. It happens when it happens, no matter who you've been around."

Starbright drew herself up and stared at Twila. "Who tell you that?"

Twila was caught. Starbright wouldn't believe anything that she'd learned in the biodome. She didn't give the mountaineers much credence, either, though that was a better prospect. Speaking from experience was the best way to convince her. "I've seen it, on the mountain," she told Starbright. "When someone gets sick, her homies take care of her, and she lives longer that way, and no one gets sick any faster. My friend Tim took care of his wife—his woman—when she got sick, and he didn't— well, their children didn't get sick from her, or their friends. Everybody gets sick eventually—" Except me, she thought. I just get to sit back and watch them die. "But it doesn't happen any faster if you take care of a sick person. I've seen it on the mountain, and I know it's true."

Starbright took a step back, as though realizing that this meant Twila had been living with sick people. "Maybe it true on the mountain," she said coldly, "but that don't mean it true here." She shook her head firmly. "No, that don't mean it true here." With that she turned her back on Twila, and she and Lacy walked away into the house.

Twila watched them go sadly. Starbright was clever, but life had made her wary and pessimistic. Trust was simply not in her vocabulary, especially when it was trust in something good and desirable. Twila wished she could teach Starbright a better way of living, teach all the Hats to give up their senseless warring and find a place where the Bariosos would not bother them, plant a garden, raise some sheep—

Twila sighed heavily and started off for the river to find Tim and Zit. One impossible task at a time, she told herself.

As Starbright had predicted, Spider did not dispute Twila's request, and they arranged to meet at dark of the

moon by the confluence of the Rio Grande and the Numex
river. He even provided her and Tim an escort back to
their rig. When they got there, Twila could not resist
handing the boys a couple of jars of peaches from their
supplies. She showed them how to open the vacuum-
sealed lid and fish out the paraffin, which kept the fruit
inside truly airtight, then ate several slices form the jar to
prove that it was not contaminated. There is a better way
of life, she wanted to tell them. But would they ever
believe it?

It was late in the day now, but Tim pushed on, trying to
get as far north as he could under cover of darkness. They
took the first bridge they found across the Rio Grande,
and finally stopped for the night on the high ground of the
west bank.

"Do you think they can be trusted?" Tim asked as he
stripped the harness from the horses and began brushing
them down with a handful of dried grass.

"As much as anything else in this plan of mine," she
replied, grabbing a handful of grass and joining him in the
task. The animals still intimidated her a little, but she had
learned to make herself behave as though they didn't.

He gave a weak laugh. "Thanks, I feel so reassured," he
said dryly. For several moments they worked in silence.
"And your friend Jon," Tim said, "will he be able to carry
off his part?"

Twila could hear the jealousy Tim tried so hard not to
show. "He's a fair hacker," she replied, "but his father
watches him too closely. He'll have to get someone else
to help him. I suggested my Aunt Trish, but I don't know
if he can contact her without drawing attention and suspicion. That's the weak link there." The horse she was rubbing down shifted its feet, and Twila skittered her toes
back out of the way. Her heavy canvas shoes were sturdy,
but they wouldn't protect her toes from several hundred
pounds of horseflesh.

"I've been thinking," Tim said. "We need to get
someone else from the Springs involved. At least one.
Someone who knows about explosives and cutting torches
and things like that. I wonder if Raul—" Suddenly he
broke off and slumped against the horse.

Twila dropped her handful of grass and rushed around

the horses to catch him, easing him gently to the ground, keeping him well away from the skittish horse's hooves. His mouth was slack, and his eyes glazed; Twila closed both and then looked around for someplace sheltered to drag him. She'd have to build a fire because the night was getting cold, and she had to keep the smoke invisible to watching eyes on the east bank. Getting him inside one of the houses here would have been preferable, but his weight was more than she would be able to haul very far without hurting one or both of them.

She managed to bring him into the lee of a building, and there she made a ring of stones and began gathering well-seasoned deadfall to make a virtually smokeless fire. When it was going, she broke into a nearby house for blankets, and soon she had Tim warmly wrapped and settled as comfortably as she could.

Dear God! she thought as she sank wearily to the ground beside him and pulled a blanket over her own shoulders. Two pregnant women, a handful of unruly savages, and a man dying of CM—this is what I'm leading against Krell.

Going to see his father always made Jon's ulcer flare up. He swigged at the chalky medicine he kept in his desk, did one of the deep-breathing exercises Carolyn had taught him, and was about to head for the door when he caught sight of the picture Desirée had painted for him that morning. It was not a picture of a thing, but just a sheet of paper symmetrically filled with splotches of bright, vivid colors. Desirée had been fascinated with her new box of paints and had simply laid out samples of one color after another across the page. Something about the harmony and the clarity of it had captured Jon. He picked it up now and studied it once more, debating within himself. Finally he took it with him and left the lab.

The lavish office his father occupied was beginning to show signs of wear. The carpet grew shiny in places, and the upholstery on the couch just inside the door was wearing thin. The whole place had a slightly tawdry feeling, that of bygone glory, of a courtesan past her prime. The man at the desk had a little of that look about him, too, with graying hair and a face wizened by care lines.

It disappeared the moment Krell looked up and saw Jon, for then he became the showman, the ringmaster, the benevolent despot smiling down on one of his subjects. "Jon! Come in. Sit down. I was just thinking about you. The board meeting is coming up, you know, and Rufus Montana is going to be retiring. I was wondering what you thought of Estelle Goldstein as a replacement."

"Estelle?" Jon hated Estelle Goldstein; she was one of the most ardent supporters of Elizabeth Modecko's philosophy for the masses—not that she practiced it herself. She had been married to Ben Markham for forty-three years and had three children who'd never seen the inside of a petri dish. Jon always thought of her as a "do as I say, not as I do" person. But she had been a contemporary of Carlton Grimm. In the coming days, people who had known Carlton well might be good to have on the board. "A conservative, like Rufus," Jon allowed. "It would keep the current balance on the board. But I'm surprised you don't want someone a little younger."

"The young will have their day," Krell told him. Then he frowned. "After I'm gone."

Jon gave a little shrug and tried to make his voice light. "You'll be around forever," he said, and squeezed out a small smile. "I just meant Estelle is only likely to serve three or four years herself before she retires. Someone like Marty Shore would give you at least ten or fifteen."

"Mm." Krell nodded a little, and for a moment the care lines reappeared on his face. "By that time I'll be thinking of retiring myself."

Never in a million years, Jon thought viciously, but he kept the emotion off his face and out of his voice. "Do you think your work will be finished by then?"

Krell glanced up at him, looking for sarcasm in his son's face and finding none. "Probably not," he admitted. "It was a passing thought. In the best of all possible worlds . . .' His voice trailed off, and he noticed the paper in Jon's hand. "What's that?"

Jon looked down at it, then held it out in Krell's direction. "Desirée made it," he said. "I thought you might like to hang it on your wall, dress up your office a little."

The emotion that swept over Krell's face as he took the painting startled Jon. Disbelief, and then gratitude, and something Jon could only describe as love transfigured the older man's features, and his eyes misted. "Thank you, son," he said thickly, and he gazed for several moments at the colorful offering. "Watercolors?" he asked finally.

Jon nodded. "Her first paint box."

Krell put the artwork on his desk and fished in his pocket for a handkerchief. "Well." He blew his nose and appeared to study the picture. "Quite the eye for color, I'd say."

"Must get that from her mother," Jon said. "I'm lucky if I can get my socks to match."

Krell laughed and wiped at his eyes. "Well, you get that from *your* mother," he chuckled. "That and your chin dimple." He looked up with a small wistful smile. "How is your mother?"

"Still angry," Jon said frankly. "Some people grow more forgiving with age, but not her." Then, "I'll be glad when Desirée doesn't need to stay with her while I'm at work. I don't want my daughter to grow up hateful."

Krell nodded, and his eyes misted again. "I often wonder," he said, "what might have happened if only she'd told me about you sooner."

Jon shrugged again. "We can't change the past," he said simply. "The future is all that's left to us." He rubbed at his face, stared at his hands, and finally said, "Dad, I want to come back on the governing board. I made some mistakes, I know that, and I was—a problem, but if you'll give me another chance I'll—" He stopped as he saw that his father was staring at him. "What?"

"Do you know," Krell said in a voice hoarse with emotion, "that is the first time you've called me Dad?"

Jon dropped his eyes guiltily and knew that it was true. "Like I said, I've made some mistakes," he mumbled. "I just—I had a hard time feeling connected to you. Now that—now that I'm a father myself, and I see how my mother can twist things . . . Now that I've got my own regrets . . ." He couldn't go on.

Krell drew a deep breath. "Are you going back to work

this afternoon," he asked, "or would you like to have a drink with me?"

Jon rubbed his chin. "I'll take the drink," he said. "I've got one experiment running in the lab, and my computer is churning out another one, so I was just going to pick Desirée up early and spend some time with her."

Krell rose and crossed to a polished cabinet on the wall. There he extracted two small snifters and a bottle of brandy that was at least eighty years old. He poured a liberal portion in each glass and brought them back to the desk; but instead of sitting behind it, he drew up a chair across from his son. "What shall we drink to?" he asked.

Jon pondered that a moment. "Second chances," he said finally.

It seemed good to Krell. "To second chances," he agreed. They touched glasses and drank.

"Good stuff," Jon observed.

"I can get you a bottle," Krell offered.

Jon wanted to refuse, to snarl at Krell that such privileges ought not to be reserved for the Medical oligarchy and their chosen favorites, that he couldn't be bought—but he bit back the objection and nodded. "I'd like that."

The effect that simple lie had on his father was amazing. Krell's whole countenance brightened.

Jon took another sip of the mellow liquor and wondered what it was doing to his ulcer. Probably, he thought, diluting the acid my stomach is churning out right now.

"Jon"—Krell swirled the brandy in his snifter, watching it coat the sides of the glass, inhaling its aroma—"when you were about—fourteen, I guess, and we had those really awful years . . ."

Jon smiled ruefully. "You mean when I used to lock myself in my bedroom the minute you came home, and refuse to come out till you'd gone back to work?" He shook his head. "I was a kid, I was—scared. Angry, because Mom sent me to you, and—I just felt like I didn't have control over anything. Not myself, not my situation, not anything."

Krell studied his son, surprised to find the boy so open. Those months in the rain forest had done him some good, then. Given him a chance to reflect. "Anyway, you once said to me that you would never choose medicine as a profession, that you didn't want to be anything like me, that you'd rather work in the waste-recycling plant than in a hospital."

Jon grimaced. "I was angry," he apologized. "I said a lot of stupid things."

"What made you change your mind?"

"Carlton Grimm." Jon knew as soon as he said it that it was the wrong thing to say; but the answer had been so reflexive he couldn't stop it. "Carlton was a grandfatherly kind of person," he went on, trying to mend it. "Patient and understanding. He told me there was more to medicine than being a physician—which, to tell you the truth, I still don't think I could do. He said I could specialize in research. And then he told me about Twila and her immunity. How it represented hope for every person in Numex—but only with good people to push the research forward." Jon took another sip of brandy. "He said you were one of the best."

"That's nice to hear," Krell said sincerely.

Jon glanced up at his father, then back down at the brandy in his glass. "I wanted to be part of that hope. I wanted to offer everyone in Numex the chance to live without the fear that had driven my mother to push me out. I—" He hesitated. "I was flattered that Carlton trusted me with the secret of Twila's immunity." Now he lifted his eyes to his father again, making sure there was no accusation in them. "I wish you had trusted me that much."

"Well." It was Krell's eyes that dropped now. "Trust doesn't come easily to me. I had my trust betrayed at an early age and, like you, I never quite got over it."

Now Jon was curious. "Your mother?" he asked. He'd known his paternal grandfather briefly—a harmless old con artist, to his way of thinking, quick with a grin and a lie—but his grandmother had simply been another woman who, in the style of Elizabeth Modecko, sent her son away at the age of eleven and never spoke to him again. At least, Jon thought, my mother kept in touch for all those years. There were several years I would not speak to *her,* but she never gave up on me.

"You never knew who she was, did you?" Krell asked softly.

"Your mother? No." And I never cared, he thought.

"Well, she didn't buy me any favors in Medical," Krell mused. "Carlton hated her. And like you, I admired Carlton very much. So I sort of buried her in my past, never spoke of her, even changed the records in PubInfo so people couldn't tell. Kept the Elizabeth, but gave her my father's family name, so no one would suspect. But she always used her own family name." He sipped his brandy. "Modecko."

The glass nearly dropped from Jon's hand. "Elizabeth Modecko?" Segregationist Elizabeth Modecko was the mother of Samuel Krell?

"Ironic, isn't it?" Krell observed. "She believed so strongly in what she preached that she sent me away; and I never believed a word of it, but I'm head of an organization whose sanction has done more to promulgate it than she was ever able to do." He shook his head. "You may not believe this, but there were times when I was every bit as angry with her as you have been with me. And after all that, I could never understand why, when it was your mother who rejected you—as mine rejected me—that it was I whom you scorned. It never made any sense to me, Jon." He lifted his eyes again, and there was a trace of bitterness there that he had never let Jon see before. "I tried so hard to win your love. I took you in, I gave you every privilege, I put up with all your abuse—and you rewarded me by loving Carlton more than me."

Jon lowered his head and shook it sadly. "I can't explain it," he said frankly. "Maybe you shouldn't have given me quite so much."

The idea surprised Krell. "What do you mean?"

"Sometimes I felt like . . . like I wasn't a person in my own right," Jon tried to explain. "That I was just your son, that everything I had came to me because of that and not because of who *I* was. Even Carlton, I think, took an interest in me because I was your son, and you were his friend. But—" He hesitated again, searching for the right words. "Carlton never let me get away with anything. If I was out of line, he told me. If I wanted something from him, I had to work for it."

"So what are you suggesting?" Krell asked. "That I

make you earn back your position on the governing board?"

"I'm not suggesting anything," Jon told him, beginning to lose patience with this game. "I'm just—trying to understand." He stood up and set his brandy snifter on Krell's desk. "I really should go get Desirée now."

"Tell her how much I enjoyed the picture," Krell said, rising and crossing back behind his desk.

Jon headed for the door but stopped, debated with himself, and then came back. He faced his father across the desk once more. "There's one more thing," he said. "You remember that activity on Carlton's old id that you . . . noticed . . . before I went to work in the rain forest?"

"What about it?"

"I heard from Twila. She's alive."

Krell sat down with a heavy thud.

"She didn't drown in the river—God only knows why not. But she's with some survivors Outside, and she located an old generator and managed to power up a computer. She's contacted me a couple of times. I'm trying to talk her into coming back Inside."

Krell's mouth worked, but no sound came out.

"I'm going to contact Twila's aunt," Jon continued, "because I think she can help convince Twila. I'm telling you up front so you know what it's about, and what I'm trying to do, and don't send Security to bust it up. Twila will listen to her aunt a lot more than she will me. I need her help."

Krell only nodded dumbly.

"Trust goes two ways," Jon said. "I'm trusting you to know about this. Trust me to follow through without interfering." Then he turned and walked out the door.

Chapter 17

"Delia."

The fourteen-year-old was sitting in a sandbox in the tiny playground near the Springs' pumping station, supervising three or four toddlers with their buckets and shovels. She lifted her head when Twila called, tucking a strand of long hair behind her ear as she did so. Her face registered surprise. "Yes?"

For an instant Twila saw another face in hers, the face of Lacy. They were near the same age, but that was all they had in common. One dark-skinned, one light, one with curly hair, the other straight, one small and childlike, the other tall and blossoming, one abused, the other loved. And my daughter? Twila wondered. Which is she more like? Either?

But she had not come to draw comparisons between this woman-child and others. She had come for help.

"Delia, you know I'm planning an—an expedition."

Delia's curiosity was open and ingenuous, as befitted Delia herself. "They say you're going to attack the biodome."

"I need to talk to a man Inside," Twila qualified. "And he won't come out unless I force him."

"Oh."

They looked at each other for a moment, Twila wondering how to begin, Delia wondering what all this had to do with her.

"Raul has fixed up some special equipment for me," Twila continued. "He and Tim are coming along to help me with it. And I have some friends—sort-of—among the gangsters, and they're coming, too. But I need one more."

Delia's eyebrows flew up. "Me?"

Twila sat down on the edge of the sandbox beside her,

and scooped up a handful of sand. She was surprised at how cold it was, for the sun was bright and warm at this time of day; but winter was coming, and the signs were all around her. "I need someone who can handle a team of horses," she said, "which I know you can. And . . . someone to take care of Tim, if he blacks out on me."

"Oh." The color rose in Delia's cheeks, and she looked down at the sand around her feet.

"I . . . I can't seem to do it right," Twila admitted, watching the sand trickle out between her fingers. "I don't know enough about it. And I'll be busy. So I need someone who—well, I'd like someone who knows him, who cares about him, and who's strong enough to do all the things that need to be done."

A small boy was burying his dump truck, one plastic shovelful at a time. Delia added her own shovelful to the pile absently. "I guess. I'll have to ask Trudy if she can watch the kids while I'm gone. Will it take long?"

"About four days, if all goes according to plan. But Delia—you must realize, there is danger involved in this."

The young face clouded. "How much danger?"

"From what I have planned, not much, not for you, because I want you to wait back out of the way with a team and wagon. But the Hats are . . . unpredictable. I don't think they'll make trouble, but they treat their women differently than mountaineers do. I just want you to be aware of that. As for the rest of it, if you stay back where I tell you, you shouldn't be in any danger."

"And Tim? Will there be danger for him?"

Twila sighed. "More than I wish. Especially because he could black out at any time."

"He could fly," Delia corrected. "You mean he could fly."

"Yes, he could fly," Twila agreed. "And it would probably be better if he stayed behind, but he won't, and to tell the truth, I don't want him to. I need him. I need his courage."

Delia gave a little smile. "I think you have plenty."

Twila took it for the compliment it was and smiled back, though a little wryly. "Only because I draw from others. My grandfather. My Aunt Trish. Even Starbright." She rubbed off the sand that clung to her palm and fingers.

"And now Tim. But I need to know there's someone to take care of him, to get him out of harm's way if he can't get himself out. Will you do that for me?"

"No," Delia said simply. "But I'll do it for Tim."

They camped in the same place Twila and Tim had camped earlier, on the south side of the Numex river, half a mile west of the enclosed city. They slipped in at dusk, hoping the domizens would either not see or not notice the horse-drawn wagon and its four occupants. Why should they care, anyway? The Springites had been traipsing up and down this road for some fifty years on their way to the city to forage for supplies. No one had paid them any attention before. The majority of domizens did not even know that anyone had survived Outside.

Leaving Raul and Delia with the wagon, Twila and Tim continued on horseback toward the river's confluence with the Rio Grande. The Hats would be coming up from the south along the west bank—provided Spider hadn't changed his mind. The moonless night glittered with stars that seemed as crisp and sharp as the wind that swept through these rolling hills. Twila was glad for the heavy coat Tanya had forced on her; its weight and warmth were a comfort. But it did not ease her disquiet when they found no one waiting at the rendezvous.

"Maybe they're waiting south of the highway," Tim suggested.

Twila shook her head, glancing around at the spattering of buildings to the south of them. "They wouldn't make that kind of mistake." Her hair began to prickle as she surveyed the derelict shops and dwellings. "I think they're here, Tim, waiting for us."

"In hiding?" he asked in surprise. "Why would they—"

"They've had clashes with the domizens before," she told him. "It might just be a precaution against being spotted, or fear of a trap. Or"—her voice dropped and gooseflesh rose on her arms—"maybe something's gone wrong. Maybe Spider isn't—"

"I got you in my sights, Bubblehead" came a voice from the darkness—Bobo's voice.

Twila froze, her heart pounding. Tim reached for the rifle strapped to his saddle, but Twila's hand flashed out to stay him. They couldn't hope to shoot what they couldn't see, and drawing the gun might force Bobo to fire. She held her breath, waiting.

"Shut up, Bobo" came another voice. "You scare the silly bitch to death, and we miss all the fun."

Relief washed over Twila as Spider stepped out of the shadows not ten meters from her, a tall, muscular shape in the darkness. "You make a deft target, though, Bubblehead," he told her. "I hope you use better sense than that in this raid you talking about."

"You'll have a chance to make sure I do," she replied, sliding off her horse and standing to face him. "We're having a council tonight, Spider. I want you and your ace kool to come; everyone else can stay here and wait."

"Oh, you'll let them do that, will you?" Spider mocked. "What if I say we all come?"

Twila did not want the entire Hat entourage to invade her camp; she worried not only for Delia, but for herself and the two men. Friction was inevitable: a Hat would make a crude remark, and Raul would flare; one would lay a hand on Delia, and Tim would intervene—no. She could not have all the Hats in her camp tonight; but neither could she let Spider know that she cared. So she shrugged. "You really want Bobo shooting his mouth off at a council?" she asked him.

"Bobo been to a lot of dances," Spider told her. "He got something to say, you best listen."

"Does he say better than you and Road Dog?" she challenged.

"Maybe I want all my Hats at my back when I walk into your camp," he said coldly, and finally Twila realized where he was going with this. Spider was walking into an unknown situation, and he was no fool—he wanted his homies there to back him up. How could she mollify him without letting the whole group tag along?

"There are just four of us," she told him. "Four Hats, no more. You can scope my camp before you walk in—you see how stupid I am, I can't hide anything from you."

He nodded. "That's righteous. Me, Road Dog, Bo—"

"Two women," Twila interrupted.

"What?"

"We have two women and two men," she said. "You

bring two women and two men. Or do you need fighters to stand up to a couple of women?"

At that he drew back, and his nostrils flared. "You think we afraid of you?"

"You tell me."

Spider muttered a string of curses. "Starbright!" he called out sharply. In a moment there was a rustling sound from Twila's left, and Starbright stepped out of the shadows with Lacy at her elbow. "How much you trust this Bubblehead?"

"I'll walk into her camp," Starbright said confidently. "Mountaineers too dumb to hurt this silly bitch; they ain't smart enough to lay a hand on me."

There was a soft sound in the darkness; Spider was laughing. "So you say!" he chuckled. "All right, then. Road Dog, you with me. So's Starbright and Lacy. The rest of you wait here. We be back by morning."

It was late evening by the time they reached the camp on the riverbank. Neither Spider nor Road Dog had wanted to get too near the horses, so Twila quickly arranged things to preserve their pride while making best use of the transportation. The horses were for the pregnant women, she said, to make the long walk easier on them. Starbright was nervous about approaching the huge beast, but Tim in his gentle, calming manner helped her mount with a minimum of difficulty. Lacy would not be separated from her friend, however, and so they settled for putting her on Tim's horse behind Starbright, and Twila rode her own. This left the three long-legged men on foot.

Light from the biodome itself illuminated the surrounding terrain enough for the Hats to get an idea of what they were facing. Spider and Road Dog turned off with Tim for a closer look while Twila took the two Hat women on into camp. When the men returned, Twila sketched out her plan—or as much of it as she wanted the Hats to know—over supper. Then she solicited Spider's opinion on the best way to deploy the Hats. After that they went round and round, Tim objecting to one part of the strategy, Spider to another. But in the end they

reached an agreement that minimized the enormous risk
and gave the best hope of achieving Twila's objective.

Then Spider and Road Dog headed back to join the rest
of the Hats. They would meet Twila and the mountaineers
the following night. Starbright and Lacy, however, were
fast asleep by the time the council finished, and it was not
difficult to persuade Spider to let them spend the night
with Twila and her friends. Finally, well after midnight,
Twila and Tim were able to curl themselves in their blankets, twined in each other's arms, and fall into an exhausted sleep.

When Twila woke the next morning, Tim was already
up and gone with Raul for a clandestine look at the biodome environs in the daylight. Starbright and Lacy were
up as well, gorging themselves on the exotic food Delia
had taken from the wagon.

"What you call this stuff again?" Starbright asked
through a mouthful.

"Bread," Delia told her. "It's made from flour and eggs
and—"

"Flowers? What kind of flowers?"

"No, *flour*," Delia laughed. "You take grain and grind it
very fine, and it makes a powdery substance we call
flour."

"Grain. Grain is like—seeds, right? Right, Twila, ain't
that what you say?"

"Yes," Twila agreed as she sat on the ground beside
them. "It's the seeds of special kinds of grasses. We grow
them in fields. We make all kinds of things from grain
flour. Remember the cookies I gave you?"

"And you eat this all the time?" Starbright asked. "Up
there in the mountains?"

"Bread, yes," Twila assured her. "Cookies we don't eat
so often, because they take a lot of sweetener, and there's
not so much of that to be had. Honey, mostly. Delia, did
you give them any cheese?"

"Phew!" Starbright wrinkled her nose. "I didn't like
that stuff. But this yellow stuff here—" She pointed to the
butter on her bread. "This is good." She went on for several minutes, then, about the other foods she had sampled,
and how different they were from Hat fare, and how
clever the Hats had to be to find enough food, but she

could see the sense in the way the mountaineers did it, and how far a walk was it into the mountains, anyway?

Tim and Raul returned and joined the women at breakfast. "How are you today?" Tim asked Lacy pointedly.

Lacy cringed back against Starbright. "It's all right, child," Starbright soothed. "He won't hurt you; I won't let him hurt you. See, he Twila's friend."

Tim smiled reassuringly, but wisely kept some distance from the frightened girl.

"How did the council go?" Delia asked.

Tim shrugged, and Twila sighed. "It has a good chance of working, I think. As long as one of the Hats doesn't get trigger happy."

"Hats know, in war you do what you told, or people die," Starbright said flatly. "Even wannabes know that. Got to do what the man say."

"This is not a war like you fight with the Bariosos, though," Twila worried. "We're not going for blood."

"Spider know that," Starbright insisted. "The man in there dis you. You want to dis him in front of his homies. Sometimes that better than blood. Spider know that."

Just then Tim reached for a wedge of melon Delia offered him, and both Hat women noticed the trembling of his hand.

Lacy scooted back, whimpering, and Starbright stared with frightened eyes. Startled, Tim looked from the terrified women to Twila for explanation. She reached forward and caught his trembling hand in her own. "It's all right," she told Starbright deliberately. "You have nothing to fear."

Starbright licked her lips. "He sick, ain't he?"

"Yes," Twila said. "Tim is showing symptoms of the disease that everyone gets—almost everyone. Sometimes he will lose consciousness, too, but it's nothing to be afraid of."

They could see Starbright's inward struggle. "The sickness is in the air, Starbright," Twila told her friend firmly. "It's in the bodies of mothers who have babies. It's like I told you before: those who are going to get it, already have it when they're born. It just doesn't show until they're much older. Being around sick people doesn't make you start shaking or fainting any sooner."

Starbright looked at Lacy, who looked from Twila's face to Starbright's and back again in confusion. "I getting old," Starbright said with a quaver in her voice. "I get the shakes soon anyway. But Lacy, she so young. I can't take no chance with her life. If he sick . . ."

"It doesn't make any difference," Twila insisted. "Lacy won't get sick any sooner by being near Tim. Or near you, if you start to shake."

"It's true," Delia chimed in, trying to add weight to Twila's words. "I've been around flyers—sick people all my life, and I'm just fine. See?" She held out a hand that did not tremble in the least.

Starlight gave her a sidelong look, wanting to believe. "Since you a baby?"

"Sure. My mother was holding me in her arms when she crossed over. Died. So they tell me, and I believe it. And I've taken care of lots of—sick people. We all do it. And hardly anyone manife—gets sick before they're twenty."

Starbright turned back to Twila. "How old you?" she demanded.

Twila hesitated. "I'm twenty-four," she answered carefully, "but I was born in the biodome—" The words died on her lips as she remembered that she *hadn't* been born Inside.

"Your mother have this sickness in her body?" Starbright pressed.

"No," Twila replied truthfully. "And it's not in the air Inside the biodome, either. That's why Bubbleheads only come out in special suits—"

"So you ain't got this."

Twila balked, but Delia jumped in. "She's got it *now*," the young girl said. "She got it when she came Outside and breathed our air."

"That right?"

Twila took a deep breath. "In my case, no," she said quietly. "I don't have the sickness, and I never will. It's what we call being immune." She heard the intake of breath from Delia and Raul; Tim gave a small sigh and seemed to close up on himself. Twila forged on.

"No one knows why I got so lucky, except that my mother was immune—and all of my children will be immune as well. Only it's not always so lucky. People who are different—good or bad—always get treated differently. It's the reason I left the biodome; it's the reason I'm worried about my children Inside. Once—" She shook her head and tried to remember a day last spring before her world changed so drastically. "Once I thought life was so boring because I was ordinary, my job was ordinary, everything about my existence was ordinary. Now I could almost wish for those days back. Almost, but not quite. Because as much as I hate what I have to do tomorrow, as much as I would like my life to be . . . peaceful again . . . I can't unlearn all I've learned because of my immunity, and I wouldn't want to. Living Outside, touching people, just meeting them face-to-face: you and Spider, Melinda and Tim—even Raul's sister Gloria—my life would be so much poorer without all of that."

Starbright stared thoughtfully at her. "Are you scared about tomorrow?"

Twila gave a weak laugh. "Of course I'm scared. But once—" She reached out a hand and laid it on Starbright's arm. "Once I was afraid to do this. Once I would have preferred to talk to your reflection instead of your face. I've been afraid of so many things, Starbright, and most of them turned out to be no harder to get through than a thunderstorm."

For a long moment Starbright held her eyes; then she seemed to come to a decision. Nodding her head, she got to her feet. "Okay," Starbright said. "Okay, I take it for true, what you say about not getting sick faster by being around people with the shakes. So if you don't mind, we hang out here in your camp till Spider come back." She dusted off her hands, and then helped haul Lacy to her feet as well. "But now me and Lacy gonna take a little walk." With that the two girls headed for a copse of trees by the river.

The others were silent for several moments. There was a heaviness in the atmosphere that had nothing to do with the cool, dry morning. They were all thinking about what Twila had just told them. "Are you really immune?" Delia asked finally.

Twila nodded. "That's why I had to escape from Krell. He was using my unborn children for experimental immunization therapy. That's why I have to confront him. I can't let him do the same thing to my daughter that he did to me."

Raul whistled. "I knew it was experiments; I didn't know . . ." His voice trailed off.

"So you'll never fly," Delia said.

A wry smile twisted Twila's lips. "No. I'll never fly. But I'll live three or four of your lifetimes. That is," she said, rising to her feet, "if I live through tomorrow."

Starbright and Lacy were a long time coming back from the river, and finally Twila went to look for them. She found them talking quietly on a sun-warmed patch of dirt; they fell silent as she drew near.

"Are you okay?" Twila asked.

"Yeah, yeah, we okay," Starbright grumbled, "we just making a plan."

"One you can tell me about?"

"If you don't tell Spider and Bobo."

Twila laughed. "Believe me, I'm not going to tell Spider anything I don't have to, and I'd be a happy woman if I never spoke to Bobo again in my life."

"Good," Starbright said bluntly. " 'Cause me and Lacy decided, we ain't going back with the Hats."

Stunned, Twila stood gaping at the two women.

"Look at this child," Starbright said, her voice low and intense as she pulled Lacy close to her with an arm protectively around the young girl's shoulders. "She gonna have a baby, and what happen to her then? If it boy, the Hats kill it; if it be girl, they keep it to give more Hat babies, but it won't ever be no proud child. And Lacy here, what happens to her? They gonna keep her and feed her if she don't give no more babies? No. So they gonna get babies on her. And you see how she is. She don't want no Hat on her no more than she want Bariosos on her. She don't want to be touched. You tell me what kind of life she have with the Hats."

It was a moment before Twila could speak. "No kind of life," she whispered. "But, Starbright, you—"

"My time short, too," Starbright told her. "I start to shake soon, and then Hats, they all walk away from me. They take Lacy, and they move their digs somewhere I don't know, and I be all by myself. I ain't never been by myself, Twila. To be sick, and all by myself . . ."

"But—Little Mako," Twila stammered. "Your son, you can't—"

"I be gone from him soon, anyway," Starbright said grimly, and Twila could see the pain in her eyes. "He a Hat, he belong with Hats. They take care of him. They won't take care of Lacy. Only I do that."

Twila sighed heavily and rubbed her hands across her tired face. In her heart there was great joy that her friend would leave the cruel way of life the Hats followed; but she felt the depth of Starbright's despair in abandoning the only community she had ever known, in abandoning her own son, to save a foster daughter who might be an emotional invalid the rest of her days. "Will you go back with the mountaineers, then?" she asked quietly.

Starbright nodded. "When Spider come back, just before you go to the dance, I pretend to shake and be sick. They walk away from me then. And when you go out to fight, Lacy and me start down that road." She pointed to the road that twisted and wound its way toward the mountains. "We be gone when the fighting done, and I don't think Spider come looking for us 'cause I be sick, and Lacy be with me and she be"—she waved a hand helplessly at her companion—"like she is," she finished lamely. "Bobo might be a problem over Lacy, but if we just gone, Spider won't let him chase after us. He think it be too late for her by the time Bobo ever find us. So we go down that road, look for those mountains. Maybe when that girl Delia come along with the wagon, we ask her for a ride. She seem like a nice girl. I think she help us."

"Yes," Twila agreed with a nod. "Yes, she'll help you. All the mountaineers will help you."

"Then, it set," Starbright said. "And you don't be telling Spider on me."

"No, I won't tell." Twila shook her head, thinking of the maturity Starbright was attaining, and of what that maturity could do for the Hats if only they would listen. "The Hats will be poorer without you, Starbright," she sighed.

"They don't know that," Starbright said bluntly. "And they never will."

Just after dark, as planned, the Hats slipped into the camp on the river. They ate and rested, and sometime after midnight they started for the biodome. The Hats had a practical lore they called "night ops," which governed a raid in the dark, and they taught it to the mountaineers. Everyone wore black, and light faces were streaked with dirt. Shiny gun barrels were grimed as well. They moved quickly and quietly in groups of two and three across the dam and into the deeper shadows on the hillside below the dome.

Her props and habit tucked in a backpack, Twila crossed the dam with Spider and Road Dog, grateful for their protection in these frightening circumstances. When they reached the far side and flattened themselves against the dirt just outside the control bunker, she looked back at Spider's face. Her heart ached for the grief she saw there, for Starbright had done her piece of acting just before Spider left camp, and it had been effective indeed. This tall, muscular youth, this warrior, this leader of his tribe, had looked for a moment as though he would crumble to the ground sobbing. Fighters he had, and any Hat woman he wanted, but he had only one sister and now she was lost to him. She had raised him, and he had protected her, and now convention demanded he walk away from her.

And walk away he had: without a word, without a sound, without a tear.

Bobo had made an ugly scene, shouting at Lacy to let go of Starbright, trying to drag her away, but Lacy had gotten hysterical and finally Spider and a couple others had hauled Bobo back and subdued him urgently while they upbraided him. They had a battle to fight; problems like this would have to wait until they returned. She was only a girl, after all, and the baby was a Barioso, and it could all wait while the fighters did what fighters were born to do. At last he'd surrendered, but the animosity raged in his eyes as he followed his leader out of the camp. The Hats murmured among themselves about the difference between his reaction and that of Spider, who had to leave his sister, too; Spider knew the way of things, they said, and that was why he was the man. You didn't see him carry on so.

But his grief showed here in the darkness outside the

control bunker. His face was set in grim lines, and his
eyes betrayed an inner sorrow. Twila knew, watching his
face, that he was thinking not only of his sister, but of
himself. One day the sickness would come to him, but his
way out would be different. There would be a battle one
day, when he felt his time growing short, during which he
would look for glory—and for death. That was the
shadow on his features now; in his grief, Spider had suddenly felt his own mortality.

Tim and Raul had been first across with the cutting
torch, but they waited until everyone else was in place
before they put the tool to its task. Here they were not
visible from anywhere in the biodome, unless someone
was clinging to the roof panels; still, they proceeded with
extreme caution. Only when there were Hats posted at the
mouth of the Security tunnel and two other dome-shaped
structures that connected to the Numex complex, did the
mountaineers light their torch and begin.

Twila forced herself to look away from the brilliant
flame, back toward the crest of the dome floating like a
ship of light upon a sea of darkness. How they had argued
with Spider that it was unnecessary and unwise to kill any
Security personnel who ventured forth in defense of the
control bunker! Draw them off, distract them, pin them
down, but don't kill them. Why not? "Because there will
be no end to the reprisals," Twila had explained. "There
are ten times ten as many Bubbleheads as Bariosos and
Hats put together; and if you kill one of them, they will
come out of their bubble city and hunt you down. If we
don't hurt them, if we only frighten them, they will leave
you alone."

Is any of that true? she wondered now as she extracted
from her pack the habit she had picked up at her grandfather's bungalow. Will they ignore the Hats after an
attack of this nature? Can I convince them there will be
no further threat?

I can if they have no immunity, she thought savagely. If
I can stop Krell's research, if they have to trust in their
SCE suits, they will not come after the Hats—perhaps not
even if someone is killed.

But I won't tell the Hats that.

It took almost thirty minutes to cut through the bolts

and seals and force the ancient door open. So far there was no stirring from within the dome. Twila did not wait but darted into the bunker, flashlight in hand, Spider at her elbow.

Jon had shown her a diagram of the interior, and it appeared to be accurate. Twila shined her flashlight around once quickly, then more slowly, trying to get a feel for the place. Unlike so many of the outbuildings attached to the biodome, this one was rectangular in construction. It was perhaps forty feet long and thirty wide on the interior, and broken by partitions into three chambers. Twila had entered the largest of these, where monitors and instruments covered three walls, glowing and humming and whirring with the activity of the hydroelectric generators. Above her head and pointing back toward the door was a small camera.

Through a doorless arch to the right, she could see the railing that surrounded a set of steps sunk into the floor. That was the way up from the biodome, the entrance from the service basement to this important place. Spider saw it, too, and stationed himself at the head of the stairs with his rifle covering the door.

"Are there light switches down there?" she asked the Hat as she fished the habit out of her pack and pulled it on over her head.

"Say what?"

Twila shook her head. "Never mind, I'll check." She slid her hands along the rails and jumped the first five steps, then trotted the remaining five to the bottom.

"Get away from that door; you crazy?" Spider hissed.

Twila wondered that herself, heart pounding wildly in her chest. "Better now than later," she told him. The switches were there, a bank of about ten. She hit them all and started back up the stairs.

Suddenly there was a shout from outside the bunker and the sound of rifle shots—two, three. From the other side of the door, Twila could hear a clanging and the incessant, brash honking of an alarm. Startled, she bolted up the stairs, almost tripping on the habit in her haste. But the lights were on, at least; she needed them for her plan. More gunfire. She almost collided with Road Dog, who lurched inside the bunker door to use it as a shield. "They

come out in two rides," he called back to Spider. "Got
the tires on one and the men pinned down behind it,
maybe three of them. The others got scared and ditched
their ride; they's behind some rocks now, shooting down
at us."

"Tim!" Twila called in panic.

"Here," he called from the farthest chamber. She raced
to it and found both Tim and Raul inspecting the panels
and displays there. "Are you sure this isn't the main control?" he asked, indicating the array of instruments in
front of him.

"Controls, yes, but not the ones I want," she told him.
"Not according to Jon. Come back this way—"

A clanging sounded at the door in the stairwell. Spider
squeezed off a shot that rang and ricocheted around the
room, causing the others to duck; but the clanging
stopped momentarily. "I suggest you leave that door
alone," Spider shouted down at it.

"This is Duty Officer Rochman," a voice rang out from
a speaker on the wall. "Leave the bunker now."

Twila spun toward the nearest camera and plucked a
cylinder from her pack. "Can you see me, Officer Rochman?" she demanded, holding up the makeshift grenade.

"I can see you—"

"This is a bomb in my hand, and this is the triggering
device," she told him, and she thumbed the safety and
plucked out the pin. "The minute I relax pressure on the
safety catch, it goes off. Now you think about that before
you do anything foolish."

There were several moments of tense silence. Twila
could feel her heart pounding, hear the blood rushing in
her ears. No sounds came from the other side of the door,
and outside the bunker the gunshots had died out.

"Just take it easy" came Rochman's voice. "Take it
easy. Tell us what you want."

Twila relaxed a bit, fought the urge to roll her neck and
relieve the tension there. "I want to talk to Krell," she told
him. "I want to talk to Dr. Krell."

There was a pause.

"It's the middle of the night," said Rochman reason-
ably. "Dr. Krell is sleeping."

Twila gave a dry laugh. "Wake him up," she snarled.

"You've got ten minutes." Then she turned her back on the camera and pretended to look around the room. No need to let them know that she knew where her objective was—that might indicate help from the Inside, and she needed them to believe she and her entourage were unassisted. Slowly her gaze moved to the doorless arch. Spider stood with one foot propped on the railing around the stairwell, his rifle still trained on the door below. She made a show of peering behind him.

Slipping through the doorway, she stopped in front of the metal grid work that surrounded a bank of controls. Rochman's voice now sounded through the speaker in this room. "Miss—miss, don't touch that, that's dangerous. It's high voltage. Miss—"

"I know what it is," she called back. "Tim, bring the bolt cutters and the wrecking bar. We need to get through this grate."

"I wouldn't touch that if I were—"

"Is it electrified?" Twila demanded.

Silence.

Twila found she still held the metal pin from her grenade in her hand. She tossed it against the grating. Nothing happened; no sizzling, no sparks. "I'm going to touch the grate," she told Rochman. "If it's electrified and I drop this canister, you know what will happen."

Still silence.

Carefully Twila reached out and laid a gloved hand on the metal. Feeling nothing, she slipped her fingers through the openings and curled them around. "You're down to nine minutes, Mr. Rochman," she called out. "Better get someone to rouse the good doctor. And while you're at it, wake up the younger Dr. Krell. I'd like to speak to him, too."

"A message has been sent," Rochman told her. "Please move away from the grate."

"I don't think so."

Tim and Raul were beside her now, inspecting the latch, applying the bolt cutters.

"What do you hope to accomplish by this?" Rochman asked her.

Twila considered what to tell him. What would get to the news nets? Nothing, not while Krell owned Security.

But if she could shake Krell's hold . . . "I hope," she said slowly, "to improve the quality of life in the biodome. I hope to begin the long process of relieving its fear. I hope . . . to give people options. As many options as I myself have."

"And who are you?" asked Rochman.

Twila smiled coldly as she watched Tim snipping away at the grate around the latch. "Mother Grimm," she said softly. "You can just call me . . . Mother Grimm."

Chapter 18

Krell's face appeared on the monitor in the corner, looking puffy and older than Twila remembered. But it was definitely Krell's face, and unmistakably his voice: rich, melodious, rational. "Twila! Twila, thank God. We all thought you were dead. Are you all right, dear?"

Twila gave a short bark of laughter. "I'm fine, Dr. Krell. And you?" She was inside the high voltage cage now, and had been studying the labels on the various switches there. But now she eased herself into a chair, which Tim had dragged in from the other room, and gazed up at the monitor.

"As well as can be expected," he replied. "But you—"

"How's my mother?" she interrupted. "And Aunt Trish. How are they?"

He sighed heavily. "I haven't spoken to them recently. I know they were devastated when you—when you left, and we thought you had drowned," he told her. "Your mother especially. She was quite hysterical."

"I can imagine," Twila said dryly, all too able to picture her mother's histrionics. "Mother never really appreciates anything until someone takes it away from her."

"We're all guilty of that, to some degree," Krell said smoothly. He was watching her intently, although his face was mild and serene. "Think of yourself, Twila." Did he find it strange that she was wearing a habit? "Don't you miss your life here?"

"Miss my monthly appointments?" she sneered. "Miss the jabs and the pokes and the medication and the uncertainty of not knowing what was wrong with me? No, Dr. Krell," she said with heavy irony, "I don't miss that at all."

He waited a beat, still studying her. What was she up

to, this little girl he'd known all her life? Was she really a threat? Did she really intend to do serious harm? If so, she was not the Twila he thought he knew. "It doesn't have to be like that anymore," he said softly.

"Oh? Do you have another victim to lay upon your operating table, your sacrificial altar?" Twila jumped to her feet and grabbed hold of the lever at shoulder height. "I can put a stop to you, Krell. I can put a stop to you anytime I want."

For a moment he held her gaze, gauging the extent of her rage, her intentions. There was always the chance she'd gone over the Edge; but somehow he doubted it. "You don't want to do that, Twila," he said finally.

"Want to? No," she agreed. "But I will, if that's what it takes to stop you."

He continued to study her a moment, trying to discern if this was an act. Then shook his head. "No, you won't, Twila. You're not the kind. I don't believe you will pull that lever."

"No?" She held up the homemade grenade. "I pulled this one. It's only my grip on the firing pin that keeps it from exploding; and if I stay here long enough, I'll get tired and my hand will slip, and I won't have to pull anything to take out your power station. Understand me?"

There was an edge to her voice he did not recognize. Was it only anger? He'd heard her angry before—and underestimated the lengths to which that anger would propel her. "Twila," he said in his most calming, soothing voice. "You're filled with rage, and I understand that. I kept secrets from you, and that was wrong—"

"My rage!" she snarled at him. "You know *nothing* about my rage! It wasn't your body that was invaded. It wasn't *your* children that were conceived without your knowledge, and butchered the same way!" Her hand strained on the power main. "And that will stop, Dr. Krell, everything about it will stop, or this entire biodome will stop. Understand *that!*"

She saw Krell watching her like a patient wolf gauging the strength of its wounded prey, and kept her face black with hatred. She let her eyes blaze, her teeth clench, and her hand tremble on the switch. There was no need to feign her anger, only to let it loose, to fuel it, to allow it to escalate. The anger itself was truly there.

In a moment he spoke again, gently. "Twila," he said. "I'm sorry. I can see that I've hurt you. Please let me—"

"Don't apologize to me," she shouted at him, letting go of the lever and taking a step toward the camera. "Apologize to my children! Apologize to the dead, Dr. Krell! They'll be more sympathetic."

His head turned aside then and spoke to someone off camera. After a moment he turned back. "What is it you want, Twila?" he asked. "What do you want of me?"

Who was off camera that he consulted with? Security? Probably. Jon? "I want you to stop," she repeated. "I want you to stop saving some lives at the expense of others. Didn't I say that? Didn't I make that clear?"

"And if I say I'll stop, will you come out of the bunker?"

She gave a short bark of laughter. "No, no, Dr. Krell!" she cackled. "It's not that easy. I need more assurances than that."

"Such as?"

"I want your public resignation as chief of staff, chief of research, and chairman of the governing board," she told him flatly. "And a complete admission of guilt."

A look of astonishment crossed his features, just briefly, and Twila smiled inwardly. Good. She'd managed to catch him off guard with that one. But the rational look returned quickly.

"What if I disassemble my lab?" he countered. "Tear down all the equipment. Will that do?"

"Too easy to fake," she informed him. "You could show me an empty room and claim it was your lab. You could move all the equipment somewhere else."

Krell was thinking, trying to come up with another compromise. "There's been a suggestion," he told her, "about a law regarding consent. What if I—"

"Laws are no better than the people who break them," she retorted. "I've told you what I want Krell. You can have thirty minutes to think about it." She stepped back and grabbed the power main again. "Until then I'll be here with my hand on the switch."

"Twila—"

"That's all, Dr. Krell!" she shouted. "If you want to talk to me again, you'll have to come out here to do it."

At her signal, Tim lifted the bolt cutters and smashed the camera.

Krell cut the transmission from his end and turned to the other two people in the room. "What do you think?"

"I think Jon's right," said Rochman. "She's walking the Edge."

Krell thought about that, wondering if Twila were truly unstable. Coming from the Outside as a baby, there was no knowing what kind of inbreeding might have produced a psychological weakness in her. Add to that the stress she'd gone through, and then leaving the dome to live with those savages . . . It was a logical assumption. But was it a valid one? He wondered again about the private conversations between Jon and Twila, and what had really been said. But Jon had confessed the contact to Krell, and that was an indication of good faith.

Yet Twila had always been so *normal.* Krell turned now to his son, who had been summoned to Security and stood with Rochman, out of range of the visicom, which allowed Krell to speak to Twila—or had. It was a dramatic gesture, breaking the camera on her end, but he believed it was just that—a gesture. He shook his head. "Twila can't pull that lever," he told Jon. "I know her, she can't do it. Her mother is in here, her aunt is in here—you're in here. She won't pull the lever."

"Twila wouldn't," Jon agreed. "But this woman . . ." He shook his head, implying that the person he saw on the monitor was not the Twila Grimm he had known. "Last time I spoke to Twila, she wasn't like this. She told me she had a way to stop you from continuing your research, but I had no idea she might turn violent. Something must have happened to her Outside."

Krell rubbed his fingers thoughtfully across his chin. He knew that life Outside was barbaric, with rival groups attacking each other like warring tribes; perhaps, like other barbarians, these survivors practiced rape. Would someone of Twila's sheltered upbringing break under the emotional assault of a gang rape? Possible. Possible. He remembered the mother, that wild woman they'd had brought Inside and decontaminated. They could not understand her language, nor she theirs, but he and Carlton had speculated that she had been assaulted numerous times. That idea had fascinated Krell—*she* had fascinated him. So primal, so unbridled in her reactions . . .

"She doesn't hang on to that lever all the time," Rochman was pointing out. "She only grabs it when she gets agitated."

"Run the footage back," Krell commanded, coming back to the problem at hand, and Rochman replayed the short interview with Twila. Krell watched it closely, watched Twila's movements, saw how far she strayed from the power main, how tightly she gripped her homemade grenade.

"She doesn't have to pull the lever," Jon said. "If someone jogs her elbow, or she loses concentration, it's all over. We have to get her out of the bunker."

Yes, Krell wanted her out of the bunker. He wanted her back Inside the biodome. He wanted it for the sake of Numex, for the sake of his research. And this time, when he had her . . .

"We can't get near her to take her out forcibly," Rochman added. "She's got too many guns around her. We estimate six outside the bunker, keeping my teams pinned down, and three men inside. One's this kid," he said, punching up a picture of Road Dog at the bunker door, taken from a monitor in the bunker, "and there's a slender blond kid, and a heavyset man that we've seen." He tapped keys and brought up images of Tim and Raul. "Someone's got a gun on the tunnel door; it might be one of them, or it might be a fourth person, we don't know. This bunker was designed for utility, not defense, so our cameras don't cover every square inch. Now we can still see her," he demonstrated, bringing back the live video of Twila seated calmly in the high-voltage cage. "But she's taken out her monitor, so she can't see us or hear us from in there. That's going to make it hard to talk her out of the bunker."

Krell's thoughts drifted away from the current problem, to how he would handle things once they had Twila back Inside. There was no question of her being allowed to roam free anymore, not after this. No, she'd have to be kept confined, as they'd confined her mother twenty-four years ago, only he'd be smarter this time. He wouldn't allow her to be held in Isolation, where the tunnel to Outside was so handy. Watching Twila now, he could see some of the savageness in her that he'd seen in the mother. No, he'd be smarter this time. He'd have a cell arranged far away from any means of escape, one whose location was known only to Security—and himself, of course . . .

"We can stage a newsnet announcement," Rochman suggested. "Hell, if we have enough time we can even pull images of the board from a history file and dummy them into the broadcast, have the computer simulate their shocked reactions. Then we pipe the 'cast to the two remaining terminals in the power station—"

"She'll never buy it," Jon interrupted. "She'll want to hear from her Aunt Trish, or someone she trusts Inside, that the message went out."

Rochman scowled, but he conceded the point. "Will the aunt lie for us?" he asked.

Krell shook his head. "Never in a million years," he said. "Has a streak of righteous indignation in her that's been troublesome in the past." He remembered the stink she'd raised when Twila was refused for advanced studies in medicine; well, she'd paid for that. He'd seen to it. Her own career had died that day.

"Maybe she could just talk to Twila," Jon suggested. "Get her to give this up. They were very close."

Krell considered that. While Trish wouldn't lie to Twila, it was entirely possible that she would cooperate in trying to talk her out of the power-station bunker. "Do you think Twila would come to one of the other monitors to speak to her?"

Rochman frowned. "We could try it. She did break off communications rather decisively."

"But what did she say?" Jon reminded the others. " 'If you want to talk to me again, you'll have to come out here.' How about sending Trish Outside?"

There was a moment of shocked silence before anyone responded. "I don't know," Krell said dubiously. He pondered the idea. It was true, a physical presence was more likely to draw Twila from her position than a virtual one.

But Trish? "Sending people Outside who've never been out before is asking for trouble. They get panicky, they get disoriented . . ."

Jon swallowed hard. "Do you want me to try?"

When Krell looked up at his son, he saw the fear in his face. Jon had been Outside only once, and it had been a disaster. It was good of him to volunteer, but you didn't send a boy to do a man's job. Krell hadn't gotten where he was without taking some risks. "No, Jon," he said. "No, it's not you she wants to talk to. It's me. It's got to be me who goes out."

"I protest!" Rochman said quickly. "You set one foot Outside, and those snipers will nail you; she'll have what she wants quick and easy. No. I forbid it."

A cold look from Krell made the other man squirm uncomfortably. "You're not in charge here."

"He's right, though," Jon said. "How do you know one of those gun-toting barbarians won't shoot you on sight?"

"I still don't think she's capable of murder," Krell insisted. "Not willful murder, not Twila. Apparently she has some kind of control over these hoodlums; and we have armored SCE suits. If I can get her to agree to talk to me—Have a close look at that grenade," he told Rochman. "If I can get my hand around hers, with the grenade still in it, will that keep it from going off? Because if it will, I know I can overpower her. If I can just get close enough . . ."

"Maybe it would help," Jon said slowly, "if you told her it was me coming out."

Krell arched an eyebrow at his son. That was not a bad idea. Let her think it was Jon coming, and agree to give him safe passage. Then, when he got close enough to her . . .

"Let's do it," he said finally. "Jon, you call out there. Ask her for safe conduct. Tell her you want to see her. Tell her anything. See what you can get."

Tim was worried. He was sitting in a chair just outside the high-voltage cage, out of range of the cameras, with Twila in his lap, cradling her close and whispering in her ear so their conversation couldn't be picked up by microphones in the room. "Do you think it's really Jon they're sending out?"

Twila was tired, weary and tired. Her hand was stiff from keeping its grip on the grenade, and she wanted nothing more than to replace the pin, nestle here in Tim's arms, and fall asleep; but that was not her privilege. Instead she considered the question, then shrugged. "Either way, I know how to handle it."

Tim hugged her and nuzzled her cheek. "I wish I had your confidence. But I keep thinking of all the things that can go wrong. I wish I could be Inside watching them right now. I wish I could hear their conversation and—"

Suddenly Twila felt the strong, comforting arms go slack around her. One instant she was being cradled lovingly, the next minute she was fighting for her balance as Tim's body slumped in the chair. Her right elbow smacked against the concrete floor as she fell and pain shot along her forearm, followed by a numbness that threatened to loosen her grip on the canister. For a moment she was terrified it would slip from her hand; but she drew the arm quickly in toward her body as she rolled into a sitting position and cradled it carefully as she shouted, "Raul! Raul, it's Tim!"

The heavyset mountaineer had been waiting in the other room with Road Dog; he arrived in time to catch Tim before he slid from the chair. "Damn!" Raul exclaimed. "Bad timing. You all right?"

"Fine, just hit my crazy bone," she replied. "Raul, get him out of here. Take him back to the wagon, back to Delia, and stay there with him. No need for you to sit in this bunker anymore." In the moonless night it was unlikely anyone would even see the pair crossing the dam; and if they did, there was precious little they could do about it, what with the Hats keeping Security pinned down just outside their tunnel.

Raul balked. "I don't like leaving a job half finished, Twila."

But she shook her head. "You've done your part, and so has he. It's up to me now, me and the Hats. It'll be easier if I know you and Tim are safe."

"Easier to do something stupid," Raul growled.

She gave him a wan smile. "This whole thing is stupid, Raul. Go. You can't change anything."

With a shake of his head, Raul hoisted Tim across his shoulders and started out. "Do you need help?" Twila asked him.

"What wrong with him?" Spider demanded, watching them suspiciously.

Hair prickled on the back of Twila's neck. "Do you need help?" she asked again, ignoring Spider's question.

"I'll be fine," Raul replied. "Delia's just the other side of the dam. I can make it that far. Just you be careful, all right? Because if he comes back from flying and finds out you're not there, I don't want to be the one to tell him."

The mouth of the Security tunnel couldn't be seen from the doorway of the power station, but Twila knew someone was coming because the word was relayed back among the Hats. So she stood in the shadows with no light behind her, shielded as much as possible by the wall of the building, and waited for her guest to clamber down the steep slope from the mesa. At the bottom he turned and started slowly for the bunker.

Twila knew it wasn't Jon the moment she saw him step onto the path. The form was too large, too bulky; even allowing for the armor of the SCE, he moved too heavily to be Jon. It had to be Krell. She left the doorway and scuttled back to the high voltage cage, where she settled in, left hand on the power main and the canister clutched firmly in her right. That was all she could do. She waited patiently for her visitor to arrive.

Jon and Rochman watched from the Security control center inside the biodome. "I don't like it," Rochman grumbled, watching Krell until he moved out of range of the camera in the Security tunnel. "It's too dangerous. She's an Edgewalker, she's unpredictable—"

"No one's made a move on him yet," Jon pointed out. "Check the interior camera, can you see him there yet?"

Rochman grunted. "They're going Outside . . . yes, here he comes. They're letting him in . . . frisking him . . . I still don't like it," he repeated, as Krell was prodded toward an open archway. "When she finds out it's not you, she could go suborbital."

Now Krell passed out of the range of that camera, and a moment later appeared on the one that showed Twila waiting in the high-voltage cage. Jon leaned casually across the console to get a better look at this new monitor. Twila stared at her visitor.

"Hello, Dr. Krell," she said.

"Hello, Twila," said Krell.

Rochman watched nervously as Krell approached the cage.

"That's close enough!" Twila called out sharply. Krell stopped where he was. "Well, well, well. Bearding the lioness in her den, are we?" she asked.

"I had to see you face-to-face," Krell told her. "Virtual communication is fine for some things, but not for solving problems. When two people meet face-to-face, it's much better."

"Don't preach to me, Krell," Twila snapped. "What do you want?"

"I've come to offer you a bargain," he said calmly, rationally. "You want my research to stop; I understand that. But what about Jon's research, Twila? Jon's research hurts no one, and it might eventually save us all. But he needs an adult donor. Your children won't be able to supply blood in the quantities he needs for . . . oh, six years yet. They're tiny things; their bodies are still growing. Don't ask them to make that kind of sacrifice."

"I'm not asking them to make any sacrifice," Twila pointed out, "you are."

"If I do what you ask," Krell continued, "will you come back Inside?"

"Inside!"

"Just for a while," he argued. "You can leave again whenever you want." His voice was smooth and rational. "Think of the advantages. You could see your mother again. She's going to be quite frantic, you know, when she learns you're alive, but here, out of reach. Don't put her through that, Twila. She's been through enough already."

"So have I," Twila said pointedly.

* * *

"She'll be frantic, all right," Jon muttered to Rochman as they watched. "He told Roxanne that Twila went over the Edge and killed herself. I wonder how he's going to explain his error?"

"Sh," Rochman hushed him. "I need to hear this."

Jon glanced over his shoulder at the monitor behind his back. Then he turned his attention back to the one Rochman was watching, heart pounding.

"And your aunt," Krell was saying. "Think of her relief. Think how she'll want to throw her arms around you and touch you and know you're real."

Twila seemed to waver a moment, and her hand eased its tense hold on the power main.

"And Jon," Krell continued softly. "You know, don't you, how much he wants you to come back Inside? And not just for his research." The suggestion in his voice was subtle, yet distinct. "You're fond of him, too, aren't you?"

Twila laughed. "Fond of him! Yes, I guess you could say that. I'm fond of Jon. Jon cared about what happened to me—me, Twila Grimm the person, not Guinea Pig Grimm, who supplied the blood for all his experiments."

"I care about you, too, Twila," Krell said gently.

Again she gave a short bark of laughter. "If you truly cared about me, Dr. Krell," she said, "you wouldn't murder my children."

Krell groaned and let his head droop a moment. "Twila," he said tiredly. "We've been over this. I do not murder—"

"You took ripened eggs from my ovaries without my knowledge or consent," she hissed, "fertilized them and started human lives; then you snuffed out those lives in the process of your research. That's murder."

"It is *not* murder!" he insisted. "Twila, if I can carry my research to its conclusion, we can save every last man, woman, and child—"

"Except mine!"

"—in the biodome! The death of a few fetuses in exchange for all of humanity—"

"Part of humanity!" she cried. "The part you want to

live, the part you deem worthy. Have you got your criteria all set up, Dr. Krell? Do you know who you're going to save first?"

"I will save all!" he roared.

"Not mine!" she shrieked, letting go of the lever to take a half step toward him. "You save yours—your son, your colleagues, your Security guards, who keep your empire intact! You had a working inoculation, Dr. Krell, and you withheld that treatment *and the knowledge of it* from all but a select few! How will it be different if you succeed in making the immunity permanent, instead of temporary?"

"Now!" Rochman coached impotently from the Security control room. "Grab her now!" But Krell was caught up in his tirade.

"There wasn't enough before!" Krell bellowed. "It was a matter of quantity! But when your children are mature, if your male children can supply sperm that produce immune fetuses, I can fertilize hundreds of eggs, thousands in a month, not just the four or five I got from you."

"Thousands a month that you can kill," Twila badgered.

"To save humanity!"

"To save one segment of society at the expense of another," she persisted. "There are words for that; words like *slavery* and *racism* and *genocide*. Hitler used an oven; you use a syringe."

"How dare you!" Krell thundered. "How dare you compare me to that madman! All I have done, I have done for the good of this biodome!"

Her hand flew up to clutch at the handle extending from its panel in the wall behind her, and inside the dome Rochman and Jon gasped collectively and held their breaths. "Do one more thing for your biodome," she challenged. "Resign. Resign and abandon your research with my children, and their children, or I will cut your power."

Krell stopped short and stared at her, stared at the wall behind her. Then he sighed heavily. "All right. I'll make an announcement on the newsnets. Give me till morning, when people are awake and starting their day. I'll go back Inside—"

"Oh, no," she said quickly, and a long metal bar was seen sliding threateningly into the picture, hovering near Krell's head. "You'll wait out here with me, Dr. Krell. It's only a couple of hours till daylight now. We'll sit right here and wait. You have someone else schedule time on the nets for you." She turned her face directly to the camera. "You got that in there? You arrange things for the good doctor. He and I are going to sit right here until you have the links ready to go. Say seven o'clock. That should give you plenty of time."

"I knew it!" Rochman hissed. "I knew he shouldn't have gone out there! Now what am I supposed to do?"

"Plan B," Jon said tightly. "We lie. We pretend to set up a link to the newsnets and let him make the announcement, but we don't transmit it farther than this room. Or, you know what might work? Get her mother. We'll bring her mother to Security, show her the announcement, and ask her to tell Twila it went out to the entire biodome. It won't occur to Roxanne that it might be a trick, whereas it would to Trish. What do you think?"

Rochman rubbed the back of his neck with a sweaty palm. "I don't like it," he growled. "I don't like any of it. But what choice do we have? All right. I'll set up the links; you contact the mother."

But Jon shook his head. "Her mother doesn't know me. She'll respect your authority more than mine. I'll set up the links for you; I know how to do that."

Rochman grunted and wheeled his chair to a visicom station. "Okay, I'll wake sleeping beauty and break the news to her that her daughter's alive. But if she gets hysterical, you send a med tech over there to sedate her."

"Done," Jon agreed, and began tapping out communication commands on a nearby workstation.

Krell struggled like a demon against his two attackers, but they were younger and stronger, and it took them only a few moments to bind him and haul him out of the bunker. He never saw Twila. They threw a blanket over his SCE suit and hustled him down a steep slope, then across a flat, level stretch of ground that he deduced was the dam, because of the roar of rushing water nearby.

Then he was loaded into a vehicle of some sort, which bounced away with him tied securely to its side.

Twila followed close behind Spider and Road Dog, who had snatched Krell as he walked out of the range of one camera and before he entered the field of the next. She'd waited while they subdued him and dragged him out, giving Jon the time he needed to patch in the phony encounter between herself and Krell, one which he and Rochman were now watching in Security's control room. Trish had constructed the videography, using her graphical and morphing skills to alter existing images of Twila in a habit and of Krell in an armored SCE suit. Knowing where Twila would make her stand, it was easy enough to drop the falsified images against the proper background, and even put Twila's hand on the power main.

They'd given Jon a count of twenty to distract Rochman from watching the monitor covering the bunker's door—which he had accomplished by simply leaning across it to look at the one where the fake video was then running—and then they had hustled Krell Outside, covered his pale SCE suit with a dark blanket, and in the moonless night had simply stolen back across the dam to where Delia waited with a wagon.

The rest of the Hats remained behind to make sure there were no immediate complications; but one by one, over the next few hours before dawn, they, too, would sneak away to safety. Bobo would be one of the last. By the time he returned to Twila's camp, there would be no trace of his sister and Starbright for him to follow.

Once the wagon gained the road south of the dam and headed west, Spider and Road Dog dissolved into the night. They would regroup with their homies at a pre-arranged location and all return to their digs together, Spider's obligation to Twila discharged fully. Raul removed the blanket from their prisoner, and the little band continued on. Raul and Delia rode on the wagon seat, Twila on horseback. Still unconscious, Tim lay supine in the bed of the wagon, next to the bound and struggling Dr. Krell. Krell began by hurling threats and imprecations, a thin disguise for his sheer panic. Security would come after them, he swore. They would pay dearly for this—those snipers on the mesa would not stop his

Security teams, now that negotiations had broken off. They had heavier weapons and—

Twila only laughed. "Why, Dr. Krell," she told him, "Security has no idea negotiations have broken off. They think you and I are still sitting in the bunker discussing philosophy. They can hear us. They can see us. They won't make a move for at least another two hours."

He fell silent. She could almost see the thoughts spinning in his brain as he pieced it together. "You haven't the technology," he said after a moment.

"Don't we?" She had discarded the habit before leaving the bunker, and was clad in dark clothing again. Her smile was a cold flash in the pale starlight. "I found a working computer in the city, and a generator to power it. I was able to tap into every resource Numex has."

He thought about that for several minutes. Then, "Jon," he said softly.

She could not see his face through the clear plate on the front of the helmet. "What about Jon?" she asked, forcing her voice to stay level.

"He was your inside man, wasn't he?"

Twila hesitated. It was no part of her plan to implicate Jon in this.

"He told me you had contacted him," Krell pressed on. "You set this up together, didn't you?" His head drooped. "It was a lie, then. It was all a lie."

"What was a lie?"

Krell wagged his head slowly from side to side, as though the helmet were suddenly too heavy for him to bear on his shoulders. "I believed him," Krell whispered, his voice barely audible through the speaker on the suit. "I thought after twenty-two years he'd finally come around, finally come to . . . respect . . ."

His pain was so genuine that Twila's heart ached in sympathy. She found herself wanting to speak words of comfort to her tormentor, but there were none to be spoken.

"What are you planning to do with me?" he asked finally. "Obviously you don't mean to kill me, or you'd have done so by now."

"We're just taking you for a little ride, Dr. Krell," she told him serenely.

The wagon bounced on. "I'll run out of air," he said.

"Air?" Twila laughed. "Why, Dr. Krell, there's air all around you. No need for you to run out of air."

After that he was silent for several more minutes. Then, "Twila," he began in his most logical tone. "You know there will be reprisals if you go through with this. You can't just take the chair of the governing board out of Numex and not expect reprisals. Think of your friends here. You may be willing to pay the price, but are they?"

"Do you really think anyone in Numex is going to care what happens to you now?" she asked cynically.

"Maybe not to Krell the man," he responded, "but this is an attack on their top official, and as such, on their sovereignty. It's an act of war, Twila. Don't start a war."

How eminently logical! she thought. No one wielded logic as deftly as the senior Dr. Krell. "No one thought it was an act of war when my grandfather was killed," she replied.

"He wasn't killed," Krell said patiently. "You know that. He was infected. It was an accident. I've paid for it a thousand times—"

"You've paid nothing!" she hissed. "You took over his work, his position, his power, and you've paid *nothing*!"

There was stony silence for a moment. Then Krell said softly, "People with power always pay."

Twila wondered if that were true. Had Krell paid, over the years? Paid in worry, paid in fear—paid, finally, with his son?

"Don't do this, Twila," he pleaded again. "Think of your friends here. Think of this young man, lying helpless. Think of that girl driving the wagon. Do you want to see them hurt? Killed? We never use lethal weapons Inside the biodome, but we have them. And Security will use them."

"Not if you tell them not to."

His body twitched in surprise, though she still could not see his face.

It was her turn to use logic. She wondered if she could put quite the attractive face on it that Krell did. "Think about it, Dr. Krell," she said. "You have a chance to leave a final legacy to the biodome. What is it going to be?

Death and destruction? Chaos and war? Or a chance at life for two communities?"

With that she urged her horse forward, out of the range of his voice.

Chapter 19

For an hour they pressed onward along the winding road. Hills and bends took the biodome from their sight, and now there was only the endless darkness of the earth and the dazzling spectacle of the star-flung sky with their tiny entourage caught between. At about four in the morning, Tim stirred in the wagon, and Delia called ahead to Twila. The little band stopped in the road.

Delia was already helping Tim to sit up when Twila tied her horse to the wagon and hurried to his side. He was smiling up at Delia, and it tore at Twila—but that was her own fault, she told herself. She had abrogated the privilege of his care, and with it the special bond between patient and nurse. It was her choice.

Then he saw her and struggled to right himself, his muscles still weak from his CM episode. He reached for her, gathering her to himself across the hard barrier of the wagon side.

"We did it," she whispered in his ear. "We did it. We got Krell out."

"I know," he whispered back. "I saw the whole thing."

Twila drew back and stared at him. "You—saw—?"

He nodded, a look of diffused joy on his face. "I flew, Twila. I lifted right out of my body, and I saw it all happen: I saw Raul pick me up, and carry me away; then I went Inside the biodome and found Krell, and I listened to them talk, and I saw Krell leave, and then when Spider and Road Dog grabbed him—I was there. My body had gone across the dam already, but *I was there.*"

"Oh, Tim!" Twila pressed her tear-damp cheek against his neck. "I'm so happy for you."

He stroked her back, her neck. "I saw him, too—Jon. He's—he's very intense."

Twila didn't want him to speak of Jon, not now. She had seen him just briefly, when he called with the phony story that he was coming out to talk to her. His face had been drawn, his eyes dark and disturbing . . . Yes, intense was a good word to describe Jon. But all that intensity, all that carefully caged passion, resided in another world.

"He has a hard time ahead of him," Tim said.

Twila drew back and searched his face. There was something behind his words, he was hinting at something . . . "What are you saying?" she asked bluntly.

"He's going to need help."

The hair prickled on the back of Twila's neck. "I can't help him anymore, Tim. I'm *persona non grata* in the biodome; they think I tried to shut down their power station. Jon will have to handle things on his own."

Tim glanced uncomfortably at Krell, who was seated next to him. "Can we take a walk?" he asked Twila.

"Sure." She let go while he climbed out of the wagon. "Raul," she said, "untie Dr. Krell. I think he and I will go on alone from here."

"It's only been seven, maybe eight miles," Raul warned.

"That should be far enough. Just keep his hands tied and make sure he doesn't get near the saddle horses."

Raul grunted and climbed off the wagon seat while Tim and Twila walked off to one side.

"What's your Dr. Krell going to do?" Tim asked her when they were out of earshot.

"I don't know," she said. "I don't think he knows at this point. I haven't put my proposition to him yet."

"I don't trust him," Tim said bluntly. "He'll say one thing and do another. Stay clear of him—he'll hurt you if he can."

"Only if it's to his advantage," she insisted. "Krell's a strange bird. He will do absolutely anything, as long as he convinces himself it's justifiable." *Any means,* she thought, *as long as it serves an end.* But she didn't think he would perpetrate violence for the sake of violence. He had lied to countless people across the years, but to no one, she believed, as much as to himself. He believed himself a hero, and the one thing he wanted more than any other was to be the savior of the biodome. Twila was going to give him that chance.

Tim shook his head sadly. "I hope you haven't over-estimated his ego. A wounded animal will do fearsome things when it's cornered. Stay clear of him, Twila. Stay well clear of him."

"I will," she promised.

He drew her to him, held her close. "If I don't see you again—"

"You'll see me," she promised. "It will be two or three days, I'm sure, before I make it back, but I'll be there. I'll come back to the Springs."

He looked at her with such sadness in his eyes that she wanted to weep. Then he kissed her—gently at first, then hungrily, as though this kiss would have to last him the rest of his life. "You don't have to," he whispered when their lips parted. "Come back, I mean. If you decide—"

"There's nothing to decide," she told him firmly. "I can't go in to Jon, and he can't come out to me. Besides, I won't leave you. Delia may take better care of you than I can, but I'm selfish. It's me that needs you, not the other way around."

Still he shook his head. "The part of me you need is ephemeral, and it will fade rapidly now. What lives on . . . will always be frustrated because it can't touch you, can't talk to you, can't help you. I felt that tonight, watching you face danger and being unable to do anything. Twila, you need someone else, someone flesh and blood."

"You're flesh and blood," she countered. "For a while yet."

He was silent a long moment. "Sometimes," he said finally, "the part of me that can touch you is frustrated, too."

Twila's throat constricted; was she really being so unfair to him? Would it be kinder just to go away and let him marry Delia?

"Are you two going to stand there sucking face all night" came a voice at Twila's elbow, "or is this wagon going to get underway?"

They jumped back, startled, and saw Starbright materialize out of the darkness, Lacy clinging to her arm. "Starbright!" Twila cried in delight.

"We was waiting just up the road," the younger woman told her, "and you go and stop down here. Now, come on—we both cookin' and we both tired, and we want to ride in that wagon thing and get some rest."

"By all means," Tim said quickly, ushering the way back to the waiting wagon. "I'll ride my horse from here—you two just make yourselves comfortable among the blankets and such there." He helped them climb in.

"What about him?" Starbright asked, pointing at Krell. "Where he gonna ride?"

"He's not," Twila said, untying her horse from the wagon. "At least, I don't think so. Did you want to go on to the Springs in the wagon, Dr. Krell? Or head back for the biodome?"

"What do you think?" he snarled.

"You gonna let him go?" Starbright demanded. "After all you went through to get him?"

Twila mounted her horse and looked down at the suited figure. "I believe in giving people choices," she said. "Sometimes their decisions can surprise you. Loosen his hands just a little, Raul," she instructed. "Once the wagon is gone, he'll need his hands free, in case he stumbles in the darkness. Or something."

Raul obeyed, then he climbed up onto the wagon seat beside Delia, and they started up the road. Twila called after them, "I'll see you in a few days."

No one responded. As the sound of the horses hooves faded into the night, she felt suddenly very alone.

Krell's voice brought her back. "Is this some kind of game?" he demanded harshly. He was tired, and frightened, and it showed in his tone.

"No game, Dr. Krell," she told him. "You're free to go any direction you like from here. Choose your destination. I'll tag along to see that you get wherever you're going safely."

He tugged the ropes off his hands. "Choose a direction, eh?" he asked bitterly. "What are my options? I've got maybe ninety minutes of air left in this suit. Where can I get in ninety minutes?"

"Well," she drawled from her perch atop the horse, "you could go after the wagon. They'll be making camp in an hour or so. If you overtake them, they'll be happy to give you a ride to their community. It's up in a canyon, about two days from here. It's a very nice place, good farmland and pastures—oh, and lots of hot water. They could use a doctor there. Raul's sister died of poisoning just recently, and appendicitis is nearly always fatal. I know you haven't done general practice for a long time, but your skills are still leagues beyond theirs. You could be quite the hero."

His answer was to begin trudging back down the road the way they'd come.

Twila clucked to her horse and began to follow, keeping a good ten meters distance from him. In the suit he could not be very agile, but she was taking no chances by getting close enough for him to reach the horse. That was an option she didn't intend to give him.

For the first mile she left him with his thoughts, keeping her horse a little behind him and to the left, just off the road. Krell was careful to pace himself, striving for maximum distance with minimum air consumption. The overall pitch of the land was downhill, but it was neither straight nor flat; there were simply more downhills than uphills. Twila knew Jon had calculated conservatively in advising her how far she needed to get Krell from the dome to force his hand, but like Tim she didn't trust the man. Krell was too devious.

After a while she broke the silence. "You actually have two choices in this direction," she told him conversationally. "The old city of Albuquerque is on the south side of this road, and that's where the Hats live. Those were my dark-skinned friends, the ones who escorted you to the wagon, remember?" Krell growled. "They're fairly savage, I'll admit—that's why I went to live with the mountaineers—but you could set yourself up in a clinic some miles away from them and live fairly peacefully. That's what my grandfather did, you know. Of course, he did have a minor problem," she admitted. "He helped people indiscriminately, you see, and a rival gang, the Bariosos, didn't take kindly to that. So they shot him. For bandaging a wounded Hat."

She looked down at the suited figure, a ghostly parody of technological man in a primitive world that was about to defeat him. He trudged on in silence, ignoring her chatter.

"Grandfather left quite a legacy, though," Twila went on. "A legacy of respect. The Hats came and buried him, and they still remember him. They can hardly remember their own parents, but they remember my grandfather." It was only a slight exaggeration. "They call him the crazy man."

"Crazy man, eh?" Krell said wearily. He didn't want to be reminded of Carlton. He'd spent so much of his life trying to do one better than Carlton, and with a fair amount of success—except with Jon. He'd never won the respect, the affection, that Jon had accorded Carlton. "You're the crazy one."

Twila laughed. "Am I? I'm not the one trying to walk seven miles through hilly country with only ninety minutes of air. The average human walks at three miles an hour on flat, level ground, did you know that?"

He stumbled in the awkward suit. "You have murdered me!" he cried in anguish.

"Have I? How old are you, Dr. Krell?" she asked. "Sixty-three, sixty-four? If you breathe the outside air and still live for fifteen years—which is the average for former domizens—that will make you nearly eighty. That's a long life, Doctor. Longer than my grandfather had. He was fifty-six years old when you infected him, and a Barioso shot him down only six or eight years later."

"I didn't infect him," Krell grated. "It was an accident." He had told the lie so often that sometimes he almost forgot it wasn't true. It could have been, after all.

"Really?" Twila reached into the pack slung from her saddle horn and pulled out her grandfather's diary. She couldn't read it by starlight, but she still had a small flashlight in her coat pocket, so she turned it on and began to read. " 'My name is Carlton Grimm, and I am a physician. I was a resident of the Numex biodome until 27 May of this year at which time I was expelled. No, let me be honest: until I was murdered. I cannot call it anything else, for I know that my poisoning with the CM virus was no accident . . . the med tech who did the lab work on my blood came to me as I sat in Isolation, waiting for the

results, and told me herself what she had found. Indeed I
was infected, but not with the airborne CM-B virus. It was
CM-A she found in my blood.' "

Krell's steps had slowed as she read. A weight descended on him, heavier than the armor of his suit. It had
gone so smoothly at the time, he had assumed either the
tech was afraid to tell anyone, or that Carlton himself was
guilty of indiscretions that could have exposed him to
the virus from another source. He'd had a story prepared,
of course, if there had been any questions—a batch of
contaminated needles. They were planted, ready for him
to discover them and solve the mystery. But the question
had never come up—till now.

"He knew it was you, Krell," Twila told him. "He knew
you'd gotten him with an infected needle when you drew
his blood."

Krell stood wagging his head slowly for a moment.
Carlton knew. Carlton knew, and he never said anything.
No accusation, no rage . . . oh, God, Carlton. Even in this
you had to outdo me, didn't you? Even in this, you had to
be a better sort of man . . . Slowly he began walking
again. "Is that what this is, revenge?" he asked the young
woman dogging him. "Dragging me out here, tagging
along to watch me die?"

"You won't die," she told him. "The seals on your
helmet are right there—you can take it off at any time and
breathe."

"I didn't infect your grandfather," he insisted. She
couldn't know for certain, after all. She must know there
were other ways her grandfather could have picked up the
disease.

"And I'm not infecting you," she replied. "You'll have
to do that yourself."

They were at the crest of a small rise, and Krell peered
into the blackness of the road snaking away from him,
trying desperately to see if a Security vehicle was coming
to his rescue. One would be coming soon, he was sure of
it. Twila's ruse couldn't fool Rochman for long. So on he
pressed, trying to pick up his speed, hampered by the
armored suit.

Behind him Twila was inclined to keep her peace for a
while, but Krell couldn't help thinking about what she'd

said. If Carlton knew . . . But he couldn't have known, not conclusively, and neither could Twila. CM-A could lie masked in the bloodstream for weeks; an infection could have been picked up a week before, or two, from another person. All it took was some intimate form of contact, an exchange of body fluids: blood, saliva, secretions of any kind. Carlton had to have had reason to doubt, or he would have said something; and if Carlton had reason to doubt, so did Twila. She must have doubts, and if she did he could still reason with her. "If Carlton believed I'd infected him," he said after a few minutes, "why didn't he accuse me?"

"Stop and think," she prodded. "What would have happened if he had? There were only three possible consequences. One, he'd have been discredited, and gained nothing but the ruin of his own reputation. Two, he'd have been believed, and you'd have been convicted and ejected from the biodome—then who would there have been to carry on the research for an immunization against CM? That was a tragedy he didn't want."

And one that wouldn't have happened, Krell thought, for he'd been prepared with the packet of contaminated needles, and a shiftless med tech to blame it on. But he'd never had to use it.

"Or three," Twila went on, "some people would have believed you, some him, and the Medical Authority—maybe the whole biodome—would have divided into two camps and torn apart the only structure holding that society together." Twila sighed. "I don't know, maybe that wouldn't have been such a bad thing. But it would have been bad for progress on the research, and that was what he cared about more than anything else. He wanted to find a way to cope with CM. He wanted the human race to have a chance at life."

"So do I!" Krell flared. "That's why I took your eggs. Why is it noble in him, and sinful in me?"

"Because you don't care what means you use," Twila told him, "or whom you sacrifice along the way. The only sacrifice my grandfather was willing to make was himself."

Still the saint! Carlton was still the saint. And this

sanctimonious granddaughter of his ... "Yet you are willing to sacrifice me," he accused.

Twila thought about that. "Yes, I am," she said finally. "I see it as an amputation—cutting off a cancerous limb to save the body. But you're right, it is a dangerous compromise. I'd be truer to my principles if I could find a way to stop you without eliminating you, but I can't."

They traveled in silence for some time then. Krell tried to reason his way out of his predicament. There must be an escape. There was always an escape. He would be rescued, he had to be. This couldn't be happening to him. He was the most powerful man in Numex, this couldn't be happening . . .

The road seemed to wind on interminably. Krell strained to see the glow of the biodome in the distance, but he was not rewarded. Surely around this bend—But around the bend was only another bend, and another and another. What did she want? She must want something, something other than his death, which she could have accomplished in a number of other more expedient ways. There had to be a purpose in drawing this out. Maybe she still wanted his capitulation. Maybe if he conceded something . . .

"Are you carrying any bottled air in your pack?" he asked her.

"No."

She was lying. Wasn't she lying? "Too bad. We could work a deal. I'd be willing to resign as chair of the governing board in exchange for enough air to make it back Inside."

"It's a nice thought," she admitted, "but there are too many ways for you to double-cross me. If you were at all trustworthy, it would be a different story, but I haven't seen anyone or anything you wouldn't betray. No, this is the only truly effective way to stop you."

They continued in silence for another half an hour. Unable to draw Twila into a compromise, Krell began to construct his own. What was his true objective? At this point, it was to get back Inside the biodome. He didn't really care anymore if he got her back for his research. It was probably better if he didn't try to recover her; Jon would make a problem of keeping her locked up. He'd just started to patch things up with Jon, he didn't want to damage that. No, let Twila stay Outside, she wasn't important now. Jon was important. Jon had finally come to him, had brought him a gift, the sweetest gift, the painting little Desirée had done . . .

Something clouded Krell's vision, and he thought maybe it was lack of oxygen already, but it was only tears. Had Jon really been part of Twila's scheme? In his head he knew it was true, but his heart ached to think of it. Why did the boy hate him so? Hadn't he taken him in, without a qualm, without a quibble, without even questioning whether he was the father? Didn't that mean anything to the boy? And what had he ever done but try to give Jon the best of everything? Fine clothes, fine food, special privileges, promotions— Damn him for his ingratitude! Didn't he understand? Didn't he understand what Krell was trying to say with all that? There were women in plenty, and protégés to choose from, and minions by the hundreds, but for all his status and power Krell had only one son . . .

Of course Jon understood. He'd sat there in Krell's office and said it: "Now that I'm a father myself . . ." It couldn't all have been lies. There had to have been truth at the core of it. You could look at a hundred young boys aged eleven, and they were just young boys, some interesting, others irritating, but when you looked at one and saw a familiar set to the jaw, and the same forehead you saw in the mirror every morning—it was different somehow. He'd never doubted Miriam when she said he was the father. To know, *this one's mine; this one is a part of me* . . .

He couldn't leave Numex now, not now. There was progress to be made—if not in his research, at least with his son. Maybe he'd give in to Twila, give up the experimentation with fetuses—Jon would be pleased with that. Perhaps he and Jon could work together then, the two of them, on the hematological research. Yes, that was it. Forget the fetal tissue, if it was a problem. They'd work on the blood serum, father and son. With two creative minds on the project, it would go much faster. It would be like the old days, with he and Carlton . . . oh, God, Carlton . . .

They rounded another bend in the road, and still there was no sight of the biodome. Krell glanced over at his guardian on her horse riding casually along the side of the road, never straying too near him. That was the answer, of course. The horse. He could ride the horse back and get Inside the biodome, and get back to Jon, get back to work. They wouldn't need Twila anymore, not with a dozen of her children to supply the small quantities of blood they would need for their research. They could conquer this disease yet. Together. All he needed was to get back to Numex. "If you gave me your horse," he said, "I could probably make it back before my air ran out."

"Could you?" Twila seemed to be running calculations in her mind. Did she know how much farther it was? "I suppose you could," she admitted.

"What will it take?" he asked. "What do you want in exchange for your horse?"

"For you to take your helmet off."

Krell couldn't believe it. There had to be something else, there had to be. "What is it you want?" he demanded in frustration. "Why are you doing this to me? What's the point?"

"The point is to make you think about what's important to you, Dr. Krell," she told him. "What it is you value in life. What you are willing to sacrifice. What you are willing to preserve. What's the purpose of your life, Dr. Krell? What is it that you want people to remember about you?"

Remember? "That I was a damn good doctor!" he snarled. "That I cared about my patients, and my community, and my species. That I did everything I could to defeat this infernal plaque!"

"How do you want Jon to remember you?"

Finally Krell realized that she really was going to do it. She was going to let him die out here. There was no going back into the dome, no working with Jon toward a serum, no wheedling his way in to see his granddaughter . . . After a moment he responded, "I want him to remember that I loved him. In spite of everything."

For a moment there was only the soft, steady sound of the horse's hooves clopping against the dark earth. "You know, I do believe that," Twila told him. "I do believe you love Jon. But I believe that if he stood between you and control of the biodome, you'd sacrifice him in a heartbeat—the same way you sacrificed my grandfather."

Despair erupted in Krell's weary heart. Unfair! The one situation wasn't anything like the other. His friendship for Carlton—his admiration for the man—were nothing like the feeling he had for his son, his own son . . . were they? Krell tried to think back, back to those days when he'd made his decision—for the good of the biodome. Carlton was getting in the way, impeding progress. He was a cautious man, and Krell was decisive . . . no, impatient. He'd wanted to try branches of research Carlton was skeptical about. But Carlton—Carlton kept getting distracted by unimportant things, wanting to spend time fighting social movements. Krell wanted to do whatever had to be done to get the job done quickly, himself, while Carlton wanted to take time to mentor the younger doctors, to let then make decisions, to get input from the board.

We'd have ambled along for years, Krell thought, *if I'd left Carlton in power. I had such a clear vision of how the community ought to be run. It would have been a crime not to take over . . . So even though I loved Carlton, even though I owed him so very much, I had to . . . But not Jon. It's different with Jon. Jon is my legacy, I could never—*

"I would never eject my son from the biodome," he told Twila.

"I'm glad to hear you say that," Twila said. "Because you were right—Jon was my inside man. He patched the phony holo in to the Security monitors, and when the forgery is discovered, your friend Rochman is going to figure that out fairly quickly. Jon is going to be in a lot of trouble. Unless . . ." She let her voice trail off.

"Unless what?" he prompted.

"Unless you intervene," she replied.

He gave a weak laugh. "And how am I supposed to do that from out here?"

"You can still communicate from the power station," she reminded him. "You're still the chair of the governing board; you could halt any investigation into the circumstances of the ruse. You could tie up all the loose ends you're leaving behind: fill vacancies, make assignments, appoint a successor . . ."

The first pale stirrings of dawn were showing in the eastern sky. "You want me to appoint Jon as my successor," he deduced.

"You need to appoint someone," she encouraged. "Otherwise there will be a lot of bickering and petty infighting, one faction against another. Numex will be like a riderless horse until someone gains power. That's going to affect research. If you want to be remembered as a man who did everything he could to defeat this plague, you need to insure stability after you're gone, and make sure Jon's research goes on uninterrupted."

Krell trudged on, turning over the possibilities in his mind. Leave Jon in charge? It had always been his plan, but the boy was still so young . . . Who would take over, though, if not Jon? Sara Wang? Rufus? They were followers, not leaders—that's why he had kept them on the board all these years, because they never questioned his authority. There was not a one of the senior staff with the breadth of vision or the strength of character to provide leadership to Numex. Twila was right; without leadership, the community would flounder, and it was to prevent that that he had wrested power from Carlton sixteen years ago. To deny the necessity now was to denigrate the reason for which he had exiled his mentor, his friend . . .

She was right about Jon, too. Young as he was, stubborn as he was, Jon was the logical person for the task. Like me, Krell thought. All these years I tried to make him like me, when that's what he already was: unmoldable, unmakable. If I couldn't control him, neither will anyone else.

"If I resign in favor of Jon," he said, "will you—"

"If you resign in favor of Jon," Twila interrupted, "you must do it because it is the right thing to do. Because that is your legacy to the biodome: a strong and principled leader, and a stable transition of government."

Krell was starting to feel short of breath now; the oxygen content in his suit was thinning. "He'll probably do it, you know," Krell admitted. "Find a way to immunize against CM. He has a genius for the work, and he's very methodical. Like Carlton. Carlton was very methodical."

"I never knew that about him," Twila said. "I just knew he was warm and loving, and gave great hugs." She drew a deep breath and let it out slowly. "I wish I'd had a chance to know more about him."

Krell's voice came in gasps now as his oxygen diminished. It added an impression of weeping to his words. "I wish . . . my granddaughter . . . could remember me as . . . warm . . . and loving . . ."

"Why shouldn't she?" Twila asked in some surprise.

"Because . . . Jon has . . . never . . . let me . . . see her."

A shiver went through Twila; Jon could be so very hard sometimes. But he could be so very tender as well. "You may see more of her from out here," she suggested, "than you did Inside. Wouldn't that be ironic."

"Give me your horse," Krell gasped. "Oh, God, Twila— give me your . . . horse."

Streaks of light were shooting up from the eastern horizon, and the stars had evaporated around them. The Sandia Mountains formed a jagged silhouette to the southeast. "That's one thing you'll like about the mountaineers," Twila predicted. "They have lots of children you can hug and hold in your lap. I'm not very comfortable with it myself yet, but . . ." She shifted in the saddle. "I think that will change. Once I have children of my own."

"Please." Krell stumbled and went down on his knees. "Your . . . horse."

"I don't think it will do you any good anymore," Twila replied. "See?" She pointed to a spot just off the road to their left where something shiny was catching the first rays of sunlight shooting over the earth's curve. "That's the biodome there. It's still a good two miles away. If you ran this horse full speed, you'd never make it before you passed out."

"Help me," he whispered, reaching out his arms to her.

"Help you get your helmet off? The seals are right there at your collar. Are the gloves giving you a problem?"

Her words were foggy in Krell's ears. How could she be so cool, so unmoved by his plight? "I'm dying," he gasped. "Help me."

"Just loosen the seals, Dr. Krell."

". . . Can't . . . breathe poison . . ."

"It won't hurt," she encouraged him. "The air is a little dryer out here, but it smells fresh and wonderful."

". . . die . . . CM . . ."

"Most people at the Springs live at least twenty years before they even show the first symptoms," she said helpfully. "And they live to be twenty-three and twenty-four quite regularly. You could have that many more years ahead of you."

". . . die . . . slowly . . ."

"And they have the most interesting experience," she continued. "When they start having catatonic episodes, they actually have out-of-body experiences. They call it psychoporting, or flying. You might want to do some research on that when you get there," she urged, dismounting and coming a little closer, though she left the horse back out of range. "Maybe there really is something in the changes CM works on the brain that cause this separation of the spirit from the corporeal body. Or maybe it's just in the people who settled there—a mutation, like my immunity. Maybe the CM is only a catalyst."

Krell's hands fumbled at the seals on his helmet.

"Or maybe it's the place itself," Twila speculated. "Magnetic fields, or lines of energy, or something like that. They tell me it has a long history as a spiritual center."

Blackness crept in on Krell. His hands felt heavy as they pawed at the two catches that would release his headgear. ". . . free . . . me . . ."

Twila knelt in front of him and thumbed the catches. "There were no explosives in the grenade," she told him. "You were right, I couldn't inflict that kind of harm on all those people in the biodome. My mother, Aunt Trish, Jon . . . I have a hard enough time doing this to you."

Slowly she put her hands over his as they struggled to twist the helmet loose. Then she gave a quick tug, and broke the seal. Air rushed into the helmet. She heard Krell take a deep breath, and begin to weep.

The sun was well up now, warming this southern slope of the mesa where the concrete bunker squatted, cool and blank, in the red soil. Higher up, a single Security vehicle sat near the rim as a suited guard tossed one last pack into it. It was an expensive parting gift for the man standing at the door of the bunker, stripped now of his useless SCE suit, but Jon had thought it appropriate, and Security had agreed. The guard waved farewell, then turned and disappeared in the direction of the tunnel, which led back to the biodome.

Leaving the shelter of the doorway, Krell rounded the corner of the building and looked back across the dam at the tiny figure on horseback. Twila had declined to come any closer while Krell entered the bunker and made his final arrangements with the governing board via the repaired monitors in the power station. Even now, with the last of Security vanishing into the tunnel, she gave no indication of coming any closer. Krell beckoned to her, walking down toward the near end of the dam to meet her.

Twila approached cautiously and halted her horse a good ten meters away from him. "How do I get there with my vehicle?" he called to her.

"The Springs?" She shaded her eyes against the easterly sun and nodded in that direction. "Head over that way, pick up the old highway. Go south a couple of miles then turn back west. Follow this road"—she turned and gestured to the road behind her, winding away through the hills along the river—"till you overtake the wagon. They'll guide you from there."

Krell nodded his head but did not turn away. "I know that culture and philosophy are acquired characteristics," he said after a moment, "but I'm not sure . . . Your mother was so savage and so wild, like nothing I'd ever seen. It was only her culture that made her so, I thought, but maybe I was wrong. Maybe there was something tough and indomitable at the core of her—there must have been. It's at the core of you, too."

Twila wondered about that woman, wondered what Krell knew of her that he'd never told. "Did she really escape?" she asked.

"Oh, yes." *Through my carelessness*, he thought. *Because I wanted her so badly. It was like some exotic fantasy, until she bit me and I was terrified I'd been infected, and in my panic I didn't care that she had slipped away from me and headed back for the tunnel and her freedom.* "Life Inside turned out to be . . . not to her liking. I wanted to go after her, but your grandfather— He had these ethics, you see. About using people without their consent."

"Is that why you infected him?" Twila asked.

Krell shook his head. How could he make her understand? It was unlikely he ever could, not while she had so few regrets of her own. "There were so many things," he said simply. "I was so young, and things looked so different then."

"You were ambitious," Twila interpreted, "and he was in the way."

Krell gave a wry smile. "Know any other young doctors like that?"

She bridled at that. "Jon's not ambitious," she denied. "Not the way you mean. He's not doing this for himself."

"No," Krell agreed. "He's doing it for you." He ran a hand across his face and looked up the slope to where the jeep was barely visible on the rim of the mesa. Then he turned back. "He wants to talk to you. You can use the monitor in the power station."

"I don't think it's very safe for me around here," Twila declined.

"Oh?" Krell pointed behind her. "Looks to me like you've got a bodyguard."

Twila whirled around to see Tim approaching on horseback across the dam. Krell left her and made his way up the slope, toward the waiting jeep.

Twila's heart pounded as she walked her horse back to meet Tim. "You were supposed to stay with the wagon," she chided.

"I just didn't trust him," Tim said.

"Was it him you didn't trust," she asked quietly, "or me?"

His shoulders sagged, and his eyes dropped to the ground. "I just had this awful feeling I wasn't going to see you again, and I'd never know what happened."

"Well, now you know," she said cheerily. "I'm fine. We can ride back together."

"After you talk to Jon."

It hurt her to see him so resigned. "At least let me say good-bye, Tim."

"Sure. Of course," he said quickly, pulling the rifle from his saddle. "Go ahead, I'll stand watch. If anyone so much as peeks over the side of that mesa, I'll fire a warning shot. You can hear it and run."

From above them came the sound of a quiet engine on the morning stillness. They glanced up and saw Krell's electric car motor away toward the east.

"I'll be quick," she promised. Then she turned her horse and trotted back to the power station.

Krell had left a terminal powered on just inside the doorway, and its monitor sprang to life the moment she entered. "Twila? Twila!"

It was not the sterile walls of Security she saw in the background, nor of anyplace in Medical. This was an apartment of some kind; there was comfortable furniture at the periphery, and artwork on the walls. One looked like a child's scribbling. "Hello, Jon," Twila said.

He himself looked worn and haggard; no doubt the conversation with his father had been difficult. Add to that the fact that he had probably not slept at all last night, had committed acts of espionage, had betrayed his father, and had thereby endangered his own life within the biodome. A lot for one night.

She slipped into a chair at the console, gazing fondly on that dark and handsome face. "How's it going?" she asked tenderly.

He gave a snorting laugh. "You've done it to me now, Twila. The board of governors is meeting in an hour to officially confirm me as the new chair, but there won't be any challenge. Not after the speech my father made. It went out to the whole city. No, the whole thing's in my lap now." There was sadness in his eyes.

"What did he say?" she wanted to know.

"To the public? Oh, it was wonderful," Jon said with ill-concealed sarcasm. "He said he'd learned there was a colony of survivors up in some mountains west of here, and that they seemed to be living longer than expected, so he was going there to do research. He said his work here had gone stale, and that I was doing all that was fresh and good, and he might as well go somewhere he could be useful. It was very touching."

"And Security? What did he tell them?"

Jon gave a wry smile. "He told them to follow orders. He told them to overlook the counterfeit broadcast from the bunker, not to ask too many questions, and just to let him go in peace."

Peace. What a wonderful concept! Twila wanted peace now, and rest. But would she ever find it? When she returned to the Springs with Tim, Krell would be there. She had no fear that he would be a danger to the community—his kind of ambition could not flourish in that society; they would not tolerate it. In fact, he would have the chance to be a more noble human being there than he could ever have been in the biodome. But every time she looked at him, she would remember . . . "I wish I could do the same," she said softly.

"Twila." On the other end of the transmission, Jon reached out and touched his monitor, wanting desperately to touch her face, her hair. "Twila, you don't have to go anywhere."

She gave a laugh that was almost a sob. "You may have power now, Jon, but not that much, not yet. Your father may have told Security not to look any further for villains, but my crime is a little too obvious."

"Maybe not." Then he told her the tale Krell had spun for Rochman: that once Outside, he'd found her a victim of the Hats, being forced at gunpoint to lure him out because some Hat leader was injured and they wanted a doctor for him; that on their way back to the ruined city, she had helped him to escape; that despite her best efforts, he simply didn't have enough air to make it back.

Twila heard the words, but could not make sense of them for a moment. She began to tremble slightly. "Why?" Twila asked dumbly. She had killed him, the same way he had killed her grandfather. "Why would he say that?"

Jon shook his head, because he wasn't really sure himself. "I guess for the research, in case we needed one more blood donor. Or maybe it was"—the corner of his mouth twitched in a nervous smile—"one last gift for me. He was always trying to give me things . . ." His eyes dropped, for he didn't want to tell her what his father had said when they parted. He didn't understand it, so he didn't want to repeat it; Krell had said something about every young man needing something wild and unfettered in his life, and good luck hanging on to her . . .

Twila sagged in her chair. She didn't know what to say. Jon looked at her again, looked at the once-innocent young woman, now aged and wisened and stronger for it. He thought of the task ahead of him, what it would require of him, and he knew how much he could use that strength to buoy him up. But she had been ill-used in here—would she trust enough to try it again? "Please," he whispered. "Come back inside."

His gray eyes pled eloquently, and Twila shook her head slowly. "I don't know." Inside? Back to classroom studies and electric lights and talking on the visicom? Back to hurrying alone from orchard to transit to building? Back to holographic dance halls, without the din of a hundred voices and the smell of perspiring bodies? "I've gotten too accustomed to—" she began, and broke off. "I can't go back to that kind of life, Jon: living in fear, not daring to touch anyone. I don't think I can ever put on a habit again."

"You wouldn't have to," Jon persisted. "You could start out living here in medical housing, where we don't, uh, suffer those strictures. And it will spread. I'm going to see that it spreads. I'm using your placebo idea, and we're going to inoculate people, I've already talked to a couple of board members." He rushed on, his face suffused with excitement, with need. "And you can come and go to the Outside, Twila. As often as you can stand the decontamination process, so you don't bring CM in with you. It's not a final decision. You can always go back out, no one will stop you."

Twila thought of Aunt Trish, of her mother, of being able to hug them . . . and Jon. There would be no inhibitions to conquer if she found herself alone with him again, and the very thought of that sent tremors of desire through her. Could she truly have it both ways? A life Inside, and another life Outside? She gave a heavy sigh and then managed a smile. "It might be worth it for a cup of real coffee and a good holo," she joked. "And a weekend with nothing to do but sleep, and dance."

Suddenly from Jon's end a small voice broke into their conversation. "Daddy, Daddy, here you are!" A petite figure launched itself at a surprised Jon, and began crawling determinedly into his lap. Twila's heart twisted. Wasn't it time now? Time for a child of her own, nurtured in her own body, to cradle in her arms as Jon cradled his daughter in his lap? Tim's child, Outside, out here where no one was afraid to touch another?

Where the child could watch all its friends die before their twenty-fifth birthdays?

Inside, where life was softer and education more complete, but fear stymied love and physical companionship?

Outside, the risk of diseases other than CM, and no adequate medical facilities. Inside, the risk of Edgewalkers, and coldness.

Jon had promised things would change Inside, but that would take time—time, and great effort. Of course, if one started with children . . .

Suddenly Twila caught her breath, for the little girl in Jon's lap was turning around to look into the monitor. As she turned, Twila saw that her dark curls framed a widebrowed face with great dark eyes and a pointed chin, and that her skin was a warm golden brown.

So that was why he'd come to Papa Joe's looking for her, and started this whole chain of events! Not because he was curious about the person whose blood he studied, but because he wanted, just once, to look upon the face of the mother of his child. "Oh, dear God . . ." she whispered.

Jon flushed, knowing he'd been found out, knowing he'd willfully kept the knowledge from her. Would she be angry? In a way, when he had stolen the unfertilized eggs from his father's lab, he had stolen from Twila as well—although he had saved this child, who was as much his as Twila's, and kept her safe from Krell. "Come through the Security tunnel," he urged. "We're all set up for emergency decontamination. Twelve hours of sleep, and you can wake up to see your mother and Trish. We've so much to do now, Twila. Be part of the process. Please be part of it." And part of me, he did not say. Part of us.

Twila tore her eyes away from the face of the child and up to Jon's anxious eyes. Work to do here, work to do at the Springs, work to do with the Hats— Seeds to scatter. Fertile, immune seeds to scatter. But the immunity must run in the Bariosos, if that was where her mother came from, and if so it would spread to the Hats through the inevitable intercourse of rape. As for the mountaineers, did they even want her immunity? It would mean those who received it could never fly. And Numex already had Twila's children. Twelve? Or did this one make thirteen?

Now the little girl poked her father in the chest. "Daddy, who is that lady?" she asked in a loud whisper.

Twila leaned forward and smiled into the monitor, smiled at the face she had yearned all her life to see echoed in a child like this. "I'm a friend of your father's," she told the little girl, "and I'd like to come and visit you. Would that be all right?" She lifted brimming eyes to Jon's. His eyes, too, swam with moisture.

"I guess so," chimed the girl. "My name is Desirée. What's yours?"

"Twila," she answered, brushing away the tears that spilled onto her cheek. "But I'd like it if you would call me Mother Grimm."

CUTTING EDGE SCI-FI
NOVELS

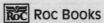